"What if I said I wanted you to kiss me?" Scarlet asked.

Mason squeezed his  the image of her looki and sad eyes. It was weakness and knew t

The hand on his chest open his eyes, he felt her palm against his cheek. She softly caressed his face, letting her thumb drag across his bottom lip. "Aren't you going to say anything?"

"It's not what I want to say, Scarlet—it's what I want to do."

She moved closer to him, pressing her firm breasts against his chest. Her whole body was aligned with his, reminding him of how she was the perfect fit for him in so many ways.

"What do you want to do, Mason?"

He couldn't hold back any longer. His eyes flew open to look down at her before the floodgates gave way. "This," he said.

Diving forward, he scooped her face into his hands and pulled her mouth to his.

* * *

The Baby Favour
is part of Mills & Boon Desire's

THE BABY FAVOUR

BY
ANDREA LAURENCE

First Published in Great Britain 2017
By Mills & Boon, an imprint of HarperCollins*Publishers*
1 London Bridge Street, London, SE1 9GF

© 2017 Andrea Laurence

ISBN: 978-0-263-92826-6

51-0717

Our policy is to use papers that are natural, renewable and recyclable products and made from wood grown in sustainable forests. The logging and manufacturing processes conform to the legal environmental regulations of the country of origin.

Printed and bound in Spain
by CPI, Barcelona

Andrea Laurence is an award-winning author of contemporary romances filled with seduction and sass. She has been a lover of reading and writing stories since she was young. A dedicated West Coast girl transplanted into the Deep South, she is thrilled to share her special blend of sensuality and dry, sarcastic humor with readers.

To Adoptive & Foster Parents Everywhere—
Whatever your reason for opening your hearts
and your homes to a child in need, thank you.

One

As a general rule, phone calls that came after midnight were bad news.

An hour ago, when Scarlet Spencer had looked at her caller ID and seen her estranged husband's name, a moment of excitement had rushed through her. The other kind of calls that came at this hour were emotional outpourings brought on by late nights and alcohol. She'd hoped that it was the latter—that perhaps he'd changed his mind about the divorce—but she was to be disappointed. Now she was walking through the front door of Cedars-Sinai Medical Center in Los Angeles just after two in the morning and she didn't know why.

All she knew was that Mason had called and asked her to come. Despite everything that was happening between them, she knew she had to do as he asked. There was something in his voice that scared her. Mason had been her rock for the last nine years. Through the ups and downs of their marriage, he had been the one to hold her hand. She got the feeling that tonight, she was returning the favor.

As she walked through the doors of the hospital, she tried to brace herself for seeing Mason again. She hadn't seen him since he moved out two months ago and she didn't know how it would feel. After nine years together, he wasn't hers anymore. He wasn't hers to hold or care for. She would have to remind herself of that as she consoled him tonight.

Before she reached the elevators, she found Mason sitting on a bench in the hallway. The first time they'd met, she'd instantly been enchanted by the beautiful surfer boy with his golden skin, eyes as blue as the sea and messy brown hair. When he smiled, his dimples had melted her insides. Just a glimpse of him now was enough to set her heart racing in her chest even all these years later.

Tonight, however, there were no smiles. He was slumped in his seat, holding his head in his hands.

He looked defeated. Scarlet had seen that in him only a few times in all these years. Most of the time, he was the confident, successful CEO of Spencer Surf Shops. The guy who never failed at anything. Who always knew the right decision to make. Sexy, bold and sure of himself. Rarely did that facade crack. Once, when he found out he couldn't give her a child. The second time, when he couldn't keep the judge from giving their adopted son back to his biological mother. The third time was when he walked out the door, leaving her and their marriage behind.

She couldn't imagine what happened tonight that could bring that look of despair back to his face. "Mason?" she asked as she approached.

Her husband shot up in his seat, turning to her with eyes more red than blue. He stood quickly, his jaw flexed tight as he tried to hold everything in. He didn't speak right away, as though if he opened his mouth, a torrent of emotions would pour out of him instead.

"What's happened? Is it Jay?"

Scarlet knew that Mason's younger brother, Jay, had been battling stage four melanoma for several months. The last she'd heard, they'd gotten the devastating news that the cancer had spread into all his major organs and they were discontinuing treatment. It wouldn't surprise her to find out that Jay had finally lost his battle. Something about the look on Mason's face, however, made her worry that this was something much worse.

"No," Mason said at last. "It's Rachel."

"Jay's wife?" Scarlet felt her chest tighten. Her sister-in-law had been like a true sister to her. As an only child, Scarlet had enjoyed having Rachel around to talk to and share marriage war stories with. The idea of Rachel raising their daughter alone after Jay passed had weighed heavily on her mind since she found out the news. Luna was only a year old and would never remember her father. "What happened?"

"She's dead."

Scarlet could only clap her hand over her mouth to hold in the painful gasp. It couldn't be true. The universe wasn't that cruel. Baby Luna was already losing her father. To lose her mother, too... "How...?" She couldn't get the words out. How could something like this happen?

"It was a freak accident. She fell down the stairs carrying a basket of laundry. I can imagine her mind has been all over the place dealing with Jay's illness. She fell in just the right way to break her neck instantaneously. Their housekeeper found her."

Scarlet didn't know what to say. Of everything that had run through her head since she received the call, Rachel's death was the last thing she expected. It was so bitterly tragic on its own, not to mention when it was compounded by Jay's illness. "Does Jay know?" she whispered through her fingers.

Mason nodded. "He's the one who called and told me about it."

She could only squeeze her eyes shut and shake her head. This wasn't the way things were supposed to happen. Her own life was a mess and she was dealing with that, but Jay and Rachel... Her heart just ached. Tears welled beneath her eyelids. A moment later, she felt Mason's arms wrap around her and she didn't fight it. Instead, she melted into him and let her tears wet the front of his dress shirt. She tried not to think about how good it felt to be in his arms again. How much she missed his scent in her lungs and his warmth surrounding her. He was just comforting her, perhaps comforting himself, and nothing more.

That thought was able to cut through the grief, stab her in her tender underbelly and remind her to keep her emotional distance. With a soft sniffle, she pulled away from him and took a step back. When her gaze met Mason's, there was a flash of pain there unrelated to the accident. It was as though he was hurt she'd pulled away so soon. As much as she might like to stay in his arms all night, that wouldn't help her get over him. It was hard enough being in the same room with him knowing he didn't want her anymore.

Despite everything, Scarlet couldn't help but wonder why he'd called her tonight. They were getting a divorce and had hardly been speaking for the last two months after he'd moved out of their Malibu beach house. He had family in town. Friends. Surely there was someone else he would want here with him instead of her. He was the one who walked away, after all. Away from her, away from their life together...

Mason cleared his throat and wiped his eyes. "I'm sorry to drag you down here in the middle of the night, but Jay asked to see us."

Scarlet frowned. "Us?"

He nodded. "He's waiting on us to come up. He's on the oncology floor."

Mason turned toward the elevator, not giving Scarlet a chance to argue with him, as usual. She followed him, both of them silent until they exited on the third floor. Halfway down the hallway, they entered a room with the name J. Spencer written on the whiteboard.

Scarlet held her breath as she stepped inside. She hadn't seen Jay in a while and she was worried about how she'd react to seeing him in such rough shape. At first, a privacy curtain blocked all but his blanketed legs, then Mason pushed it aside.

The man lying in the bed was half of the robust brother-in-law she'd once known. He'd easily lost fifty pounds on a tall frame that needed every bit of it. His thick brown hair, so much like Mason's, had thinned. His skin was sallow. But the Jay she knew was still in there somewhere—the life of the party, the comic relief, the easygoing counterpoint to Mason's perfectionism.

"Hey there," Jay said in a raspy voice as he spied Scarlet slipping into the room. She reached out and took his extended hand as he offered it to her. "You're looking beautiful as always, sister."

Scarlet bit at her bottom lip to keep from crying. "I won't be able to keep it up if you continue to interrupt my beauty sleep," she quipped. Jay preferred to keep things light even in the darkest moments, so she'd do her best to comply.

"I know." Jay's gaze grew distant as he stared off for a moment. "It couldn't be avoided. Did Mason tell you what happened?"

Scarlet could only nod as she slipped down into the chair beside the bed. "I'm so sorry, Jay."

Jay shook his head. "Don't worry about me. I won't be wasting away without her. She and I will have a happy reunion before too long. But I asked you both here because I'm worried about what's going to happen to Luna."

Scarlet felt stupid. She'd focused on the trauma of the loss and hadn't even considered the fact that Luna would be orphaned soon. No wonder Jay was up in the middle of the night worried about his daughter's future.

"We want you to raise her. The paperwork officially just names Mason as her guardian for some reason our lawyers explained but I never understood, but of course we intended to leave her to both of you. I know how badly you both wanted a child. This isn't the way I expected it to happen, but I hope that you're open to the possibility of adopting Luna and raising her as your own."

"She'll always be your child, Jay," Mason said.

Jay shook his head. "She won't remember us, Mason. You and Scarlet will be the mother and father she knows and I'm okay with that. When she's older, you can tell her about us and about how much we adored her. But I hope you'll embrace this opportunity and raise her with all the love and support that Rachel and I would've given her."

Scarlet's heart lodged in her throat as she realized the implications of Jay's words. She couldn't make a sound, she could only sit stunned and listen to the two brothers discuss her life like nothing had changed between them. Mason hadn't told his brother they were getting a divorce yet. Jay was speaking about their future as though he expected them to raise his daughter together. What were they going to do?

Mason reached out and took Scarlet's hand, squeezing it tightly to silence her concerns. Her gaze met his for a moment and she knew that he sensed her panic. "Of course we will," he said.

"Promise me," Jay said.

Mason swallowed hard, squeezing his eyes shut before nodding. "I promise, Jay. Luna will want for nothing. She will have all the love that we can give her."

Jay finally seemed pleased. He relaxed back into his bed and took a deep, labored breath. "Thank you. You know, when you write your will, you never imagine you'll actually need it. At least you hope you won't. In the morning, I'll have my attorneys start the process of having you declared her legal and physical guardian, Mason. I can't fill that role from my hospital bed, and before long, you'll be all she has anyway. Once I'm gone, I hope the two of you will consider adopting her."

"Of course," Mason said. His grip on her grew ever tighter as Jay spoke. "You don't need to worry about a thing."

"You haven't told your brother that we're getting a divorce?"

Mason halted his quick pace. They were just exiting the hospital and heading toward their cars when she finally confronted him. He was thankful she'd waited that long so no one could overhear the truth he desperately wanted to keep from his brother. He pivoted on the asphalt and turned to look at his soon-to-be ex-wife.

He'd tried not to react to seeing her again for the first time since he moved out, but not even his grief could suppress his response to Scarlet. Even now, after spending the last hour with her under the worst possible circumstances, his heart still skipped a beat when their eyes met. There was an undeniable connection between them that time and distance hadn't dulled. He didn't know if anything could.

She was the most beautiful women he'd ever seen in person, and LA was filled with beautiful people. In his eyes, no one could compare. Scarlet had long brown curls that trailed down her back, soft brown eyes and a disarming smile that had immediately caught his attention when they met. That was just the beginning of her appeal, he soon learned. She was also talented, smart, sensitive and a wonderful mother. At least for the short period of time she had been able to be one.

"No, I haven't told him. I didn't tell anyone in my family about the divorce yet."

"Why?"

"Why?" Mason repeated, running his fingers anxiously through his hair. "Because my brother has spent the last few months of his life battling terminal cancer. My parents are a wreck, barely holding it together. I didn't want to dump more on them. And really, the demise of our marriage seems fairly inconsequential in comparison, don't you think? They've been too caught up to even notice they haven't seen you in weeks."

"Of course it doesn't compare, but it's hardly insignificant. Now, because you haven't told anyone, Jay thinks we're going to raise Luna as one big, happy family." Scarlet's large brown eyes reflected the panic that he'd felt the moment he realized what Rachel's death would mean for him.

"I know," he admitted. "But how could I possibly tell a man in his position no?" He remembered his brother asking about putting him in the will not long after Luna was born. He'd agreed. Of course he'd take his niece in an emergency. He just never expected there to be an actual emergency. Or if there was, that it would happen at the worst possible time in his own life.

His lawyer had just sent him a draft of the mediated divorce settlement to review. Once they agreed on terms, it was a matter of signing off and filing it with the judge. Mason had moved out of the house he and Scarlet had bought together in Malibu and got a place in the Hollywood Hills. The new place was definitely a bachelor pad, not a single-dad pad. It was a midcentury modern design decorated with lots of glass, wood and chrome, completely unsuitable for an infant just starting to walk.

Then again, the home he'd shared with Scarlet in Malibu would be perfect. It still had a decorated nursery in it. She'd shut the room up and left it as it was the day they took their adopted son, Evan, back to his birth mother. The home also had an open floor plan with soft, safe surfaces that were fully baby proofed over a year ago.

It also had Scarlet, the mother that Luna would desperately need. That was where Luna should be. Mason was happy to have children with Scarlet when she wanted them, but the idea of being a single father to his niece was horrifying. He didn't know anything about babies, and he was certain Jay wouldn't leave Luna to him if he knew Scarlet was out of the picture.

The trick was convincing her to go along with this. After their adoption plans went south, she swore she would never go through that again. Was asking her to take in Luna, even temporarily, going to aggravate the wound? He didn't know. All he did know was that he'd made a promise to his brother and he would do whatever he had to to keep his word.

"I know that I have no reason to ask you for anything and you have no reason to go along with it. But you were there in Jay's hospital room, Scarlet. You heard him beg me—*us*—to take care of Luna. He was worried enough about leaving Rachel all alone, and now he's powerless to do anything but leave his daughter behind. I know our situation is complicated, but I couldn't tell him no. I need your help."

Scarlet crossed her arms over her chest. He knew from years together that it was her defensive posture. She was uncomfortable with this entire situation. "What are you asking of me, Mason? Do you want us to get back together just so you don't have to do this alone?"

"No, of course not." But what *did* he want? He really hadn't had enough time to process what all this would mean. Life-changing moments that arrived in the wee hours of the morning were hard to work through with a combination of stress and sleep deprivation. He couldn't process a long-term plan at this point; he could only focus on his next steps. The most important things were to make sure Luna was safe and Jay was at ease.

"For now, I just need you to do me two favors. First, please let's keep the divorce a secret from Jay and the rest of my family until after..." Mason couldn't finish the sentence. He still hadn't fully accepted the fact that his brother had only weeks left to live. Skin cancer was supposed to involve removing a bad mole and getting a lecture about sunscreen. It wasn't supposed to strike down an otherwise healthy father in his early thirties.

Scarlet watched him silently with dark eyes that didn't betray what she was thinking. She was always too hard for him to read. Whatever happened inside Scarlet's head was a secret from Mason. To this day, he wasn't sure if she blamed him for the fact that they couldn't have children. It was his fault, really, but did she look at him and see a barren future because of him? He didn't know. He also didn't know if she felt he was responsible for everything that happened with Evan. Had he fought hard enough to keep him? Had he hired all the best attorneys their money could buy to keep their son in their home? He thought he had, but it hadn't been enough.

All he knew was how he felt, and he felt like a failure where Scarlet was concerned. Mason wasn't the kind of man who failed at anything. He turned a small Venice Beach surf store he started in college into a chain with locations at every major beach in California, Florida and Hawaii. Spencer Surf Shops was more successful than he'd ever dreamed. But none of that mattered to him when he saw the brokenhearted look on Scarlet's face the day they took Evan away. He had failed her in the one dream she longed to fulfill more than any other.

"Okay. What's the second favor?" she asked at last.

"I need to move back into the house." He held up his hand to stop her inevitable protest. "Not forever. I don't want you to think I'm just trying to sweet-talk you into taking me back so I have a permanent babysitter. But I want to create the illusion of a secure future for Luna with the two of us to give Jay some peace of mind. Everyone thinks we're still together."

Scarlet flinched. "You walked out on me and now you just expect me to let you move back in?"

Mason tried not to let her reaction hurt his feelings. He was the one who had left, although he didn't like the idea that she'd already gotten used to living without him. They were together nine years. "Yes, that's what I'm asking, but you know I wouldn't if I had any other choice. It's just for however much time Jay has left. It will also give me some time to get my place ready for a baby. Our house has a nursery ready to go."

Scarlet's already pale skin seemed to blanch at his words. "Evan's nursery? You want to put Luna in Evan's room?"

Mason's jaw tightened. Scarlet's protection of Evan's space was something that he'd never challenged before. He knew it wasn't healthy to keep the room like a shrine to a child who was never returning, but pushing the issue with her seemed like a cruel fight to pick.

"It's an unused nursery," Mason clarified. Evan was never going to use it ever again. It was just a room with a crib, a changing table, and some baby supplies and toys that would help ease the situation they were in. "I'm not saying Luna has to stay there forever."

Scarlet's lips flattened into a tight line of displeasure, but she didn't argue with him. Instead, she seemed to be considering his request for a moment, finally dropping her arms at her sides. "Okay, fine. You can stay at the house and bring Luna. But," she emphasized, "I'm not going to be your nanny, Mason. I've got a new gallery opening in San Francisco in two weeks, not to mention a large commissioned piece for a hotel in Maui. I'm behind on it because of everything that's happened between us and I have to get it done."

"That's fair," Mason said cautiously. "What do you need to make this work for us?"

"I'm happy to keep up appearances for Jay's sake, but you need to get a nanny to take care of Luna. I won't—no, I can't—go into Evan's room. I don't even like the idea of Luna using it, but I know that's unreasonable. You can use it, but don't expect me to be in there singing lullabies and rocking Luna to sleep. Please don't ask me to."

Mason watched as frustrated, glassy tears formed in Scarlet's eyes. It had been over a year since the judge awarded Evan back to his biological mother, but it may as well have been yesterday as far as Scarlet was concerned.

He had hoped that she might enjoy the time with her niece, but that didn't appear to be the case. She actually seemed repelled by the idea, which surprised him, but he wouldn't push the issue. If she agreed to the two favors that really mattered, he would find a way to make it work even if Scarlet was hands-off with Luna.

"I understand. Thank you for doing this. I'll see about a nanny first thing in the morning."

"Where is the baby now?" she asked.

"With my parents." It gave them something to focus on other than the grief. Luna was the same happy baby she always was. For her, nothing was different and that was a good distraction for them. "They'll probably keep her until Rachel's memorial service."

Scarlet nodded and reached into her purse. She pulled out a key and handed it to him. "This is to the house. I had the locks changed after you moved out. Just let me know you're on your way before you show up. Remember this isn't your place anymore."

Without another word, Scarlet turned and headed toward her car in the hospital parking lot. Mason watched her drive away with an aching feeling of disappointment in his stomach. He hadn't been able to shake that feeling the last few years of their marriage as they battled to start a family. He'd hoped that maybe when they were apart, the feeling would go away. It only got worse.

Scarlet had agreed to do him these favors, but he could tell she didn't want to. She had loved her little niece, but she resisted the idea of being hands-on with her. He hadn't had time to ponder the possibilities of what Luna could mean for their relationship, but it was clear that those ideas would just be fantasies. She didn't want anything to do with Luna. She wanted a child of her own. Once they were divorced, there was no reason for her to even pretend to be a family. Hell, that was why he'd left in the first place, so she wouldn't be held back from her dream.

That meant that once Jay passed away, Mason was going to be raising his niece all on his own.

A feeling of overwhelming panic started to wash over him. It felt like the first time he'd caught a huge wave surfing and had been engulfed by the harsh cone of water. He could only brace himself for the inevitable wipeout, knowing he was in way over his head.

Two

"You just need to go in there. Get it over with."

Scarlet turned to her manager, April, with a frown. They were sitting on her poolside deck overlooking the Pacific Ocean. "All right, you're cut off. No more wine for you." She picked up the bottle of chardonnay from the table and moved it out of her friend and employee's reach.

"I'm not drunk. I'm serious, Scarlet. Do it right now. I'll even go with you. Just open the door and step into the nursery. I think once you do it you'll feel better. It's just a room. It doesn't have any power over you that you don't give it."

"Thank you, Dr. Phil. I'll take that under consideration, but I'm not going in there right now." April was Scarlet's best friend, but she was regretting confiding in her about her latest situation with Mason. She was from the school of tough love and wouldn't pull any punches if she thought Scarlet needed to hear the truth.

"Does anyone go in there? Ever?"

"The housekeeper goes in to clean once a week."

"Did Mason ever go in there?"

Scarlet hesitated to answer, the memories of that night flooding through her mind like it was yesterday. "He did once. The night they took Evan away. He sat on the floor and cried. Losing Evan was hard on us both. Adopting that beautiful baby boy was a dream come true for us after struggling so long with infertility and sitting on the waiting list to get a baby. It was the best four months of my life. And then when the mother changed her mind..."

April reached across the table and took Scarlet's hand. "I know it was hard on you. And I'm not going to be the jerk who tells you to move on and forget about him, because that's never going to happen. You loved that little boy more than anything. Hell, I couldn't get you to put him down long enough to paint. But I do think that you're being unreasonable about the nursery. It's just a room filled with furniture like any other room. Once Mason and Luna move out, maybe you need to redecorate."

Scarlet snatched her hand away. "Redecorate?"

"Yes. Donate the furniture and baby clothes to a needy family. Paint the walls. Maybe turn it into an office or a yoga studio. Something that won't haunt you every day about what you lost."

Scarlet took a large sip of wine and sat back in her

Adirondack chair. April was right. She knew she was right. She just hadn't been able to make herself do it. In her heart, it was Evan's room. It was their chance at a baby, as brief as it was, and changing that room meant that she was giving up on that part of her life. Or at least it felt that way.

"After they move out, I'll consider it," she agreed reluctantly. That answer would hopefully be enough to appease April, but not require her to march into the house and do something about it right that instant.

April gave her a satisfied smile and took a bite of the homemade guacamole and chips she'd brought with her for their girls' night in. "When is Mason moving in?"

"The funeral service for Rachel is tomorrow, so probably tomorrow night or the next morning."

"Are you prepared for having your soon-to-be ex-husband living in the house again?"

Scarlet sighed. She wasn't really sure how she felt about it. "It's hard to say. This whole situation is so complicated. On one hand, he hasn't been gone that long, so having him back in the house may just feel like he's been on an extended business trip. Then again, he'll be in the guest room, not in bed beside me."

"You could always invite him into the bed beside you," April said with a sly wink.

Scarlet responded with a nervous giggle. "Yeah, right. I'm sure he'd bite, because that won't complicate matters at all. Anyway, if my feminine wiles were that powerful, I wouldn't have lost him in the first place."

April ignored her sarcastic tone. "I still don't understand how you two could break up. You were the perfect couple. Your marriage was what I was striving for. Now you're divorcing and living in separate houses. It makes me feel very dubious about my own love life. I don't get it."

No relationship was perfect, although it might look like it from the outside. "We had issues. There were a few things that bothered me before the baby thing came up, but I thought we could work through it. In the end, I'm not the one who left, April. You'll have to ask Mason why he decided to give up. I know things between us had become...strained... And then he told me he wanted a divorce."

It had been only a couple months since their marriage unraveled, and the moment was still fresh and painful in her mind. She knew she hadn't been herself. Not since they lost Evan. But she'd been getting better. She was trying to reimagine her future without a child in it, and that took time to come to terms with.

"What reasons did he give for wanting the divorce?"

"He said he didn't want to hold me back from my dream of having a family. Since he was the one who couldn't have children, he said he thought it was best to step aside and let me find someone who could."

April's mouth fell open. "That's the most romantic breakup I've ever heard of."

Scarlet shook her head. "I don't know that I believe it was entirely selfless. It sounds noble, but I know Mason. He can't stand to fail at anything. Mason doesn't do well when he isn't on top. He'd rather walk away from something if he can't succeed. He's done it before. Did you know he was a vice president at his father's company before he quit and started the surf shop? That he dropped out of grad school? This was the same thing. Staying married to me would be a daily reminder that he failed and couldn't give me a child. And by that point, we'd started growing apart. If you'd asked me two years ago about us ever divorcing, I would've laughed in your face. But we'd become strangers living in the same house."

She knew most of that was her fault. Once they started to try having a family, she'd become obsessed with the idea. As the only child of two only children, Scarlet had always wanted a big family. Three or four kids at a minimum. For the first five years of their marriage, she and Mason had been focused on their careers and they'd been very successful. It wasn't until they decided to finally try for a family that things started to come apart.

Their passionate nights became dominated by ovulation kits and monthly disappointments. Then romance went out the window entirely in the face of sterile doctors' offices and medical exams that uncovered that Mason was infertile. It had been a huge blow to them both, but Mason seemed especially devastated by the diagnosis. She had tried to convince him that she didn't care, that they could adopt a child who needed a home. When that fell apart, too, they had no hope left for their marriage to cling to. At that point, Mason did what he always did—he made a decision without consulting her, and moved out.

"Do you think things will be different with him back in the house again? Now that he has custody of Luna, perhaps you could reconcile."

Scarlet didn't really think that was an option. Being back together would be awkward at best, contentious at worst. She imagined them tiptoeing around each other, trying to adapt to a new dynamic that flew in the face of nine years together. "This won't really be the right environment to rekindle our romance. We'll have Luna here. And the nanny."

April set down her empty wineglass and turned in her seat to look at Scarlet. "May I ask what the nanny is about?"

Scarlet's brow furrowed at her friend's silly question. "I'm on deadline. That massive humpback whale oil painting is due next week. You of all people should know that. And we're on the verge of opening up the Fisherman's Wharf gallery. That's going to keep me busy."

April didn't look convinced. "So busy that a woman desperate for children can't make time in her day to care for her orphaned niece, who needs a mother more than anything in the world?"

Scarlet frowned at her insightful friend. So she wasn't *that* busy. They would need help with Luna, though. She'd rather have an in-home nanny than put her in day care while they worked.

"Tell me that you're not putting up these walls as a self-preservation mechanism," April said.

"A what?" Scarlet snapped.

"You got attached to Evan and you lost him. Are you deliberately keeping distance between you and Luna so you don't get attached to her, too?"

That question hit a little closer to home than Scarlet cared for. Best friends saw too much sometimes. "It's not my baby, April, and Mason and I aren't reconciling. I know this whole thing seems like a terrible twist of fate that will reunite us and give us the child we've always wanted, but that's just not the case. Mason made it very clear to me that this is all for show, to put Jay at ease."

She sat back in her chair with a sigh. "Of course I love Luna as my niece, but no… I'm not going to let myself fall head over heels for her when Mason is her sole legal guardian. I basically have no rights in the matter. When he decides the time is right, he's going to take her away from me and carry on with his life. I'll be alone again, and brokenhearted, because he decided I need to go out and have a child of my own. No." She shook her head. "I'll do what he asked of me, but I can't let myself get attached to another child that isn't mine. That's why I refused to try adoption a second time after we lost Evan. I couldn't go through that again."

"So there's no chance whatsoever that you and Mason will call off the divorce and raise Luna together?" April looked at Scarlet with big, hopeful eyes.

Scarlet understood. It was a beautiful fantasy to have. They really had had a marriage that made other people jealous. They'd started out their careers together, had common goals and interests, and aesthetically they were a match made on a Hollywood film set. Losing Mason had been doubly hard because she really didn't think she'd ever find another relationship like that one. It was one of a kind and she hated to let it go, but she couldn't figure out how to hold on to it either.

She'd once held that kind of hope for her marriage,

but she'd realized she was being naive. "No, April. While it might seem like our divorce was all about kids, it isn't that simple and adding a baby won't fix everything. Mason and I are not getting back together no matter how things might look."

Mason's gaze kept drifting from the white casket covered in pink roses to his wife and niece beside him. The service had been beautifully done. He was surprised, really, considering they had everything arranged for Jay and nothing arranged for Rachel. Fortunately, the funeral home had handled most of the details, and they'd purchased their plots months before after Jay's grim diagnosis.

To Mason's other side, Jay was seated in his wheelchair. It was hard for Mason to look at his younger brother. He was like a shriveled skeleton inside the black suit he'd worn last when he was fifty pounds heavier. A hospice nurse had come out with him to check on his oxygen and make sure he didn't overdo it. Even though it was July, he had a blanket over his lap and a pink rose clutched in his hand. All things considered, he was holding together pretty well.

Mason wished he could say the same about himself. On the outside he looked calm and collected enough, but on the inside he was a bundle of raw nerves. Just a glance at Jay or Scarlet was enough to set him on edge, and for very different reasons. He'd even done a shot of whiskey to get him through the service.

Every time he looked at his brother, he thought about Luna and the future he never expected. Being a father was an idea he'd taken for granted until it couldn't happen. Once he realized it wasn't in the cards for him, he'd let it go along with his marriage. The concept of being Luna's father once Jay was gone—and a single father at that—scared the hell out of him. Would he make the same choices Jay would've made for his daughter? Would he screw the kid up by levying the same unrealistic expectations of perfection on her the way his parents had done to him? That was the vicious cycle, right?

Each time he turned away from his brother, he caught a whiff of Scarlet's perfume on the air. He knew the scent well, having bought her a bottle of it every year on her birthday for the last nine years. The scent reminded him of her hair spilled across pillowcases, of his lips pressed against the hollow of her throat, tasting her pulse, and of her wrapped in nothing but a towel getting ready for the day.

He'd been desperate when he'd asked Scarlet to play house with him for a few weeks. Now a part of him regretted it. Leaving her the first time had been hard enough, but it was something he knew he had to do. Being back under the same roof might make it impossible to leave a second time. But he had no other choice. He couldn't give her what she needed, despite what she might say to the contrary.

Glancing over at her, he saw Scarlet weeping silent tears as she clutched baby Luna in her arms. They'd decided that their time as a reunited couple needed to start at the service so there was one less worry on Jay's mind. Once it was over, Mason would unload his stuff from the back of his Range Rover into the beach house. He'd also packed a bag at Jay's house with Luna's clothes and some toys. He'd move the rest of her belongings directly into his new place once the time came.

Thankfully, along with her stuff, Mason was also able to bring over Luna's nanny, Carroll. She was happy to stay with the baby and keep her job, which would ease the transition for everyone involved. It would also give Luna a familiar caregiver when her whole world was changing around her.

Who was going to help Mason as his whole world changed around him?

The pastor ended his short graveside sermon and began the commitment prayer. "We thank You for Rachel's life here on this earth, and we recognize that the body that lies before us is not Rachel, but rather the house in which she lived. We acknowledge that Rachel is rejoicing, even now, in Your very presence, enjoying the blessings of Heaven. Father, we commit her body to the earth, from which our bodies were originally created, and we rejoice in the fact that her spirit is even now with You. We thank You, Father, that in the days, weeks and months to come, these realities and the abiding presence of Your Spirit will especially strengthen, sustain and comfort Rachel's friends and family until they can join her there. In Jesus's name, amen."

The pastor gestured to Jay and the nurse rolled him forward to place his rose on top of her casket. Jay placed his palm flat against the smooth white wood and closed his eyes. "I'll see you soon, baby."

Once he moved back, the pastor thanked everyone for coming and the crowd started to disperse so the team could complete the burial. With Jay needing to return immediately to the hospital, the family had opted against a wake, so it was done. Mason was relieved it was over, even though the next step he had to take might be even harder.

Mason squeezed Jay's shoulder. "We'll bring Luna to see you in a day or two, okay?"

His brother nodded and turned to the ambulance that had pulled into the cemetery. "My ride is here. Take good care of her."

Mason, Scarlet and Luna stood by the grave as the crowd cleared away and Jay was taken back to the hospital. When they could stall no longer, he turned back to her. "I guess we'd better go. I've got a lot of stuff to bring in and get settled."

Scarlet wiped her damp cheeks and nodded. Luna had fallen asleep in her arms. They walked to the car like the family everyone thought they were, loading Luna into her car seat and climbing into the front together.

Driving down the highway back to Malibu with Scarlet in the passenger seat and a baby in the back was a moment that brought back uncomfortable memories for Mason. It felt so easy, so normal, and yet it reminded him of Evan and their short stint as parents.

He'd thought they had a great marriage. He'd had no doubt that they would be together forever. They complemented each other well, had common interests and were very compatible in their day-to-day lives. He enjoyed spoiling Scarlet. He could tell her anything without feeling judged. It was a far cry from the family he'd grown up in, where his father was always needling at him to push harder and do better. He'd meant well, of course, wanting Mason to succeed, but in the end, all he'd done was create a man with an inability to accept failure.

When they'd brought Evan home from the hospital, he had been only four days old. Mason remembered holding his son in his arms, looking at Scarlet and thinking their life was really complete now. Their perfect marriage had now become the perfect family, despite his inability to give her a child of their own. He'd started to think that perhaps he hadn't failed in this endeavor at all. Scarlet was happy, Evan had a loving family...things had worked out the way they were meant to.

It wasn't until they got the call from their attorney telling them that Evan's birth mother had changed her mind that he believed otherwise.

Scarlet pulled the gate opener out of her purse and Mason waited for it to open, allowing them to pull onto their property. "I'm going to put her down to finish her nap," she said, getting out of the car and unfastening Luna.

Mason went to the back of his SUV and opened the hatch. He hadn't packed much—a couple of suitcases' worth of clothes, toiletries and random items he might need, like his laptop and tablet.

As he stepped through the ground-floor entry of their former home, Mason hesitated. He'd moved on instinct up until this moment, but he realized things were different now. Some of the furniture had changed. His favorite chair and big-screen television had moved with him. There was a large floral arrangement on the dining room table in a vase that he didn't recognize and a bright-colored rug in the entry that was way too loud for his taste.

It was obvious this wasn't his house any longer and he wasn't sure where to go next. "Where am I sleeping?" he asked. Initially, he'd thought he'd be in the guest room, but that was where the nanny would sleep. Their four-bedroom house had a master suite, a nursery, a guest room and Scarlet's art studio.

Scarlet paused and turned to look at him. "I guess we'd better make that decision before the nanny arrives with her things. I think you'll have to sleep on the futon in my studio, with Carroll staying in the guest room that adjoins the nursery. Since my studio is upstairs near the master, it's probably a better choice anyway. Even the nanny will think that we're sharing a room."

"We can't just share a room?"

"Uh, no. I'm going along with this whole thing for Jay's sake, but if you think you're going to take liberties with me, you're wrong. I think it's best you sleep in the studio."

Although the idea of toughing it out on a futon didn't appeal to him, she was right. "I don't want to clutter your workspace. Will I be able to put my clothes and toiletries in your bathroom?"

"I suppose." Scarlet placed the sleeping baby into the Pack 'n Play they'd set up in the living room. "Just don't make a mess," she added with a smile.

Mason chuckled as he turned to the stairs and carried his bags up to the second floor. They both knew that Scarlet was the messy one. Mason was the oldest child, raised to the highest standards possible. He was as perfect as he could be. He was tidy. He cleaned up after himself. He always put his clothes in the hamper and his shoes on the rack. He even made the bed. Or at least his side if Scarlet was still in it.

Scarlet was an artist. She was an only child and was raised to be a free spirit. She saw nothing wrong with leaving a cereal bowl on the counter overnight or leaving a glob of toothpaste in the sink. Most of the time she was splattered in paint.

They were different, but he'd loved that about her. Really, Mason had been envious of her ability to let things go. In the few months they'd had Evan, Mason had been on edge over the mess. "Babies are messy," Scarlet would tell him with a happy smile even as she wiped away spit-up. He'd tried to loosen up then, but he had more than thirty years of training from his father to overcome.

At the top of the stairs, he turned toward the bedroom to unpack his clothes. He paused just inside the French doors, staring at the king-size bed he used to share with her. At least it looked like the same bed. She had changed the bedding to an ivory-and-purple floral print, and the walls had been painted a pale purple color that almost looked gray. It was a far more feminine room than he'd left behind.

It hadn't changed enough for him to forget everything that had happened in there, though. The sight of the headboard alone was enough to bring back the memories of passionate nights spent together in this very room. It made his whole body start to tighten in a way furniture shouldn't elicit.

Despite the ups and downs of their relationship, he and Scarlet had always enjoyed a very physical and satisfying love life. From the first time they'd made love on the beach at midnight to the final time the night before he decided to move out, they'd had that spark. Thoughts of that last night together flooded his mind and sent jolts of electricity south to other parts. That memory had haunted him the last few months, knowing he'd never touch her again that way and it was his own fault. His response tonight was compounded by the scent of her perfume, which was stronger in here than anywhere else in the house. It filled his lungs as he tried to take a deep breath and wish away his response to Scarlet.

"Carroll is here!" Scarlet called to him from downstairs.

"I'll be right down," he answered and set his bags to the side. He'd unpack later. Now he needed to focus on getting his body and mind on the same page or this would be a very uncomfortable few weeks.

Three

Scarlet couldn't shake the feeling that she was a horrible person.

It had been only three days since Mason, Luna and Carroll moved into her house, but she felt awful from virtually the moment it happened. Not because she didn't like having people in her space or that she resented the situation. It was because she did like it. She liked the scent of Mason's shampoo lingering in the heavy air of the bathroom after his shower. She liked hearing a baby's giggles downstairs. It reminded her of the happiest time of her life. And because of that, she had to keep her distance and close herself off from everyone else in the house.

And *that* was why she was a horrible person.

She hadn't held Luna since she laid her down for her

nap after the funeral. She hadn't fed her, bathed her, played with her or even so much as stepped a foot into the nursery to check on her in the night. There might as well not even be a baby in the house. Scarlet tried to reason with herself that it was the nanny's job. That was why she'd insisted they have one, after all. Scarlet was just for show—a make-believe mom for a make-believe family, to soothe Jay's worries. So she could keep her distance, go along with her agreement with Mason and come out of this situation unscathed.

April was right—this plan was entirely centered on her self-preservation. But who could blame her? What woman with a ticking biological clock and a love of children wouldn't fall head over heels for Luna? She was the sweetest, most laid-back baby Scarlet had ever encountered. She had a head of crazy brown curls, Mason's big blue eyes and his dimples. There was plenty of Rachel and Jay in her, too, like Rachel's pert little nose and Jay's pouty mouth, but unfortunately all Scarlet could see were the bits of Mason's genetics in her.

The pieces that their own biological child would've had if they could have had their own.

It wasn't easy to keep her distance. It was just in her nature to want to care for people. When she heard a baby cry, she wanted to soothe it. When Mason swore, she wanted to rush down and see if he'd hurt himself. But she had to remind herself time and time again that this wasn't her baby and this wasn't her husband. If she let herself think otherwise, even for a moment, her heart would be crushed when it ended.

As it was, her heart still hadn't recovered from its

last major hit. She wasn't entirely sure how she could recover when her too-sexy soon-to-be ex-husband was sitting on her couch watching a ball game and working on his laptop.

So far, she had made the excuse that she had to work. And it was true. In her studio, a massive three-panel canvas took up most of one wall, waiting to be painted. When she was done, it would be disassembled, photographed, boxed and shipped to Hawaii to hang in the lobby of the Mau Loa Maui hotel.

Scarlet took a step back and eyeballed her work. The painting was coming along. So far, she'd focused mainly on the background with the three humpback whales roughed in, but not yet done. Locking herself in her studio for hours on end had been helpful for that, at least. As long as she didn't glance over at the futon with Mason's neatly folded blankets and pajamas stacked on top of it.

She put down her paintbrush and stretched her hands out. Damn. It had been a long time since she'd worked such long stretches without stopping. How long had it been? Scarlet looked at her watch. It was almost seven in the evening. She hadn't even stopped to eat, drink or use the restroom since noon.

That was it for tonight. She rolled her shoulders and reluctantly stepped out into the hallway. She could hear the sounds of the television downstairs. It was about Luna's bedtime, so Carroll was probably giving her a bath.

Scarlet crept down the floating staircase and went into the kitchen. She was surprised to find Carroll there, making herself a cup of hot tea. Her face looked a little puffy and her nose was red. "Good evening, Mrs. Spencer," she said as though her nose were pinched closed.

Scarlet frowned. "You sound awful, Carroll. Are you coming down with something?"

Carroll shook her head. "I don't know. I hope not. I almost never get sick and I know now is a horrible time. You're so busy, and if I give this to Luna, she won't be able to visit her father at the hospital."

That was true. The chemotherapy had basically destroyed Jay's immune system along with the cancer. Unfortunately, the cancer had recovered better than Jay had from the treatment. He would catch any bug he was exposed to and, at this point in his illness, a bout of the flu could be deadly for him.

Carroll set down her tea and launched into a fit of sneezes, followed by a rattling cough that Scarlet didn't like the sound of. She reached out to touch the woman's forehead and it was burning up.

"You've got a fever. I think you'd better take your tea and get to bed right now. I have some medicine upstairs you can take. I suggest you visit the walk-in clinic first thing in the morning. That flu medicine has to be administered within so many days of symptoms for it to work."

"What about Luna?"

That was a good question. What about Luna? Scarlet squeezed her eyes shut and resigned herself to her fate. She'd tried, she'd fought, but in the end, fate won out. "We can handle her until you're feeling better. I've made a lot of progress on my next painting."

Carroll's eyes grew wide. "No, no. Maybe I could call someone..."

Scarlet would have none of it. "No arguing. Now get to bed right this instant. Is Luna already down for the night?"

"No, ma'am. Mr. Spencer is playing with her on the deck. I asked him to keep her for a minute while I made tea."

That wasn't ideal. Scarlet was hoping the baby was already asleep so she could avoid the nursery for as long as possible, but she would do what she had to. "Okay. The two of us can take care of her until you feel better. Now, to bed!"

Scarlet watched as Carroll reluctantly carried her mug with her out of the kitchen toward her room. She steeled herself for what she had to do and went out to the deck to look for Mason and Luna, the two people she'd been trying to avoid.

The deck was empty, as was the pool. Curious, Scarlet walked around to the gate and steps that led to the beach. There, she found Mason and Luna playing in the sand. She stepped down to the beach, kicked off her shoes and walked through the sand to where they were playing.

The summer sun had finally set, but the sky was still bright and people still walked up and down the beach. There was a nice breeze for a summer's night, reminding Scarlet that she'd spent too much time working and not enough time enjoying the property they'd worked so hard to afford.

"Look, Luna. Your aunt Scarlet has come out to

play with us!" Mason picked up the baby and turned her to face the house where Scarlet was walking toward them.

The baby immediately lit up when she saw Scarlet. She grinned wide and dropped her handfuls of sand to reach out for her.

"Someone has missed you," Mason said.

Scarlet stopped short, biting at her bottom lip. She ached to scoop the baby up into her arms and cradle her to her chest. To smell the top of her head and draw in the endearing scent that reminded her of nights rocking Evan to sleep.

Instead, she crouched down out of arm's reach. Holding her during Rachel's funeral had been hard enough. "I doubt that," she said in a soothing voice she used for babies. "What are we doing out here?"

"We are playing in the sand. I figured she's about to have a bath anyway, so why not?"

Scarlet nodded. "Well, it appears as though Nanny Carroll has the flu, so I've sent her to bed. This dirty little girl is ours to deal with for the next few days."

Luna reached down to pick up a little red plastic shovel and then dropped it. "Uh-oh!" she declared. So far, she'd mastered *mama*, *dada*, *no*, *uh-oh* and *dog*.

"Uh-oh is right," Mason repeated. "Are we going to be able to handle her on our own?"

"She's a baby, not a wild animal," Scarlet said. "I'm sure we'll be fine."

"And what about you?" he asked. His dark blue eyes focused on hers, saying far more than his words ever would. "Will you be fine?"

Scarlet bit at her lip and stood up, dusting sand from her hands. "I guess we'll find out."

"Have you gone into the nursery yet?" Mason asked as he followed suit and lifted Luna into his arms.

For a moment, Scarlet was struck by the image in front of her. Her tall, strong Mason casually holding a baby in his arms. It was a simple thing—hardly unusual to any passersby—but it was enough to make her heart catch in her throat.

"No," she replied, turning away. As her gaze fell on the ocean, she spotted the splash of a pod of dolphins not far offshore. "Look!" She pointed out at the sea.

Mason turned and pointed the animals out to Luna. "Look, Luna. There are dolphins. They're jumping out of the water. Aren't they silly?"

Luna's eyes grew wide and her tiny little mouth formed an O of excitement. She started to clap enthusiastically as they watched them leap out of the water.

"They're dolphins. Can you say *dolphin*, Luna? *Doll-fin*."

"Dafin!" she exclaimed. "Dafin!"

Scarlet smiled, turning away from one of her favorite creatures on earth to look at Mason and Luna. The two of them together watching the sea with excited grins made her chest ache. This was the life she'd lost. The future she'd never have with him because he'd decided what was best for her instead of asking what she wanted.

"I think our job here is done," Mason said at last with a satisfied smirk. "She loves dolphins. Next, we just need to get her a baby wet suit and a surfboard."

Scarlet's smile dimmed a little. She remembered him

making the same threats about teaching Evan to surf. The idea had terrified her at the time, although they'd never gotten that far. "I think she needs to master walking more than a few steps without falling down before she starts shooting the curl, don't you?"

Mason sighed with feigned disappointment. "I suppose. We need to get her in baby swimming lessons, though. She's already behind all the kids that started with those 'mommy and me' classes. She's going to be doing the backstroke before her second birthday."

Scarlet just shook her head and headed back to the house with Mason and Luna on her heels. "Don't tell Jay about all this. He'll think you're out to drown his baby."

"Don't be silly, Scarlet. If Luna knows the backstroke, there's no way she'll drown."

Mason awoke with a start. It took a moment for him to get his bearings in the dark, unfamiliar room. Then, from the crick in his back, he remembered that he was on the futon in Scarlet's studio.

Then the wail of a baby sounded louder and he realized what had woken him up. He was about to fling back the sheets and go downstairs, but he heard footsteps down the hallway and Scarlet's soothing voice. "I'm coming, Lulu. I'm coming, baby girl."

Mason held his breath, waiting to see what would happen. The night before, Scarlet had let him give Luna a bath and put her to bed. In exchange, she'd made some dinner for them both while he was doing it. If he was right, she was about to step into the nursery for the first time in a year.

He got up and crept across the floor as quietly as he could, then peered out the door. Luna's bedroom was near the foot of the stairs. He saw Scarlet stand there for a moment, just outside the threshold. Then she took a deep breath and stepped inside. After a few seconds, the crying stopped and he could make out the calming mumbles Scarlet said to soothe her.

A few minutes later, Scarlet came out of the bedroom with Luna in her arms. He watched them go into the living room, where Scarlet sat in her favorite chair to rock Luna back to sleep. He remembered her doing the same with Evan. It had worked like a charm every time.

After about ten minutes, he moved quietly down the stairs. "Is everything okay?" he asked in a hoarse whisper.

Scarlet nodded and continued to rock. Luna was snuggled in her arms, already sleeping. "We just needed a new diaper and someone to love on us a little bit."

Mason settled onto the couch beside her. He watched the way Scarlet looked down at the sleeping baby and immediately understood why she'd chosen to be so closed off the last few days. It was to keep from falling in love with the sweet bundle in her arms. She looked at Luna the same way she'd looked at Evan, as though the sun rose and set on that tiny baby.

He'd thought at first that she just didn't want to be around her. Scarlet had made it very clear after they lost Evan that she didn't want to try adoption again. She couldn't risk falling for another baby only to lose it. He understood that. He didn't really think of Luna that way, but he supposed in Scarlet's eyes it was the same. It wasn't her child, so she wasn't going to get attached. Scarlet wanted her very own baby; he knew that. Perhaps spending this time with Luna would light the fires in her to settle down with someone else and start a family.

"Motherhood always did look good on you," he said without thinking.

Scarlet froze for a moment, staring at him before taking a breath and gazing back down at the sleeping baby. "Christian Dior always looks good on me, too, but that doesn't mean I should wear it all the time."

"What is that supposed to mean?" he asked, speaking louder than he expected to.

Scarlet raised a finger to her lips, then gingerly stood up. "I'm going to put her back to bed before I answer that question."

Mason waited as she returned Luna to her crib and shut the nursery door. When she came back, she beckoned for him to follow her out onto the deck. He stood up and traced her steps, noticing for the first time that she was wearing nothing more than a tiny pink cotton chemise with lacy white trim. It fit tightly to her full bust, then flowed freely over her hips to midthigh. It wasn't exactly lingerie, but it wasn't your grandmother's nightgown either.

He found himself instantly responding to the innocent outfit as though it were some racy black teddy. His pulse started racing and his mouth was suddenly bone-dry. He attempted to lick his lips, but it didn't help. It only made him think about her lips and how long it had been since he'd kissed them. Too long.

After he stepped outside, Scarlet pulled the glass door closed behind them. The sky was an inky black sprinkled with as many stars as the LA lights would allow. The moon was hovering overhead, almost full, casting a silvery glow to Scarlet's figure.

"What I meant was that just because something looks good on you doesn't mean you get to wear it. Motherhood might suit me, but it appears that life may have other plans."

Mason frowned. "I don't know why you would say that. You've got plenty of time to still be a mother, Scarlet. You're beautiful and talented... Surely you'll meet a man who will give you the family that you want."

Scarlet looked at him as though he'd reached out and slapped her. "Stop saying that."

"Stop saying what? It's true. That's why..." He trailed off. *That's why I left you.*

Scarlet crossed her arms over her chest, pressing her breasts up against the deep V of her nightgown. "I don't know why you think that just because you're divorcing me I'm going to waltz out the door and find another man I'll love as much as I loved you. Do you think they just have men lined up at the shopping mall and I pick one out and live happily ever after?"

Mason tried not to note her use of the past tense where he was concerned. He was the one who left, but that didn't mean he had to like the idea of her moving on. "Don't be silly," he said. "I'm trying to be serious here. I don't want you to give up on your dream of having your own family, Scarlet. Not because of me. You can still have it. Sure, it won't drop in your lap tomorrow, but you can have it."

"Maybe. Someday. But I sure as hell can't move on with you here. It's so hard to have you here and not think about everything else. About us. About Evan. About what a mess our lives have become…"

"Do you think it's any easier on me? Christ, Scarlet. The last three days have been torture."

Scarlet flinched. "This is what you wanted. How has it been torture?"

He ran his fingers through his sleep-tousled hair and then rubbed his palm over his face. "Do you know how hard it is for me to be around you and not want you? I am crazy with wanting you. You're my wife."

"I *was* your wife," she said in a cold, accusatory tone she'd never used during their marriage. "You *left* me."

"I left you because I can't have you, Scarlet. Not and let you have what you need to be happy."

She narrowed her gaze at him and took a step closer. "How do you know what I need, Mason? You always do this. You've always treated me like I'm a part of the company that you have to manage. You're always making decisions for me, thinking you know what's best, instead of asking me what I want or listening to me when I tell you things."

Mason hesitated in his reply. He knew it probably seemed that way. He did listen. He just didn't believe her. No matter how many times she said she was okay not having children, he knew it was a lie. She was settling. Because of him. And he wasn't about to let her do that for something so important. Even when he didn't like what he had to do, he'd do it because it was in her best interests.

"You bought this house without asking me."

"I bought your dream house on Malibu. You don't like it?"

"I love it," she argued. "But what if I didn't? You never consult me. You chose our honeymoon. You hired Nanny Carroll without asking me what I thought. You bought me that Mercedes and just left it in the driveway."

"You don't like your Mercedes?"

Scarlet sighed. "That's not the point. The point is that you never consult me on anything. You just make a decision. It's not just about the car. Or the divorce. It's everything. You never ask what I want."

He took a step closer to her, leaving only a few inches between them. When he was this near to her, he could feel the warmth of her skin and her soft breath on his lips. "So what do you want, Scarlet?"

She placed her hand against his chest and looked up at him with her large dark eyes that spoke volumes even as she stood silent. He prayed she couldn't feel his heart pounding in his rib cage or hear the blood rushing through his veins at top speed. That, combined with the nearby crashing of the waves, was a dull roar that filled his ears. Mason kept his hands at his sides. They curled into fists as he fought to hold still and keep from sweeping her into his arms.

That was the absolute wrong thing to do. Right? He'd distanced himself from her intentionally. Filed for divorce. Moved out of the house. All to give them both a chance to start over. Except he didn't want to start over. Not really. But being around Scarlet stirred up so many confusing emotions inside of him. Among the desire, he also fought the feelings of inadequacy and frustration that he couldn't shake. As much as he wanted to be around Scarlet, he also wanted to stay away from her. That wasn't what a marriage was supposed to be like. He was convinced they would be happier apart than together.

And yet, if she leaned in and kissed him right now, he wouldn't stop her.

"What if I said I wanted you to kiss me?" she asked.

Mason squeezed his eyelids tightly shut to block out the image of her looking up at him with those full lips and sad eyes. It was as though she could sense his weakness and knew that she was it. Why else would she ask for the one thing he was reluctant to give her? The one thing he was desperate to give her?

The hand on his chest lifted, but before Mason could open his eyes, he felt her palm against his cheek. She softly caressed his face, letting her thumb drag across his bottom lip. "Aren't you going to say anything?" she asked.

"It's not what I want to say, Scarlet, it's what I want to do."

She moved closer to him, pressing her firm breasts against his chest. Her whole body was perfectly aligned with his, reminding him of how she was the perfect fit for him in so many ways. This close, he had no doubt that she could feel his desire for her through the thin cotton of his lounging pants.

"What do you want to do, Mason?"

He couldn't hold back any longer. His eyes flew open to look down at her before the floodgates gave way. "This," he said.

Lunging forward, he scooped her face into his hands and pulled her mouth to his. They collided with the passionate force of a nuclear blast. Weeks and months of frustration, tears and need coursed through his veins as he threatened to devour her. Her mouth was open to him and her lips were soft, just as they always were. His hands were nearly shaking with the rush of adrenaline that came from finally being able to touch her again. The taste of her, the scent of her skin, the soft whimper against his lips…it was everything that he'd thought about, fantasized about, in all the weeks he'd lain alone in his new house in the Hollywood Hills. Scarlet was addictive and quitting her cold turkey had left him miserable and wanting.

But wouldn't this just make it worse?

Fighting his instincts, Mason pulled away, leaving Scarlet unsteady and gasping for breath. What was he doing? They'd gone through so much to put an end to this and here he was, practically attacking her on the back deck. This was why he'd kept his distance from her. Why he needed to continue keeping his distance from her. He had no self-control where Scarlet was concerned.

"What's the matter?" she asked.

Mason could only shake his head. "Things are so complicated for us, Scarlet. I just don't think what we're doing is going to help matters."

"And lying to everyone while we pretend to be a happy family will help?" With a sad shake of her head, Scarlet turned back to the house and disappeared through the sliding glass door.

With a curse, Mason dropped down into one of the deck chairs. He cradled his head in his hands and prayed that his body could forget just how badly it wanted her.

Four

Despite her late night with Mason, Scarlet found herself awake just as the sun came up. She sat for a moment, reliving the thrill of his kiss and the sting of his words, before she realized she needed to get up and try to put last night behind her. Despite their attraction to one another, which had never waned, he was right about their relationship being so complicated.

Over time, it had simply become one of those situations where being together hurt more than being apart. Seeing each other was just a reminder of everything that had gone wrong. At least for Mason. He intended to maintain his distance while they were stuck in this situation together, and so she needed to respect that, no matter how fast he made her heart race and her skin tingle from his touch. Attraction didn't solve any of their issues.

She wrapped up in her silk robe and crept downstairs as quietly as she could. As she did every morning, she started a pot of coffee, took her vitamins and stared blankly into the refrigerator for something to eat. When she found nothing, she shut the fridge and found herself looking at the nursery door just beyond it.

Last night, with Luna crying, she'd ignored the sense of anxiety that normally kept her from going inside that room. She'd suppressed it all, scooped the crying infant from her crib, changed her diaper and run out into the living room as quickly as she could. She hadn't allowed herself to look around at the cheery blue walls, the stuffed animals on the shelves or the fabric sign over the crib that read "Evan." She didn't need to. She knew every inch of that room despite having not gone in it in nearly fourteen months.

This morning, there was no baby crying. No reason for her to charge in. Even so, she wanted to check on Luna while the coffee was brewing. She went to the door and stopped. It was harder than she'd expected to reach out and grab the doorknob without Luna's cry urging her on. It was a simple action, yet an important one for her. The only sound in the whole house seemed to be her heart pounding in her chest as she moved her hand closer. As her fingers wrapped around the cold metal, she hesitated again.

Scarlet didn't know why this room meant so much. Why it was so important. It felt like all she had left of Evan, but that wasn't really true. He wasn't in that room. It was just wasted space filled with unused baby things. At least that was what Mason had tried to tell her.

A few months after they lost Evan, he'd encouraged her to redecorate. If they weren't going to try to adopt again, what was the point of keeping it a nursery? They could turn it into a home gym. Or a library. Or a storage room. He didn't care, as long as it wasn't a pale blue shrine to the child they'd lost. Scarlet had been aghast at the mere suggestion. That was where the conversation had stopped until Luna needed a place to stay.

He was right. She knew that. Taking a deep breath, Scarlet turned the knob, allowing the door to click open. The early-morning sunlight streamed in through the window, highlighting the crib and the very awake baby in it. Luna had used the rails of her crib to pull herself up and was standing there with a slobbery grin on her face when she saw Scarlet. Apparently, the baby was a morning person.

"What are you doing awake?" Scarlet asked.

Luna immediately started babbling and bouncing up and down while she held to the rail. Scarlet couldn't suppress her grin as she watched her niece. She had always been such a happy baby. It was unthinkable that she should have so much tragedy in her life so early. She supposed it was good that Luna wouldn't remember any of it, but at the same time, she also wouldn't remember what a good mother Rachel was, or how much Jay doted on his baby girl.

That was the thought that propelled Scarlet one step, then two steps into the nursery.

As she got closer, Luna reached out to her to be picked up. Without her grip on the crib, she lost her balance and fell backward, hitting her head with a loud crack on the wooden crib back. The grin vanished, followed by a loud howl of pain and fear. Scarlet didn't hesitate to rush forward and scoop Luna into her arms. The baby was instantly red-faced with tears streaming down her fat cheeks.

"Mama-a-a!" Luna wailed, making Scarlet's chest ache as she thought about the mama who wouldn't come.

Scarlet cradled Luna against her breast, rubbing her back and mumbling the first soothing words that came to mind as they rocked back and forth. Gently, she let her hand smooth over the back of Luna's head as she checked for a cut or a scrape, but she didn't find any. Luna might have a bit of a knot in a few hours, but mostly she'd just scared herself taking a tumble.

After just a few minutes with Luna curled up in her arms, the sobbing finally subsided. When Scarlet looked down, Luna was watching her with big blue eyes that were so much like Mason's. Both he and Jay had the same unusually blue eyes and Luna had inherited them from her daddy. She also had the dark curly hair and dimples of the Spencer side of the family. Scarlet imagined that a stranger would have no problem thinking Mason was Luna's father.

It made her chest tighten to think that any babies they could've had would have looked like Luna. They would've made beautiful babies if they'd been granted the ability to do so. As she looked down at her, Luna reached her fingers up to touch Scarlet's face. Her eyes started to tear up at the innocent gesture and she felt the last of her resolve starting to crumble.

It wasn't supposed to be like this. She was supposed to keep her distance so she didn't get too attached to another baby she couldn't keep. This baby was going to be raised by her husband. Her future ex-husband. Not her. That meant she was at a high risk of getting her heart broken again, the one thing she swore she'd never let herself do. Scarlet knew how she was—any baby turned her to butter. A beautiful, happy baby who needed a mother more than anything in the world? That was impossible to resist. Perhaps she was wasting energy fighting it.

Once Luna was soothed, Scarlet was able to take a deep breath and realize that she'd been standing in the nursery for a good five minutes. Nothing had happened. It was just a room filled with furniture and things. The specter of her lost baby didn't haunt her the way she thought it would. It was a relief, and yet the relief was tempered by the fear that she was happily embarking on another path to heartache.

Looking down at Luna, Scarlet realized there was nothing she could do about it. She could try to stay objective, try to remember that this situation was temporary, but telling herself that she could resist this baby girl was a damn lie. She wanted to smell her baby shampoo and rock her until she fell back to sleep.

In fact, she decided to do just that. Scarlet walked over to the rocking recliner and sat down for the first time since she'd handed over her adopted son to child services.

Sitting in the rocker with him had been one of her favorite things. Some nights, Mason had to force her to put Evan in his crib because she wanted to just stay in her chair and hold him all night while he slept. Cradling Luna in her lap now felt different, but still good.

Before long, Luna had drifted back to sleep and Scarlet felt her own eyelids getting heavy. She closed her eyes for what seemed like a second and a half.

"Scarlet?" a voice whispered.

She opened her eyes and saw Mason standing in the doorway of the nursery. He looked just as surprised to see her in the nursery as she was to see him fully dressed in one of his suits and surrounded by late-morning sunlight. Scarlet winced at the glare coming through the window where there had only been soft dawn light a moment before. "What time is it?"

"After eight. I've got to go into the office today. Carroll just left to see the doctor. Will you be okay with Luna by yourself? Do I need to call someone to help?"

She hadn't just blinked; she and Luna had both dozed hard for almost two hours. She'd slept better in this chair holding her than she had in months. In a year, even. How was it that having a baby in her arms made her so much more contented and relaxed? Suddenly, it felt silly for her to demand a nanny around to care for Luna while they were staying with her. She obviously didn't need the help. It was only to keep her from getting too close. She feared that was an unavoidable risk, nanny or no.

"No, we don't need help. I'm sure we'll be okay," Scarlet said.

Mason watched her curiously for a moment, narrowing his gaze at the two of them sitting in her rocking chair. "You're sure? I could call Mom."

Scarlet shook her head vigorously. "Don't you dare drag your mother into this. Really, just go. We'll be fine. I think we'll have some Cheerios and maybe a little fruit, then go play on the beach for a bit. It looks like a clear, sunny day for splashing in the ocean. Maybe we'll even get in the pool if it's warm enough."

"Okay." Mason seemed reluctant, but whatever was going on at work would trump his concerns. It always did. You didn't turn a single store into a national chain by sitting idly by and letting things evolve naturally. "I'll see you later this afternoon. Call me if you need anything," he said before slipping from the doorway and disappearing down the hall.

With him gone, Scarlet looked at Luna. She was awake now and chewing on one slobbery fist. With all that chewing and drooling, she was probably getting some more teeth. She made a mental note to check Luna's bag for a teething ring she could put in the freezer. "I think someone is hungry. What do you say we get that diaper changed, find us both an outfit for today and have some breakfast? Does that sound good to you?"

"Dafin!" Luna said.

"Dolphin?" Scarlet repeated. She was surprised Luna remembered her new word from yesterday. Seeing them must have made quite an impression on her. "Do you want to go see the dolphins again?"

Luna just grinned, showing off the four little baby

teeth that had come in up front. That looked like a
yes to her. Scarlet stood up and laid Luna out on the
changing table. She unsnapped her onesie pajamas and
put on a clean diaper. As she pulled on the last of the
new outfit she'd chosen for her, Scarlet eyed the nursery wall. The wall the crib was on had no windows. It
was just a big expanse of blue with Evan's name sign
strung across it.

It was time for that to come down, Scarlet decided.
She propped Luna on her hip and reached up to unhook
the ribbon that was tied around one nail, then the other.
The plush fabric letters fell to the floor in a heap. She
held her breath as she looked back up at the now bare
wall for the first time since they'd hung that sign over
a year ago.

It felt good. She thought she might burst into tears
at the sight of Evan's sign crumpled on the ground, but
it actually made her feel as though a weight had been
lifted from her chest. Mason had been right, although
she wouldn't ever admit that to him.

Taking a step back, she looked around the room.
There were some other things in here that were due
for a change—baby boy clothes that could be donated,
some toys that Luna was too old to be interested in, all
that could go to make room for more of Luna's things.
And as for the big empty wall, Scarlet had an idea brewing for that.

With a satisfied smirk, Scarlet looked at Luna. "I
think we're going to do a little redecorating today."

Luna grinned and clapped her chubby little hands
together. She was a girl after Scarlet's own heart.

* * *

It ended up being a longer day at the office than Mason anticipated. He had planned to help take care of Luna so Scarlet wouldn't feel overwhelmed with Carroll gone, but he couldn't get away, and then he got stuck in the infamous LA traffic.

Mason wasn't quite sure what he was going to come home to that day, but he never would've bet on what he actually found. Carroll's car was still gone, making Mason nervous that Scarlet had been alone with Luna all day. He rushed through the front door, then stopped to listen. The living room and kitchen were empty and quiet. He couldn't see anyone through the wall-to-wall windows along the back of the house, so they weren't outside on the deck. Then he heard a giggle.

He set down his briefcase by the door and slipped out of his suit coat. He tossed it over the back of a chair as he made his way toward the nursery. There, he stopped short.

Finding Scarlet in the nursery that morning had been a surprise. Finding Scarlet back in the nursery— this time on a stepladder with a paintbrush in her hand—was another matter entirely. She was wearing a tank top and a pair of cutoff shorts that made her legs look four feet long. Her hair was pulled up into a messy knot on top of her head, exposing the long line of her neck and shoulders. She wasn't wearing makeup or even a bra as she worked, but Mason was captivated by her as usual.

Seeing her like this reminded him of the early days in their marriage when he would interrupt her work because he couldn't stand not to make love to her right that second. Things had been so easy between them then. Children were a far-off idea, not a recent source of constant heartache. It made him want to go back to the times when he could use his fingertip to play connect the dots with the tiny splatters of blue and green paint that decorated her pale skin after she worked.

Luna squealed, drawing his attention to where she was sitting and dousing any thoughts of messing around with his estranged wife. Luna was buckled into a bouncy chair on the floor, playing with a Taggies blanket that she seemed to prefer over her head. Behind her was all the nursery furniture that Scarlet had moved to the opposite wall so she had room to paint the mural.

Not just any mural, but a Scarlet Spencer original of dolphins swimming in an enchanting underwater scene. There was kelp drifting through the water like undersea trees, colorful schools of fish and coral providing highlights against the dark blues and greens of the water…and two half-painted dolphins as the centerpiece of the scene.

Scarlet had done a couple large-scale murals on the sides of aquariums and such, but she'd turned down repeated requests to paint a mural in a private residence. It made sense that the first one she did was in her own home, though. He just wondered why it had taken over seven years for her to think about doing it here.

Mason had always loved watching her work. When she was painting, her focus was 100 percent on her piece. Her canvases were typically so large that painting was almost like a ballet for her—reaching and turning and flicking her wrists to apply color in just the right place. When they had Evan, she switched to nontoxic paints and put an air purifier in her studio because she couldn't stand being apart from him long enough to work. She would swaddle him in a Boba Wrap, tucked against her chest, and he would sleep happily while she painted. Watching them move together was one of the most beautiful things he'd ever seen.

And watching her try to paint after they lost him was one of the most heartbreaking things he'd ever witnessed. He was suffering from the loss of their son, too, but somehow watching Scarlet go through her stages of grief had been harder than feeling it himself. Perhaps because he blamed himself for all of it. Somehow, he'd managed to hurt—not even hurt, nearly destroy—the one person he loved more than anything else. More than himself. That was why he'd walked away to give her a chance to be happy.

Capturing this perfect moment made him glad to see her so light of spirit again, but it also scared him. Was bringing Luna into her life temporarily going to hurt her again? Was coming back here with Luna going to ruin everything he'd done to help Scarlet move on with her life?

He hadn't thought about it that way when he asked her to play along with the marriage for Jay's sake. He'd only been focused on his grieving brother. When Scarlet took a distant stance from him and Luna, he'd almost been offended by it. But now that he saw what it truly meant for her to let her guard down and let Luna, at least, into her life, he understood how much he'd really asked of her.

He felt guilty, but it was too late to change it now. All he could do was hope that being with Luna for a few weeks would help her heal and move on from losing Evan. Maybe it would even inspire her to find that new family with someone who could give her the biological children that she wanted.

Mason watched Scarlet dip her brush into a gray paint and start to fill in the space where one of the dolphins would be. He knew from watching her that there would be layer after layer of color and highlight on top of this, but it was a start. Considering she'd begun the mural when he left for work, she was moving along amazingly fast. That typically took a big dose of inspiration for Scarlet.

"Wow," he said, the words slipping from his lips.

Scarlet's brush hand stiffened and pulled away before she turned to look at him. She smiled and set the brush on the tray so it didn't drip down the wall and ruin her work. "Hello there. I didn't hear you come in. Luna and I have been very busy today."

"I noticed. What's all this about?" he asked.

Scarlet climbed slowly down the stepladder and wiped her hands on the jean shorts that were already speckled with a million different colors of paint. Before she could answer, Luna pointed at the wall and said, "Dafin!"

They both looked at Luna and smiled wide. "That, right there," Scarlet said, "is what it's all about. That's all she's been saying since she saw that pod yesterday.

Today I decided that this room needs a face-lift and who better to paint her a mural with dolphins than me?"

It all seemed perfectly logical when she said it, and if he hadn't battled with Scarlet for months over changing this very same room, he might be able to follow along. Instead, his gaze fell on the stack of boxes and bags in the corner. Evan's things. "What about all that?" He gestured to the pile.

Scarlet followed his gaze and nodded. "We're starting fresh. Luna isn't going to use any of that stuff, so I decided to donate it to someone who could. Right now, it's just in her way. Isn't it?"

She turned her attention to Luna in her bouncy chair. Luna grinned and flung her Taggies blanket out of reach. Scarlet unsnapped Luna's safety belt and lifted her up out of the seat. As she held her, Luna reached out to touch a smear of dried blue paint across Scarlet's cheek.

"Am I messy?" she asked, but the baby just grinned. Instead, she turned to Mason. "Do I need to hose down in the yard?"

"It's not that bad. I think the shower will be adequate."

Scarlet frowned and walked over to the mirror that was attached to the dresser. "You're a liar. I'm an absolute mess."

Mason just shrugged. "You know I always liked you messy. Just like you always liked me with saltwater hair and wet-suit tan lines."

Scarlet smiled for a moment, both of them thinking back to the happier times where painting, surfing and being in love had been the center of their lives and their marriage. Then her smile slowly faded and she rubbed absently at her cheek. "I'd better get in the shower," she said.

"I'll take Luna," he offered. "Where's Carroll?"

Scarlet handed the baby over to him and he noticed just how careful she was not to touch him in the process. He supposed that was his own fault after the way he reacted the night before. It wasn't that he didn't want to touch her. He wanted that more than anything. Kissing her last night had relit a fire inside him that he'd tried unsuccessfully to squash the last few months. If he didn't walk away then, he knew that he would want to touch her, make love to her...and then where would they be? He wanted Scarlet; he just knew that he shouldn't want her. Even then, he couldn't help but feel slighted by her avoidance.

"She has the flu. She got the medicine, but the doctor said she's contagious for another twenty-four hours, so she's staying with her sister. She's hoping she'll be back tomorrow afternoon. The day after at the latest."

Whether it was good or bad for Scarlet's situation, he had to admit he was relieved that she was okay caring for Luna. Mason wasn't entirely sure what he would do in this scenario if the nanny was sick and he had to take care of the baby on his own. He had been thrown into the deep end of the parenting pool without warning or a life preserver. Scarlet was all he had to cling to in a time like this and he was very grateful for her help.

"It sounds like you deserve a treat. How about after your shower, we go to Rico's for dinner? That's still your favorite, right? We can relax, have some good food, a nice night out just the three of us."

Scarlet looked at him curiously before nodding slowly. "It's still my favorite. Are you sure you want to do that, though? We could just as easily order takeout. We'll have to play the public couple if we go out and run into someone we know."

That was true. They really hadn't had to try since the funeral. Carroll didn't seem too interested in their business at home. "To be honest, we've been apart for such a short time compared to how long we were together, it's easier to pretend to be a couple than to try to be apart. Unless you mind...?" He stopped, waiting for her to say she didn't want to be seen in public with him.

"No, I don't mind."

With a sigh of relief, he smiled. "Then go get ready."

"Okay." Scarlet smiled and disappeared up the stairs to the master suite.

Mason watched her climb the staircase, her cutoff shorts creeping higher with every step. His mind easily made the leap to running his hands over her smooth skin and wrapping those legs around his waist. He'd missed that. Missed her.

Then Mason looked at Luna and cursed silently. He didn't know what he was thinking, fantasizing about Scarlet like that. Just because she had warmed up to Luna didn't mean that they were on their way to being one big, happy family. Scarlet still wanted and needed her own family. They were just pretending, and when Jay was gone, they'd both go back to living their own separate lives.

The wheels of their divorce continued to turn, no matter how attracted they might be to each other or how natural it felt to be in the same house again. They were miles away from raising Luna together.

And it was his own fault.

Five

"Do you want dessert?"

Scarlet looked at him and shook her head. "Not only am I full enough to burst, but this one is about to pass out in her high chair."

They both glanced over at Luna. Her eyes were getting heavy and she was weaving steadily in her seat. It was a late night for her. Dinner had been nice, but it hadn't been a fast process. He hadn't really considered that when he chose this place. They'd never attempted to come here as a family before with Evan, so time hadn't really been a factor he'd considered. Thankfully, Luna hadn't fussed once. She was happy in her chair with a bottle, some finger nibbles and her favorite stuffed bunny.

"I bet she's going to be asleep before we leave the parking lot," he said. "If she lasts that long."

Mason paid the tab and, when they were ready, lifted Luna up out of her high chair. She curled against his chest, resting her head on his shoulder. On instinct, he pressed a kiss to her forehead. She had that baby smell he remembered from giving Evan baths—a distinct mix of milk and baby shampoo.

It reminded him that he hadn't really spent that much time caring for Luna. Carroll was doing most of the work, with Scarlet filling in for her while she was sick. Thank goodness Scarlet had stepped up. A nanny was nice, but they couldn't be there every second, as this bout of flu had proven. Scarlet had been the one to take on most of Evan's care while he worked long hours expanding his business into Florida. He didn't know a thing about babies, really. He didn't know what he would've done without her.

Hopefully, Carroll would continue on with him once they moved to his place in the Hills, but he would need to work on a secondary backup option, as well. Scarlet wouldn't always be there to bail him out. He might be doing okay with a happy, sleepy baby, but a cranky one, a fussy one, or basically any other ailment that caused a baby to scream or spew fluids...he'd be thoroughly clueless.

He stopped just as they reached the front door and found Scarlet watching him with a curious look on her face. "What?" he asked. "Is she drooling on my lapel?"

"No, your suit coat is fine. You two just look sweet together. She's so comfortable there that she's already fallen asleep in your arms," Scarlet said as she propped open the door and they stepped outside the restaurant.

"I always had a way with the ladies."

"You put them to sleep?" Scarlet asked with a grin.

"Pretty much. You stayed awake, though, so I married you."

Scarlet opened the car door so Mason could fasten Luna into her car seat. "So, that was the determining factor, eh? I thought it was my sparkling personality."

Mason shut the door and turned to look at her. Scarlet was leaning against the driver's-side door with her arms crossed, surveying him. Her wavy hair was loose around her shoulders, covering the bare skin that her flimsy strappy top exposed. For some reason, she looked younger tonight. More like the girl he'd fallen in love with at the beach. That Scarlet never looked at him with disappointment in her eyes the way his wife Scarlet did.

It took everything he had not to reach out and touch her. He wanted to brush a strand of dark hair from her eyes, run his fingertips down her bare arm and kiss her against the side of his Range Rover until she was breathless. His brain just couldn't seem to convince his body that she wasn't his any longer.

"Your sparkling personality certainly helped." He leaned into her, bracing his hand on the roof of the car. "So did the fact that you were beautiful, talented, smart and yet stupid enough to be attracted to me. I had to jump on that before some other guy snatched you up."

Scarlet smiled, then reached out to touch his face. It was a simple, casual touch, and yet it made his blood heat in his veins until he was forced to loosen his tie.

"I've missed you, Mason."

Mason couldn't think of a smarter response in the moment while she was touching him, so he opted for honesty. "I've missed you, too." He had. More than he ever expected to. Every night he had to convince himself not to call her. She couldn't move on if he didn't get out of her life.

"What happened to us?" she asked. "I would've told anyone who would listen that you and I would be together for the long haul. And here we are, on the verge of finalizing our divorce. Sometimes I look around our empty house and wonder what the hell went wrong."

"I let you down," Mason said. "That's what happened."

Scarlet's dark eyes widened and caught the reflection of the parking lot lights. She seemed surprised by his words, although he didn't know why. It seemed obvious to him.

"You let me down? Are you serious?"

Mason flinched at her words. "Yes, I'm serious. You and I both know that our problems started when I couldn't give you the children you wanted."

Scarlet's hand moved from his face to his chest, where it pressed insistently. "You stop right there. We've already had this fight ten times, but you don't ever seem to listen to me when I tell you that I don't blame you for that. Yes, I wanted children, but you certainly didn't let me down. It's out of your control. Life doesn't always work out the way you expect it to, Mason. You've got to roll with the punches."

"And our attempt at adoption was certainly a one-two punch to the gut."

Scarlet sighed and shook her head. "We had some bad luck, that's true. I'll admit that it scared me enough not to want to try adoption a second time. But again, that isn't your fault. You know that, right? There's nothing we could've done to convince the judge once Evan's birth mother changed her mind. I feel like I've been talking to a wall for the last year and nothing I say or do has any impact on you aside from just pushing you further away."

She might not blame him, but he certainly blamed himself. "You aren't pushing me away. I left all on my own."

Scarlet's hand dropped to her side, stealing the warmth of her body from his chest. "I know. You've made that clear, but it doesn't make any sense to me. Tell me the real reason why you left me because I still don't understand."

Mason looked Scarlet in the eye, but the pained expression on her face stole the words from his lips. She looked tired, older in that moment, like the last few years weighed as heavily on her shoulders as they did on his own. He hated that he was the one responsible for it.

She did deserve an answer, though. They'd never really had this fight. Not exactly. After everything happened with Evan, they'd just drifted apart until they were two people moving around one another in the same house. Their conversations never seemed to stray beyond what they would have for dinner and when the trash needed to be taken to the curb. That wasn't a marriage and he knew it. He just didn't know what to do about it.

"I told you before. I left…to give you a chance at happiness."

"Bullshit."

Scarlet's sharp words startled Mason from his next response. "What?" he asked instead.

Her face flushed as red as her name as she shook her head. "Don't you dare walk away from our marriage and then have the audacity to tell me that you did it for me. This is not what I wanted. This is not what I asked for. Yes, I wanted a family, but until you walked out that door, Mason, *you* were my family. Now I have nothing. No baby, no husband."

"But you have the hope of something better than what I could give you. A month, a year, even two years from now, the right man could walk into your life and give you everything you wanted."

"And what if all I really wanted was to be happy?" she asked. "With you."

Mason was at a loss for words. He had a hard time believing she really, truly felt that way. She might now, but in fifteen years when her opportunity had passed, she would resent him. He didn't want his wife to harbor animosity toward him, now or in the future.

"If I thought I could make you happy, I'd tear those divorce papers up in a heartbeat."

Scarlet stood silent and still as she watched his face. He couldn't tell whether she was hoping he would call off the divorce or was terrified by the idea of it.

"But I don't think I can," he continued, watching her face fall and her gaze drop to the ground. "I think being back together for this short time has just confused things between us. Pretending to be married, raising Luna together… I worry that this situation will make us think we're feeling things again when we really aren't."

Mason thought he was saying the right things, but the look that formed on Scarlet's face told him otherwise.

She put her hand back on his chest. "So when I feel your heartbeat speed up when I touch you… I'm not really feeling that?"

"Well, I…"

Scarlet's hand traveled down his stomach and located the desire he'd tried hard to hide from her. "And this?" she asked. "Am I imagining that, too?"

"No." There was no sense in arguing that. "I've never stopped wanting you, Scarlet. Our divorce has never been about that. It's been—"

"Stop," Scarlet said. "Stop saying things that you and I both know don't really mean anything. You're letting your mind get in the way of how your body feels. I know what it wants. And I know what I want. At least for tonight. Forget about the divorce and what you should or shouldn't do right now. Tonight, show me how you feel about me, Mason, and kiss me."

Scarlet's palm pressed hard into the fly of his suit pants, and what little restraint he had left vanished. Lunging forward, he captured her face in his hands and pinned her body back against the side of the car. The night before, their kiss had been almost like that of teenagers, getting a feel for new territory. Tonight, they were old lovers reunited.

The way her tongue grazed along his…the way her back arched and pressed into his body…the way she gave herself to him in every way he demanded… That was like coming home. His whole body responded to the familiar stimuli, his nerves lighting up and demanding more.

And if he was honest with himself, he wanted more. He wanted everything he'd missed out on since their relationship disintegrated in his hands. If he set aside all the reasons why they couldn't be together, just for tonight, he wouldn't be able to stop from claiming her as his own. But he didn't want to do it in a restaurant parking lot with Luna asleep a foot away. As much as he hated to, he pulled away, giving himself some distance and perspective. It was possible that the moment would pass and he wouldn't get this opportunity again, but it didn't matter.

Scarlet looked up at him with the sleepy, passionate eyes that he recognized from their years together. She wasn't finished with him. Not even close. "Now take me home, put Luna to bed, and let's finish this properly."

Scarlet was thankful that Luna slept like a rock. They carried her inside, changed her into a clean diaper and pajamas, and put her down in her crib without her so much as squirming or making a cry of complaint.

They shut the door of the nursery and found themselves standing at the bottom of the staircase together.

It was now or never.

She might regret this later, but right now she didn't care. She couldn't remember the last time she'd made love to Mason. Things had been so strained. Even if this was the one and only time they gave in to their desires for each other, she was okay with that. But she was going to burn tonight into her memories forever.

Reaching out to him, she took his hand and led him upstairs. In the bedroom they'd once shared, she walked over to the wall of windows and opened them up to let the sea air and night breezes blow through. Outside, the sky was as inky black as the sea with the moonlight highlighting the crest of the waves as they washed ashore. In the distance, the lights of ships were visible as they disappeared into the horizon.

As she watched the water, she felt the heat of Mason's body come up behind her and envelop her. She leaned back against him, letting him snake his arms around her waist and pull her close. Scarlet had always loved the feel of being in Mason's arms. She'd never been the daintiest or most graceful of women—at five-ten and with a solid build that inevitably weighed more than anticipated on the scales, she'd been envious of the petite women with their tiny shoes, tiny clothes... Any man could lift them into his arms and carry them into the bedroom to make love to them.

That wasn't ever the case with Scarlet. At least before she met Mason. He was six-one with a large, strong build, and when he'd held her, he'd made her feel feminine and delicate for the first time. And on their wedding night, he had carried her over the threshold of their home, something she never thought would happen to her.

"I've missed this," he said as he swept her hair over one shoulder to expose the line of her neck. "I've missed touching you. Kissing you."

Scarlet closed her eyes to fully experience every sensation as his mouth ran from her shoulder up to the hollow behind her ear. It felt like sparks flickering across her skin, the heat making her shiver despite the warm night air. She couldn't remember how long it had been since he touched her like this, but she wanted to remember this moment for as long as she could.

Mason slipped the flimsy straps of her top off her shoulders along with her bra straps. She held her breath in her lungs as she waited for his touch. Her breasts ached to be held again.

Mason didn't disappoint. He unsnapped her bra and let it fall to the floor along with the top, which slipped over her hips and gathered at her feet. His large hands immediately covered her bare breasts, his warm touch making her nipples pebble against his palms.

The air rushed out of her lungs on a pleasurable sigh. She melted into him, rolling her head back over his shoulder and exposing her throat and chest for Mason to do as he pleased. He pinched and teased at her rippled flesh, knowing just how to ride the line between pleasure and pain and drawing a cry from the back of her throat.

As he held one breast firmly in his left hand, Mason's right hand strayed down her soft belly to the waistband of her skirt. He slipped beneath it, moving aside her panties to find her silky center with his fingertips.

Scarlet gasped and arched into his hand. "Mason…" she whispered.

"It's been too long," he said. "A woman like you isn't meant to go without a man's touch. You're already ready for me. I guess that means we can save a long night of foreplay for another day."

A ping of awareness went off in Scarlet's brain. Did tonight mean more than she thought it did? It didn't sound as though he was working under the premise of one night for old times' sake.

Did it matter? Not right now. She would deal with the fallout in the morning. She wasn't about to put on the brakes while he was stroking her center so expertly. He had been right about one thing—she was ready for him. He'd barely touched her and she was aching to have him. One stroke across her sensitive parts had put her on the edge. If he wanted to, he could send her over with the flick of his wrist.

And he knew it.

"Are you close?" he asked. "I want to hear you come apart for me. That sound has haunted my dreams these last few months without you in my bed. Let me hear it again. I thought I never would."

Scarlet barely had a choice in the matter. He placed a breathy kiss against her neck and stroked her hard and fast. In half a heartbeat, she found herself trembling in his arms.

"Yes," he coaxed as the pleasure washed over her like the crashing waves down below.

Suddenly, her knees were like butter, her throat was raw from her cries, and if not for Mason's support, she'd be pooled on the floor with her clothes. He held her tight through the whole thing, finally walking her backward to the bed. She didn't have enough energy to do anything other than exactly what he guided her to do.

With the backs of her calves pressed against the bed, she fell onto the mattress. Mason moved quickly to her hip, where he located the zipper to her skirt and slid it down. She lifted her pelvis just high enough for him to pull the skirt and her panties down the length of her legs.

Scarlet expected him to join her on the bed, but instead he simply stood there, admiring her. "What is it?" she asked.

"You're just so beautiful," he said.

She squirmed under his scrutiny. "I look the same as I ever have."

"Exactly. You were beautiful then and you're beautiful now." He started unbuttoning his shirt with his eyes still fixed on her naked body. "I'd tried to convince myself that you weren't as sexy as I remembered. That I'd embellished your appeal in my mind. But I was wrong. You're even more alluring than you were in my memories."

Mason tugged his shirt off and threw it aside. Scarlet tried not to stare too much at his broad chest and strongly carved arms, but she couldn't help it. It was her favorite part of him. Years of paddling his surfboard out into the sea had created a hard, defined body. She could even remember the first time she'd seen him walk up onto the beach with his wet suit peeled down to his waist. Her tongue had suddenly become so large in her mouth that she could barely speak when he said hello to her.

The years had added a few pounds and a manly scattering of chest hair, but she liked it. She was especially happy to see his trousers declaring he felt the same way about her. Scarlet licked her lips in anticipation as Mason unfastened his belt and slipped out of his pants.

She pushed herself into a seated position and slid farther back across the bed. As she inched away, Mason moved forward until his large body was hovering over her own. The heat of his skin so near to her own chased away the chill of the sea air. It made her want to curl against him. Instead, she lay back and wrapped her arms around his neck to pull him into a kiss.

Mason propped on his elbows and settled against her body as his lips touched hers. The heat of his skin pressed against hers sent a chill through her and a wave of goose bumps in its wake. She couldn't get enough of him—his kiss, his touch, his scent.

Scarlet had tried to be strong as she watched their marriage fall apart—as Mason started sleeping in the guest room before finally moving out entirely. He had pulled away from her and taken with him everything that she loved, everything that was important in her life. Now, as she held everything precious to her in her arms and cradled him between her thighs, she wasn't sure whether to hold on tighter so she wouldn't lose him again, or to cling to her heart instead. She could only choose one.

Tonight could be just tonight. Or it could be a few days, a few weeks of enjoying the physical side of their relationship while they could. There was no way to know. Once Jay passed, everything would change, and Scarlet wasn't sure how she wanted things to end. Did she dare hope to keep Mason and Luna in her life? To hope, only to lose them both, was something she wasn't sure she could go through again.

"Get out of your head," Mason whispered in her ear.

He'd caught her overthinking this. It was the risk of giving herself to someone who knew her almost better than she knew herself. Before she could respond, he pressed into her. As his firm heat pushed farther inside of her, setting off sparks of pleasure through her body, all the thoughts and worries disappeared. This moment, right here, was all she needed to focus on. She needed to enjoy it. Cherish it.

Scarlet pulled her knees up to cradle his hips and draw him deeper inside. He groaned and swore softly against the bare skin of her shoulder before nipping gently at it. She gasped and arched her back, urging him on.

Mason thrust into her, apparently setting aside any thoughts of a slow, romantic seduction as his need took over everything else. She raised her hips to meet his every advance, feeling the familiar tension in his body increase even as her own release built up inside her again.

"Are you going to come for me again?" he asked in a rough voice that betrayed how close he was. "Please say yes. I need to hear it again." Mason slipped his hand between them to stroke her center.

"Yes," she gasped. "I…" was all she managed to get out before Mason thrust hard inside of her and she came apart. Like glass shattering, the pleasure shot through her in every direction and then rained down all over her body.

Through her own cries of passion, she heard Mason's own low groan as he stiffened and poured into her. Rolling to his side, he collapsed onto the bed beside her.

After a few moments of rushed breath and racing heartbeats, the room grew awkwardly quiet. Now that the wave of passion had faded, they seemed to be at a loss for words. She wasn't sure what to do. Normally, she would've curled against him and fallen asleep. That felt a bit too comfortable, too familiar for where they found themselves now. That was the risky part of falling back in bed with an old lover—moving too far, too fast. She didn't want to do that and ruin the moment, along with any chance of future moments.

But the mood had probably already soured. Scarlet could almost feel the tension, as if a cloud of regret was settling down over them both. It had come even more quickly than she ever anticipated.

The loud cry of Luna echoing from downstairs provided her the out she desperately needed. "I'll get her," she said. Rolling out of bed, she pulled her robe out of the closet and slipped it on before disappearing from the room.

As though things weren't already complicated enough without the reminder of why they were really together.

Six

Mason awoke the next morning back on the futon in Scarlet's studio. She hadn't asked him to leave the night before, but the speed at which she fled their bed had made it obvious that she had some regrets over what had happened. He had a few of his own, although they hadn't been enough to stop him from sleeping with her again.

While she had been downstairs with Luna, he'd gathered up his clothes and carried them back to the studio with him. She hadn't come looking for him. He hadn't even heard her come back upstairs. Instead, he was awakened by sunlight and the sound of Luna squealing with laughter.

He knew he needed to go downstairs and talk to Scarlet about what happened. They were adults. Married adults at that. He was supposed to be able to tell her anything, but he was dragging his feet because he wasn't sure what kind of conversation he wanted to have with her.

Mason opted for a shower instead to gather his thoughts first. As he stepped into the streams of steamy water, he was reminded of the warm oblivion he'd found in Scarlet the night before. He'd missed it. That much had been obvious. Their physical relationship had been passionate and nearly overwhelming. That hadn't changed even as their circumstances had. But was it the right thing for both of them? Especially for Scarlet?

Leaving her had been hard. Walking out of their home with luggage in his hands had been one of the most difficult things he'd ever done. He never thought he and Scarlet would divorce, much less that he would be the initiator. The only thing that had propelled his concrete-filled shoes down the driveway to his car was the knowledge that this was the best thing for her. She didn't believe that, but it was true.

They'd both survived the separation. Like riding out a rough withdrawal, they'd made it through to the other side only to backslide. Now he had to decide if he was going to continue to indulge in something he knew he shouldn't, or if he was going to put himself through the hell of getting over her a second time.

If he'd actually gotten over her the first time.

He'd fallen into her bed so quickly it made him think otherwise.

Once he was dressed and had made it downstairs, he found Scarlet in the nursery painting again. She was back on the ladder in one of his old T-shirts she'd long ago claimed and a pair of yoga pants smeared in blue and orange paint. Luna was lying on the baby jungle activity mat on the floor, alternating between laughing and chewing on a toy tiger that hung from the bar overhead.

"Good morning," Scarlet said without turning away from her work. Her voice was frustratingly neutral, giving him no clue to which outcome she was hoping for today.

"Morning," he replied with the same noncommittal voice. "It's looking great."

"Thanks. I should have it done today or tomorrow depending on how much Lulu lets me work."

An idea came to Mason's mind. "I was actually thinking of taking her to see Jay today before I went into the office. That would give you a couple hours to work uninterrupted." *And give us some time apart to think.* "Then Carroll should be back soon, right?"

Scarlet set down the brush and nodded. "That's what she said, but I told her that if she's still feeling bad she should stay with her sister. She may not be contagious, but she'll be miserable and that's not good either. I'm not worried about it, although you taking Luna to see Jay is a great idea. She's fed and dressed for the day. You'll just need to pack a diaper bag to take with you. There's a bottle made up in the fridge."

Mason hadn't thought that far ahead. Running an errand with a baby in tow was a completely different scenario. It was something he'd managed to stay ignorant of when they had Evan. Scarlet had stayed home with him while he was at work. This time, it would be just him and Luna. He had to remember the diapers, the wipes, the toys and the food. He had to know how to set up the stroller and how to change a diaper without it sliding right off.

Carroll would be there to help in the future, but he needed to know these things, too, if he was going to be a single father. The idea was terrifying. He owned and ran a major retail chain he'd started from a cart on the beach. He could handle any crisis, and yet this tiny human threw him for a loop. He wouldn't tell his brother or Scarlet or anyone else how he felt, but it was true.

"Thank you," he muttered, turning in search of the diaper bag she'd referenced. After a moment of searching in vain, he heard the creak of the ladder as Scarlet climbed down.

She went straight to the bag, lifting it over onto the changing table. She grabbed a handful of diapers and stuffed them inside the bag. "This is more than you'll need, but better safe than sorry. There's already wipes in here and a change of clothing in case of disaster."

"Disaster?" Mason frowned.

"Yes, either she spits up all over herself or she has a massive diaper malfunction."

"Oh," he said with wide eyes. Those were possibilities that hadn't even crossed his mind.

"There's a container of Cheerios left over from last night and, like I said, a bottle in the fridge."

Mason lifted the bag. "Thank you."

Looking up, he noticed that Scarlet was making eye contact with him for the first time since the night before. "You'll be fine. You'll learn all this soon enough."

He was glad she had confidence in him. He wasn't
so sure. Before he forgot, he grabbed the bottle from the
refrigerator and tucked it into the diaper bag. He slung
it over his shoulder and picked Luna up off the floor.
"Thanks, Scarlet." The words felt odd in his mouth.
There was a time when he never said her name. Scarlet's name was "babe." But despite last night, it didn't
seem appropriate. Things were…unresolved at best.

"Say hello to Jay for me," she said before picking up
a brush and returning to the mural.

"Will do." Mason and Luna headed out the door and
loaded into the car. Since the funeral, Jay had been
moved from the hospital to a hospice care facility. Some
terminal patients returned home, but with Rachel gone
and Luna with Mason, there was no point. The nursing
facility was closer to Malibu, so they were there in less
than twenty minutes.

After they signed in, they were directed to the hallway where Jay was now staying. He readjusted Luna
on his hip and knocked at the door.

"Come in," his brother's voice responded. At least
it sounded like a version of his brother's voice. It was
weak and shakier than he'd ever heard it before.

Mason pushed open the door and stepped in. "You've
got a very small visitor, Daddy."

Jay's eyes lit up the moment his gaze fell on Luna.
"Hello, my beautiful girl," he said, reaching out to hold
her.

Luna squealed with a wide grin and reached for
Jay. Mason gently settled her into Jay's arms, making
sure she wasn't pulling on any of his IVs or monitor-

ing wires. Once he was certain she was steady, he sat in the guest chair and gave them a moment together. They had precious few left.

"Thank you for bringing her by," Jay said after a couple of minutes chatting with her and getting big hugs. "She's the best medicine I've received in days."

"How are you feeling?" Mason asked.

"Truthfully?" he asked with a heavy sigh. "Like I'm about to die. But I've felt like this for several weeks now. Now that we've stopped treatment, I almost feel better. The chemo was so hard on my system. But even so, I know I'm counting down the hours."

Mason wanted to argue with his brother and tell him that negative talk wouldn't help matters, but he held his tongue. They were past the point of trying to be ridiculously positive. Cancer had won the war and they both knew it.

"How have things been with you and Scarlet lately?"

Mason sat bolt upright in his seat, an undisguised look of panic on his face. "What? What do you mean?"

"I mean how has it been for you two having Luna around? You've spent most of your marriage just the two of you. Suddenly having a baby in the house has to be different. Or even difficult, considering how long you two struggled to start a family."

Mason sighed in relief and shook his head. "It's an adjustment, I won't lie. We brought Carroll over, but she's had the flu the last few days, so we've been on our own. Scarlet has adapted to having a baby in the home faster than I have, of course—she was the one home with Evan while I was at work."

"You seem to be doing fine. Luna wasn't screaming when you came in, so she must like you."

Mason chuckled softly. "Well, that's just because she's a mellow baby and we've had her less than a week. I don't know how I'm going to handle the idea of every week from here on out. School, boys, makeup, broken hearts…"

Jay looked at his daughter as she snuggled against his chest. "You'll handle it like every other father handles it. You learn. You make mistakes. You get better. As long as she grows up to be a relatively functional member of society, you've done your job."

"You make it sound deceptively simple."

"It is that simple," Jay said. "And that hard. And that wonderful. You and Scarlet will do just fine. I have all the faith in the world that the two of you will be good parents. You might even be better at it than Rachel and I would've been because you two have wanted a child for so many years."

Mason's gaze dropped to the floor. He couldn't look his brother in the eye and not tip him off that something was wrong. Lying to Jay about the divorce had seemed like a good idea at the time. Now, facing him, it felt awful. Mason's only consolation was knowing that no matter what happened between him and Scarlet, Luna would be as well cared for as humanly possible. But he still couldn't tell Jay the truth. He couldn't bring back Rachel or cure his brother's cancer, but he could ease Jay's worries about Luna and her future.

So he would keep his damn mouth shut.

* * *

Scarlet and Luna were sitting on the beach together the following afternoon when her cell phone rang. She picked it up, spying her manager April's number on the screen.

"Don't eat the sand," she said to Luna as she answered the call.

"I'll try," April replied.

"Very funny." Scarlet wiped the sand off Luna's face and handed her the little plastic shovel to play with instead.

"I'm calling to be polite and warn you that I'm on my way to your place. I hate to just arrive unannounced."

Scarlet frowned at the ocean. "Thanks for the heads-up. Why are you coming by again?"

"Have you forgotten what day it is?"

She ran through a dozen options in her brain without landing on something relevant. "Thursday?"

"It's *Wednesday*. And no, that's not why I'm coming. I'm coming to pick up the Maui mural. You said you'd have it done by today. I've got to get it copied and crated to ship. It's done, right?"

"Yes, it's done." Thankfully, Scarlet had finished it up the day before as she attempted to avoid Mason when he got home from his visit with Jay. There might still be a couple tacky spots where it wasn't fully dry, but it was done. She'd set some fans up the night before to help it along.

"Good. I'll see you in ten."

The phone went dead. With a sigh, Scarlet stood up

and dusted the sand off her shorts. "We've got to go back inside, Lulu. Auntie April is on her way to get our whale picture for Mr. Bishop."

Luna stuck out her bottom lip and gave a yelp of displeasure as Scarlet picked her up off the beach towel. Settling the baby on her hip, she tossed the shovel into the bucket and picked up the towel with a shake. Back inside the house, she put Luna into her playpen. There, she immediately forgot about the beach and was content to find some of her favorite toys. With Luna happy, Scarlet went upstairs to check on the painting.

All things considered, it might just be one of her favorite pieces. It would be perfect for the Mau Loa Maui. She'd toured the hotel a few months back when she was desperate for a reason to get out of the house for a few days. Things at home had reached a fever pitch with Mason and she thought a break would help things between them.

It hadn't.

But the trip hadn't been completely in vain. The owner of the hotel, Kal Bishop, had given her the freedom to paint whatever she wanted to. Seeing the space where the painting would hang in the hotel helped her visualize what kind of piece to create and what scale would fit it.

It was also an inspiring trip. Seeing the humpback whales breaching just off the shore of the hotel had made it easy to decide what to feature. In the late winter and early spring months, the humpback whales traveled to the warm Hawaiian waters to mate and give birth to their calves. Typically, the mother and calf would be joined by a male escort who was there to protect them and hopefully get the chance to be the next calf's father. That was why she'd chosen to paint a large-scale image of three humpback whales—the mother, the calf and the escort.

As Scarlet was picking up the first panel to carry it downstairs, she heard the doorbell ring. She hauled it to the first floor and left it leaning against the wall to open the door.

April was standing there, looking smart in her linen suit and Gucci sunglasses. "You're not lying to me, right?" she asked without saying hello. "The painting is finished?"

"Finished, yes. Completely dry and ready to ship, perhaps not. You may want to wait a day or two before you get it photographed and scanned for the catalogs and prints. Then it should be dry enough to wrap it and box it up."

"I'll take it." April pushed into the door and turned to inspect the panel beside her.

Her critical eye had always been helpful to Scarlet. Sometimes she didn't know when a painting was truly finished. Usually "done" was determined by when April snatched it from her hands.

"What's it called?" she asked.

"New Life in Maui," Scarlet said.

"I could use a new life in Maui," April quipped. "There's three pieces?"

"Yes."

"I'll go lay down the seats of my Lexus."

Scarlet carried down the other two panels and they

were able to set them in the back of April's SUV without any wet-paint disasters. She expected April to take off, but instead she shut the trunk and followed Scarlet back into the house.

"Is it wine o'clock yet?"

Scarlet shrugged. "I've got a bottle of chardonnay in the chiller even if it isn't."

"Perfect."

April poured herself a glass while Scarlet checked on Luna. She looked like she was ready for her afternoon nap. After picking her up out of the playpen, she carried her into the nursery. Just as she got Luna settled in, she heard April's loud voice behind her.

"What the hell is that?" she shrieked.

"Shh!" Scarlet hissed before turning back to check on Luna. She looked a little surprised, with wide eyes, but after a moment of her little music box playing, she eventually closed her eyes again. Having dodged that bullet, Scarlet scooted April out of the room and shut the door behind her.

"I'm waiting," April said in a quiet yet annoyed tone.

Scarlet took her by the arm and led her over to the living room, where they sat on the couch. "It's just something I painted for Luna," she said at last.

"Luna, the little girl you were keeping your distance from? Luna, the baby that your soon-to-be ex-husband has custody of? Luna, the adorable chubby-cheeked child that has obviously wormed her way into your heart?"

That was a lot to take in all at once, but Scarlet listened and finally nodded. Thankfully, Mason was at the office and not around to hear all that. "Yes," she vocalized.

"Care to tell me what's changed since the last time I saw you?"

Not really. But Scarlet knew she needed someone to talk to. Things had gotten a little complicated lately. Wishing she had a glass of wine of her own but not wanting to drink while Luna was in her care, she took a deep breath and started at the beginning. She began with the first few awkward days, the late-night kiss, the nanny's illness and finally falling back into bed with Mason. The more she spoke, the more April's eyes seemed to widen. "And now we're avoiding one another," she said, finishing off her sordid tale.

"Uh-huh," April replied before taking a large sip of her wine. "It's hard to believe you've lived a life that dramatic and yet still managed to paint a huge panel piece and a mural."

"When I wanted to avoid Mason, I worked."

"Remind me to thank him later."

"Don't thank him just yet. I don't know that he deserves it."

"Why? Was the sex…?" April tilted her hand side to side in a "so-so" gesture.

"No! It was…well, it was just like it was before. Even more like it was early in our relationship. I'm just worried."

"About what?"

Scarlet sighed. "About everything. Mason walked away from me and bought that place in the Hills. Then the next thing I know, he's moving back in and kissing me. He makes love to me, and then he avoids me. Was I just a convenient outlet for pent-up sexual energy or did it mean something more to him? I don't know what to think of all of this. It's certainly not the fairy-tale reunion you're hoping for, I'm sorry to say."

April considered her words thoughtfully for a moment. "Well, there might be more to his motives than just sex or rekindling your romance. Do you think he's trying to win you back just so Luna will have a mother? Or more to the point, so he doesn't have to be a single father?"

Scarlet blinked a few times. She hadn't considered that before. He'd been the one pushing the divorce from day one. She'd never wanted it, but he wouldn't listen to her, as usual. This sudden turnaround once Luna entered the picture could be seen as suspicious. Did he really want *her* back or was he just unwilling to face his unexpected and scary future all alone?

"I don't know," Scarlet admitted. "But I do know he hasn't mentioned anything about a future together or calling off the divorce. Our night together felt very in the moment. As far as I know, all this ends once Jay is gone, since it's all for his benefit."

"Sleeping with you wasn't for Jay's benefit."

"True. That might've just been an unintended side effect of our arrangement. But he's acted weird since then. I think he regrets it."

"And do you regret it?"

More than ever, Scarlet wished that April had loaded up those panels and taken them to the shop instead of loitering around and digging into her personal business. These weren't easy answers. She wasn't about to let this go, though.

"I do and I don't. I regret that it complicated matters between us and strained what little friendship we had left. But at the same time, it was so amazing to be in his arms again. I've missed him. I wouldn't admit that to anyone but you, but I have. This whole scenario—pretending to be a family, living together again, having a baby to care for, making love—it has me all turned around. I don't know whether I'm coming or going anymore."

"Well, for your sake," April said, "I hope you're coming, or it's hardly worth the trouble."

"April!"

Her manager laughed and drained the last of her wine. "I kid, I kid. Just trying to keep things light. There's entirely too much drama in your life. Of course, you're an artist. You thrive on drama."

Scarlet wrinkled her nose. She hated drama. She wasn't a van Gogh out there pining for her lost love and painting her feelings. She painted what she saw. And yet, as an artist, she knew how her moods could affect her work. The mural in Luna's room had been a joyful piece because of how she felt painting it. So maybe April was onto something. "Whatever you say, manager lady."

"Can I get that recorded so I can hear it when you're being contrary or moody with me? No? Okay, fine." April set her wineglass down on the table and stood up. "I'm going to get those panels ready to go, and then I'm heading up to San Francisco to oversee the last-minute details of the gallery opening. All this drama isn't going to interfere with that, is it?"

"I don't think so." The only thing she could envision being an issue was if Jay were to pass, but there was no way of knowing when that would happen. April should know that was a possibility, so there was no reason to mention it to her and start her worrying unnecessarily.

"Well, I hope not. Opening your gallery without you there is kind of pointless. We've gotten over a hundred and fifty RSVPs from art connoisseurs in the area. They're coming to meet you and admire your work. I intend to sell more than a few of your pieces that night and I need you there to shake their hands and talk up your work. Got it?"

Scarlet sighed. This was hardly her first gallery opening. She knew how it would work. Mingle, sip wine, smile and sell herself to the art-appreciating public. Normally, it didn't bother her. She much preferred days spent painting in dirty overalls with her hair in a ponytail, but dressing up every now and then to sell her work made those other days possible. "I'll be there with bells on."

"That's what I want to hear. My assistant will email you your itinerary and hotel information. I'll see you up there. Oh, and when you're done with that mural—" she gestured toward the nursery "—let me know. I'll send someone over here to photograph it and get it cataloged. I don't want any Scarlet Spencer originals floating around without my knowledge. It all goes into the portfolio."

"It's just a mural for Luna," Scarlet argued.

"If I had painted it, sure. But when an internationally recognized wildlife artist paints a giant mural of her subject of choice, it's not just decoration in a baby's room any longer. You should've opted for teddy bears if you didn't want me putting prints into production. Sorry."

Scarlet got up and walked April to the door. "Okay. I'll see you next weekend."

"All right. Keep me posted on how things are going with the ex. If necessary, we can book a second ticket and you can bring him with you."

Scarlet flinched. "Bring Mason with me to the opening?"

"Why not?" April asked. "If you two are still together publicly, wouldn't you want him to come? And even more importantly, don't you think some time alone with him could help you figure out what he really wants from you?"

She had a point, Scarlet had to admit. "I'll keep that in mind," she said. "We'll have to stop avoiding each other first."

April just smiled and slung her purse over her shoulder. "You two can't avoid each other for long. You've got more chemistry than a sophomore in high school."

Seven

Scarlet was at the store and Luna was taking a nap, since she'd been a little fussy all afternoon. Mason was finally getting more comfortable having the baby with no one else around, but he was certainly feeling more confident with Luna asleep. Carroll was planning on coming back tonight after several days of misery on her sister's couch, so soon neither he nor Scarlet would have to watch Luna every second of the day.

That was good. He had a company to run and Scarlet was headed to San Francisco soon to open her latest gallery. Neither of them had really had the chance to adapt their lives to the addition of a baby. If Scarlet could've gotten pregnant or they were going through the adoption process, they would've had months to plan and prepare before a child arrived. Luna was simply there one day. Carroll had been convenient to slip into their lives, but adjustments still needed to be made.

Especially once he was on his own without Scarlet.

She knew exactly what to do when it came to handling babies, while he was completely clueless. He wasn't entirely sure how she got so comfortable around them, but he admired her for it. A lot of it just seemed like a mother's instinct.

Mason was about to consider a nap of his own when he heard a sudden, angry wail coming from Luna's nursery. He didn't know much, but he was pretty certain that something was wrong. It didn't sound like her usual cry for food or a change of diaper. He opened the door to the nursery and found that she had gone from fussy to a complete meltdown.

She was standing in the crib, gripping the bars with her tiny fists. Her face was bright red with both tears and a stream of snot running down her face. He picked her up and held her close, her cheek brushing across his. He nearly flinched from the contact because her skin was burning up with fever.

Mason tried not to panic. Babies got sick. That was just what happened. But he didn't know exactly what to do. At the same time, he didn't want to call for help either. If he was going to raise Luna, he needed to be able to figure this out on his own.

He carried her over to the changing table and opened the drawers until he found one filled with creams, medicines and something that looked like a weird flashlight. Picking it up, he realized it was actually an in-ear thermometer. He tested it on himself, then carefully pressed it to Luna's ear.

After a few seconds, it beeped and the screen read 100.9 degrees. It was higher than his, but he wasn't sure how high was too high for her age. He carried her into the kitchen to look up the pediatrician's phone number where they'd posted it on the refrigerator for Carroll. He was fishing his phone out of his pocket while holding a squirming and still screaming Luna when Scarlet came in through the garage with her hands full of grocery bags.

Her dark brown eyes widened as she took in the scene in the kitchen. "What's wrong?" she asked and placed the groceries on the ground.

He'd never been so happy to see Scarlet in his life. He didn't want to call for help, but if she was here, he could at least watch and learn. "She woke up from her nap with a fever and a runny nose. I was about to call the pediatrician to see if we need to take her in or not."

"Did you take her temperature?"

"Yes," Mason said, thankful he'd at least gotten the first step right. "Yes, it's just under 101."

"That's good. Any higher can be dangerous. Did you give her some baby Motrin?"

He shook his head. "Not yet. Is that what you give babies for fever?"

Scarlet nodded. "It's in the guest bathroom cabinet. I'll go get it. That should help bring down her fever, and if we can't get her to the doctor until tomorrow, she'll at least be more comfortable."

"How do we get her to swallow a pill?" Mason asked, trailing behind her.

"It's a liquid." She pulled the box from the bathroom and showed him the bottle with the dropper. "She won't take pills until she's quite a bit older."

Mason felt both stupid and relieved at the same time. He remembered trying to get the family cat to take a pill once and it had been a nightmare. He couldn't imagine doing that to an infant. He had so much to learn; it was more intimidating than college. No matter how this new family had come about, Mason wanted to do a good job. He didn't want Luna to cry for her nanny when she was hurt or sick. He wanted her to want him, like she would her real daddy. That meant knowing how to handle these kinds of situations, and he was starting from the very bottom.

He held Luna as Scarlet filled the dropper and squirted it into Luna's open mouth. The sudden arrival startled her out of crying for a moment as she swallowed the medicine. Her bottom lip pouted out—he imagined the flavor wasn't so great—and then she began to cry again.

"What now?"

"I think we make her a cool bottle of electrolyte water so she doesn't get dehydrated and I'll call the doctor."

"Okay." Mason rocked Luna back and forth on the balls of his feet while Scarlet disappeared into the kitchen to make the call he'd tried to make earlier. By the time she'd gotten off the phone, Luna had calmed down a little, so he carried her into the living room and sat down in a recliner. He rocked back and forth, petting her back and trying to soothe her as much as he could. Eventually, her cries faded to a fussy sort of whining that was much easier to take.

He didn't like this at all. Mason was the CEO of his own company. He was used to being able to handle any situation. He snapped his fingers and a dozen people ran out of the room to make things happen. There was nothing he could do to fix this. They could give her medicine and make her comfortable, but an illness usually had to run its course. He didn't like seeing Luna miserable, and this was just a fever. He couldn't imagine her being seriously ill or hospitalized.

Scarlet came into the room with a bottle. "The nurse said that the fever is low enough not to bring her in tonight. At this point, they can't be sure if it's just a cold or if Carroll gave her the flu. They said to keep an eye on things and bring her in tomorrow morning. If she develops any other flu symptoms, they can give her the medication for that."

Mason was relieved they didn't think it was serious, but their response still left him with questions. "So what can we do for now? She's pretty miserable."

"Give her this for a start," she said, handing over the bottle of water. "If she'll drink it. The medicine should kick in pretty soon and her fever will go down. We can give her a cool bath. Hold her a lot. Basically, just love on her and keep her from getting overheated."

Mason offered the bottle to Luna and she took it, sniffling sadly as she suckled on it. "How do you know all this stuff?" he asked her when Luna appeared to be settled for the moment. "You were an only child. You weren't raised around any other kids, were you?"

"No. But when we found out we were getting Evan, I read a lot so I'd be prepared on day one. I was so worried I was going to screw something up and they'd take him away."

Mason's jaw tightened. Her worst fears had been realized through no fault of her own and he hated that, but it was another scenario he had no control over. Child-rearing was far more stressful than business any day. "I don't know how I'm going to manage this on my own."

Scarlet sat back on the couch and looked at him. "You're doing just fine."

"Because you came home just in time."

"No," she insisted with a shake of her head. "You checked her temperature and you were about to call the doctor. They would've told you what to do even if you weren't sure. You could've handled this. You're going to be a great father. I always thought you would be."

He wasn't so sure of that, but he knew she was destined to be a great mother. Part of him wanted her to be that mother to Luna, but he wouldn't force that on her. If she wanted her own children, she deserved that.

"I remember you sitting in that same chair holding Evan not long after he came to us," she continued. "I was so enamored with him I'd hardly put him down for a week, but I was desperate for a shower. You took him while I washed my hair, and when I came downstairs, the two of you were just like this."

Mason remembered that day. He'd been terrified by the idea of holding such a small baby, but he'd done just fine. At least for fifteen minutes or so. Evan slept most of the time, so it hadn't been as much of a challenge as today had been. "You had the magic touch with Evan. The minute you picked him up, he'd stop crying."

"It's not magic," Scarlet said. "It's love and trust. The baby bonds with you and you with it. When they know that you'll do whatever it takes to keep them safe and happy, that's where they want to be. Eventually, Evan would've been just as contented with you as he was with me. And the same goes for Luna. You're going to be her whole world and she'll love you more than anyone else on the planet, and you'll feel the same way. When you run across a speed bump, you'll figure it out. That's just parenting. You can't expect to know everything, but you adapt and the baby learns to trust in you."

Mason looked down at Luna, who had let the bottle slip from her lips as she fell asleep, then back up at Scarlet. "I never wanted to do this without you. Whenever I imagined a family, it had you in it."

"Life doesn't always turn out the way you plan," Scarlet said with a sad, distant look in her eye. "You two will be just fine."

Mason watched as she turned and walked back into the kitchen to deal with the groceries and end the conversation. He hoped she was right.

Things had begun to return to normal after a day or two. The new normal, anyway. Carroll was back, Luna was on medication and was feeling better. They were starting to settle into a groove. At least it felt that way.

Scarlet was feeling anything but settled. She felt like

the world was tipping on its axis and the scariest part of it all was that she liked it. It was far too easy to return to the life she had with Mason, especially adding the piece of her life she always felt was missing. Having Luna made almost everything fall into place for her. That was what made it frightening. This couldn't possibly be her happily-ever-after, could it? Could the Fates really give her everything she wanted and let her be happy? She just couldn't believe it. There had to be a catch.

She was pretty sure that catch was Mason. She just wasn't sure if he felt the same way about how things were going between them. They hadn't really talked about the night they'd spent together. Both of them had artfully dodged the situation, and with Luna getting sick, it was easy to do it. She wasn't sure where they stood long-term. What she did know was that she wasn't going back into this relationship again just because he was scared to care for Luna alone. That was a recipe for disaster.

He'd walked away from their marriage once because he didn't feel like he could give his best to her. Before she could trust her heart in his hands a second time, she had to know that he was in it for the long haul, no matter what challenges came their way. Those things were inevitable, but they were easier to tackle with someone else than alone. At the same time, she didn't want him coming back just because he was afraid to face those scary things without her help.

When she came home from her office that evening, she found the house quieter than it had been since everyone else moved in. She'd stayed late getting things ready for the grand opening but was still surprised by the stillness.

"Hello?" she called as she stepped through the foyer.

"Hello," Mason's voice answered back.

She followed the sound through the sliding glass doors to the deck. Mason was sitting out there with his laptop and a half-empty bottle of beer. "Where's Luna and Carroll?"

"Luna is down for the night and Carroll is reading in her room, so I came out here to work. You stayed pretty late at the office tonight."

She nodded. She did most of her work at home, but she did have an office she went into occasionally to handle the business side of her art. Today, it was going over all the plans April had put together, overseeing the shipment of works up to the new gallery, finalizing the catering arrangements and approving the hiring of the employees who would be manning the new location.

"Gallery openings are exciting and wonderful and stressful all at once."

He nodded. She'd watched him go through the same anxiety every time he opened a new surf shop. "Well, grab a glass of wine and join me out here. It's a beautiful night."

That was an excellent suggestion. As a couple before children came into the picture, they'd spent more evenings than she could count out on this deck talking. Over a bottle of wine, they'd catch up on their busy work lives, reconnect emotionally and enjoy the soothing rush of the waves at their back door. She didn't realize how much she'd missed those moments with him until she joined him on the porch with a full glass of merlot.

This was where they'd always had their important talks. Something about the sea and the safety of their deck retreat made it easier to share their feelings. Maybe by the time she'd gotten halfway through this wine, she'd have the nerve to bring up their brief encounter the other night. On an empty stomach, the first two sips were strong, warming her blood and loosening her tongue.

"I'm glad we have this moment together to talk. I feel like things have been so hectic lately."

She nodded, deciding to let him say what was on his mind first. It might make whatever she wanted to discuss moot. "It's been a whirlwind since you and Luna arrived."

"Scarlet, things have really been...nice...since I came back. Being here feels just like before. Sitting on this deck with you, it's like the last year and a half never even happened. I probably shouldn't say this, but I hate my new house."

"Why?" She hadn't been there, of course, but she had no doubt it was superluxurious. Mason strived for the best in all things. Building in Malibu had been their dream, but his place in the Hills was hardly a shack.

"Because it's not home." He looked around their backyard, which included the Pacific Ocean, and reached out to take her hand. When he leaned in, the spicy scent of his cologne mingled with the sea air and tickled at her nose. "This feels like home."

Scarlet couldn't pull away although she knew she

should. She liked the feel of her hand in his. The warmth of his skin enveloped her, and he was right, it did feel like home. It hadn't until he came back. The big house had seemed hollow when she was alone and she'd spent many nights walking around wondering how she could ever fill it.

At the same time, she couldn't shake the worry about his timing. Without Luna, he wouldn't be here saying these things to her. This was still the man who left her, and she had to keep reminding herself of that, especially when he leaned in close and smiled at her this way.

"When I realized Jay was leaving Luna to me, it was like the whole world was collapsing around me. I didn't know what I was going to do. I know moving in on your life and pretending like our breakup never happened wasn't ideal, especially for you, but I don't regret it. Being here, raising Luna together, has shown me a lot about the life we never got to have."

She knew what he meant. Even as they avoided the consequences of the physical relationship, she understood how easily it had happened. Slipping back into their life was so easy. So comfortable. She had to fight not to let herself get carried away by the fantasy they created when it was everything she had ever wanted in her life.

"I'm sorry I couldn't give this to you. I'm sorry that I couldn't keep Evan home where he belonged. All you wanted was to have a family with me, and no matter what I seemed to do, I just made it worse."

"None of it was your fault."

"It feels like my fault. But even if all of that was out

of my control, leaving you *was* my fault. I hurt you and I'm sorry for that."

"Thank you," she said, accepting the apology he offered. "I'm sorry for disappearing on you the other night."

"I didn't blame you," Mason said as his thumb brushed over the back of her hand. "We didn't plan that, and I don't think either of us were ready to deal with what it meant, if anything, to ourselves and to each other."

"I think we both needed some comfort and a release after everything that has happened."

He nodded. "It was more than that for me, though. That, more than anything else, really made me feel like I'd come home. This place, this life, making love to you again...it was amazing, Scarlet. And I can't stop thinking about it. Thinking about you."

Scarlet held her breath as she anticipated what he would say next. This whole conversation had been unexpected for her. They'd tried to keep their focus on Luna and the situation, but this was treading into unexpected territory.

"I don't know what to do, honestly. I still feel like letting you start a new life is the best thing for you. But if I'm being totally selfish, I want you back. Not just in my bed, but in my life. I want you in Luna's life. She deserves a mother like you would be. When I see you two together, I know that's the way Rachel and Jay wanted it to be."

The words he was saying sounded nice, but Scarlet still wasn't hearing what she wanted. Yes, he liked being back, but was he more interested in the life they'd make for Luna than just being with her again? He hadn't said that he still loved her. That he wanted to be with her no matter what. That he wanted to call off the divorce proceedings. Just that Luna needed her for a mother.

Things were going well enough now, but it wouldn't always be such smooth sailing. Would he turn and run again if something bad happened, like before? Would their fragile peace be destroyed by the finality of Jay's death? His brother's health was deteriorating day by day and their stability could change with a single phone call.

"What do *you* want, Scarlet?"

The question startled her out of her thoughts. It was a question she wasn't used to answering. Mason was bad about making decisions without consulting her. He always insisted he was acting in her best interests, but sometimes people didn't want what was best for them. They just wanted what they wanted. Now that he was asking, she was afraid to throw caution to the wind and be completely honest with him, or with herself.

"I don't know," she said. "These last few weeks have been a taste of the life I've always dreamed of. But I'm afraid it won't last."

"What do you mean?"

"I mean Luna seems to be the linchpin that's holding our relationship together at the moment. But when Evan was pulled from our lives, things fell apart. What if something happens to her? What if someone in Rachel's family takes you to court for custody and you lose? Or she gets sick. Or in a car accident. I feel like what we have would go into a tailspin without her. That scares me."

"Why do you think that?"

"Because you can't deal with failure, Mason. At the slightest sign that something won't work out for you, you bail. I can't have you bailing on this marriage twice."

Mason frowned at her. "No, I don't."

"When grad school got too hard, you dropped out. When your first big project at your dad's company went south, you decided to quit."

"I did both those things so I could focus on starting my own company. Considering how successful the store chain has become, that was the right choice, don't you agree?"

"And did you leave me to focus on starting your own company? No. You did it because you couldn't stand to live each day with me as a reminder that you'd failed at making me a mother. Maybe leaving so I could start over was how you legitimized the decision in your own mind, but with you, I know you're always going to pull away when things get too difficult. Your father programmed you to succeed at all costs. It's not good or bad, it's just the way you are."

Mason let go of her hand and sat back in his seat for a moment to take in everything she said. After a bit, he sighed and nodded. "I guess I do. I've never thought about it that way. I'm sorry you feel like you can't rely on me."

Scarlet shook her head. "Enough apologies for tonight. I just need you to know that I need someone who will stand and fight for this. For us. No one ever said marriage was easy, and raising a family is even harder. You and I have chemistry, there's no doubt of it. But passion alone isn't enough for me. Staying together is a choice you have to wake up and make every day."

Passion faded; she knew that. And if it did, she was in a very precarious position with Mason and Luna. Unless he allowed her to legally adopt the baby after Jay died, she had no rights to Luna. Just like with Evan, she wouldn't have a leg to stand on in court if they separated again and battled for custody. Losing another child would destroy her and she wasn't sure she could recover from it a second time while also coping with her marriage finally ending. She was already enamored with her niece. But losing her daughter, if she let it go that far, would be devastating.

"Before I can let myself even consider a future with you and Luna in it, I need to know that I'll be able to count on you, especially when things get hard."

Mason listened patiently to everything she had to say. When she was finished, he reached over and cupped her face in his hand. She couldn't resist closing her eyes, leaning into the warmth of his touch and drawing the scent of his skin into her lungs. He was her weakness, and she knew it. All he had to do was say the right words and she'd believe him because she was desperate to believe.

When she opened her eyes again, he was watching her with a serious expression lining his face. "I'm not going to run this time, Scarlet."

He leaned in and followed his promise with a kiss.

Scarlet didn't resist. This was what she wanted, even if she was afraid to want it again. She knew this kiss would lead them upstairs and, eventually, would lead her heart down a path of no return. But even then, she kissed him back with all her heart and soul and could only hope for the best.

Eight

Things were going well. Too well.

Mason wasn't known for being the most optimistic person. Running his own company had taught him to always watch for the other shoe to drop. After his talk with Scarlet the other night, things had made a turn for the better. They seemed to really be giving this a chance. He was actually sleeping in their bedroom again, leaving her studio and the lumpy futon behind. Now he got to fall asleep every night with the scent of Scarlet's shampoo on his pillowcase and the warm curve of her body pressed into his.

He could almost forget that the drama of the last year or so had ever happened. And that was what worried him the most. He was not one to get lulled into complacency. That was when fate would throw a curve ball and hit you squarely upside the head. He just wasn't sure what direction the threat would come from next. Would Scarlet decide that she really did want her own child? Would something else drive them apart? Jay's death? Something with Luna? He didn't know. There was no way to know. That was just life. He just needed to be ready for the eventuality.

When Mason pulled his car into the garage that evening, there were no curve balls in sight. When he stepped inside, he could hear commotion out back and saw that Scarlet, Carroll and Luna were playing in the pool together. He stood for a moment at the window, watching Scarlet and Luna.

Scarlet's dark hair was twisted into a messy knot on the top of her head to keep it dry. She was wearing the red halter bikini he'd chosen for her at one of his shops a few years before. She was bouncing up and down, holding on to a little floaty chair that kept Luna upright in the water. The baby was wearing a hot-pink zebra swimsuit with giant sunglasses that nearly covered half her face. She was happily splashing her hands and giggling as the water went everywhere.

The look on Scarlet's face as she played with her niece was enough to make a man melt. Devotion, wonder, joy, amazement…all of those things and more were wrapped up in the wide smile that crossed her face. She was meant to be a mother. He'd always known that, he just hadn't been sure how to make it happen before Luna came into their lives. He might never be able to provide that opportunity the old-fashioned way, but he'd brought a child into her life nonetheless.

He hoped it was enough.

The smile on his own face faded away as he realized what it had cost his family to make it a reality. It was hard to focus on the happiness, on this second chance they'd been given, when it was costing them both Rachel's and Jay's lives. That was a high price, and not how he ever would've wanted it to happen. And yet, here Luna was, in need of a home just as surely as Scarlet needed a child. It was kismet.

Turning away from the window, he noticed his cell phone beeping at his hip. It needed charging. He opened the nearby drawer in search of a cable and immediately forgot all about his phone. Stashed away there was the finalized copy of their divorce agreement. Scarlet's copy.

At this point, there was no reason not to look it over. His copy was probably on hold with no one to sign for it at his new house. There weren't many surprises. They'd gone back and forth after the mediation to get everything settled between them. When Rachel died, the paperwork had become something he'd hardly given a thought to. He supposed that in the back of his mind he knew his attorney was getting things drawn up and ready to sign, but his lawyer didn't know anything about Luna and how much had changed in the last few weeks.

It could change everything. Or nothing. Mason liked to think they were on the path to reconciliation, but he wasn't naive enough to think that a baby could turn everything around. That oversimplified their situation. Yes, losing Evan had pushed them to the end, but they wouldn't have gotten there if they'd been able to communicate better. If he'd been able to understand what Scarlet really needed, not just what he thought she needed.

And maybe he was just presuming that what she wanted or needed was him. Yes, she'd warmed up to him during their time together, but he couldn't be certain he was the sole cause for the smile that returned to her face. More than anything, Scarlet wanted a baby and she seemed really taken with Luna. When he'd drawn Scarlet into this situation, a part of him had hoped that she would fall for the baby and they could reconcile as a complete family at last. Finally being able to give her what she wanted made him feel like he was less of a failure in their marriage.

What he didn't anticipate was that he would feel like the third wheel in his own marriage. Scarlet seemed more devoted to the baby than she was to him. He had to wonder if it was really their marriage she wanted back, or the baby that would now come with the reconciliation package.

Mason would be the first to admit that he was the one who walked away from the marriage. Scarlet was stubborn enough to stick it out no matter how miserable she was with him. But when he walked away, she didn't try to stop him either. The air of tension in the house had become so thick that there was almost a feeling of relief when he told her he was moving out. That, more than anything, had convinced him he was making the right decision.

Looking down at the paperwork now, he wasn't so

sure. Now that Scarlet was back in his bed, he had a taste of the family they'd hoped for. Scarlet might be cautious where the two of them were concerned, but that would change with time. Or it should, but he'd have to stand his ground. That was perhaps the hardest part.

It wasn't that Mason was afraid to work hard. He'd work harder than anyone to achieve what he wanted. But he was also realistic and knew when he was banging his head against a brick wall. If he wasn't going to be successful, it didn't seem like a good use of his time. He'd rather stop and change course than go down with the ship. From the outside, he supposed that might look like quitting when things got tough.

He didn't want to quit on Scarlet. Not again. But did he dare to put his whole heart into this reconciliation when he wasn't certain what the future would hold for them?

Mason was about to stuff the papers back into the drawer when he noticed a handwritten note from her attorney. He knew he shouldn't read it, but when he caught a glimpse of Luna's name in the loopy script, he couldn't stop himself.

Scarlet—here's the draft we agreed to with Mason's attorneys. My advice is to hold off on moving forward with the divorce for now. If the situation changes, we want to make sure that the custody and support arrangements for Luna are included. Hope the adoption attorney I recommended was helpful.

He read the note three times before he stuffed it back in with the other pages. He wasn't entirely sure what the note meant. Did she plan to drag out the divorce long enough that she could take custody from him? Or did the lawyer mean that in the event they decided to divorce anyway, they should include something to address the situation with Luna? He didn't feel like Scarlet was working him, but he could be wrong.

Either way, it didn't sound good, and it didn't sound like the words of an attorney who didn't think the divorce was right around the corner. They were discussing adoption attorneys. Was that Scarlet's idea or just her attorney pushing her to cover her bases in a worst-case scenario?

Mason sighed as an ache of worry started to pool in his gut. That was why you never read anyone else's mail. You learned things you didn't really want or need to know. He shoved the kitchen drawer closed and tried to pretend he'd never read that note.

He tried to tell himself that those papers had been in the works for quite some time. She could've discussed this with her attorney long before they got back together. He knew that at this point, he didn't think he wanted to sign and neither did Scarlet, despite what that paperwork might imply. A lot had changed in the last two weeks. It was too early to decide either way. He wouldn't mention the divorce again until he knew for certain. Then they could either tear it up together or sign together and make a plan to move forward.

Until he knew where he stood, however, Mason was going to tread very carefully. He wanted things to work out with Scarlet, but if they didn't, he needed to be mentally prepared for that. The last time, he spent three days in a bourbon-fueled stupor. He couldn't lose it like that with Luna in his life now. He had to be responsible, do the adult thing. And that meant keeping his heart secured until he knew it was safe.

If safe was even an option.

After Luna went down for the night, Scarlet opted for a bubble bath upstairs. It had been a long time since she'd indulged in something so luxurious, but she needed it. Keeping up with her career and a one-year-old was enough to bring on a Calgon moment. She needed to unwind and relax if she was going to make it through the next week. The trip to San Francisco loomed heavy ahead of her.

As she turned off the water and sank, naked, into the bubbles, she felt her tight muscles instantly start to unwind. Her hair was still on the top of her head from the pool, so she was able to lean back onto the bath pillow and close her eyes.

Scarlet was anxious about the San Francisco opening. She really hadn't had the time to think about it with everything else going on, but she was worried. She wasn't entirely sure why. Maybe it was just the idea of being away from her family that bothered her.

Her family?

That was the first time a thought like that had crossed her mind. While it was easy to think of Mason as her husband—technically, he still was—thinking of the whole household as her family was a big step. She'd developed a sense of attachment to them as a whole. Even Carroll. But especially Luna. She had very quickly become Scarlet's baby girl.

Going to San Francisco meant leaving them all behind. Luna and Carroll would fare fine without her, but she still disliked the idea of going. At least right now when everything was so fragile. Especially with Mason.

Of course, she could always ask him to come with her to the gallery opening. The more she soaked, the more she realized that she wanted that. April had planted the bug in her ear when she picked up that painting and now she couldn't imagine going through such a big night without him. But would he go? She'd never asked him to come with her to these things before because it seemed like such an imposition, and that was when their marriage was okay. They seemed to be in such a delicate place at the moment, especially with Jay clinging to the edge of death a few miles up the road. She wasn't sure if Mason would want to go all the way to San Francisco under the circumstances.

But they both said they were going to try harder this time. Communicate better instead of making presumptions. This was important to her, so she was going to ask. It was possible he wouldn't be able to attend, but she should at least give him that option.

When she got done in the tub, she drained the water and wrapped herself in a fluffy white towel. She was going to head downstairs to talk to him, but when she went into their bedroom, she found him sitting up in bed with a mountain of pillows behind him. He was wearing his favorite pair of striped cotton pajama pants and faded Pepperdine T-shirt from his college days. He had a pair of reading glasses perched low on his nose to see while he was working on his laptop, looking over the top of them to watch a baseball game on the television. The sound was muted so he didn't disturb Scarlet's bath.

"Hey," she said as she approached the bed.

"Hey." Mason shut the laptop and set it on the comforter beside him. He admired her messy, damp hair and nearly inadequate towel over the tops of his glasses with a small smile curling his lips.

"What's with the glasses?" she asked. He'd never worn glasses in the nine years they were together. It seemed strange for something to change about him without her knowing about it. They hadn't been apart that long, but it was apparently long enough.

Mason slipped the black framed glasses off and put them on top of the laptop. "Yeah, those. My optometrist said I needed to start wearing them when I'm on the computer. Eyestrain."

"Put them back on," Scarlet said.

He complied, modeling the new look for her. They were square black frames that mimicked the lines of his jaw nicely. "What do you think? Can I pull off the sexy nerdy look?"

Scarlet smiled. She actually really liked the glasses on him, even if they did give off a bit of the geeky hipster vibe that clashed with the tanned surfer boy she was used to. "You look…"

"Smarter?"

She shrugged. "Maybe. It's a different look for

you. But I like them. How long have you been wearing them?"

"About a month. Since I've never worn glasses before, I keep forgetting to put them on. Now that you
know, you can nag me about wearing them."

"I'll add that to the list of other things I nag you
about, like wearing sunblock and putting the recycling
on the curb."

"Very good." Mason slipped the glasses back off and
set them aside. "Did you enjoy your bath? You weren't
in there for very long."

"I'm not good at sitting still, even when I try to. I
thought of something and I got out to talk to you about
it. My opening is Saturday. I was wondering if…" Scarlet hesitated. She didn't know why she was so nervous
to ask. Perhaps because Mason hadn't been to any of her
other openings. This was a big one, though. Her biggest.
And she wanted him to be there with her. Somehow it
felt like she was asking a boy to prom instead of asking her husband to support a work event.

"If what?" he asked.

She walked around to his side of the bed and leaned
her shoulder against the wall. "If you wanted to come
with me."

Mason's brow raised curiously. "Really?"

"Yes. I know I've never asked you to come to any
before, and I wasn't sure if you had time to go up to
San Francisco with me this trip. This event is a lot bigger than some of the others. I'm more nervous about
this one. I think April said the mayor RSVP'd. I understand if you—"

"Of course I will," he interrupted.

Scarlet had been on the verge of accepting his excuses as to why he couldn't make it when she realized he'd actually said yes. "You will?"

He nodded. "I realize I haven't made it to the others, but I thought that was what you wanted, since you never asked me to go. Those openings are so stressful for you and I know what it's like opening one of my new stores. Everything comes together at the very last moment. I figured that I would just be a distraction for you on your big nights."

Scarlet could only shake her head. He wouldn't be a distraction. He would be her saving grace. Just the touch of his hand would keep her ship sailing smoothly on the rough seas. "I always just thought you were too busy. I didn't want to bother you with my work when you already had plenty to worry about, running your own company."

Mason peeled back the blankets and stood up, closing the gap between them and putting his hands reassuringly on her upper arms. His skin was warm against hers, sending a shiver through her body even in the comfortable evening air. "I know I work too much, but don't ever think I won't take time out for what's important. My career isn't any more important than yours is. You've done amazing things and I couldn't be prouder of how far you've come as an artist since you first walked into my little shop to sell your paintings. All you have to do is ask me and I'm there."

Scarlet looked up into his sea-blue eyes and knew he meant what he said. Maybe she was wrong about all of this. She'd worried that their physical draw was nothing more than a comfortable distraction from their grief of losing Rachel and soon Jay. That it was easier to fall into bed and forget about reality than to think about the future and what it might mean for them.

Especially when she could sense there was still a distance between them.

It was hard to put her finger on, but she could feel it. There was a part of him that wasn't fully committed to this reunion. Perhaps she could more easily pick up on it because she was doing the same thing. She was scared to take his words at face value, trust him with her heart and get crushed again. Maybe both of them were too nervous to think this second chance was truly a second chance.

Then again, those weren't the words of a man just looking for a distraction or a mother for the child he'd inherited. He meant it when he said he would make time for her. That he was proud of her. So maybe she was imagining things. Or perhaps the distance was natural after everything they'd been through and the gap between them would close in time. If they put in the effort.

"I would like you to come. It's black tie. April really went all out for this one. I'm so nervous I'm going to screw this opportunity up."

"I don't know why you'd be nervous, Scarlet. You're an amazing artist. San Francisco is lucky to have one of your galleries and all those people coming to the opening know it. Everyone is going to want a Scarlet Spencer original hanging above their mantel." Mason stopped and, with a frown, turned to their own bedroom fireplace. "You know, *we* don't even have a Scarlet Spencer hanging above *our* mantel. We just have some dumb old flat-screen television."

Scarlet smiled. "Thank you for agreeing to come with me." She leaned into him, snaking her arms around his waist and resting her head against his chest. "I'll see what I can do about the fireplace art," she added with a chuckle.

"You do that," he said with a low laugh that rumbled against her cheek. "And while you do that…" Mason began just as she felt her bath towel slip to the floor. "Oops." He grinned.

Scarlet didn't resist. Instead, she pressed her damp skin against him, letting her hard, chilled nipples dig into his shirt. She hadn't thought about having some alone time with Mason while they were on the trip, but the idea certainly intrigued her now. A nice hotel room. No baby. No nanny. No household to deal with. It sounded perfect.

Her worries about her opening faded as Mason tipped her backward over his arm and brought her up-tilted breast to his mouth. He drew hard on the dark pink flesh, nipping just enough with his teeth to make her gasp and suck a ragged breath into her lungs.

"Shh…" Mason whispered as he brought a finger to his lips and then dragged it lazily between her breasts. "We don't want to wake Luna. But this weekend, you can make all the noise you want. No one will be around to hear you scream my name until you're hoarse."

"And what exactly do you have in store for me that will make me scream like that?"

Mason stood her up and flashed and evil grin. "You'll just have to wait and see."

Nine

This was Scarlet's biggest and fanciest gallery opening yet. They had a prime location at Fisherman's Wharf near one of her murals. It would draw in plenty of tourist foot traffic along with fans who were deliberately coming to the gallery itself, and she'd need every one to support the rent in such a pricey area of town. She felt like she should've been focused on every detail of the event, from which painting hung where to what hors d'oeuvres were being passed by the waiters, but she found her mind was elsewhere tonight. She knew April could handle it. That was what she paid her for. She was the management, Scarlet was the talent.

"Did we leave Carroll with the pediatrician's phone number in case Luna gets sick again? She was still a little sniffly when we left."

Mason came up behind her as she stood in front of the mirror, putting on her earrings. His black Armani tuxedo fit him like a glove, highlighting his broad shoulders and narrow waist from years paddling out on his surfboard. It had been a long time since she'd seen him dressed up like this. He wore suits almost every day, but he only pulled this tux out for special occasions. Like their wedding day.

That felt like an eternity ago, and yet he hadn't changed a bit. Well, maybe there was a stray strand of gray at his temple and a few lines around his eyes, but he was still the man she said yes to all those years ago.

He smiled and patted at her bare shoulder. "Yes. She has all the numbers, I promise. The house is filled with enough food and baby supplies to last through a nuclear winter. It's just a two-day trip. Carroll knows what she's doing. Everything will be fine."

Scarlet fastened her earring and turned around to face him with a wry smile twisting her lips. "I'm being *that mom*, aren't I?"

He just smiled. "A good mom, yes. Good moms worry. But tonight, I want you to focus on you. It's your big opening. Everyone is coming out to see your work. I want you to focus on that and only that." He leaned in and pressed a soft kiss to the tip of her nose so her lipstick didn't smear. "Are you almost ready? The car is waiting downstairs."

Scarlet nodded and took a deep breath before grabbing her beaded navy clutch. "How do I look?" she asked, before turning to face him.

The look on Mason's face said it all. His blue gaze

took in every inch of her body, from the navy-and-silver lace cap sleeves to the fitted, beaded bodice and full, draped skirt. She thought the color would look nice against her skin and complement the ocean colors of the paintings in her gallery. He seemed to agree. By the time his eyes met hers again, there was a huge, devious smile crossing his face. Even his dimples were showing.

"I think we should skip it," Mason said. He pressed up against her and rested his hands at her waist. "I think you need to take that dress off right now so I can start all those wicked things I promised to do to you."

Scarlet smacked him on the chest with her bag. "Well, I'm glad you approve of the dress, but that isn't happening. I can't be hoarse when I greet all my guests. But after we get back…" She trailed off with a seductive smile as she twisted out of his grasp. "Let's go."

Reluctantly, Mason followed her out of their suite and down to the lobby. Under the portico of the hotel, as predicted, a black town car with the name "Spencer" in the window was waiting for them.

It didn't take long to get to the gallery. They'd chosen a hotel only a few blocks from Fisherman's Wharf. They pulled up to the back entrance, where they could slip inside and check on things before the guests arrived.

"We're opening the doors in five," April barked into her headset as she blew past them in a black beaded cocktail dress. She stopped short in front of them. "Good, the guest of honor is in the building." She smiled, paying particular attention to Mason in his tuxedo. "You both look lovely tonight."

Scarlet caught a hint of a blush on his cheeks. "Thanks. Are we ready to go?"

April looked down at her watch. "Yep, let's get this party started."

From there, the first two hours were a blur. Mason stayed at her side for support but allowed himself to blend into the background while Scarlet took center stage. As she moved across the dance floor to greet guests and speak with people about her work, she would look over her shoulder and catch glimpses of him beaming with pride over his half-empty flute of champagne.

It was going well. At least she thought so. One of her massive original oils had been purchased for a solid six figures before Scarlet had finished her first drink. Smaller pieces were flying off the walls, figuratively, even with five-digit price tags. Almost everyone was leaving with at least an autographed coffee-table book or print. It was a great start to the gallery, which would need the capital to recoup the expense of opening up a new location.

It wasn't until she finally sat down at a table to rest her feet that she was able to consider the event a success and relax. She had been too busy to worry about Luna or Mason or anything else aside from keeping a smile on her face, but the event was winding down at last.

She took a sip of her wine and turned to look for Mason. He'd slipped away for a moment while she was talking to the mayor, but he hadn't returned yet. That was when she spotted him on the far side of the room. His back was to her as he admired a painting on the wall. When he turned around and his gaze met hers, she felt a sizzle run across her skin. She missed the heat of his body at her side, the gentle press of his palm against her lower back. The expression on his face promised all that and more when the opening was over.

He finally strolled back across the gallery and stopped just in front of her. "Come with me," Mason said as he held out his hand.

The look he gave her made her knees like butter and she wasn't sure she could follow him onto the dance floor even if she wanted to. Knowing there were quite a few guests watching, however, she smiled and forced herself to follow him.

A few couples were dancing around the center of the gallery. When the gala was over, one of her bronze sculptures would go in the open space, but for tonight, there was enough room for a dozen couples to dance to the soft jazz the band was playing.

They found an open spot and Mason wrapped his arm around her waist and held her tight against him. Scarlet adjusted in his arms and let him guide her in a soft rocking motion. Neither of them were very accomplished when it came to dancing, but they made do at events like this. It helped that she was always so aware of Mason's body. Every inch of him pressed into her, so she noted every twitch of muscle, every motion to guide her one way or another. She could almost anticipate his moves.

For the first time since they touched down in San Francisco, Scarlet felt like she had a moment to breathe. Even though April handled most everything, Scarlet still felt as though she had to double-check it all, practically rearranging artwork as Mason shoved her out the door so they could return to the hotel and change. Once the guests arrived, it was chatting and smiling and autographing books. She wasn't an introvert at heart, but there was no denying this was exhausting.

She was happy to just be in Mason's arms now. A month ago, it was a place she never thought she'd be again. On lonely nights, she'd lain in bed trying to remember the last time he'd kissed her, or the last time they'd made love. She couldn't even begin to recall when they'd danced. Maybe on the cruise they took to Mexico for their fifth anniversary.

"I can't remember the last time we had a night like this," he said in a low voice after a few quiet moments of dancing together. It was as though he could read her thoughts sometimes.

"Like what?" she asked, curious of how he'd come up with it.

"Just the two of us together. Dancing, drinking adult beverages and chatting about idle pursuits. There's no talk of babies or ovulation, family law attorneys or sperm counts. It's just you and me, enjoying a night together for the first time in forever. The last few years of our marriage were taken over by our quest to have a child. It's nice to just be Mason and Scarlet Spencer, married couple out for a night together, for a change."

Scarlet felt a rush of blood flood her cheeks in embarrassment. That probably wasn't the reaction he was expecting, but she couldn't help it. She knew that most of that life disruption was her doing. She was the one who got obsessed and dragged him along with her. "I'm sorry I let all that get in the way of us. I just went baby crazy and forgot all about our marriage."

"You didn't forget about our marriage," he soothed. "You just got focused on our family. There are worse things."

"Yes, but we lost each other along the way."

"We didn't lose each other. We just forgot we were supposed to face those trials as a team. Somehow we turned into adversaries instead."

It had felt that way for a while, even though she knew, practically, that it wasn't true. There was no bad guy to blame their fertility difficulties on, no villain to accuse of stealing Evan away. It was just life making a turn in a direction that neither of them knew how to handle. They'd accomplished everything they'd set out to do in life, but this one thing had just been out of their reach.

"Are we playing on the same team now?" she asked. "For good?" It was a question she'd been afraid to pose since Mason moved back into the house. When the temporary started to feel permanent, how was she to know what was real anymore?

"We are, Scarlet. I told you I wasn't going to run away again. I meant it. I've been happier with you these last few weeks than I've been in a long time. I'm not letting that slip away again."

He looked down at her with his big blue eyes and she felt the last of her fears slip away. This was really happening. They were reconciling, and not just because of the baby, but because they wanted to be together. They realized they were better together. Luna was just the fluffy pink icing on the cake.

"I'm happy to hear you say that," Scarlet said.

Mason smiled. "And I'll be happy to sweep you off your feet and back to our hotel suite. How long do we have to stay?"

Scarlet eyed the dwindling crowd and April in the corner rubbing her feet. Once her manager's shoes came off, it was safe to call it a night.

"Not a minute longer."

Mason was glad to be back at their hotel. As he tugged at his bow tie and pulled it out from under his collar, he could only shake his head. "Are they always like that?" he asked.

Scarlet's reflection in the mirror smiled at him as she stepped out of her shoes and pulled off her jewelry. "That one was fancier than normal, but yes, they're all basically the same. I suck up to people, they buy my art." She walked up to him and then turned her back toward him. "Can you unzip me, please?"

"With pleasure." Mason reached for her zipper at her neck. Tonight, she'd worn her long dark hair twisted up into an elegant sort of knot. The whole back of the gown was navy lace, giving glimpses of her bare back down all the way to the swell of her hips. Grasping the zipper tab, he slowly followed the curve of her spine until it settled at the bottom.

Before she could pull away, he pushed the lace aside with his hands and exposed her back. The cap sleeves moved easily down her arms until the dress was pooled around her waist. The mirror she'd stood at moments before now gave him the perfect view of his wife's full, bare breasts. He watched their reflection as he snaked his arms beneath hers and cupped her breasts in his hands.

Scarlet sighed and leaned back against him. He loved the feeling of her body pressed into his own. He loved the warmth of her skin, the scent of her hair, the soft sounds she made as he teased and pinched her nipples into tight buds... He watched her face contort with pleasure as he caressed her the way he knew she liked to be touched. She was his wife. His everything. They'd been together for almost his entire adult life. He knew that a kiss just below her earlobe would make her crazy with need. He knew that she was ticklish behind her knees. He didn't need a road map for her body because he already knew it by heart. Returning to the familiar territory had been both comforting and exciting after the months apart.

Now that she was back in his arms, in his bed and in his heart for good, the thought sent a surge of desire and possessiveness through his veins. She was his now, and no paperwork from their lawyers was going to change that.

Scarlet tipped her head enough to reach up and pluck a few pins from her hair. It was enough for the entire twist to come tumbling down over her shoulders. The scent of her skin mingled with her styling products to surround him with a smell that, when his eyes were closed, instantly brought to mind images of her in their bathroom. He leaned in and buried his face in her hair, letting the silky strands brush over his skin before drawing a deep breath of her into his lungs.

She arched her back and shimmied her hips just enough for the gown to fall to her feet. That left the ample curves of her thong-clad rear end to press into the desire that strained against his tuxedo pants. He growled low in her ear as the sensation radiated through his lower extremities.

"Do you know how badly I wanted to rip that gown off you tonight?" he whispered. "I wanted to make love to you on the floor of the stock room and I didn't care if April caught us in the act. That's why I had to walk away for a while. I couldn't take it."

"Well, it's out of your way now," she said. She stepped out of her dress and moved away from him, leaving him suddenly cold and alone. When she turned to face him at the foot of the bed, she was wearing nothing but a nude lace thong that blended into her skin and nearly vanished.

He couldn't tear his eyes away as he slipped out of his tuxedo jacket and unbuttoned his shirt. "Good. I'd hate to ruin a perfectly nice dress."

Still in his tuxedo pants, Mason closed the gap she'd created between them and placed his hands on the soft curve of her hips. He tugged her against him, pressing his need into her stomach. "Do you have any idea what you do to me? What you've always done to me?"

Scarlet wrapped her arms around his neck and laced her fingers through the short strands of his hair. "I've got a pretty good idea." She looked up at him with her big doe eyes and batted her lashes coquettishly. "But maybe you should show me just to make sure."

She knew just how to play to his base instincts. With a growl, he scooped her up off the ground. She squealed and clung to him, wrapping her legs around his waist as he carried her over to the bed. The sound of her carefree laughter was like music to his ears after all the seriousness they'd faced lately. He was glad that this time, he was the one making her smile.

Once he reached the bed, he laid her down with her legs still entwined around his waist. He surged forward, pinning her against the mattress and pressing his length against her lace-covered center. She moaned at the contact, but his mouth quickly sought out hers and swallowed the sound. He drank in the taste of her, relishing in the mix of dry white wine and sweet chocolate truffles that still lingered on her tongue from the party.

She squirmed beneath him, and the next thing he knew, he could feel her palm pressed against the fly of his trousers. He shuddered and ripped his mouth away from hers. "Quit that," he groaned.

Instead, she slipped her hand beneath his waistband and wrapped her fingers around his length. He swore against the pillows before propping on his elbow and tugging her hand away. He sat back on his knees, and gripping both her wrists together in one hand, he pinned them against the mattress over her head. She tried to break free from his grasp, but she wasn't getting away.

"You're naughty, and this is your punishment."

Scarlet looked at him with wide, innocent eyes, then

lifted her hips to drag the crotch of her panties against him. Apparently, she didn't need hands to torture him.

"Do you want to be in charge tonight?" he asked.

She answered him with a grin. Fair enough. He released her arms and rolled to the right, taking her with him until he was lying on his back and she was straddling him.

"I'm all yours," Mason said.

"You always have been," Scarlet replied.

Mason pressed his fingertips into the flesh of her hips and looked up at her with a serious expression in a previously light moment. "I always will be."

Scarlet stilled over him. Her eyes grew glassy for a moment before she smiled through her tears. She didn't respond. Instead, she sat back on her heels and lifted her hair up with her arms, putting on a little show for him. He wanted to reach for her and tug her close, but he was letting her have tonight. It was her big night, anyway.

She stretched, arching her back and letting her silky chestnut waves rain back down onto her shoulders. She rocked her hips with the movement, torturing him further through the cursed pants he'd made the mistake of leaving on. As if she could anticipate his discomfort, Scarlet climbed onto her knees and reached down to unfasten his pants. She slid them and his silk boxers down his legs, then let him kick them off onto the floor.

Reaching between them, she wrapped her fingers around him, and this time he didn't complain. Mason closed his eyes and exhaled hard through his nose as sparks of pleasure danced across his skin. She stroked the length of him once, twice, and then he felt her velvet heat envelop him.

He opened his eyes to find Scarlet straddling him with a look of divine contentment on her face. She started rocking slowly, making him clench his teeth. He wasn't sure how long he could stand her moving like this. "Come here, baby," he managed through his tightly flexed jaw.

Thankfully, Scarlet opted not to torture him any longer. She leaned forward, planting her elbows on the mattress beside his head. Now she was close enough for him to lean up and capture her lips. As their tongues and breath mingled together, she continued to rock back and forth. Wrapping his arms tight around her waist, he stilled her movement and began thrusting into her from beneath.

Her sobbing gasps against his mouth were enough to tell him that she didn't mind his interference. He could feel her body stiffen against him as she came closer to her release. He waited with anticipation for the moment to come. Maybe even more so than for his own orgasm. Watching the beautiful woman he called his own come apart in his arms was something he could never tire of. He longed for it, needed it for his own satisfaction to be complete.

"Yes," he whispered against the line of her jaw, following his words with soft kisses. He gripped her hips harder, thrusting into her with renewed enthusiasm. "Please, baby. I need to hear it. Be as loud as you need to be tonight."

Scarlet closed her eyes then, her mouth open in anticipation of the tsunami coming for her. When it hit, he held her tight, riding the wave with her as she cried out into the room. "Mason!" She pushed herself up, gripping his shoulders and bucking her hips against him.

Mason felt her muscles tighten and flutter around him, pushing him toward his own end. When she collapsed against his chest, he wrapped his arms around her. The feel of her skin on his, her breath at his ear, her moist core wrapped around him…it took only a few more thrusts before he lost himself inside her.

For a few minutes, all Mason could hear was the sound of their breathing and the rapid pounding of his heart in his chest. It was the first time in a long time that the beat of his heart tapped out a joyful rhythm instead of a somber dirge. With Scarlet still in his arms, he felt happy. Really, truly happy.

Reluctantly, he let her finally roll back onto the bed. They crawled beneath the blankets together and switched off the lamp before he turned on his side and pulled her back against him. It had been a great night. He almost didn't want to close his eyes and have it end, but sleep was winning the fight tonight.

Mason was very nearly on the edge of sleep when he heard his cell phone ringing on the nightstand. Rolling over in bed, he picked up his phone and his heart sank when he saw the number. The fleeting moments of happiness he'd just cherished seemed to crumble in his hands as he looked at the screen. The last time he got a late-night call like this, it was Jay telling him that Rachel had an accident and was dead. This time, with the hospice number flashing across the screen, there was only one eventuality and he wasn't prepared for it.

Ignoring the call wouldn't change anything, however. He hit the button to answer. "Hello?"

"Hello, this is Karen with New Horizons Rehabilitation Center. Is this Mr. Spencer speaking?"

He closed his eyes and hesitated to answer, knowing his life was about to change forever. "This is he."

Ten

It felt surreal to be back to the cemetery so soon. They all knew this was where they were going to return, but that just wasn't something Scarlet had been ready to face.

Today, they were seated in a short row of chairs in front of the casket. That made it easier to hold the squirming Luna in her arms. For some reason, holding the baby made her feel grounded. It couldn't hide the ugly reality of the situation from her, though. As her gaze strayed from Jay's casket, she noticed the grass hadn't even started to grow over Rachel's grave. They'd removed the last of the dead flowers from her service to prepare Jay's final resting place.

A new wreath of white roses was placed behind the newly installed headstone Rachel shared with her husband. All his information was complete aside from the date of his death, a date that Scarlet would never forget. Up until the moment they received that call, it had been one of the best days of her life. Since then, everything had fallen apart.

They'd called the airline after getting off the phone and made arrangements to catch the first flight back to LAX. They didn't even bother going back to sleep. Instead, they'd taken showers, packed and checked out of the hotel in the small hours of the morning.

Mason had said almost nothing since he got the call. He'd hung up the phone and said, "Jay's dead. I'm sorry, but we need to get back to LA." That was basically it. He'd muttered the occasional inconsequential thing about packing and spoken briefly to the TSA agents at the airport, but Scarlet was suddenly invisible.

At least that was how she felt. She wanted to hug him. To say she was sorry about Jay. But he wouldn't make eye contact long enough to engage her in any kind of serious conversation. After they got back home, things weren't much better. He immediately threw himself into dealing with Jay's funeral arrangements. He met with Jay's estate attorneys and busied himself with paperwork for Luna's adoption.

Scarlet tried not to notice that he never once mentioned her adopting Luna. She wasn't sure if that indicated a change in how he felt about their relationship or not. What she did know was that it felt like before. Like the months leading up to their separation. The warm, affectionate Mason seemed to have vanished with that phone call. He hadn't touched her. Some nights, he hadn't even come upstairs to go to bed.

This morning, like the night before, she'd woken up to a cold, pristine space beside her in the bed. It was amazing how quickly she'd gotten used to having him back there. It was where he belonged. Scarlet just wasn't sure if he felt the same way any longer.

She'd held her tongue so far. She understood that Mason would need time and space to grieve. His younger brother had been his best friend. That didn't mean she wasn't worried. If Mason retreated too far into himself, if he didn't lean on Scarlet for support the way a husband should lean on his wife…she worried that he was going to run.

Mason had sworn he wouldn't run again. He said that he wanted her, that he wanted this. But Jay's death was their first real test, and a serious one at that. If his instinct was to flee from the reality of losing his brother, he might be several miles down the road before he realized that he was doing it again.

It felt like running. As she turned to look at Mason, he was like a stone statue. No emotion, no movement. She hadn't seen him cry a single time since he got the call about his brother. He'd instantly gone into "handle it" mode. She wished he would cry. Then she could feel like comforting him wasn't a misplaced gesture. He was sitting a mere five inches away from Scarlet, but it felt like she was losing him all over again and she didn't know what to do.

Scarlet turned away from Mason and looked to the minister. The same man had overseen Rachel's service.

She was certain his words were comforting, but she had a hard time focusing on him. She was trying to keep from letting her feelings get the best of her for Luna's sake. The baby might not understand what was happening, but she could feel the emotional energy Scarlet put out. She didn't want Luna wailing through the service. It would break everyone's hearts to hear the dead couple's baby so distraught.

"Let us give thanks today, even in our grief, for Jay's brother, Mason, and his wife, Scarlet."

Scarlet perked up at the sound of her name spoken by the minister.

"For even in this moment of sadness and mourning, we are celebrating the beginning of a new family for Luna when she needs one the most. For many years Mason and Scarlet have longed for a child, and now they have found what they always hoped for. The Lord works in mysterious ways, bringing joy to some even as grief is brought to another. But may we find peace in knowing it was God's plan for Rachel and Jay to be together in the Kingdom of Heaven, and for Luna to remain on Earth with her new family."

Scarlet looked out of the corner of her eye at Mason. He seemed to be even more uncomfortable than he had been before. He obviously didn't like the attention shifted onto them, as though they had somehow benefited from his brother's death. She was certain no one looked at it that way, but still, he seemed visibly uneasy.

She turned her attention to Luna instead. The baby was enamored with the stuffed monkey they brought with them today. It was one of the few items they could take that didn't jingle, beep, play music or otherwise disrupt the service. Luna chewed at the monkey's ear, indicating another tooth was coming in. A milestone her parents would miss.

And then, as soon as it had begun, the service was over. Mason and Jay's parents approached the casket to say goodbye, and then Scarlet stood and went with Mason. She watched as Mason laid his hand against the smooth white surface. He said something she couldn't understand, then turned and walked down the hill to the car. She followed behind him, struggling to catch up in her heels as he nearly ran from his brother's grave site.

By the time she reached the Range Rover, Mason was inside and the engine was running. Scarlet cautiously buckled Luna into her car seat and climbed in front. "For a moment I wasn't sure if you were leaving without us," she said quietly after she shut the door.

Mason didn't look at her. He just put the car into Drive and pulled away from the curb. "Don't be ridiculous," he replied.

"It felt like you were running."

"I…" He hesitated. "I just needed to get away from there. It was too much all at once."

Scarlet turned to look at him. "Not from the service. It felt like you were running away from me."

He considered her words for a moment before pulling out into traffic and taking the turn to merge onto the freeway. "Maybe I was," he admitted with a heavy sigh.

Scarlet didn't know what to say to that. She had expected him to argue with her. To tell her she was being too sensitive and this wasn't about her. To reassure her that he wasn't running away, he'd promised he wouldn't do that, and that he just needed some time. She'd gotten the exact opposite and it stunned her into silence.

The ache of worry started to pool in her stomach. Had she misjudged this entire situation?

She sat back against the soft leather of the passenger seat and took a deep breath. Mason had only asked her to play along with the relationship for Jay's sake. Once his brother passed, the charade was supposed to end. She knew that. But hadn't things changed between them? Hadn't they made love, made promises that they weren't going to let their marriage fall apart when things got hard? She hadn't imagined that things had evolved past the original agreement, had she?

And yet she knew that was Mason's modus operandi. When he couldn't control things, he retreated. And now, despite everything he may have said before, everything he promised to change, he was distancing himself from her and their marriage. She could feel it: the same anxious ache of losing something and being unable to stop it that she'd felt before he left the last time.

Tigers didn't change their stripes.

Scarlet could feel things spiraling out of her control. She hadn't wanted the divorce last time and it hadn't made any difference. Once he pulled away, there was nothing left to hold on to. She wanted to work through this, to raise Luna with him the way Jay had always intended. She just wasn't certain if Mason was going to give her that choice.

Luna.

Scarlet closed her eyes tight and clutched at the

leather armrest as she realized how much more was at stake if he ran away this time. He wouldn't. He couldn't. After weeks of insisting he wanted them to be a family, he wouldn't take the baby away just when she'd given in and fallen in love with her. Or would he? If the situation was uncomfortable enough for him, she wasn't so certain.

"And were you running from Luna, too?" she asked.

Mason exited the freeway and pulled to a stop at a red light. His jaw tightened as he gripped the steering wheel and considered his words. "Of course not. I told my brother that I would raise Luna like she was my own daughter and I intend to keep my promise."

"And what about all the promises you made to me?" she asked.

He didn't answer.

Mason felt like crap. There was no candy coating it.

He was used to things going to plan. In his business, he was in charge of every detail and had built his success on knowing the right decisions to make and executing them flawlessly. Real life wasn't as simple as choosing which brand and style of beach towels to stock in the stores. There was an X factor of emotion that threw everything into a tailspin no matter how hard he tried to keep things steady.

As he sat at the dining room table, staring at his laptop and surrounded by paperwork, he could feel that X factor at play. Nothing was going the way he expected it to. Or at least the way he wanted it to. That just added a foul mood on top of his other problems. He missed his brother, missed his wife, missed feeling like his life made any sense at all…

He'd seen the way Scarlet looked at him since the funeral. He'd earned that scowl, there was no question of it. But for now, he needed his space. He needed room to breathe, to think. Being with Scarlet made him happy. This was not the appropriate time to be happy.

It was like some kind of self-imposed penance that he was sure Scarlet wouldn't understand. All he knew was that the moment before he'd received the call about Jay's passing, he'd been happier than he'd been in years. He had his wife back, his home back, a child he adored, things were going well… It was almost enough to make a man forget that his sister-in-law was newly buried and his brother was clinging to life in a hospice facility. That the baby they cherished—the one who had salvaged their marriage and made their lives complete—had only arrived through the direst of circumstances. Rachel and Jay had to lose everything, including their lives, for Mason and Scarlet to be happy again.

Mason felt guilty as hell. That was the long and short of it. His life was better than ever and he'd forgotten in the moment that he had no business celebrating at a time like this. The only way he knew to make up for it was to make his brother's needs his number one priority. The funeral arrangements were an easy and obvious way to fill his time. From there, he spent hours with the estate lawyers determining what needed to be done with Jay and Rachel's property and holdings. It would all be liquidated and put into a trust for Luna. Jay had already put that provision in his will.

In preparing for Luna's adoption, his brother had also put together an account for her care. It was generous enough that the monthly interest generated on the principal would handle most of her expenses. Not that a one-year-old had many outside of the usual food, diapers and care. Later, however, it would provide for private school and the best colleges she could get into.

Mason would've happily paid for all of that himself. He told Jay he would raise Luna as his own daughter and that meant he wouldn't skimp when it came to anything she might need. At this point, he'd feel better about things if he was financially supporting Luna. But Jay hadn't allowed for it. It was typical Jay to handle all the details so Mason didn't have to do anything but make the most of his time with Luna.

But that was the hardest part of all. At least for Mason.

Luna wouldn't remember her parents, or know why she was here instead of the home she'd been born in. But Mason knew, and every time he looked at her, all he could see was everything she'd lost. Each milestone she achieved would be bittersweet, knowing Rachel and Jay had missed it.

"There you are."

Mason looked up to find Scarlet peeking at him from around the corner. He had set up his computer in the dining room, which was in plain view, but was also the most secluded and unused of the rooms in the house. "Hey."

Scarlet leaned against the wall and crossed her arms over her chest. "Do you know that's the first thing you've said to me all day?"

He frowned. It wasn't intentional. At least he didn't think so. "I've been working on some things today."

She nodded thoughtfully. "Just like yesterday. And the day before. And every day since Jay died."

Mason sat back in his chair and slammed his laptop lid shut. "Someone has to deal with things, Scarlet. My parents can't handle it."

"I know. And I understand. But you don't have to abandon your own family to do it, Mason."

"I don't know what you're talking about, Scarlet. I'm right here. I haven't gone anywhere."

"Physically, no. Mentally, you've checked out of this marriage. And of this family, too."

Mason pushed his chair back and stood up. He grabbed his drink off the table and carried it into the kitchen for a refill. He needed something to do instead of sit there while she leveled accusations at him. "Don't you think you're being a little overdramatic about all of this? My brother died. Can't I have a little time to process everything?"

Scarlet followed him into the kitchen. "Absolutely. And if I thought you were actually working through your brother's death, I wouldn't mind at all. But you're hiding from it just as surely as you're hiding from us. I know this feeling, Mason. You're getting ready to run."

Mason set his glass on the counter and turned to face her. "Do I look like someone about to run away?" He was wearing cargo shorts and flip-flops.

"I didn't think so. I thought you really meant it when you said you wanted to try again."

"I did want to try again. But then I saw this and I

wasn't sure you felt the same way." Mason opened the kitchen drawer and pulled out the divorce papers she'd stashed there.

Scarlet took the pages from him. "This is just the draft we agreed upon weeks ago. I haven't spoken to my attorney about this since we decided to reconcile. I thought you didn't want the divorce."

"I don't want the divorce," he said. "But I'm still worried that you do. What is that note in there about consulting an adoption attorney?"

Scarlet flipped through the pages and found the note her attorney had hand scribbled in the package. "That was nothing."

"It didn't look like nothing. It looked like you might be trying to cozy up to me long enough to get what you really wanted—custody of Luna—then you'd walk away from me."

Scarlet's mouth dropped open. "My attorney recommended I talk with someone just so I had a better idea of my rights, since Jay left her to you alone. That's all. I didn't even end up calling him. Do you really think that all of this—all these weeks, all those nights together—was just about luring you back in so I could have the baby, then leave you high and dry? Honestly? That's what you think of me?"

Mason shook his head. "I didn't know what to think. That's why I didn't bring it up. I wanted more time to figure it out before we discussed it again."

She put the papers down on the counter. "I think we're discussing it now."

Mason closed his eyes. He wasn't mentally prepared

to have this talk. Not now. At least not if he wanted it to end well. He shouldn't have brought up the divorce papers. He could tell she was going to push the issue, though. He had shut her out, and she was tired of it, but he didn't know what else to do. Was he supposed to tell her that he couldn't stand to be happy with her because he felt guilty? That every kiss, every touch, every laugh they shared made him feel more and more like a thief who stole his brother's life?

"Scarlet, please," he said, his voice on the edge of begging. "Can we not do this today?"

"When, then, Mason? You're not exactly known for facing issues head-on. Are you going to drag it out for months this time and then walk away when I'm least expecting it?"

"What does it hurt to wait instead of acting in haste or on an emotional response? I'm dealing with a lot right now. I don't understand why you can't give me the space I need so we can have this discussion when we're better prepared."

"Because…every moment I spend with you and Luna is just another memory that's going to haunt me once you're gone."

That snapped Mason to attention. He looked up at her, the words surprising him. "What?"

Scarlet just shook her head and let her gaze fall to the floor. His brilliant artist, his loving wife, looked completely broken. Her tall, strong frame seemed to be swallowed by her sweatshirt, and her messy ponytail seemed more the result of stress than its usual casual ease. There were gray smudges beneath her dark eyes that he hadn't noticed before. The last few days had obviously been harder on her than he'd allowed himself to notice. He'd been too wrapped up in himself.

"I think I'm done, Mason."

"What do you mean by 'done'? Do you mean done with us?"

"Yes, I'm done. I can't handle any more of this emotional roller coaster. I can't be with you. I can't be in a relationship with someone that I can't depend on. You wanted this second chance, but I feel like you're just throwing it away, and me with it. Your brother is dead. I'm sorry. But you're not. I feel like you're punishing yourself for that, and punishing all of us in the process. I can't just sit around and wait for you to decide you don't want to do this anymore."

Mason watched Scarlet reach for the paperwork on the counter. She flipped through it, searching for the final page. She hesitated only for a moment before she reached for a pen and signed her name on the line. Mason held his breath in his throat as he watched her go through the motions of ending their marriage. She'd always fought to stay together before, but he could tell she was tired of fighting.

"There," she said, looking up at him with a shimmer of tears in her dark eyes. "If you're really truly done, if you want to leave for whatever reason, I'm not going to be the one who keeps you here against your will. If you want to go, sign the papers and send them to your attorney. If you don't, tear them up and snap out of this haze you're in. But I'm tired of being in limbo with you, so you have to choose."

Setting down the pen with an angry slap against the granite, Scarlet avoided eye contact with him and walked out of the kitchen.

Mason stood stunned for a moment. He wasn't entirely sure what to do. Things had escalated between them faster than he'd anticipated. Apparently, his internal struggle had pushed Scarlet to the edge. Walking up to the counter, he picked up the papers and looked at her angrily scribbled signature on the last page.

Her name in ink on their divorce papers was a jarring sight. Maybe this whole exercise for Jay's sake had just been putting off the inevitable. For a while he'd thought that maybe they could have that happy family they'd talked about and dreamed of. Now he knew it was just a pipe dream.

He and Scarlet were done. They'd been done for months. They just hadn't wanted to admit it to themselves because the alternative was scary for them both. But it didn't change the truth.

Mason carried the papers over to the dining room table with everything else and slammed them onto the top of the pile. One more thing to deal with.

Eleven

Scarlet stayed at the office as late as possible. She didn't want to go home because she knew what she would find—an empty house and an empty heart. Mason hadn't said a word to her since their discussion, but he'd returned to sleeping in her studio that night. She saw him packing up a few things from the bathroom as she left this morning. That meant he would be gone by the time she got home. And if he was gone, that meant everything she loved would be gone, too.

She knew the minute she signed those papers that she'd made the wrong choice. She had given him an out, letting him decide once and for all if he wanted to be with her or not. She was giving him the freedom to make that choice without guilt. But as she'd signed the papers, essentially giving up on him, she'd watched the expression on his face completely crumple.

Up until that moment, it was what she thought he wanted. Mason was the one who never talked about their future together in concrete terms. The moment he seemed to break down and say yes, he would commit to this marriage and this family, he seemed to take a huge step back from everything. After the funeral, he'd been more distant than he had been in the weeks leading up to his moving out the first time. It had become clear to Scarlet that he was pulling away now that Jay was gone. She'd assumed that in his mind the game they'd been playing was over.

When he pulled out those divorce papers, his response to them had thrown her completely off guard. Somehow, he was upset with her because he thought she'd been conniving behind his back to steal custody of Luna away. That was hardly the case. Did he really think she was capable of seducing him, luring him into her life, then just casting him aside once she was able to secure the baby she wanted? They'd been together too many years for him to accuse her of something like that.

Her heart had broken in that moment—what was left of it at least. There had only been fragments when he came back into her life and now there was nothing. She'd given what she had left to him and Luna.

When she walked into their home tonight—the home that had been so full of life and excitement the last few weeks—she knew it wouldn't be the same. It would be silent. Hollow. She'd experienced that before, although it would be so much worse this time because she wasn't just losing Mason, she was losing Luna, too. She'd given the sweet baby extra kisses this morning before hurrying out the door so Carroll couldn't see her tears.

A rush of movement passed Scarlet's office door, then the figure stopped and leaned back. It was April, with a perplexed look on her face. "What are you doing here? I thought you were taking some time away after the funeral."

Scarlet could only shrug. If she opened her mouth, she would start to cry. She hadn't told anyone about what had happened between her and Mason. She wasn't sure if she was ready to say those words out loud. She'd spent the hours focused on going over the San Francisco opening numbers and orders for the next month.

"I am," she managed to say.

April backed up and came into her office, sitting down in her guest chair. "What's going on? You're almost never in the office. Things at home must be rough. Is Mason taking his brother's death hard?"

"You could say that. He's also taking the divorce hard." Once the *D* word slipped from her lips, Scarlet felt a rush of emotion and heat warm her cheeks. Tears spilled down her face before she could squeeze her eyes closed.

"Divorce? Wait. What happened? Oh, honey," April continued, holding a tissue out to Scarlet.

Scarlet reached out to take it and press the thin paper to her face. It was hardly enough to hide behind, but it soaked up a few of her tears and made her feel a little better. She hated to fall apart in front of other people.

April gave her the space she needed, thankfully. She sat quietly for a few moments before she pressed Scarlet to talk again. "So tell me what's happened."

She crumpled the tissue into a ball in her fist and shook her head. "It's done."

"Was that his decision this time or yours?"

"I don't really know." Scarlet bit at her bottom lip. She knew how ridiculous that sounded, but it was true. She didn't want the divorce, but she wasn't going to sit around and wait for him to leave her either. Either they were staying together forever or she was going to end it while she still had some of her heart and pride left to salvage.

"He was pulling away like last time. I could see it happening no matter how hard I tried to engage him. So this time, I pushed him instead of trying to pull him back. I thought maybe that would snap him into fighting back. Fighting to be with me or at the very least standing up and saying, 'Relax, I'm not about to leave you every time I need some space.' But I think I pushed too hard and he thought I wanted him gone, because he just walked away. So I guess it's my fault. But I couldn't sit around and wait for him to leave me in good time. I would rather the break be clean and fast."

"Are you taking it better this time? Being clean and fast?" April asked.

"No." Scarlet broke down into tears again. She hated April seeing her cry, but she couldn't stop the emotion from pouring out of her even if she wanted to.

"If you don't want this, why don't you talk to him? Tell him that you're just scared of losing him and you don't really want a divorce. It's not too late to change things."

"He's already moved out."

"He's moved out before and come back. That doesn't mean anything."

"The only reason he came back before was to make his brother happy. Whatever I may have thought the last few weeks were, or ended up being, it all started as a ruse. Maybe I was a fool for seeing more to it than there really was."

April got up and came around the desk. "Give me a hug," she insisted. Scarlet got up and let herself be embraced by her significantly smaller manager. It reminded her of the hugs from her grandmother who had been just shy of five feet tall. She gave the best hugs, though, making Scarlet feel safe and loved even when she had far outgrown her lap.

"You need to go home," April said as they finally parted.

Scarlet shook her head adamantly. "I can't. I can't bear to see the house empty again. I had everything I ever wanted in my hands and I let it slip away because I was too frightened to hold on tight enough."

"You can't sleep here. You can stay here for a week and it won't change what's at home. Face your fears. Go home. Think about what has happened and see if you're inspired to do the brave, hard thing."

"And what's that?"

"Going to someone with your heart on your sleeve and saying you were wrong. That you were scared. There's no way to judge how Mason will take it, but it's possible that he feels the same way but you two don't know how to talk to one another. Share your feelings."

"And what if he doesn't feel the same way?"

"Then you'll have me over for drinks, we'll have a good cry and you'll move on knowing you did everything that you could."

She was right. Scarlet knew she was right. With a sigh, she reached for her purse and shut down her computer. "Okay. Thank you."

"Call me if you need me," April said as Scarlet slipped out the door.

Her manager's pep talk got her into her car, but it didn't help for the long drive home through LA traffic. With every mile the anticipation built. Anticipation for what she would find at home. For how Mason would take her confession. She knew that all of that was out of her control. April was right about doing what was in her power, telling him how she felt and letting the cards fall where they may.

When the garage door opened, it revealed, as expected, that both Mason's and Carroll's cars were gone. There was a part of her, up until that moment, that thought she was wrong about what she would find there. That maybe Mason might've decided to fight for her love instead of walking away again. That instead of doing what he thought was best, he would tear up the divorce papers and say, "No, I'm not letting us throw our relationship away again, no matter what it costs us."

Those were just the kind of heroics that happened only in movies and romantic novels. In real life, the garage was empty, the house was empty and so was the cavernous hole in her aching chest.

She opened the door, cautiously peeking into the quiet, dark kitchen. The house was perfectly still, reminding her of those days before Mason returned. With a sigh, she came inside and shut the door behind her. The silence was familiar, at least, as was the heartache. She knew how to handle that.

There was a new element to this emptiness, however, that she wasn't so sure about. Setting her purse on the kitchen counter, she looked around. There were no glass bottles in the dish rack with Mason's travel mug. No brightly colored plastic spoons mixed in with the other hand-washed utensils. She continued into the living room. His laptop wasn't on the coffee table and there was no Pack 'n Play by the couch.

Her heart was pounding in her ears as she turned toward the nursery door. It was as though it was once again the closed shrine she never entered. The monument to her lost child. She knew she couldn't let it become that way, no matter what was on the other side of the door.

She turned the knob and let the door swing open. There was nothing. Mason had taken the furniture, the toys, the clothes…nothing remained in the room but the mural she'd painted for Luna. She wished he could've taken that, too. Now, when she looked at it, all she could see was Luna's toothy grin as she squealed and tried to say *dolphin*.

That was the moment. The moment everything changed. Scarlet knew, she just knew how all this would end. That was why she'd insisted on the nanny and the hands-off approach for both Luna and Mason. She knew her heart would get captured by the tiny child and the bumbling uncle who was in over his head. And she'd done it anyway. She'd let herself fall back in love with her husband, let herself get attached to a child who wasn't hers, and it all fell apart.

Standing in the middle of the room, Scarlet looked up at the mural and felt her knees give out from under her. She sank to the plush gray carpet and, now that she was well and truly alone, let her grief unravel.

Mason looked out the massive window of his Hollywood Hills home at the valley below and missed the ocean more than ever. It had been nearly two weeks since he'd moved out, but it hadn't taken him five minutes to know he'd made a huge mistake. He'd known that immediately, felt it in his bones when he walked through the front door.

He wasn't the only one. Luna didn't like it either. She didn't say as much, of course, but she'd been miserably fussy lately. Carroll did her best to soothe her, but there was nothing that warm milk or her favorite toy could do. She wanted Scarlet.

And so did he.

There just wasn't anything he thought he could do about it now. He'd promised not to run away from her, and the moment things got tough, that's what he'd done. He hadn't realized it at the time. As always, he'd found a way to justify what he was doing. Someone needed to handle things. And that was true. But there wasn't so much to be done that he needed to withdraw from his wife and family.

He'd felt guilty, scared, unsure of the future, and he screwed up. Yes, Scarlet's signing the divorce papers had hurt, but in retrospect, he realized what she was doing. She'd pushed him to see which way he would turn under stress, and he did just what she was afraid of. He bolted back to Hollywood even though it was the last thing he really wanted to do.

Mason frowned at the layer of smog blanketing the valley and shifted his gaze to the courtyard below. Carroll and Luna were playing outside. He'd already called about having a swing set put in. In the meantime, Luna was happy with the small plastic playhouse with a window and a tiny slide.

Carroll helped her down the slide and Luna broke into a wide grin as she reached the bottom. It was the first time she'd smiled since they moved here. Maybe she was starting to forget Scarlet. She was so young. It would be a tragedy, though.

The last thing he wanted to do, especially after all their prior heartbreak, was to take a child away from Scarlet. Even when faced with the knowledge that she might be planning to take Luna from him, he would've said he couldn't do it to her. He'd seen how devastated she was losing Evan. Although he'd blamed himself for their inability to have a child, Scarlet insisted it wasn't his fault.

But losing Luna was his fault. He had taken her away. And just because he had every right to do it didn't make it okay. It wasn't what Rachel and Jay wanted. It wasn't what Scarlet wanted. And it certainly wasn't what he wanted. He just wasn't certain if what he wanted was what he should have.

Climb down from the cross, Mason. We don't need another martyr in this family.

The night before, Mason had shot up in bed in a cold sweat. He'd heard those words, his brother's words, as surely as if Jay had been sitting on the bed speaking to him. For a moment, Mason expected to actually see Jay sitting in the chair. Then he remembered his brother was dead and gone.

Perhaps it was his conscience telling him what Jay would say if he were alive. Out of the two brothers, Mason was driven by success and Jay was driven by happiness. Oddly enough, they were both successful in their own ways, but Jay's focus on being content had served him well. Mason felt guilty for being happy after his brother's life had imploded, but he failed to realize that Jay wouldn't see it that way at all. Jay would want his older brother to be happy, especially if that happiness resulted in a better life for Luna.

Jay would've reached out from his hospital bed and smacked Mason across the back of the head if he'd thought for one moment that Mason would sacrifice his own happiness out of guilt over Jay's and Rachel's deaths. He would be furious that Mason wasn't living his life to the fullest when he was lucky enough to still have one to live.

Of course, that just made Mason feel even guiltier. He couldn't win.

But if he was damned if he did, and damned if he

didn't, he might as well choose to be guilty *and* happy, right? Jay would say yes. Scarlet would say yes. Why couldn't he let himself say yes, too?

He wanted to. He wanted to hold his wife again. The guilt would pass, but he needed to work through it. He wanted to see Luna fall asleep in Scarlet's arms. He'd promised Jay that he would give Luna the best possible upbringing. Didn't that mean having a mother who would love and care for her more than anything else?

And if he did choose to be happy, if he did want Scarlet back in their lives, was it a decision come too late?

Mason turned his back to the window and walked over to his desk. It was overrun with paperwork now instead of the kitchen table at the beach house. On top was the divorce paperwork with Scarlet's signature still on it. Mason hadn't signed. She probably thought that he'd signed and filed the paperwork the next day, but he hadn't. He couldn't make himself do it. That was admitting failure, and if there was one thing that made Mason more uncomfortable than guilt, it was defeat.

And if he refused to be defeated, he had to try to win Scarlet back. He sat on the edge of his bed trying to think about what he could do to woo his wife. The years had taught him that flowers, jewelry and the usual items were appreciated, but not particularly Scarlet's style. She was the kind that was impossible to shop for, the one who wanted something thoughtful and from the heart.

What could he possibly give her?

He would think of something and give it his best shot. If Scarlet wouldn't take him back, there was nothing he could do about it. He'd made his bed and now he had to lie in it. But he at least had to try. When he left before, he'd done it because he wanted her to have the family she really wanted, instead of believing that what she really wanted was him. He'd worried this time that Luna wouldn't be enough for her, but those doubts flew out the window the day he came home to the mural in progress.

Scarlet might not want to take him back, but that was a risk he'd have to take. He would march into the house with his heart on his sleeve and see what happened. Either way, he knew in his heart that he couldn't take Luna from her.

Wait…that was it.

Mason walked back over to his desk and started shuffling through the papers until he found the folder of adoption paperwork. He had been named Luna's physical and legal guardian prior to Jay's passing, but now they were starting the process of legal adoption.

Even when they were giving things a second try, Mason had been loath to have Scarlet adopt Luna right away. He could always do it himself, then have Scarlet do it down the road when Luna was a little older. All it changed, really, was the name on the birth certificate, nothing more. Luna wouldn't love Scarlet any less and vice versa. Given the discussions she'd had with her attorneys, it made sense to wait.

But now he knew he couldn't.

Mason had never been able to give her the biological child she wanted. He hadn't been able to do what was necessary to keep their adopted son. He'd basically taken Luna from her the same way. But he could fix this. He could offer Scarlet the chance to adopt Luna now. That way, neither of them could take the child from the other. Scarlet could feel secure. Mason would know that if they stayed married, it wasn't just to keep Luna in her life, and Scarlet would know that he wasn't just keeping Scarlet around because he was afraid to parent on his own.

It was perfect.

Flipping through the pages, he found the number of the family attorney handling the adoption. It took a few minutes for him to explain what he wanted. Since his lawyer was aware of the separation, he knew it was an odd request, but he was adamant about it. In the worst-case scenario, Luna would still have two parents who loved her, and that was the most important part. That was what he'd promised Jay.

The updated paperwork would be ready tomorrow for him to pick up. Once he had it in hand, he would go straight to the beach house. Hopefully, in the next twenty-four hours, he would figure out just what to say when he got there.

Mason hung up the phone and merrily took the stairs two at a time until he very nearly collided with Carroll at the bottom. "Sorry about that," he said, flattening against the wall out of her way.

Carroll looked at him suspiciously. "Are you okay, Mr. Spencer? You seem different. At least, different since we've moved out here."

"Well, I'm trying to work on something that might change everything." Mason didn't want to tell the nanny too much and get her hopes up. Of course, she might abandon him to go live with Scarlet and Luna if given the choice. He hadn't been the best boss or roommate lately as he skulked around the house.

"Well, I hope what you're working on is a big, fat apology to Mrs. Spencer so she takes you back."

Mason couldn't help being curious about her response. "Why is that?"

She looked around the house and held her arms out. "It's a perfectly nice house in a good neighborhood. I'm sure you paid a fortune for it. But I don't like it here. Luna doesn't like it here. I daresay that you don't even like it here. I don't know what happened between you and Mrs. Spencer, but I hope that whatever has you smiling all of a sudden is going to fix this mess and we'll get to move home."

Mason grinned and patted her on the shoulder. "I hope so, too, Carroll. I hope so, too."

Twelve

Scarlet was going stir-crazy.

It had been two weeks without a word from Mason. Surely by now he'd filed the divorce papers, but not even her attorney had called. She was going to go insane from the deafening silence of the empty house.

She'd tried to get away from it. Despite April's protests, she'd gone into the office every day. Her work there wasn't impacted by her broken heart. That was at the core of her creativity. Until she was healed, the brushes were useless. She might as well work on spreadsheets and inventory so she could be productive in her grief.

It was Sunday, however. April told her that if she showed up today, she would change the alarm codes on her and all the alarms would go off when she tried to get in. That threat, albeit hollow, was enough to keep her home today, at least. She didn't really want to deal with the police and explain to them why her own employee had basically locked her out of her building.

Scarlet settled for sitting on the deck, watching the ocean. The roar of the waves was a soothing white noise that allowed her to simply disengage. That was the best she could hope for at this point. Eventually, she would pick up and move on, but not yet. She was allowing herself the grace to get through this in her own time so she could heal. If she could heal.

The sound of the doorbell echoed from inside the house. Scarlet frowned as she got up from her chair. She wasn't expecting company.

She whipped open the front door and froze in place when she saw Mason standing on her welcome mat. He was wearing his favorite blue jeans and his worn brown leather jacket he'd had since they started dating. She blinked her eyes twice to make sure he was real and not her imagination conjuring the Mason of her past. He was still there. Scarlet bit at her lip, unsure what to do now. She hadn't been prepared for this at all, and it probably showed.

"Hello, Scarlet."

Mason gave her a soft smile that threatened to undermine her resolve to stay strong. She wasn't sure why he was here, but she knew she shouldn't get her hopes up. He probably forgot his laptop charger or something and had to stop by and pick it up. He didn't even have the courtesy to bring the baby with him for the visit. Maybe that was for the best, though. Space would help. She hoped.

"I wasn't expecting you today," Scarlet said, skipping the pleasantries. "I wasn't expecting you ever again, actually. Did you forget something at the house?"

Mason shook his head. "No, Scarlet, I just came to talk to you."

To talk? "About what?" she asked.

He looked around the front stoop awkwardly and shuffled on his feet. "Can I come in?"

As much as she knew she shouldn't, Scarlet was desperate for someone to be in the house other than herself. Without replying, she took a step backward and allowed him to enter.

He brushed past her as he stepped into the house, smelling like leather and his favorite cologne. She tried not to breathe it in but had to draw in a breath before she turned blue. "What can I do for you today?" she asked as she casually led him to the couches in the living room. She thought about offering him a beverage but decided she was being hospitable enough as it was.

She sat down in a chair, forcing him into the couch across from her. Mason settled into his seat looking as uncomfortable as she felt. "Luna is doing well," he offered. "I think she misses you."

Scarlet gritted her teeth together. It was bad enough that she was miserable; she didn't want to know that Luna missed her. She'd already lost too many people in her young life.

"I miss you, too, Scarlet."

She froze in place, her breath held captive in her lungs. She didn't know what to say. Was it better to be honest and admit she missed him as well, or to be stoic and let him think she was over him? "Divorce is hard," she said, opting for another tactic: avoidance.

Scarlet watched as his blue eyes searched her face for something. He hunched over in his seat, gripping his hands together between his knees. He appeared to be considering his options. She wasn't sure what those options could be, or why he was even here, telling her these things. Could he really be missing her? Could he be here trying to reconcile and she was stonewalling him?

"I miss you, too," she added quickly.

A bit of hope appeared in Mason's eyes, but it didn't make it to his smile. "The other day, when you signed the divorce papers, I didn't know what to do. I didn't want a divorce. I was happier than I'd ever been with you and with Luna. It was the last thing I wanted."

"You didn't seem happy. You were distant and moody. You completely withdrew from everyone."

"I know. And I'm sorry. I was having trouble reconciling my happiness with my guilt over my brother losing everything. Being without you these few weeks has helped me realize that Jay would want me to be happy. He would want a loving, joyful home for Luna, and I was letting my grief ruin it for everyone."

"So, what…you want to come home?" Her brain warred with itself over what the answer would be if he said yes. Fool me twice…she didn't want to be a fool again. And yet, a part of her would always be a fool where Mason was concerned.

"Yes, I would. We all would. But before you say yes or no, I want to give you something."

Scarlet hadn't noticed anything in Mason's hands but

a manila envelope. She presumed it had something divorce related in it. It certainly wasn't flowers or something like that stashed away. Not that she was a fan of flowers.

"Scarlet, when we got married seven years ago, we wrote our own vows. Do you remember?"

That was a silly question. Who forgot their wedding vows? "I do."

"And do you remember the part where I vowed to do anything to make you happy? That I'd give you the moon if that was what you wanted?"

Scarlet felt the prickle of tears in her eyes at the mention of that moment. He'd looked so handsome, his hands trembling slightly as he read his handwritten vows to her. She had no doubt in that moment that he loved her more than anything on earth and he would give her the moon if she asked for it. Young, idealistic love. "I remember. But that was a long time ago, Mason."

He shook his head. "It doesn't matter how long ago it was. It's as true today as it was seven years ago. I know what you want, Scarlet. More than anything. You want a baby. No, not a baby. You want Luna. And I'm going to do whatever it takes to make that happen."

Scarlet flinched. He couldn't be serious. "Are you offering her to me in the settlement?" she joked.

Mason smiled. "No, of course not. She's not a vacation home, she's a child. But I am offering you the chance to be her mother. Legally. Forever." He held up the envelope. "I've had the paperwork drawn up for both of us to adopt Luna. When this is finalized, you will have just as many rights to her as I do. You will be her mother in every way that counts and no one, including me, is going to take her away from you. No matter what happens with us."

Scarlet's jaw dropped open the longer he spoke. He was dead serious about this. When he was done, she held up her hand. "Wait, you're saying that you're willing to do this even if I still want the divorce? That we'll share custody of Luna no matter what?"

"Yes." He looked as serious as he had when he said *I do.*

"Why?" It was all Scarlet could say. He didn't have to do this. It wasn't her baby. She wasn't related to Luna by blood. If he was doing this, it was because he knew how much it was hurting her to lose another baby. "You don't have to do any of this."

"I'm doing it because Luna deserves a mother who loves her as much as you do. What kind of father would I be to her if I took her away from you?"

Scarlet covered her face with her hands as the tears started pouring from her. She couldn't stop them. After a moment, she felt his hand on her knee. When she opened her eyes, he was kneeling in front of her, holding a handkerchief.

"Here," he offered.

She took it, dabbing at her eyes and drying her cheeks. "Thank you" was all she could say. For the handkerchief, for the adoption papers…for everything. "I appreciate it, even if I don't understand it."

"To be honest," Mason said, "it's not entirely selfless on my part."

"How is that?"

"Well, I don't just want a mother for Luna. I want my wife back, too."

Scarlet looked at him with puffy, red eyes, making it hard to gauge how she really felt about what he'd said. He waited a moment to let the words sink in before he continued. "I screwed up. I did the one thing you were afraid I would do. I wasn't sure how to cope with everything, so I retreated when I should've held my ground. I don't want the divorce, Scarlet."

She shook her head. "I don't want it either. But how do we stop it? You've already filed, haven't you?"

"Nope. I actually never even signed the papers."

Scarlet sat back in her seat, stunned. "You didn't? I thought for sure after I signed and you moved out that you would've pressed forward with the process."

"You'd think so. But I couldn't. They're sitting on my desk just as you left them, as I flip-flopped back and forth on what to do. I rationalized, as I did before, that you might be happier with another man who can give you everything you want. I know that I can't give you the family you hoped for. Luna is the only child I will ever have. But I'm willing to share her with you, no matter what. That's why I wanted to tell you about the adoption first. I didn't want you to say yes to taking me back just because of Luna. You will have her in your life. I want you to want me because you truly want me as I am. I just hope that I'm enough for you."

Scarlet covered his hand with hers. "You've always been enough. I just couldn't convince you of that."

Mason sat back on his heels. "You really mean that? You'd be happy just you and me and Luna?"

Scarlet nodded. "Absolutely. I know you might find this hard to believe, Mason, but I love you. Even when I signed the divorce papers, I loved you. I was just trying to make the smart choice for me."

Mason's excitement dulled. "What do you mean?"

"We've talked about this before, Mason. You run. I told you how hard it was on me the last time and you did it anyway. I knew it was coming, and that's why I tried to push you away. I was trying to protect myself and make our breakup my decision this time. But it didn't make any difference in the end. You were still gone and I still felt horrible."

"And now?" His heart stilled in his chest as he waited for her answer. Just because she loved him didn't mean she would take him back. Perhaps he'd screwed up too much. He would understand if she was afraid to trust her heart to him again. He wasn't sure he'd believe himself if he promised not to run again.

"And now, I still worry, to be honest. If we're going to raise a child together especially, I need to know I can count on you to be there, Mason. Bad things are going to happen. I can guarantee it. You need to learn a better way to cope with disappointment and pain. I need you to turn to me instead of running away from me. I need you to tell me when you're feeling overwhelmed so we can work through it together like a couple should."

Mason heard her words and he understood. His parents had never been much of a team. His father handled the office and his mother managed the home. Mason had tried to do both and got overwhelmed when it didn't work out perfectly. "You're right. I just have this feeling like I have to do it all on my own. But that's not what a marriage is about, is it?"

Scarlet shook her head. "If we're going to do this, we have to both promise to do it together. You and me and Luna against the world. Can you promise me that?"

"I'll promise you that and more. I promise I'll love you more than any man has ever loved a woman. I promise that I'll do anything to make you happy. All you have to do is ask. Remember, I promised you the moon and I'll find a way to climb up there and snatch it from the sky if you asked."

"And if you start to feel overwhelmed or stressed?" she pressed.

"I'll talk to you about it. Maybe I'll try a fishing trip in Tahoe or something to clear my head the next time. But I promise to always come home to you. I mean that."

Scarlet's dark eyes surveyed his face for a moment before her lips softened into a smile. "I love you," she said before lunging out of her chair and into his arms.

Mason straightened up to catch her. He wrapped his arms around her waist and buried his face in her neck. The scent of her shampoo was like a welcome home, a reminder that the familiar was once again in his grasp. "I love you, too," he whispered into her ear. "More than you will ever know."

Scarlet pulled away to look down at him. She cradled his face in her hands. "I know." Then she leaned down to give him a kiss. Her lips were soft and hesitant at first, almost embodying how she felt about everything between them. It didn't take long, however, for her to give in to the kiss and leave her reservations behind.

It felt amazing to hold Scarlet, and know that this time he was never going to let her go. She was his, for always. He relished every moment of their embrace after going two long weeks without touching her. He wanted to hold her in his arms and kiss her until they were both out of breath, but he knew they had other things to attend to. They could pick up where they left off tonight. And every night from here on out.

Finally, reluctantly, he pulled away. Mason stood, taking Scarlet's hands and pulling her up from her chair with him. Every step they took from here was on the path of their new life together. He couldn't wait to see what was in store for them.

"Let's call Carroll and tell her the good news. I'm sure she'll immediately start packing to come home."

He laughed. "We will, but we have something we need to do first."

Scarlet looked up at him with confusion. "What?"

Mason held up the envelope in his hand. "We have to sign the adoption papers and drop them off at the attorney's office. It takes forever to process them and get them in front of the judge as it is." He took her by the hand and led her over to the dining room table. He opened up the envelope, flipping through the legal pages until he reached the one where they both had to sign. He held out a pen to her. "You first."

She took it from him, her hand trembling with excitement or nerves, he wasn't sure which. Gripping the pen, she signed the page, and unlike when she signed the divorce papers, her name was written in her neat cursive penmanship. When she was finished, she handed him the pen and he did the same.

When he was done signing, he slipped the pages back inside and capped the pen. Turning to look at Scarlet, he noticed she had tears shimmering in her dark eyes. "What's the matter?" He wasn't expecting her to cry at a moment like this. Excitement, joy, sure, but not tears.

"Do you realize that you've fulfilled your promise from the day we married?"

Mason's brow furrowed. "To love, honor and cherish you until death?"

"No. You said you'd do anything for me and you did that with Luna. You've given me the moon."

Epilogue

Scarlet didn't recognize the number when the phone rang that afternoon. She was in the midst of preparations for Luna's second-birthday celebration. The deck had been transformed into a pink extravaganza. Caterers were setting up the food, the cake had been delivered moments ago and guests would be arriving within the hour. Any other day she might've been able to identify the number of their adoption attorney's office.

"Hello?" she said.

"Hello, Scarlet? This is Peter Vann. Do you have a moment?"

"Of course. Is something wrong?" Scarlet tried not to let her concern be evident in her voice. She settled down at the dining room table, expecting bad news. *Not today*, she prayed. Not on her baby's birthday.

Luna's adoption had been finalized months ago, but the way things had ended with Evan taught her that nothing was ever final in that regard. Perhaps one of Rachel's relatives had come forward to fight for the baby—and more likely, the sizable estate that came along with her.

"No, nothing is wrong. I'm actually calling because I have some good news you and Mason might be interested to hear. I just received a call from child services."

Good news from child services? "Yes?" she pressed.

"It seems they have taken a little boy into custody and they're looking for a home to place him in. The mother has terminated her rights, so he's eligible to be adopted. They contacted us directly because they thought you and Mason might be interested in him."

She winced at his words, torn between the fantasy and reality of what this could mean for their family. Both she and Mason were content in just having Luna. "I don't know, Peter. I told you before that Luna was the exception. I don't think either of us are willing to chance another adoption scenario after what happened before. It's too risky."

Peter chuckled. "I think you'll be very interested in this one. He's two and a half years old, brown hair, brown eyes, in good health, and his name…is Evan."

Scarlet's heart skipped a beat. She couldn't believe she'd heard the attorney correctly. "Evan? Our Evan?"

"The very same. If you want him back, he's yours, Scarlet. They reviewed his history and wanted to give you two the first chance to adopt him before he gets placed elsewhere."

She could barely focus on his words as Peter continued to talk. All she needed to know was that her baby boy was coming back to her. Scarlet stood up and placed the phone against her chest to muffle her voice as she shouted, "Mason! Come quick! Evan is coming home."

* * * * *

If you liked this story of a billionaire tamed by the love of the right woman—and baby— pick up these other novels from Andrea Laurence!

THE PREGNANCY PROPOSITION
THE BABY PROPOSAL
THE CEO'S UNEXPECTED CHILD
HIS LOVER'S LITTLE SECRET
MORE THAN HE EXPECTED
Available now from Mills & Boon Desire!

* * *

And don't miss the next
BILLIONAIRES AND BABIES *story*
THE CEO'S NANNY AFFAIR
by Joss Wood
Available August 2017!

* * *

She was pregnant. Very pregnant.

He had a million questions and didn't have time to nail down a single one before Rita threw herself into his arms.

"Jack!" She hugged him hard, then seemed to notice he wasn't returning her hug, so she let him go and stepped back. Confusion filled her eyes even as her smile faded into a flat, thin line. "How can you be here? I thought you must be dead. I never heard from you and—"

"Not here," he ground out, giving himself points for keeping a tight rein on the emotions rushing through him. "Let's take a walk."

"I'm working," she pointed out, waving her hand at the counter and customers behind her.

"Take a break." He needed some answers and he wasn't going to be denied. She was here. She was pregnant. Judging by the size of her belly, he was guessing about six months pregnant. That meant they had to talk. Now.

* * *

Little Secrets: His Unexpected Heir
is part of the Little Secrets series: Untamed passion, unexpected pregnancy…

LITTLE SECRETS: HIS UNEXPECTED HEIR

BY
MAUREEN CHILD

First Published in Great Britain 2017
By Mills & Boon, an imprint of HarperCollins*Publishers*
1 London Bridge Street, London, SE1 9GF

© 2017 Maureen Child

ISBN: 978-0-263-92826-6

51-0717

Printed and bound in Spain
by CPI, Barcelona

Maureen Child writes for the Mills & Boon Desire line and can't imagine a better job. A seven-time finalist for a prestigious Romance Writers of America RITA® Award, Maureen is an author of more than one hundred romance novels. Her books regularly appear on bestseller lists and have won several awards, including a Prism Award, a National Readers' Choice Award, a Colorado Romance Writers Award of Excellence and a Golden Quill Award. She is a native Californian but has recently moved to the mountains of Utah.

To my mom, Sallye Carberry,
because she loves romance novels
and shared that love with me.

One

Jack Buchanan listened to his interior decorator talk about swatches and color and found his mind drifting… to *anything* else.

Four months ago, he'd been in a desert, making life-and-death decisions. Today, he was in an upholstery shop in Long Beach, California, deciding between leather or fabric for the bar seats on the Buchanan Company's latest cruise ship. He didn't know whether to be depressed or amused. So he went with impatient.

"Which fabric will hold up better?" he asked, cutting into the argument between the decorator and the upholsterer.

"The leather," they both said at once, turning to look at him.

"Then use the fabric." Jack pointed at a bolt of midnight blue cloth shot through with silver threads. "We're building a fantasy bar. I'm less interested in wear and more concerned with the look of the place. If you want black leather in the mix, too, use it on the booth seats."

While the decorator and the upholsterer instantly jumped on that idea and put their heads together to plan, Jack shifted his gaze to encompass the shop. Family-owned, Dan Black and his sons, Mark and Tom, ran the place and did great work. Jack had seen that much for himself.

The shop itself was long and wide and filled with not only barstools, but also couches, chairs and tables being refinished. A chemical scent hung in the air as two men at the back of the room worked on projects. The low-pitched roar of an industrial sewing machine was like white noise in the background and the guy seated at it moved quickly, efficiently. Their work was fast and good enough that they'd also done jobs for the navy and Jack figured if they could handle *that*, they could handle his cruise ship.

But why the hell was Jack even here? He was the CEO of Buchanan Shipping. Didn't he have minions he could have sent to take care of this?

But even as he thought it, he reminded himself that being here today, in person, had all been his idea. To immerse himself in every aspect of the business. He'd been away for the last *ten* years, so he had a lot of catching up to do.

Jack, his brother, Sam, and their sister, Cass, had all interned at Buchanan growing up. They'd put in their time from the ground up, starting in janitorial, since their father had firmly believed that kids raised with all the money in the world grew up to be asses.

He'd made sure that *his* children knew what it was

to really work. To be alongside employees who would expect them to do the job and who had the ability to fire them if they didn't. Thomas Buchanan raised his kids to respect those who worked for them and to always remember that without those employees, they wouldn't have a business. So Jack, Sam and Cass had worked their way through every level at the company. They'd had to buy their own cars, pay for their own insurance and if they wanted designer clothes, they had to save up for them.

Now, looking back, Jack could see it had been the right thing to do. At the time, he hadn't loved it of course. But today, he could step into the CEO's shoes with a lot less trepidation because of his father's rules. He had the basics on running the company. But it was this stuff—the day-to-day, small but necessary decisions—that he had to get used to.

Buchanan Shipping had interests all over the world. From cruise liners to cargo ships to the fishing fleet Jack's brother, Sam, ran out of San Diego. The company had grown well beyond his great-grandfather's dreams when he'd started the business with one commercial fishing boat.

The Buchanans had been on the California coast since before the gold rush. While other men bought land and fought with the dirt to scratch out a fortune, the Buchanans had turned to the sea. They had a reputation for excellence that nothing had ever marred and Jack wanted to keep it that way.

Their latest cruise ship was top-of-the-line, state-of-the-art throughout and would, he told himself, more than live up to her name, *The Sea Queen*.

"Mr. Buchanan," the decorator said, forcing Jack out of his thoughts and back to reality.

"Yeah. What is it?"

"There are still choices to be made on height of stools, width of booths..."

Okay, details were one thing, minutiae were another.

Jack stopped her with one hand held up for silence. "You can handle that, Ms. Price." To take any sting out of his words, he added, "I trust your judgment," and watched pleasure flash in her eyes.

"Of course, of course," she said. "I'll fax you a complete record of all decisions made this afternoon."

"That's fine. Thanks." He shook hands with Daniel Black, waved a hand at the men in the back of the shop and left. Stepping outside, he was immediately slapped by a strong, cold breeze that carried the scent of the sea. The sky was a clear, bold blue and this small corner of the city hummed with an energy that pulsed inside Jack.

He wasn't ready to go back to the company. To sit in that palatial office, fielding phone calls and going over reports. Being outside, even being here, dealing with fabrics of all things, was better than being stuck behind his desk. With that thought firmly in mind, he walked to his car, got in and fired it up. Steering away from work, responsibility and the restless, itchy feeling scratching at his soul, Jack drove toward peace.

Okay, maybe *peace* was the wrong word, he told himself twenty minutes later. The crowd on Main Street in Seal Beach was thick, the noise deafening and the mingled scents from restaurants, pubs and bakeries swamped him.

Jack Buchanan fought his way through the summer crowds blocking the sidewalk. He'd been home from his last tour of duty for four months and he still wasn't used to being surrounded by so many people. Made him feel on edge, as if every nerve in his body was strung tight enough to snap.

Frowning at the thought, he sidestepped a couple of women who had stopped in the middle of the sidewalk to argue about a pair of shoes, for God's sake. Shaking his head, he walked a little faster, dodging gawking tourists, teenagers with surfboards and kids racing in and out of the crowd, peals of laughter hanging in their wake.

Summer in Southern California was always going to be packed with the tourists who flocked in from all over the world. And ordinarily Jack avoided the worst of the crowds by keeping close to his office building and the penthouse apartment he lived in. But at least once a month, Jack forced himself to go out into the throngs of people—just to prove to himself that he could.

Being surrounded by people brought out every defensive instinct he possessed. He felt on guard, watching the passing people through suspicious, wary eyes and hated himself for it. But four months home from a battlefield wasn't long enough to ease the instincts that had kept him alive in the desert. And still, he worked at forcing himself to relax those instincts because he refused to be defined by what he'd gone through. What he'd seen.

A small boy bulleted around a corner and slammed right into Jack. Every muscle in Jack's body tensed until he deliberately relaxed, caught the kid by the shoulders to keep him from falling and said, "You should watch where you're running."

"Sorry, mister." The kid jerked his head back, swinging his long blond hair out of his eyes.

"It's okay," Jack said, releasing both the boy and the sharp jolt of adrenaline still pumping inside him. "Just watch it."

"Right. Gotta go." The boy took off, headed for the beach and the pier at the end of the street.

Jack remembered, vaguely, what it had been like to be ten years old with a world of summer stretched out ahead of you. With the sun beating down on him and a sea breeze dancing past, Jack could almost recapture the sensation of complete freedom that everyone lost as they grew up. Frowning at his own thoughts, he concentrated again on the crowd and realized it had been a couple of months since he'd been in Seal Beach.

A small beach community, it lay alongside Long Beach where he lived and worked, but Jack didn't make a habit of coming here. Memories were thick and he tended to avoid them, because remembering wouldn't get him a damn thing. But against his will, images filled his mind.

Last December, he'd been on R and R. He'd had two weeks to return to his life, see his family and decompress. He'd spent the first few days visiting his father, brother and sister, then he'd drawn back, pulling into himself. He'd come to the beach then, walking the sand at night, letting the sea whisper to him. Until the night he'd met *her*.

A beautiful woman, alone on the beach, the moonlight caressing her skin, shining in her hair until he'd almost convinced himself she wasn't real. Until she turned her head and gave him a cautious smile.

She should have been cautious. A woman alone on

a dark beach. Rita Marchetti had been smart enough to be careful and strong enough to be friendly. They'd talked, he remembered, there in the moonlight and then met again the following day and the day after that. The remainder of his leave, he'd spent with her, and every damn moment of that time was etched into his brain in living, vibrant color. He could hear the sound of her voice. The music of her laughter. He saw the shine in her eyes and felt the silk of her touch.

"And you've been working for months to forget it," he reminded himself in a mutter. "No point in dredging it up now."

What they'd found together all those months ago was over now. There was no going back. He'd made a promise to himself. One he intended to keep. Never again would he put himself in the position of loss and pain and he wouldn't ever be close enough to someone else that *his* loss would bring pain.

It was a hard lesson to learn, but he had learned it in the hot, dry sands of a distant country. And that lesson haunted him to this day. Enough that just walking through this crowd made him edgy. There was an itch at the back of his neck and it took everything he had not to give in to the urge to get out. Get away.

But Jack Buchanan didn't surrender to the dregs of fear, so he kept walking, made himself notice the everyday world pulsing around him. Along the street, a pair of musicians were playing for the crowd and the dollar bills tossed into an open guitar case. Shop owners had tables set up outside their storefronts to entice customers and farther down the street, a line snaked from a bakery's doors all along the sidewalk.

He hadn't been downtown in months, so he'd never

seen the bakery before. Apparently, though, it had quite
the loyal customer base. Dozens of people—from teenagers to career men and women waited patiently to get
through the open bakery door. As he got closer, amazing scents wafted through the air and he understood
the crowds gathering. Idly, Jack glanced through the
wide, shining front window at the throng within, then
stopped dead as an all too familiar laugh drifted to him.

Everything inside Jack went cold and still. He hadn't
heard that laughter in months, but he'd have known it
anywhere. Throaty, rich, it made him think of long, hot
nights, silk sheets and big brown eyes staring up into
his in the darkness.

He'd tried to forget her. Had, he'd thought, buried the
memories; yet now, they came roaring back, swamping
him until Jack had to fight for breath.

Even as he told himself it couldn't be her, Jack was
bypassing the line and stalking into the bakery. He followed the sound of that laugh as if it were a trail of
breadcrumbs. He had to know. Had to see.

"Hey, dude," a surfer with long dark hair told him,
"end of the line's back a ways."

"I'm not buying anything," he growled out and sent
the younger man a look icy enough to freeze blood.
Must have worked because the guy went quiet and gave
a half shrug.

But Jack had already moved on. He was moving
through the scattering of tables and chairs, sliding
through the throng of people clustered in front of a
wide, tall glass display case. Conversations rose and fell
all around him. The cheerful jingle of the old-fashioned
cash register sounded out every purchase as if celebrating. But Jack wasn't paying attention. His sharp gaze

swept across the people in the shop, looking for the woman he'd never thought to see again.

Then that laugh came again and he spun around like a wolf finding the scent of its mate. Gaze narrowed, heartbeat thundering in his ears, he spotted her—and everything else in the room dropped away.

Rita Marchetti. He took a breath and simply stared at her for what felt like forever. Her smile was wide and bright, her gaze focused on customers who laughed with her. What the hell was she doing in a bakery in Seal Beach, California, when she lived in Ogden, Utah? And why did she have to look so damn good?

He watched her, smiling and laughing with a customer as she boxed what looked like a couple dozen cookies, then deftly tied a white ribbon around the tall red box. Her hands were small and efficient. Her eyes were big and brown and shone with warmth. Her shoulder-length curly brown hair was pulled into a ponytail at the base of her neck and swung like a pendulum with her every movement.

Her skin was golden—all over, as he had reason to know—her mouth was wide and full, and though she was short, her figure was lush. His memories were clear enough that every drop of blood in his body dropped to his groin, leaving him light-headed…briefly. In an instant, though, all of that changed and a surge of differing emotions raced through him. Pleasure at seeing her again, anger at being faced with a past he'd already let go of and desire that was so hot, so thick, it grabbed him by the throat and choked off his air.

The heat of his gaze must have alerted her. She looked up and across the crowd, locking her gaze with his. Her eyes went wide, her amazing mouth dropped open and she lifted one hand to the base of her throat as if she, too, was having trouble breathing. Gaze still locked with his, she walked away from the counter, came around the display case and though Jack braced himself for facing her again—nothing could have prepared him for what he saw next.

She was pregnant.

Very pregnant.

Her belly was big, rounded and covered by a skin-tight, bright yellow T-shirt. The hem of her white capris ended just below her knees and she wore slip-on sneakers in a yellow bright enough to match her shirt.

He saw and noted all of that in a split second before he focused again on her rounded belly. Jack's heartbeat galloped in his chest as he lifted his eyes to meet hers. He had a million questions and didn't have time to nail down a single one before, in spite of the crowd watching them, Rita threw herself into his arms.

"Jack!" She hugged him hard, then seemed to notice he wasn't returning her hug, so she let him go and stepped back. Confusion filled her eyes even as her smile faded into a flat, thin line. "How can you be here? I thought you must be dead. I never heard from you and—"

He flinched and gave a quick glance around. Their little reunion was garnering way too much attention. No way was he going to have this chat with an audience listening to every word. And, he told himself, gaze dropping to that belly again, they had a *lot* to talk about.

"Not here," he ground out, giving himself points for keeping a tight rein on the emotions rushing through him. "Let's take a walk."

"I'm working," she pointed out, waving her hand at the counter and customers behind her.

"Take a break." Jack felt everyone watching them and an itch at the back of his neck urged him to get moving. But he was going nowhere without Rita. He needed some answers and he wasn't going to be denied. She was *here*. She was *pregnant*. Judging by the size of her belly, he was guessing about six months pregnant. That meant they had to talk. Now.

She frowned a little and even the downturn of her mouth was sexy. Which told Jack he was walking into some serious trouble. But there was no way to avoid any of it.

While he stared at her, he could practically see the wheels turning in her brain. She didn't like him telling her what to do, but she was so surprised to see him that she clearly wanted answers as badly as he did. She was smart, opinionated and had a temper, he recalled, that could blister paint. Just a few of the reasons that he'd once been crazy about her.

Coming to a decision, Rita called out, "Casey," and a cute redhead behind the counter looked up. "I'm taking a break. Back in fifteen."

"Right, boss," the woman said and went right back to ringing up the latest customer.

"Might take more than fifteen," he warned her even as she started past him toward the door.

"No, it won't," she said over her shoulder.

Whatever her original response to seeing him had been, she was cool and calm now, having no doubt figured out that he deliberately hadn't contacted her when he got home. They'd talk about that, too. But not here.

People were watching. The redhead looked curious,

but Jack didn't give a damn. He caught up with Rita in two steps, took hold of her upper arm and steered her past the crowd and out the door. Once they were clear of the shop, though, Rita pulled free of his grip. "I can walk on my own, Jack."

Without another word, she proved it, heading down the block toward the Seal Beach pier. The tree-lined street offered patches of shade and she moved from sunlight to shadow, her strides short, but sure.

He watched her for a couple of minutes, just to enjoy the view. She'd always had a world-class butt and damned if it wasn't good to see it again. He'd forgotten how little she was. Not delicate, he told himself. Not by a long shot. The woman was fierce, which he liked and her temper was truly something to behold. But right now, it was his own temper he had to deal with. Why was she here? Why was she *pregnant*? And why the hell hadn't he known about it?

His long legs covered the distance between them quickly, then he matched his stride to hers until they were stopped at a red light at Ocean Avenue. Across the street lay the beach, the ocean and the pier. Even from a distance, Jack could see surfers riding waves, fishermen dotting the pier and cyclists racing along the sidewalk.

While they waited for the light to change, he looked down at her, and inevitably, his gaze was drawn to the mound of her belly. His own insides jumped then fisted. Shoving one hand through his hair, he told himself he should have written to her as he'd said he would. Should have contacted her when he came home for good. But he'd been in a place where he hadn't wanted to see anyone. Talk to anyone. Hell, even his family hadn't been able to reach him.

"How long have you been home?" she asked, her voice nearly lost beneath the hum of traffic.

"Four months."

She looked up at him and he read anger and sorrow, mingled into a dark mess that dimmed the golden light in those dark brown eyes. "Good to know."

Before he could speak again the light changed and she stepped off the curb. Once again he took her arm and when she would have shaken him off, he firmly held on.

Once they crossed the street, she pulled away and he let her go, following after her as she stalked toward a small green park at the edge of a parking lot. Just beyond was a kids' playground, and beside that, the pier that snaked out into the sea.

The wind whipped her ponytail and tugged at the edges of his suit jacket. She turned to look up at him and when she spoke, he heard both pain and temper in her voice.

"I thought you were dead."

"Rita—"

"No." She shook her head and held up one hand to keep him silent. "You *let* me think it," she accused. "You told me you'd write to me. You didn't. You've been home four months and never looked for me."

Jack blew out a breath. "No, I didn't."

She rocked back on her heels as if he'd struck her. "Wow. You're not even sorry, are you?"

His gaze fixed on hers. "No, I'm not. There are reasons for what I did."

She folded her arms across her chest, unconsciously drawing his attention to her belly again. "Can't wait to hear them."

Two

Rita was shaking.

Her hands clenched, she tried to ease her galloping heartbeat and steady her breathing. But just standing beside Jack Buchanan made that almost impossible. She slid a glance at him from beneath lowered lashes and her breath caught. Even in profile, he was almost too gorgeous. That black hair, longer now than it had been when they met, those ice-blue eyes, strong jaw, firm mouth, all came together until a knot of emotion settled in her throat, nearly choking her.

For one magical week six months ago, she had been in love and she'd thought he felt the same. Then he was gone, and she was alone, waiting for a letter that never came. So the last several months, Rita had been convinced he was dead. Killed in service on his last tour of duty. When they met, she knew he was a Marine on

R and R. Knew that he would be returning to danger. But somehow, she'd convinced herself that he would be safe. That he would come back. To her.

He'd promised to write and when she didn't hear from him, Rita had mourned him. She'd had to face the stark, shattering truth that he was never coming home again. That he'd made the ultimate sacrifice and everything they'd found together so briefly was over.

And now, he was *here*.

"How did you find me?"

He shook his head. "I didn't. I was just walking down the street. Heard your laugh and it stopped me cold."

Oh, God. Just an accident. A whim of Fate. He hadn't been looking for her. Had probably forgotten all about her the moment he left her six months ago. And what had she done? *Mourned. Grieved.* The memory of that pain fueled her next words.

"I thought you were dead," she finally said, and hoped he couldn't hear the pain in her voice.

He took a breath, blew it out and said, "I wanted you to."

Another blow and this one had her reeling. He'd *wanted* her to mourn him? To go through the pain of a loss so deeply felt that it had been weeks before she'd even been able to *function*? The only thing that had kept her going, that had gotten her out of bed in the mornings, was her baby. Knowing that Jack had left her with this gift, this child, had given her strength. She'd gone on, telling herself that Jack would want her to.

Now she finds out he *wanted* her to believe he was dead?

"Who are you?" she asked, shaking her head and

blinking furiously to keep tears she wouldn't show him at bay.

"The same guy you used to know," he ground out.

"No." She stiffened her spine, lifted her chin and glared at him. "The Jack I knew would never have put me through the last six months."

For an instant, she thought she saw shame flash across his eyes, but it was gone as quickly as it had appeared, so Rita put it down to wishful thinking.

"This isn't about me," he said quietly and she heard the tight control in his voice. "You're pregnant."

"Very observant." God. She wrapped her arms around her belly protectively.

"How far along?"

Shocked, Rita bit back the words that first flew to her mouth. Temper spiked, and she had to wrestle it into submission. She knew what he was asking—*who's the father?* And she didn't know if she was more hurt than angry or if it was a tie between the two.

"Six months," she said pointedly. "So your cleverly veiled question is answered. You're the father."

Not that she was happy about that at the moment. She loved her baby, *had* loved its father. But this stranger looking down at her through icy cold eyes was someone she didn't even recognize.

"And you didn't tell me about it."

Before she could stop it, a short, sharp laugh shot from her throat. Shaking her head in complete wonder at his ridiculous statement, she countered, "How was I supposed to do that, Jack? I had no way of contacting you. You were going to write to me with your address."

A muscle in his jaw twitched and his eyes narrowed, but she didn't care.

"I don't think sending a letter addressed to Jack Buchanan, United States Marine Corps, somewhere in a desert would have found you."

"Fine. I get it." He pushed the edges of his jacket back and stuffed his hands into his pockets. The wind lifted his dark red power tie, turning it into a waving flag. His hair was ruffled, his eyes were cold and his jaw tight. "Like I said, there were reasons."

"Still haven't heard them."

"Yeah. Not important right now. What is important," he said, his gaze shifting to the mound of her belly and back up to her eyes again, "is my baby."

"You mean *my* baby," she corrected and instantly wished she hadn't come to work that day. If she'd taken the day off, she wouldn't have been in the bakery when he walked by and none of this would be happening.

"Rita, if you think I'm walking away from this, you're wrong."

"Why wouldn't I think that?" she argued, moving away from him, instinctively keeping a safe distance between him and her child. "You walked away before. Never looked back."

"That's not true," he muttered, letting his gaze slide from hers to focus on the ocean instead. "I thought about you."

Her heart twisted, but Rita wouldn't allow herself to be swayed. He'd walked away. Shut her out. Let her *mourn* him, for heaven's sake. *I thought about you* just didn't make up for the misery she'd lived through.

"And I should believe you?"

He slanted her a glance. "Believe or not, it changes nothing."

"That much is true anyway," Rita agreed. "Look, I have to get back to work."

"Your boss won't fire you if you take more than fifteen minutes."

She laughed a little, but there was no warmth in it. "I *am* the boss. It's my bakery and I have to get back to it."

"Yours?"

"Yeah," she said, turning away to head back up Main Street.

"Why did you come here?" he asked and had her pausing to look over her shoulder at him. "I mean, *here*, Seal Beach. You lived in Utah when we met."

Rita stared at him and whether she wanted to admit it to herself or not, there was a jolt of need inside her she couldn't quite ignore. With the sun pouring down on him, he looked both dangerous and appealing. He was tall and broad-shouldered and even in an elegant suit, he looked…intimidating. Was it any wonder why she'd fallen so hard for him?

That was then, she reminded herself; this was now.

"I moved here because I wanted to feel closer to you," she admitted, then added, "of course, that's when I thought you were dead. Now, the only thing that's dead is what I felt for you."

When she walked away, Rita felt his gaze fix on her. And she knew this wouldn't be the last time she'd see him.

And that was both worrying and comforting.

That afternoon, Jack went back to the bakery, took a table that allowed him to keep his back to a wall and ordered coffee. A seemingly never-ending stream of customers came and went, laughed, chatted and walked out

with red bakery boxes. This was her place, Jack thought
with admiration. The shop was small but it had an old-
world elegance to it.

Gleaming wood floors, dark blue granite counters,
brass-and-chrome cash register, glistening glass display
cases boasting pastries and cookies. There were brass
sconces on the walls and pots of flowers and trailing
greenery in strategic spots. It looked, he thought, just
as she wanted it to. Like an exclusive Italian shop.

His gaze tracked her employees as they hustled to
serve their customers, then shifted to land on Rita herself. She was still ignoring him, but he didn't mind.
Gave him time to think.

Jack's mind was still buzzing. Not only at news of the
baby but at seeing Rita again. He'd worked for months
to wipe her out of his memories and now everything
came rushing back in a tidal wave of images.

*He saw her standing at the water's edge, moonlight
spearing down on her from a cold, black sky. December
at the beach was cold and she was wearing a jacket,
but she was holding her shoes in one hand and letting
the icy water lick at her toes.*

*Her hair was a tangle of dark brown curls that lifted
and swirled around her head in the ever-present wind.
She heard him approaching and instantly turned her
head to look at him. He should have walked on, cut
away from her and headed for the pier, but something
about her made him stop. He kept a safe distance between them because he didn't want to worry her, but
as he looked into her big brown eyes, he felt drawn to
her like nothing he'd ever experienced before.*

"Don't be scared," he said. "I'm harmless."

*She smiled faintly and tipped her head to one side.
"Oh, I doubt that. But I'm not scared."*

*"Why not?" he asked, tucking his hands into the
pockets of his jeans. "Empty beach, in the dark, strange
guy..."*

*"You don't seem so strange. Plus, I'm pretty tough,"
she said. "And I run really fast."*

*He laughed, admiring the way she stood there, so
calm and self-assured. "Noted."*

*"So," she said, "I'm a tourist. What's your excuse
for being at the beach when it's this cold?"*

*Jack turned to look out over the spread of black
water dotted with white froth as it tumbled toward
shore. "I've been away for a while, so I want to appreciate this view."*

"You're in the military?" she asked.

He glanced at her and smiled. "That obvious?"

"It's the haircut," she admitted, smiling.

*"Yeah," he scrubbed one hand across the top of his
head. "Hard to disguise I guess. Marines."*

*She smiled and he thought she was the most beauti-
ful woman he'd ever seen.*

*"Well, thank you for your service," she said, then
added, "do you get tired of people saying that?"*

*"Nope," he assured her. "That never gets old. So, a
tourist. From where?"*

"Utah," she said, smiling. "Ogden, specifically."

*"It's pretty," he said. "Though it's been a few years
since I've been there."*

*Her smile brightened, nearly blinding him with the
power of it. "Thanks, it is gorgeous, and I love the
mountains. Especially in fall. But—" she half turned,*

letting her gaze slide across the ocean "—this is hard to resist."

"Yeah, I've missed it."

"I bet," she said, tipping her head to one side to look at him. "How long have you been gone?"

He shrugged, not really wanting to bring the desert heat and the memory of gunfire into this moment. "Too long."

As if she understood what he wasn't saying, she only nodded and they fell into silence until the only sound was the pulse and beat of the sea as it surged toward shore only to rush back out again.

At last, though, she reached up to push her hair back out of her face, smiled again and said, "I should be getting back to the hotel. It was nice meeting you."

"But we didn't," he interrupted quickly, suddenly desperate to keep her from leaving. "Meet, I mean. I'm Jack."

"Rita."

"I like it."

"Thanks."

"Do you really have to get back, or could I buy you a cup of coffee?"

She studied him for a long minute or two, then nodded. "I'd like that, Jack."

"I'm glad, but you sure are trusting."

"Actually," she said quietly, "I'm really not. But for some reason..."

"Yeah," he answered. "There's something..."

He walked toward her and held out one hand. She took it and the instant he touched her, he felt a hot buzz of something bright, staggering. He looked down at

*their joined hands, then closed his fingers around hers.
"Come with me, Rita. I know just the place."*

"Excuse me."

The tone of those words told Jack that it wasn't the first time the woman standing beside his table had said them. It was the redhead. "I'm sorry, what?"

"Rita says to tell you this is on the house," she said, setting a plate with two cannoli on it in front of him.

He frowned a little.

"Yeah, she told me you wouldn't look happy about it," the woman said. "I'm Casey. Can I get you more coffee?"

"Sure, thanks." She picked up his cup and walked to the counter, but Jack stopped paying attention almost immediately. Instead, his gaze sought out Rita.

As if she was expecting it, she turned to meet his stare and even from across that crowded room, it felt to Jack as it had that first night. As if they were alone on a deserted beach.

Well, damn it.

Casey was back an instant later with a fresh cup of coffee. Never taking his eyes off Rita, Jack leaned against the wall behind him and slowly sipped at his coffee. They had a lot to talk about. Too bad it wasn't *talking* on his mind.

A couple of hours later, the customers were gone and Rita was closing up. He'd already seen the sign that advertised their hours—open at seven, closed at six. Now as twilight settled on the beach, he watched Rita turn the deadbolt and flip the closed sign. Jack had had enough coffee to float one of his cargo ships and he'd had far too long to sit by himself and watch as she moved through the life she'd built since he'd last seen her.

"Why did you stay here all day, Jack?" She walked toward him. "This is borderline stalking."

"Not stalking. Sitting. Eating cannoli."

Her lips twitched and he found himself hoping she might show him that wide smile that he'd seen the first night they met. But it didn't come, so he let it go.

"Should you be on your feet this much?" he blurted.

Both of her eyebrows lifted as she set both fists on her hips. "Really?"

"It's a reasonable question," he insisted. "You're pregnant."

Now her big brown eyes went wide with feigned surprise. "I am?"

Jack sighed at the ridiculousness of the conversation. "Funny. Look, I just found out about this, so you could cut me some slack."

She took the chair opposite him, sitting down with a sigh of relief. "Why should I? It's not my fault you didn't know about the baby. You could have been a part of this from the beginning, Jack, if you had written to me." She reached over and plucked a dry leaf off the closest potted plant. Then she looked at him again. "But you didn't. Instead, you disappeared and let me think you were dead."

Yeah, he could see this from her side, and he didn't much care for the view. But that didn't change the fact that he'd done what he thought was necessary at the time. He'd had to put her out of his mind to survive when he went back to his duty station. Thoughts of her hadn't had any place in that hot, sandy miserable piece of ground and keeping her in his mind only threatened the concentration he needed to keep himself and his men alive.

Sure, at first, he'd thought that having her to think about would get him through, remind him that there was another world outside the desperate one he was caught up in. But two weeks after returning to deployment, something had happened to convince him that images of home were only a distraction. That keeping her face in his mind was dangerous.

So, he'd pushed the memories into a dark, deep corner of his brain and closed a door on them. It hadn't been easy, but he'd been convinced that it was the right thing to do.

Now he wasn't so sure.

"Why?" she asked, folding her hands on top of the small round glass-topped table. "You could at least tell me that much. Why did you never write, Jack?"

His gaze locked on hers. "It really doesn't matter now, does it? It's done. We have to deal with *now*."

Shaking her head, Rita sat back in the chair, and tapped the fingers of her right hand against the tabletop. "There is no *we*, Jack. Not anymore."

Beside him, a wide window overlooked Main Street. Late afternoon sunlight shone on the sidewalks, illuminating the people strolling through the early evening cool. It looked so normal. So peaceful. Yet seeing even that small crowd of pedestrians had Jack's insides going on alert. He didn't like the fact that he couldn't really relax around a lot of people anymore, but he had to accept that fact. So he turned away from strangers to look at a woman he'd once known so well.

"As long as there's a baby, there's a *we*," he told her.

"If you think I'm going to walk away from my own kid, you're wrong."

Instinctively, she dropped her hands to the curve of her belly and he realized she made that move a lot. Was it something all women did, or was Rita feeling threatened by seeing him again?

"Jack—"

"We can talk about it, work it out together," he said, interrupting her to make sure she understood where he was on this. "But bottom line, I'm here now. You're going to have to deal with it."

"You don't get to give me orders, Jack." She gave him a sad smile. "I live my own life. I run my own business. I raise my own child."

"And mine."

"Since your half and mine are intertwined," she quipped, "yes."

"Not acceptable." And this conversation was veering into the repetitive. It was getting him nowhere fast and he could see the flash of stubborn determination in her eyes that told him she wasn't going to budge. Well, hell. He could out-stubborn anyone.

"I really think you should go, Jack." She stood up, rubbing her belly idly with one hand.

He followed that motion and felt his heart trip-hammer in his chest. His child. Inside the woman that had been his so briefly. Damned if he'd leave. Walk away. It probably would have been better for all of them, but he wouldn't be doing it.

"I'll take you home," he said, standing to look down at her.

She chuckled. "I am home. I live in the apartment upstairs."

"You're kidding." He frowned, glanced at the ceiling as if he could see through the barrier into what had to be a very small apartment. "You live over a bakery."

She stiffened at the implied insult. "It's convenient. I get up at four every morning to start the baking, so all I have to do is walk downstairs."

"You're not raising my kid above a bakery."

When her eyes flashed and one dark eyebrow winged up, he knew he'd stepped wrong. But it didn't matter how he'd said it if the end was the same. His kid was not going to live above a bakery. Period.

"And, the circle is complete," she said, walking to the front door. She unlocked it, opened it wide and waved one hand as if scooping him out the door. "I want you to leave, Jack."

"All right." He conceded on this point. For now. He started past her, then stopped when their bodies were just a breath apart. When he caught her scent and could almost feel the heat shimmering off her body. Everything in him twisted tight and squeezed. Giving in to the urge driving him, he reached out, took her chin in his hand and tipped her face up until her eyes were locked with his. "This isn't over, Rita. It's just getting started."

Sitting on her couch in her—all right, yes, tiny apartment—Rita curled her feet underneath her as her fingers tightened on her cellphone. "What am I supposed to do, Gina?"

Instead of answering, her sister called out, "Ally, do *not* pour milk on the dog again."

"But *why*?" A young, loud voice shouted in response.

In spite of everything going on in her life at the moment, Rita grinned. Ally was two years old with a hard head, a stubborn streak a mile wide and a sweet smile that usually got her out of trouble.

"Because he doesn't like it!" Gina huffed out a breath, came back on the line, and whispered, "Actually he *does* like it, idiot dog. Then he spends all night licking the milk off himself, my floor is sticky and he smells like sour milk."

It was times like these that Rita really missed her family. Her parents. Her sister. Her two older brothers. All of her nieces and nephews. They were all in Ogden, working at the family bakery, Marchetti's. Rita's family was loud, boisterous, argumentative and sometimes she missed them so much she actually *ached* to be with them.

Like now, for instance.

"Michael and Braden Franco!" Gina shouted. "If you ride your skateboards down the steps and one of you breaks another bone, I will burn those boards in the fire pit—"

The five-year-old twins were adventurous and barely containable. It's what Rita loved best about them.

Gina broke off with a satisfied sigh. "Another crisis averted. Sorry sweetie, what were you saying again?"

Back to the matter at hand. "Jack. He's alive. He's *here*." Rita bit down hard on her bottom lip and blinked wildly to keep the tears filling her eyes from falling. Though there was no one there to see her cry, she didn't want to give Jack the satisfaction.

Hadn't she already cried rivers for Jack? After two months had passed without a word from him, Rita had known that he was gone, no doubt killed in action somewhere far away. What other reason, she'd told herself, could there have been for him not to write her?

They'd had such an amazing connection. Something strong and powerful had grown between them in one short week. She'd loved him fiercely even after so short a time. But then her mother had always told her that time had nothing to do with love. If you knew someone five days or five years, the feelings didn't change.

It had taken Rita much less than five days to know that Jack was the one man she wanted. Then he was gone and the pain of loss had crippled her. Until she'd discovered she was pregnant.

"He's *there*?" Gina whispered as if somehow Jack could overhear her. "At your apartment?"

"No," she said, though she tossed a quick look toward the door at the back of the building that opened onto a staircase leading to a small parking lot. She half expected Jack to show up on her landing and knock. Shaking her head, she said, "No, he's not here, here. He's here in Seal Beach. He came into the bakery today."

"Oh. My. God." A moment or two passed before Gina continued. "What did you do? What did he say? Where the hell has he been? Why didn't he write to you? Bastard."

A short laugh shot from Rita's throat. She heard the outrage in her sister's voice and was grateful for it. How did anyone survive without a sister?

"I nearly shrieked when I saw him," Rita confessed. "Then I hugged him, damn it."

"Of course you hugged him," Gina soothed. "Then did you kick him?"

She laughed again. "No, but I wish I'd thought of it at the time."

"Well, if you need me, Jimmy can watch the kids for a few days. I'll fly out there and kick him for you."

Rita sighed and smiled all at once. "I can always count on you, Gina."

"Of course you can. So where's he been?"

"I don't know."

"Why didn't he write?"

Rita frowned. "I don't know."

"Well, what did he say?"

Rita picked up her cup of herbal tea and took a sip. "He only wanted to talk about the baby."

"Oh, boy."

"Exactly." Sighing more heavily now, Rita set the cup down on the coffee table again. "He was…surprised to find out I was pregnant and he didn't look happy about it."

"We don't need him to be happy. But why wouldn't he be? Who doesn't like babies? Hold on. I'll be right back."

While she waited, Rita's head dropped back against the couch. Her apartment wasn't tiny, it was cozy, she thought in defense as her gaze swept over the space. A small living room, an efficiency kitchen, one bedroom and a bathroom that, she had to admit, was so small she regularly smacked her elbows against the shower door. But the apartment walls were a soft, cheerful green and were dotted by framed photos of the beach, the mountains and her family.

"There," Gina said when she was back. "I took the baby to Jimmy. I have to pace when I'm mad."

Rita laughed. "Gina, I'm okay, really. I just needed to talk to you."

"Of course you did, but we're Italian and I need my hands to talk as much as I need to move around. Besides, I just finished feeding Kira. Jimmy can take her for a while."

Her sister had four gorgeous kids, the youngest only eight months old and a husband who adored her. A small pang of envy echoed in Rita's heart. Then to ease the hurt, she rubbed the mound of her baby with slow, loving strokes, and reminded herself that she had a child, too. That she wasn't alone. That it didn't matter that Jack had walked away from her only to suddenly crash back into her life.

"So," Gina said a moment later, "what're you going to do about this? How are you feeling?"

"I'm not sure, to both questions." Pushing up off the couch, Rita walked to the window overlooking Main Street and smiled, thinking Gina was right. Italians thought better when they could move around. Looking down on the street, she enjoyed the view that was so similar to the one she grew up with. Historic 25th Street in Ogden also had the old-fashioned, old-world feel to the buildings, the lampposts and the bright, jewel-toned flowers spilling out of baskets.

But as pretty as it was, it wasn't home. Not really. She was alone in the dark but for a slender thread of connection to her big sister.

"I don't know what to do," she admitted, "because I don't know what he's planning."

"Whatever it is, you can handle it." And, as if Gina had read her mind, she added, "You're not alone, Rita."

Her mouth curved slightly. "Not how it feels."

"You still love him, don't you?"

Rita laid her hand on the glass, letting the cold seep into her skin, chilling the rush of heat Gina's question had awakened.

"Why would I be foolish enough for that?" she whispered.

Three

"What's going on with you?"

Jack looked up. His father walked into the office that, up until four months ago, had been his. Thomas Buchanan was a tall man, with salt-and-pepper hair, sharp blue eyes and a still-trim physique. Though he'd abdicated the day-to-day running of the company to his oldest son, Thomas maintained his seat on the board and liked to keep abreast of whatever was happening. That included keeping tabs on his son.

"Nothing," Jack answered, lowering his gaze to the sheaf of papers on the desktop. "Why?"

"Well," Thomas said, strolling around the room, "you nearly bit Sean's head off when he couldn't get the shipping schedule up on the plasma fast enough."

"It's his job," Jack said, being perfectly reasonable. "He should be able to accomplish it when asked."

"Uh-huh."

Jack knew that tone. He glanced at his father, saw the wary curiosity-filled expression and looked away again. He wasn't in the mood for a chat and couldn't satisfy his father's curiosity. He knew that ever since he'd returned to civilian life, his family had been worried about him and no one more than his father. There didn't seem to be anything Jack could do about it, though. He didn't need therapy or sympathy and didn't want to talk about what he'd seen—what he wanted to do was forget about it and pick up his life where he'd left off. So far of course, that wasn't happening.

Rather than try to explain all of that to his dad, Jack chose to ignore the man's questions, even though he knew it wouldn't get him anywhere. The worry would remain, along with the questions, whether spoken or not. After a few seconds of silence from him, though, Thomas seemed to understand that it was a subject Jack wasn't going to address.

"Still don't understand why you changed the office furniture around," his father said, surprising Jack with the sudden shift of topic. "My father's the one who put that desk in front of the windows. I don't think it's been moved since then. Until now."

Jack squirmed slightly in his oversize black leather chair. He'd made a few changes since he'd stepped into his father's shoes. The main one being that he had moved the old mahogany desk across the room so that he could have his back to a wall and not be outlined in a window.

Yes, he knew it was foolish without anyone pointing it out to him. He didn't have to worry about snipers here, but it was hard to shake ingrained habits that had kept him alive.

"I like it where it is," Jack said simply.

"Yeah." His father gave a resigned sigh, then admitted, "I wish you could talk to me."

His father's voice was so quiet, so wistful, Jack's attention was caught. He looked up and found his dad watching him through concerned eyes.

He didn't enjoy knowing that his family was worried about him. In fact, it only added to the guilt and the pain that were crouched on his shoulders every day. But he couldn't ease for them what he couldn't ease for himself.

"We do talk," Jack said.

"Not about anything important," his father answered. "Not since you got back. It's like you're still too far away to reach."

"I'm right here, Dad," he said, trying to help, knowing he was failing.

"Part of you is," his father agreed, "but not all of you. I wonder every day when my son will finally come home."

So did Jack. It was as if a piece of him had been left behind in the heat of a desert and he didn't know when or if he'd find that part of himself again. Jack sat back and let a long breath slide slowly from his lungs. "I'm doing my best here, Dad."

"I know that." Thomas stuffed his hands into his pants pockets and rocked uneasily on his heels. "I just wish there was something I could do to help. That you would *let* me do. I thought that stepping down, having you take over here, would make a difference. Drop you back into the world and, all right, *force* you to find your life again. But you continue to shut yourself off. From me, from your sister and brother. Hell, you haven't even been on a date since you got back, son."

"I don't want to date." Lie. Everything in him wanted Rita, but he wouldn't give in to it. He was in no shape to be in her life and he knew it.

"Right there should tell you that there's something wrong."

"I'm fine," Jack said, hoping to head his dad off at the pass. He'd heard this before. Knew that his father had the best of intentions. But Jack couldn't give the older man what he wanted most.

Thomas shook his head, then nodded. "You're not, but you will be. I wish you could believe me on that." He walked toward his son, laid both hands on the desk and leaned in. "I know you don't. Not yet. But someday you will, Jack. Just give yourself a chance, all right?"

"I am." He looked into his father's eyes and lied again. "Everything's good. I swear."

Nodding, the older man pushed up from the desk. "Okay. We'll leave it there for now."

Thank God, Jack thought in relief.

"On another subject entirely," his father said, "I'm headed down to San Diego tomorrow. Sam and I are taking the boat out fishing for the weekend. Want to join us?"

The Buchanan Boys, as his mother used to call the three of them, had gone on hundreds of fishing weekends together. And in the old days, there had been nothing Jack liked more than getting away with his younger brother and his father. But now, the thought of being caged on a boat in the middle of the ocean with a too-curious father and brother sounded like a nightmare. They'd hammer him with questions, he'd resent being prodded and they'd all have a crappy time.

Besides, he told himself, there was Rita. Decisions to be made.

"I can't," he said. "I've got plans I can't get out of." Not that Rita knew of his plan to corner her into talking with him about their baby.

"Plans?" Thomas gave him a pleased smile. "That's good, son. Really good. To prove how happy that makes me, I won't even ask you what you're going to be doing."

"Thanks," Jack said wryly.

"All right, then." His father slapped his hands together then gave his palms a good scrub. "I've got to go by the house, pick up my fishing gear. Then I'm headed to San Diego. I'll have my phone with me if you need to contact me."

"I won't," Jack assured him. "But thanks. And say hi to Sam."

"I will."

Once his father was gone, Jack took a long, deep breath and willed the tension out of his body. It didn't work, so he got up, walked across the well-appointed office without even noticing the familiar furnishings.

Beige walls, dark red carpet, thick and plush enough to take a nap on, and twin couches facing each other across a low wood table. Windows were on two walls and Jack had moved the desk out of the line of sight of both of them.

Now, though, he walked to a far window and looked out over the sea. He didn't look at the beach below or the crowd of early-summer sun worshippers spread out on the sand. Instead, he watched the steady rise and fall of the water as wind and its own weight formed ripples and waves that seemed to go on endlessly.

It was quiet in the office and normally he treasured

that. But now, that silence tapped at the edges of his mind like a persistent knock on a closed door. As that door opened, images of Rita flooded his brain, from before, from yesterday, until he half expected her to simply appear physically in the office. But that wasn't going to happen.

Rita would never come to him, she was too angry and he couldn't blame her for it. But that wouldn't stop him from doing what he had to do. She was pregnant with *his* child and damned if he'd ignore that.

There was a knock on the office door just before it opened and his assistant stepped inside. A middle-aged woman with a brisk, no nonsense attitude, Linda Holloway said, "Excuse me, Mr. Buchanan, you've got a twelve-thirty meeting with the captain of *The Sea Queen*."

In the last four months, Linda had been responsible for Jack's seamless takeover of his father's position. She kept meticulous track of his schedule, his tasks and anything involving Buchanans. He was grateful, but right now, he didn't appreciate the interruption.

"The captain will meet you at the dock so you can take a walk-through of the areas you didn't see on your visit last month."

"Yeah," he said. "I remember." *The Sea Queen* was their latest ocean liner. And yes, he did have to meet the captain if only to go over any last-minute concerns about the ship's maiden voyage coming up in about a month. But not today.

"Cancel it," he snapped and stalked across the office.

"What?" Linda watched him, eyes wide. "But the captain has come in from his home in Arizona specifically for this meeting."

Yet one more guilt straw landed on the bale already situated on his shoulders, but he accepted it and moved on.

"It can't be helped. I've got personal business to take care of. Put the captain up in the best hotel in the city and tell him we'll meet tomorrow morning."

"But—"

"Eight o'clock on the dock. I'll be there and we can take care of this business then."

He snatched his suit jacket out of the closet and shrugged into it. What good was being the boss if you couldn't make the rules?

"But—"

"Linda," he said firmly, "I have somewhere to be and it can't wait. Make this happen."

"Yes, sir," she said, the slightest touch of defeat in her tone.

He didn't address it. "Thanks," he said and walked around her to leave without a backward glance.

"Tall, dark and dangerous is back."

Rita glanced at her friend and bakery manager, Casey. "What?"

She jerked her head toward the small cluster of tables in one corner of the bakery. "The guy who swept you out of here yesterday? He's back and looking just as edible as ever."

Rita's pulse skittered as she slowly, carefully, looked over her shoulder. Jack was sitting at the same table he'd spent hours at the day before. He wore a black suit, with a black dress shirt and a dark red tie. He looked exactly how Casey had described him. Dangerous. Edible.

As if he sensed her looking at him, he turned his

head and his gaze locked with hers. Instantly, her blood turned to a river of fire and the pit of her stomach fluttered with nerves and expectation. He'd had that same effect on her from the beginning.

The minute he took her hand that first night on the beach, she'd felt it. That something special. Magical. There was a buzz between them that was electrifying.

She hadn't been afraid when he'd walked toward her out of the darkness. Maybe she should have been, but instead, it had felt almost as if she'd been waiting for him.

They walked to a small café, took a table on the sidewalk and ordered coffee. There they sat for three hours, talking, sharing their lives, though Rita did more of that than he did. He hadn't talked about his family or where he lived, only that his name was Jack Buchanan and that he had a week to be back in the real world and how he didn't want to waste a moment of it.

And when he walked her to her nearby hotel, neither of them wanted to say goodnight. He escorted her through the lobby to the bank of elevators with mirrored doors and she looked at their reflection as they stood together. He was so tall, she so short. But they seemed to fit, she thought, as if they'd been made for each other.

He turned her in his arms and asked, "Tomorrow? Be with me tomorrow, Rita."

"Yes," she said quickly, breathlessly.

"Good, that's good." A brief smile flashed across his face and warmed his cool blue eyes. "I'll be here early. Nine okay?"

"How about eight?" Rita asked, wanting to be with him again as soon as possible.

"Even better." He cupped her face in his palm and held her there as he bent his head to kiss her.

Rita held her breath and closed her eyes. Once, twice, his mouth brushed hers, gently, as if waiting for her response to know if there should be more.

And she wanted more. She wanted it all. Never had she felt for a man what Jack made her feel. Just talking with him stirred everything inside her and now that she knew the taste of his mouth, she hungered for him.

Rita answered his unasked question by wrapping her arms around his neck and leaning in to him. Her breasts pressed against his chest and her nipples ached as her body hummed. He actually growled and that sound sent her head spinning as he grabbed hold of her and deepened the kiss. Devouring her, his tongue tangled with hers, his breath mingled with hers and Rita felt as if their souls were touching, merging. Every inch of her body lit up and awakened as if she'd been in a coma all of her life and was only now truly living.

Neither of them cared about who might be watching, they were too lost in the fire enveloping them. Lightheaded, loving the feel of his big strong hands sliding up and down her back, Rita could only think how badly she wanted him, but she wasn't a one-night stand kind of woman and didn't think she could pretend she was, even for Jack.

When finally she thought she might never breathe again, he broke the kiss and leaned his forehead against hers while they both fought to steady themselves.

"You are a dangerous woman," he whispered, a half smile curving his mouth.

"I never thought so, but okay."

His grin flashed. "Trust me."

She smiled back at him and felt her equilibrium disintegrate even further. Honestly, he didn't smile often, but when he did, it was a lethal weapon on a woman's defenses. Her mouth was still tingling from his kiss and the taste of him was flooding her system.

"Looking into those brown eyes of yours makes me feel like I'm diving into good, aged whiskey," he murmured, reaching out to smooth his fingers over her face. "Makes me a little drunk just losing myself in them."

"Your eyes remind me of the color of the sky after a mountain storm," she said, "clear, bright, with just a hint of shadow."

His smile faded then and Rita wished she could pull her words back. She hadn't meant to say anything about the darkness she saw in his eyes, but her urge to ease those shadows was nearly overwhelming.

"I've shadows enough, I guess," he admitted, letting his hand drop to his side. "But when I'm with you, I don't notice them."

"I'm glad," she said and went up on her toes to kiss him again.

Putting both hands on her shoulders, he held her in place and took a long step back. He shook his head and said, "If I kiss you again, I'm not going to be able to let you go."

That sounded pretty good to Rita, but she knew it wasn't smart to go to bed with a man she just met no matter how much she wanted to.

"So," he continued, "I'm going to leave while I still can."

"Probably a good idea," Rita said though, inside, her mind was whimpering, demanding that she beg him to stay.

"You keep looking at me with those whiskey eyes and I'm not going to be able to walk away." His voice was wry, his eyes flashing with heat.

"Then I will," she said, reaching out to punch the elevator call button.

"I do like a strong woman," he told her.

"Not so strong at the moment," Rita admitted when she looked at him again and felt a rush of heat settle and pool at her core. *"But I will be. So, good night. I guess I'll see you at eight."*

"Seven," he said.

"Even better," she said, throwing his own words from earlier back at him. The elevator dinged and the doors swished open. She stepped inside, then turned to look at him again. *"Seven. I'll be ready."*

"Good," he said as the doors slid shut on a whisper of sound, *"because I'm ready now."*

Alone, Rita leaned against the wall of the car, smiled to herself and lifted one hand to her mouth as if she could capture his taste and hold on to it forever. As the elevator rose to her floor, she told herself she wouldn't be getting much sleep tonight, but her morning was going to be wonderful.

"Rita?" Casey's voice and an insistent shake of her arm. "Hey, Rita? You okay?"

"What?" she tore her gaze from Jack's and looked at her friend. Coming up out of that memory that had been so filled with sensation and sound was like breaking the surface of the water when you were near drowning. You were back in reality but still too stunned to accept it easily. "Sure," she said, nodding for emphasis. "Yes. I'm fine. Really. Just…tired."

And sexually frustrated and angry and hurt and confused and far too many other emotions to even name.

"You sure?" Casey tried to steer Rita toward a stool.
"Maybe you should sit down."

"No." Rita shook off all those unwelcome emotions
and smiled. "I'm fine. Really. Um, will you keep an
eye on the front while I go in the back to restock the
cannoli tray?"

"Absolutely," Casey said, "as long as you call out if
you need me."

"Don't be such a worrier," Rita told her with a pat
on the arm.

Hurrying through the swinging door into the kitchen
where she could get a couple of minutes to herself, Rita
gave a sigh of relief to be on her own. She needed a little time to settle. Do the *ahooom* thing until she could
breathe without feeling like she was going to shake
apart at the seams.

"Get a grip, Rita," she mumbled as she snatched an
apron off the hook by the door. Slipping it on over her
head, she drew the string ties around her ever-expand-
ing belly then tied it down. The simple, familiar task
helped her get steady again.

She scrubbed her hands in the kitchen sink, dried
them on a fresh towel, then turned to survey her do-
main. She might have chefs come in to help her, but
this bakery was all hers, right down to the last cookie.

She was most comfortable in the kitchen. Rita and
her brothers and sister had grown up working in their
parents' Italian bakery in Ogden. From the time she
was a little girl, barely tall enough to reach the mixing table, Rita had been helping the bakers. Even if it
was just sprinkling flour on the cool white marble so

dough could be rolled out. She loved the scent of baking cookies, cakes, pastries. She loved the feel of getting her hands into a huge bowl of dough to knead it. She'd worked off a lot of temper by working bread dough into shape.

"But there's not enough dough in the world to help me through *this*," she whispered, laying out paper doilies on a stainless steel tray. Then she moved to the end of the counter and carefully set fresh cannoli, some draped in shiny chocolate, on each doily. To her, presentation was as important as taste so before it went out to the shop, it would be perfect.

Once she was satisfied that all of her cannoli were lined up like soldiers, Rita checked on two more bowls of rising dough, punched them down, then covered them again, so they could do a second rise.

She'd be making bread before the bakery closed because her customers liked picking up a fresh loaf on the way home from work. Then she checked the meticulously aligned steel racks against one wall and made a note to have Casey get someone back there to box up the maple-nut biscotti.

"And I'm stalling," she said aloud to the empty room. "Question is, why?"

Her eyes closed on a sigh as Jack's deep voice echoed all around her. Of course he wouldn't be ignored. He was the kind of man who got exactly what he wanted *when* he wanted it. A trait that was both sexy and annoying.

"You shouldn't be back here, Jack."

"Your friend Casey said you weren't feeling well."

She rolled her eyes and told herself to have a little chat with Casey. Wouldn't do any good, of course. If a gorgeous man asked Casey to stand on her head, the girl would. And they just didn't come more gorgeous than Jack, so Casey really had been putty in his hands.

Rita surrendered to the inevitable and turned around to face him. "I don't have time for you right now, Jack. I'm working."

She walked to the tray of fresh cannoli, but before she could pick it up, Jack swooped in and snatched it from her. "You shouldn't be carrying this. It's heavy."

A thread of pleasure whipped through her at his instinctive urge to protect, even as it irritated her that he clearly thought she was either helpless or a delicate blossom.

"I carry heavy things all the time. I'm pregnant, not an invalid." He opened his mouth to argue the point, but she rushed on before he could. "I'm careful, too. I don't take chances with my baby—"

"Our baby."

"*The* baby," she corrected meaningfully. "Now, give me the tray."

"Don't be stupid," he said and turned for the door into the front of the shop.

"I'm stupid now?" she said to his retreating back.

"I said *don't* be stupid. There's a difference."

When the door swung open, snatches of conversation rushed toward her, along with Casey's prolonged sigh of "Thank you so much."

Rolling her eyes so hard it was a wonder they didn't simply pop out of her skull and skitter across the floor, Rita pulled down the decorative biscotti boxes. She'd pack them herself and that would give her yet another reason to stay back here and keep her distance from Jack. Of course she should have known that wouldn't work.

He came back through the swinging door, holding an empty tray and shook his head at her. "Do you have to do everything around here personally?"

"My business, my responsibility." She lifted a tray of biscotti off the rack and turned for the counter, dodging Jack when he would have taken it from her. "So yes, I do. I want things done a certain way and I can't expect everyone else to do all the work."

She expertly folded the box into shape, slid a dozen biscotti inside then closed the box and slapped a gold *Italia* sticker in place. Automatically, she started on the next one while Jack came closer. Rita didn't even look up from her task when she asked, "Why are you here again, Jack?"

He picked up a biscotti and took a bite, shrugging when she gave him a hard look. "I'm here because you are. Because my baby is. And I'm not leaving until we work this out between us."

"Fine." She continued boxing the biscotti in the bright red *Italia* containers, keeping her eyes on the job, rather than him. If she looked at Jack again she'd feel that torn sensation—yearning and betrayal.

He'd allowed her to mourn. Let her believe he was dead. How did you forgive someone for that when they wouldn't even explain *why* they'd done it? And how did you get past those old feelings that continually slipped in despite the pain that should have smothered them?

"You want to talk, let's talk," she said. "I'll start. I want to know why you disappeared."

"That's not on the table."

Now she did risk a quick glance at him and his features were tight, closed, his eyes cold and icy.

"So we talk, but only about what you're willing to

discuss?" Shaking her head, she sealed another box and set it aside, automatically reaching for the next.

"I'm not looking to recapture anything here, Rita."

A sharp stab of pain stole her breath at the blunt honesty. She looked into his eyes. "Wow."

He flinched slightly, but otherwise remained stoic. "I'm not saying that to hurt you."

"And yet..."

He looked down at the biscotti in his hand and then lifted his gaze to hers again. "This isn't about us, Rita. It's about the baby."

A sinking sensation opened up in the pit of her stomach. Her mouth went dry and her hands shook, so she set the box she was holding down onto the counter so he couldn't see it. How had they come to this, she wondered. Where had it all gone so terribly wrong?

What had made him shut her out when he left her to go back to his duties? What had turned him away from what they'd found, what they'd been to each other for one amazing week?

And how had he become so cold that he could stand just inches from her and look at her as if she wasn't really there?

"What is it you want, Jack?"

He set the biscotti down, planted both palms on the counter and said, "I want you to marry me."

Four

Rita actually *felt* shock slam into her like a physical blow. Whatever she'd been expecting hadn't been this. She knew she was staring. Knew she should say *something*, but for the first time in her life she was absolutely speechless. He was serious, that much she could see. But surely he didn't expect her to agree.

He laughed shortly, but it was merely a harsh scrape of sound against his throat. There was no humor in his eyes and no easing of the tightness of his mouth. "Not the usual reaction when a man proposes."

Finally she found her own voice. "It's not the *usual* situation, is it?"

"No," he admitted solemnly, "it's not."

"Jack, you don't want to be married to me." God, how it hurt to say that, because six months ago, at the end of their week together, Rita had had dreams. She'd believed that when he came home from war, they would get married, have kids, live happily ever after. All the normal fantasies that women spin when they meet a man who makes their blood burn and their heart sing.

But that dream had died with him, or so she'd believed at the time. Now he was here, but it was a different Jack who faced her asking her to marry him. It was a colder, harder man than she'd once known and the loss of that rang deep and true inside her.

He pushed one hand through his hair then scrubbed the back of his neck. "No," he admitted, looking directly into her eyes. "I don't want to be married. To anyone."

"Then what is this about?"

"I also don't want my kid born without my name."

Rita sighed heavily. "Of course you'll be on the birth certificate, listed as the father."

He frowned. "Not what I'm talking about. I want us married when the baby's born," he told her firmly. "After that, we can divorce and I won't bother you again."

Just when she thought the shocks couldn't be more earth shattering, he said something else that ripped away what was left of the earth beneath her feet. "Seriously?"

Moments ago, she'd worried about a custody battle, but in reality he wanted nothing to do with his own child? What kind of man was he?

He blew out a breath, shoved his hands into his slacks pockets and admitted, "I'm not asking you to understand—"

"Good," she interrupted. "Because I don't. If you don't want me, then fine. I get it. But how can you not want anything to do with your own child? My God, who are you?"

"Still me," he insisted, but she didn't believe him.

When she first met him, he'd been more quiet than chatty, more solemn than happy, but there hadn't been such a marked coldness about him. Now it was as if he'd submerged his old self under a layer of ice.

"Think whatever you like about me. Can't change it. But I want my kid born into the Buchanan family." His mouth tightened and the muscle in his jaw twitched as if he were grinding his teeth together. "After that, you can raise it."

It. So impersonal. So distancing. Rita hadn't wanted to know what her baby was, preferring to be surprised. But now, at her next appointment, she would ask. Because she wanted Jack to see their child as a *person.* But that was for later. "So you'll just put your baby aside like you did me and move on, is that it?"

He scrubbed one hand across his jaw. "You're putting words in my mouth."

"Because you're not explaining any of this."

"Damn it, Rita, you don't have to make this harder than it already is."

"No, I don't," she said sadly. "Because *you* did that just fine on your own."

"I'll make sure you're taken care of."

Her eyes nearly popped out of her head at that insult on top of everything else. Rita had reached her limit. She walked around the edge of the counter, leading with her belly, and didn't stop until she was standing in front of him. "You think I want *money* from you?"

He met her gaze and Rita would have given anything to be able to read what he was thinking, feeling. But there was no clue there for her. He was a blank slate. Deliberately. This new Jack had such a tight handle on his emotions, she couldn't see past the facade.

"No," he said, shaking his head. "I know you don't want money."

"That's something, anyway," she muttered, still looking up into his eyes, still looking for some shred of the man she'd loved.

"Do this, Rita," he said quietly.

"Why would I marry you knowing you don't want me?"

"Because I need it," he admitted and it looked as though it cost him to give her that much. "I need to know my kid has my name. That I did the right thing."

"The right thing." She huffed out a breath and folded her arms across her growing middle. "This isn't the '50s, Jack. Single mothers do just fine on their own and so can I." She didn't believe in what he was saying, but Jack clearly did.

Rita knew she would be fine raising her child alone. She had her family's support. She had her own business, a home and the strength to do whatever she had to do to succeed.

"It's not a matter of that," Jack argued. He picked up the biscotti again and when his hand fisted around it, let crumbs fall to the marble counter. "I know you *could* do it. I don't want you to. I get you don't owe me a damn thing and I've got no right to ask for this. Still, this is important to me, Rita. I don't want my kid knowing his parents weren't married."

"Oh, for heaven's—"

"Look, this is the best answer for all of us," Jack said quickly.

"How is a meaningless marriage the best for any-one? You're crazy."

"That's been said before," he admitted wryly. "But not about this. This is important enough to me that I'm not going to back off or give up until you agree."

She laughed shortly, turned her back on him and went back to boxing biscotti. "Good luck with that."

"I'm a rich man, Rita," he said and brought her up short.

Money again? What was he getting at? A tiny nug-get of fear settled in the pit of her belly as, wary now, she asked, "How rich?"

"Very."

She took a breath. He was watching her, waiting for her reaction and she wasn't sure what that should be. Rita didn't care if he had all the money in the world or nothing at all. So what was the point of this?

"Congratulations to you," she finally said. "But why should I care?" Even as she asked that question, though, her brain was racing. A *very* rich man? She'd had no idea.

But then, there was so much she didn't know about him. He hadn't talked about himself a lot during their week together and she'd told herself that the informa-tion would come. That they could learn about each other in letters, phone calls. But that had never hap-pened, so she was as much in the dark now as she had been then.

A very rich man, though, had power. The question was now, would he use that power to manipulate her, to take custody of her child?

"I can take care of the baby," he said.

She stiffened. "So can I."

"Rita, you live above a bakery," he snapped. "I can get you a nice place. On the beach."

"Are you trying to bribe me?" she asked, astounded at the turn this conversation was taking.

"No. Look, it's my kid, too." He took a moment to gather his thoughts and said, "We get married, I get you a house and after the baby's born, we split up."

"And if I don't want to marry you?"

"You will."

"Don't take any bets on it."

"I will bet on it." He held out one hand. "Five bucks."

"For a *very* rich man, you don't have much faith in your ability to persuade me." She shook his hand and deliberately ignored the zip of heat she felt. "Twenty dollars."

"Even better," he said and completely knocked her feet out from under her.

Even better. It reminded her of that first night, of his smile, his kiss, their eagerness to be together. And when she looked into his eyes, she saw a gleam of amusement and knew he was remembering, too. Her heart turned over at the tiny glimpse of *her* Jack. Maybe he wasn't as lost as she'd thought. Maybe he was reachable.

He let go of her hand but the heat engendered remained. The tiny moment of shared memory was over, the hint of humor gone from his eyes and she was left with this gorgeous stranger again. How could he make her feel so much while apparently feeling nothing himself? How could she allow herself to marry a man for all the wrong reasons when she once would have given anything to marry him for *love*?

"It won't work, Jack."

"We'll see, Rita."

It took her only a week to surrender.

A week of Jack coming to the bakery daily, helping out, making sure she got off her feet. He ignored his own business and showed up in jeans, scuffed cowboy boots and T-shirts, making her heart skip just looking at him. He stacked pallets of supplies, carried trays of cookies, rang up sales and won Casey over. That last part wasn't hard at all, Rita allowed. But as for the rest, he wore her down with his relentless pursuit and dogged determination.

"You owe me twenty bucks," he said when she told him she'd marry him.

"This isn't funny." Should she have held out? Refused him? Possibly. But in the last week, she'd caught repeated glimpses of the old Jack, and though they were brief, they'd given her enough hope to think that just maybe it was worth trying to get past the ice he'd packed around his heart.

"No one's laughing."

"I'll marry you, but I can't get married without my family there," she said. "They'd never understand."

They weren't going to understand a quickie wedding or a divorce so soon after that wedding, either, but one problem at a time.

"Fine. Us. Our families. Small ceremony," Jack said like he was ticking things off a to-do list.

"And I don't want anyone to know this is a…business deal," she said for lack of a better way to put it. "Also, I don't want you to buy me a house."

"Nonnegotiable," he said. "When we split, you can pick something out or I will."

It didn't make sense to argue with him now, but

Rita could be as stubborn as Jack. And she wouldn't be bought off or given a "going away gift." But this, too, was a worry for another day. God knew she had enough for today already.

"Okay, then," she said, sighing heavily. "I guess we're getting married."

He grabbed a black leather jacket off a hook by the back door and shrugged into it. "I'll take care of the details. I'll send packers to get your stuff out of your apartment. Bring it to the penthouse."

She blinked at him. "Packers?"

He stopped, looked at her. "You want this to look real, then we'll be living together at my place."

At his place? She didn't even know *where* he lived! Oh, this wasn't something she'd even thought about.

Before she could say anything to that, though, he was gone.

"It's a surprise, that's all I'm saying," Jack's sister, Cass, said for the tenth time in the last hour. "I'm glad you found someone, but it would have been nice to meet her before the wedding."

He looked at Cass and read the worry in her eyes. God, would he ever get used to seeing that emotion on his family's faces? And if not accustomed to it, could he please, God, reach a point where it wouldn't tear at him? "It was sudden. I met her six months ago—"

"Clearly," Cass said wryly.

"Right." The baby. His family had been shocked not only with the announcement that he was getting married, but that he was going to be a father. Soon.

Cass flipped her long brown hair behind her shoulder, threaded her arm through his and watched Rita with her family. "I like her already."

"Good. That's good." Jack nodded thoughtfully and kept his gaze locked on his wife. *Wife.* He swallowed hard and told himself it would be all right. The important thing here was that he'd done the right thing by his kid. He could survive three months of marriage and then his life would go back to what it had been. Quiet. Alone.

"Jack?"

He looked at his sister and nearly sighed. She was watching him so closely, trying to read every expression on his face, he might as well have been under a microscope. But judging by her own expression, she wasn't happy with what she was seeing. In fact, she was giving him the serious, concerned look he was pretty sure she gave her patients.

As a general practitioner, Cass was adept at cutting through the bull to make a diagnosis and it was clear to him she didn't like what she was seeing in him.

"Relax, Cass," he said, "I'm fine."

"Sure. It's what you've been saying for months."

"Then you should believe me," he said, patting her hand on his arm.

"No, you remind me of this one patient. He's ten. And he always insists he's fine even when his fever is spiking or his throat is sore." She shook her head. "He doesn't want me asking questions, you see. And neither do you."

"Yeah," Jack said, giving her a tired smile. "But I'm not one of your patients."

"Good thing," she told him. "We'd butt heads even

more than we do now. Jack, I have to ask you something. Will you let her in?"

"What?" He looked down at her and tried to hide his impatience. It wasn't the family's fault that he couldn't give them what they wanted. *Be* who they wanted.

Cass moved to stand in front of him and put both of her hands on his forearms. "I'm asking you. You're married now. Going to be a father. And yet I still see that distance in your eyes."

He let his head fall back and he stared unseeing at the overcast gray sky for a second or two. The steady roar of the ocean was a constant white noise in the background. The sea itself was as gray as the sky and the waves rolling to shore just a few feet away were edged with foam that looked like lace.

"Cass…"

"Don't bother to deny it. We all know it's true. You've shut down, Jack and we don't know how to reach you." She leaned in and looked up into his eyes. "Will you let Rita try?"

What no one understood was, he couldn't allow himself to be reached. Couldn't be pulled from the shadows because the darkness was where he belonged now. He felt his own helplessness rise as he watched his sister's face.

Jack wished he could reassure his whole family. Wished that this marriage was changing something. But the truth was, *nothing* had changed for him. He was who he was now and everyone would eventually accept what he already had.

The old Jack Buchanan died on his last tour.

Cass must have read the resignation on his features because she sighed, went up on her toes to kiss his cheek. "I love you, Jack. Give yourself a chance to be happy."

He nodded again, gave her a quick hug, and then sighed in relief when she walked off to join her family. Jack looked to his father and brother as they stood with Rita's parents, laughing and talking. There was no respite for Jack today. He'd dropped himself into a crowd. Yet he was still a man on the sidelines, watching as life went on around him.

Both families were gathered and they seemed to be getting along fine. His sister's family, husband and two kids and his brother Sam's group, wife and three kids, actually looked small compared to Rita's.

Her parents, her sister and two brothers with all of their kids and spouses made quite a crowd. Her sister's four kids, each brother had five and one of the wives was as pregnant as Rita. The Marchettis were clearly devoted to family and Jack was glad to see it. When this marriage ended, when he was out of her life, Rita would have their support to help her through.

Another straw of guilt dropped onto his shoulders and he nearly winced at the added weight. Had he done the right thing here? Marrying her with the promise to divorce in three months? Setting her up to have to explain what went wrong to a loving family who were assuming she was marrying for love? Wouldn't it have been better to just tell everyone the truth up front?

Easier for him, maybe, he acknowledged. But for Rita? His gaze went to her and locked on with a laser focus. Tension gripped him as every cell in his body tightened, buzzing with the kind of need only *she* had ever awakened in him. He wanted her with every breath and knew he couldn't have her because he had nothing to offer her. Not now.

All he could give her was this marriage and a house and the promise to stay the hell out of her way once this was done and over. She deserved at least the pretense of a real marriage for her family's sake, he told himself. Hell, she deserved so much more than he had.

Her curly brown hair was pulled up on top of her head to cascade down past her shoulders in a riot of wind-tossed curls. She wore a long dress of some filmy material that almost seemed otherworldly. The color was a soft lavender so pale it made him think of moonlit fog. Her eyes were bright, her mouth curved in a smile as she hugged her sister. Then those aged, whiskey eyes found his and his insides fisted. He was caught in a trap of his own making.

Married to a woman he wanted and couldn't have. Living in a shadow world, yearning for light. Wanting to bury himself inside her warmth to ease the cold that was always crouched within him. He was outside a window staring in at what he most desired, but unable to reach out and touch it.

And maybe that was his penance, he thought. The price he had to pay for living.

"You look too solemn for a man on his wedding day."

Somehow Jack's father had sneaked up on him. Damn. He'd been hyperalert for months, but looking at Rita was enough to distract him from everything but her.

"Just thinking," he said.

Thomas turned to follow Jack's gaze to Rita. "Well, I don't know how you can look at your bride and be thinking thoughts dark enough to put a scowl on your face."

Chagrined, Jack realized he hadn't been paying close enough attention. He'd let his mask slip and shown people what he was feeling and that wasn't something he wanted to happen. No point in those he loved worrying even more than they already were.

He forced a smile and hoped it looked more real than it felt. "You like her?"

Thomas smiled and slapped his back. "What's not to like? She's beautiful, kind and she's giving me another grandchild." His voice trailed off. "I only wish your mother was still here to enjoy all of these kids running around."

Jack smiled wistfully. His mother had died five years before and had only seen a few of the grandchildren she would have enjoyed so much. "She would have loved this."

"Yes, she would," his father said. "But I have a feeling she's here, somehow. I can't imagine your mother *not* being around when something big was happening to one of her kids."

True, Jack thought. And his mother never would have worried about him from afar. She would have hammered at him relentlessly until she'd dragged him kicking and screaming out of the darkness and back to where she wanted him. Carla Buchanan had been a force of nature. And Jack honestly didn't know if he was more sad or relieved that his mom wasn't there to see what he'd come to.

"Come on now," his father said. "We're all going over to *The Queen Mary* for the wedding brunch."

He had to smile. Once his father had heard about

the wedding, he'd insisted on taking care of a celebratory brunch. And of course, he'd arranged for a private dining room on *The Queen Mary*. Nothing his father liked better than ships, and in his defense, Jack was sure their out-of-town guests would enjoy visiting the historical ship.

"You go ahead," Jack said, "I'll be there in a minute."

"All right then."

Thomas walked off to join the others and Jack took a breath, steeling himself to join in, to be a part of the festivities. The stretch of beach had never looked longer to him. A cold sea wind whipped past him and tugged at the edges of his jacket. He headed for their families, but with every step he took, he felt the sand shifting beneath his feet and the sensation reminded him of too much.

Awakened too many memories that were always too close to the surface. His insides tightened and a heightened sense of awareness took over. Sounds were more defined, until he could hear shrieks from down the beach and screams that had him whirling around and crouching as if he were under fire. Then his gaze locked on a screaming girl as her boyfriend carried her into the icy water.

Heartbeat racing, hands fisting at his sides, Jack took a breath to steady himself. The wind pushed at him, but instead of scenting sea spray on the air, he smelled the stale, flat air of a desert country that had claimed too much of him. His spine stiffened, but he turned back and kept walking, determined to keep what he was feeling to himself.

To stay half in the shadows even as he pretended to be in the light.

Rita walked up to meet him and he looked into her eyes, focusing on her, only her. Staring at her, the swamping sensations nearly drowning him faded, to be replaced by a different kind of tension. She was so beautiful she stole his breath. And now she was his wife.

God help her.

Five

"I didn't let anything slip to Mom and Dad," Gina was saying. "*But*, I know there's more to this whole sudden wedding thing than you're telling."

Rita glanced past her sister to the people in the private dining room. Sure that no one could overhear, she said, "Okay, yes. There is more. Thanks for not saying anything, and I'll tell you about it at some point, I promise. Just… I can't right now and I don't want Mom and Dad worrying."

"I know how to keep a secret." Gina's eyes narrowed on her. "So I'll stay quiet. But I'm warning you, Rita, if he's a jerk, I expect you to tell me so I can kick him."

Rita laughed a little as relief trickled through her. She had enough on her mind and heart at the moment without worrying about her family worrying about *her*. Gina was always as good as her word. If she said she'd keep a secret, nothing and no one would be able to pry it out of her.

If her family knew she'd gotten married with the promise of a quickie divorce looming, there would no doubt be hell to pay. As it was, her brothers kept giving Jack a hard eye like they'd prefer to take him outside and deal with the man who'd left their sister pregnant and alone. But her parents at least were believing Rita's story of finding Jack and the two of them reigniting the love between them.

If only, Rita thought with an internal sigh.

"I promise. But, I might kick him myself before you get the chance."

"I can live with that," Gina said, sipping on a mimosa in a crystal champagne flute.

While her sister was quiet, Rita had a minute to think about her wedding day. The ceremony had been small, just hers and Jack's families on a roped-off area of the beach. The early June weather of dark skies and cool winds had kept the beach mostly deserted, so it had been intimate in spite of being so public.

When they exchanged vows, Rita remembered looking deeply into Jack's eyes and for one brief moment, she'd seen that quick glimpse of *her* Jack hidden inside him again. And that gave her hope. Maybe there was a way to reach him. To *actually* reignite what they'd shared so briefly six months ago.

Their kiss at the end of the ceremony had started off perfunctory, but after a split second, it was as if Jack had forgotten that they were putting on a show. He'd pulled her in to him and cradled her against his body as his mouth took hers in a slow, seductive kiss that had nearly blown Rita's short veil right off her head.

If there was *that* between them still, that heat, that magic, couldn't there be more? Heat didn't exist in a vacuum. Emotions, feelings, had to be there, too, right?

Was she being deliberately foolish? Probably. But if you didn't try, you couldn't win. If you didn't ask, the answer was always no.

"You're thinking."

"That's a bad thing?" she asked, a small smile curving her mouth.

"I haven't decided yet," Gina admitted. She half turned to look at Jack, across the room, standing somewhat apart from everyone else. "He's gorgeous, I give you that. But he doesn't seem the sociable type. Won't that drive you nuts?"

Rita shook her head. "No, I talk enough for both of us."

"True." Gina laughed.

"You know, he wasn't like this when we first met," Rita said quietly. "Oh, he never talked as much as I do, but he was warmer. Less…closed down. I don't know how to explain it."

"You're doing pretty well," Gina said thoughtfully, studying the man they were talking about.

"Gina, the thing is, every once in a while," Rita continued, "I see the real Jack hiding behind his eyes."

Her sister gave her a cool look. "And you think you can bring him out of hiding?"

"If not me, who?" Rita asked. "If there's a chance, I have to try."

Gina dropped one arm around her shoulders. "Sweetie, sometimes people are hiding for a reason."

She might be right, Rita acknowledged. But if she didn't find out for sure, the what-if would haunt her forever. "But what if that reason can be dealt with? Fought?"

"Oh, God," Gina murmured, shaking her head. "You're trying to save him, aren't you?"

Was she? Oh, Rita didn't like the sound of that. How many times had she seen friends fall for a guy with "issues" and then try to fix him? Get him to change. Help him deal with his demons? Is that what she was doing?

No, she argued with herself silently. This was different. *Jack* was different. Something specific had happened to him and whatever it was had affected him deeply. Even if it was because of what they'd once had, or the fact that they'd created a child together... Didn't Rita owe it to him to at least make the attempt to help him?

"Is that so wrong?" She looked at her sister, really curious to hear what she had to say.

"No, I guess not," Gina said, resignation clear in her tone. "If it's something you feel like you have to do, there's no stopping you anyway. Just make sure you don't lose yourself in the effort."

"I won't," Rita said and knew that keeping her promise wasn't going to be easy. Because in spite of everything that had happened between them, Jack was the one man in the world who could still cause her pain.

"Uh-oh," Gina said suddenly, "I've gotta go save Jimmy. Mom's just dropped Kira into his lap, so he's got all four kids and is seriously outnumbered."

Rita smiled on cue, but she wasn't thinking about her brother-in-law. Her thoughts were with Jack, standing apart and alone at his own wedding. Backlit by the light flooding in through the wall of windows he stood in front of, he looked so solitary, it broke her heart.

He'd done all he could to make this faux marriage beautiful for her. From the ceremony itself to this family reception. *The Queen Mary* was a beautiful old ship and this private dining room in its five-star restaurant was old-world elegant. Windows lined both sides of the ship and she imagined that when the old ocean liner was still sailing, the views were incredible.

Where Jack stood, there was a sweeping vista of the sea and other boats bobbing on the surface. The sun had finally broken through the clouds and slanted off the water like gold dust. But Jack was silhouetted, defining his aloneness, and that tore at Rita.

"We're staying in town for a few days," Gina was saying. "As long as we're here, figured we'd take the kids to Disneyland."

Rita glanced at her. "They'll love it."

"Yep," Gina mused. "Hope Jimmy and I survive it." She grabbed Rita's hand and squeezed. "If you need me for anything, call me. I'll be there."

"I know," she said, returning that squeeze briefly. "Thanks, Gina. I'm gonna be fine."

As Gina moved away, Rita heard her own words echo in her mind and she hoped she was right. Because at the moment, her heart was aching for the man who'd cut himself off. He'd gone to so much trouble for her, but he wasn't being a part of this at all. Even in the heart of his family, he was determinedly alone. That didn't equate with everything he'd told her about his family when they met. Back then, he'd laughed at the stories of fishing trips with his father and brother, of his sister being outwitted by her five-year-old daughter, of how devastated their family had been when they'd lost Jack's mother.

Now, though, it was as if his family wasn't even in the same room with him. She'd seen his father, brother and sister try to connect with him and eventually give up. She'd watched Jack keep to the sidelines as if punishing himself, somehow. Rita didn't have the first clue how to go about reaching him, but she knew she had to try. Because if there was even a tiny chance she could find *her* Jack, it would be worth the effort.

Smiling and nodding to her family as she passed, Rita walked to Jack. He was staring out at the ocean and Rita came up right beside him.

He didn't look at her, but he must have sensed her presence. "Everything all right?"

"It's fine," she said, staring up at his profile, waiting for some flicker of—she didn't even know what. "Are *you* okay?" she asked.

He turned his head then and looked down at her. She felt that stare sizzle in her blood. One look from him and she burned.

"Yeah," he said finally, quietly. "I'm just not good in a crowd of people."

His words, so simply stated, tugged at her heart as she realized just how important this marriage must have been to him. He'd dropped himself into a situation that would make him uncomfortable because this meant something to him. He'd stood up against what plagued him to make sure she had what she needed at the wedding. He'd brought her family in, and seen to it that everything was beautiful for her in spite of his own misgivings. Just another sign to Rita that her Jack was in there somewhere. That only strengthened her resolve to discover what had happened to change the man she'd once thought was her one and only.

But today, she only wanted to be here. With him. To let him know he wasn't alone, even if that's what he believed he wanted. Going on instinct, she slid her hand into his and was rewarded when his fingers curled around hers and held tight.

Jack lay wide awake in bed, alone on his wedding night.

Rita was down the hall in the penthouse guestroom and he couldn't tear his mind away from the image of her. His whole body ached for her, just as it had from the first moment he'd met her.

No other woman had ever affected him as she had. While he was overseas, he'd worked on convincing himself that what he'd felt with her was nothing special. He'd had to, just to survive. Clinging to the real world and the memories of a woman with a warm heart, soft body and wild, raw laugh had only made his reality that much harder to endure.

Then, when everything went to hell one afternoon, Jack had sliced every emotion out of his life because it was imperative to survival. He hadn't written to her because he couldn't lie to her about what was going on and he couldn't have told her the truth. He didn't look for her when he came back because he was in no shape to be around anyone. And because by then, he knew he could never again be the man she had once known.

"But Fate's a nasty bitch," he muttered into the darkness. His own voice seemed to echo, low and harsh in the empty room.

The gods of irony had conspired against him. He'd put so much effort into avoiding her that the gods laughed and threw her in his path, making it impossible to ignore her. And now they were married.

Shaking his head, he draped one arm across his eyes to dim the moonlight spearing into his bedroom. He had the terrace doors open, because he couldn't stand to be closed in. He needed that swirl of air, even when it was cold. Needed to smell the sea, remind himself that he was here. Home. And not in that hot, desperate situation that had nearly driven him over the edge.

His room was big, with a black-and-white-tiled gas hearth on one wall, bookcases and a television on the other walls. There were chairs, tables and a bed that was so big it felt even emptier than it actually was.

"My choice," he reminded himself and gritted his teeth against the roiling heat and tension coiled inside him.

It would be so easy to go down the hall, walk into her room and relive a few memories. Make some new ones. No guarantee she'd let him in, but then he remembered how she'd held his hand at the reception. As if she'd known, somehow sensed, that he'd needed that touch to ground himself in the moment.

She was good like that, he thought. Always had been. They'd connected so deeply in one week that it had been almost like they could read each other's minds. He hoped to hell she couldn't pick up on his thoughts now, but back then, it was different.

He was there the next morning to pick her up at seven, as agreed. She was in the lobby, waiting for him, clearly as eager as he was for them to be together again. Just seeing her in her jeans and dark green sweater had made his mouth water.

When she smiled at him, he went hard as stone and

damn near killed himself just trying to walk across the floor toward her. Then she reached out for him, took his hand and he was lost in need, heat, a fire that built with every breath.

They had breakfast on the beach, coffee and bagels shared over laughter and a breathless sense of expectation. Looking into her whiskey-brown eyes was mesmerizing. Intoxicating. On that deserted winter beach, they were alone in the world but for one or two hardy surfers out challenging the waves.

Hands linked, they walked along the beach for what felt like miles, then they hiked back to the car and drove down the coast. Music pumping, wind roaring through the open windows and the two of them, still holding hands, as if unable to bear not touching.

Two hours later they were in San Diego and stopping for lunch at a tiny inn outside La Jolla. The once-dignified old Victorian mansion clung to the cliffside and waves pounded against the rocks in a steady, rhythmic heartbeat.

"It's beautiful here," Rita said, letting her gaze slide across the water, the cliffs and the meticulously tended gardens.

"Yeah, it is," he replied, his gaze locked on her. With the wind in her hair and the winter sun shining in her eyes, Jack thought he'd never seen anything more lovely. And he knew if he didn't kiss her soon, it would kill him.

"You're not even looking at the view," she chided with a half smile.

"Depends on what you consider a great view." He snaked one hand across the small round table and cov-

ered hers. He felt her pulse pounding in time with the relentless sea and knew that beat matched his own, too.

She licked her lips and he fought to breathe. She curled her hand beneath his and the heat that blossomed between them should have set the grounds on fire.

Her gaze locked with his. "What's happening here?" she asked, her voice nearly lost in the wind and the roar of the waves.

"Whatever it is, I'm all for it," he admitted and stroked his thumb across her palm. Her eyes glazed over and her breath quickened.

"Oh, I am, too."

"You're making me crazy, Rita. Couldn't sleep last night. I kept thinking about you. About today. About..."

She pulled in a shaky breath. "I've been thinking about...too."

Oh, yeah. If he didn't have her soon, he was a walking dead man. He'd never make that two-or three-hour drive home with his body and mind so entangled with nothing but thoughts of her. All he could think of was touching her, stroking her skin, sliding his body into hers and being surrounded by her heat.

"You know, maybe we should book a room here at the inn. Neither one of us slept much last night. We could get some sleep before that long drive back up to Orange County."

Her tongue slipped out again to slide across her bottom lip and his gaze tracked that motion as if his life depended on it. Fire, he thought. It felt like he was burning up from the inside and if his body got any harder, he'd have to crawl from the table because walking would be impossible.

Nodding, she said, "That's probably a good idea. A nap, I mean. Tired drivers can be dangerous."

"Yeah," he agreed. "Safety first."

Her smile was fleeting, but brilliant, taking his breath away. "I'll see if they've got a room where we can...rest. Just wait here."

When he stood up, Rita took his hand and squeezed. "Okay, I'll wait. But hurry. I'm really tired."

That was all the encouragement Jack needed.

In ten minutes, they were entering their room on the second floor. Jack swept her up close to him, kicked the door closed and gave the dead bolt a fast turn. She laughed up into his face and he felt something inside him turn over. She was more than he'd ever had. More than he'd ever thought to find. And for now, she was all his.

"Oh," she said, tearing her gaze from his to give the room a quick look. "Isn't it lovely?"

He hadn't noticed. Now he did. White lace curtains at the windows, a brass bed with a detailed flower quilt across the mattress. There were two chairs before a tiny hearth outlined in sea-blue tiles and a table held a carafe of water and two glasses. There was a door that led to a private bath and photographs of old San Diego dotted the pale gold walls.

He supposed it was very nice, though it could have been a cave for all he cared. "Yeah," he said tightly, not caring about the room.

When she looked up at him again, she gave him a knowing smile. "Ready to nap?"

"More than you know."

"Then let's get to sleep," she said, throwing her arms

around his neck, holding on as she lifted her face for his kiss.

When their mouths met, merged, it was like the whole damn world lit up. Or maybe it was just the fire inside, blazing brighter than ever. Seconds ticked into minutes and still they stood, locked together, bodies pressed tightly to each other, heartbeats hammering in time.

Finally, he tore his mouth free, fought for enough breath to admit, "I have to touch you."

"Please, yes," she said softly, hungrily, "Now. Touch me."

In seconds, they were naked and falling onto the bed together. Afternoon light poured through the windows and winter sun painted a soft, golden slash across the polished wood floor to lie on the bed and shine in Rita's eyes.

His gaze raked over her lush curves, and everything in him stirred to a fever pitch. Jack felt as though he'd been waiting for this one moment his whole life. He bent his head to take one of her nipples into his mouth. Tasting, nibbling, working his teeth and tongue across her sensitive skin. Every whispered moan and sigh that slipped from her fed his hunger until it was like a closed fist around his throat, making breathing almost impossible. Her fingers slid through his military-short hair, nails scraping along his scalp as she arched up and into him, silently asking for more. And he had plans for a lot more.

Lifting his head, he stared down into her eyes. "This could be the longest nap on record."

"Oh, good," she said on a long sigh, "because I'm really tired."

He grinned. "And I'm really glad to hear that."

She pulled his head down to hers and this time she claimed his mouth in a kiss that seared him right to his bones. He let her lead, let her devour and gave back all that she was giving him and still, it wasn't enough.

Jack moved over her, running his hands up and down her body, discovering every curve, exploring her soft silky skin until they were both trembling with an explosive need. Her small hands moved over his chest, his shoulders and every stroke of her fingers felt like licks of flame.

They rolled across the bed, tasting, touching. Her heavy brown curls spread out beneath her head like a wild, tangled dark halo. He was lost in her, her scent, her touch, the hunger raging inside him. Body raging, mind fogging over, Jack stood poised on the brink of a cliff.

"Now," she whispered, lifting her hips, rocking into his hand as he cupped her center. "Jack, now. I can't take this anymore."

"Hold on. Just hold on." Before he lost control completely, he reached down for his jeans, dug into the pocket and pulled out the condoms he'd tucked in there only that morning.

"Boy," she said, "I really love a man who's prepared to take a nap."

He grinned at her as he sheathed himself. "Babe, ever since the moment we met, I've been prepared to nap."

"So glad to hear it." She opened her arms to him, lifted her hips again and welcomed him inside her.

That first slick, hot slide into her body stole his breath and would have finished him completely if he hadn't fought for control and held on to it. She moved into him, and the slippery threads of control fell away.

Together they climbed, staring into each other's eyes as they rode the crest of what they created. Mouths mating, breath mingling, they moved in an ancient dance as if they were born to be one. Together, they raced toward completion and together, they fell from the precipice, wrapped in each other's arms.

What could have been minutes or hours later, when breathing was easier, Rita cupped his face in her palm and whispered, "I hope you're still as sleepy as I am. Because I think I need another nap."

He turned his face into her palm, kissed it, then grinned down at her. "It's important to get enough sleep."

Jack groaned tightly as the memory faded and he was alone again in a room that suddenly felt too small, too quiet. Too empty.

He could still feel her small hand on his face, see her smile, taste her kiss. His body was tight, hard, eager. His mind raced with possibilities, before he shut them all down and accepted the cold reality.

Jack had a penance to pay and being this close to Rita without touching her was only the latest toll to be taken.

Jumping out of bed, he stalked through the open doors to the terrace and there he stood, letting the icy wind off the sea blow away the lingering heat still haunting him.

The next few days weren't easy.

Rita had to acknowledge that finding her way to the real Jack was going to be far more difficult than she'd anticipated. She was gone before he woke in the morning, heading down to the bakery where she worked to stay busy enough to keep thoughts of Jack at bay. Then in the evening, Jack did his best to avoid her completely. It was as if she was an unwanted guest he was trying to convince to leave.

Okay, yes, she'd agreed to a temporary marriage, but only because she'd caught those glimpses of *her* Jack. And now, he seemed determined to not let that happen again. He was pushing her away and expected her to simply give up and go when their time together was up.

"Well," she muttered to herself, "I'm not that easy to get rid of."

"Glad to hear it."

Rita closed her eyes, groaned quietly at being overheard—and by Jack's sister no less—then turned to face Cass. "Hi."

"Hi," the other woman said, walking farther into the kitchen. "I didn't mean to eavesdrop, but you were talking out loud so it was hard to miss."

"Sometimes," Rita admitted sheepishly, "I have to talk to myself because I'm the only one who really understands me."

Cass laughed. "Boy, I know that feeling. Between my practice, my husband and my kids, sometimes I talk to myself just to make sure I'm still there."

Rita relaxed her defenses a little. She'd liked Cass immediately when they'd met at the wedding. And listening to her now, Rita realized that with time, the two of them could be good friends. The question was, would she have that time?

"Look, I hope it's okay that I'm back here. The redhead out front said I could come in."

Casey again. "Of course it's okay. Have a seat. I'm just getting these loaves of bread ready for the ovens."

"God, it smells wonderful in here." Cass took a deep breath and sighed as she pulled a stool up to the marble work surface. Glancing around the room at the trays, the racks of cooling biscotti, bread and cannoli shells, she sighed. "Bread, cookies... I could live here."

Rita laughed and ran the blade of her knife along the elongated loaves of bread, making a few slices to give the dough room to grow while baking. "I love being in the kitchen."

"Well, clearly you have the talent for it," Cass said on a heavy sigh. "My husband has banned me from ours. He says what I call cooking, modern science calls poison."

"Oh, ouch."

Cass shrugged. "Yeah, it would be painful if it weren't true. So we have a cook and everyone's happy."

She looked at a tray of thumbprint cookies with their glossy chocolate centers and sighed again. "Can I have one?"

"Sure."

She bit in. "Wow. Just wow."

Rita laughed and said, "Thank you."

"Oh, my pleasure." Cass watched her as she readied the bread loaves and the silence spun out for several seconds before she finally blurted out the reason for her visit. "I'm really happy you married Jack."

Oh, Rita hated guilt. She'd grown up Italian Catholic and nobody did guilt better than they did. Her mother was a master at making her kids feel guilty and so Rita recognized the sensation when it slapped her. She'd lied to her family. To Jack's family.

Maybe even to herself, it was too soon to tell. "Cass…"

The other woman waved one hand and shook her head. "No, you don't have to say anything. I just mean, I wanted to let you know that we're all glad he has someone. Jack's been…sort of shut down since he came home from his last tour."

Rita watched her, unsure what to say, or even what she *could* say.

"We've all tried to get through, but it's like trying to catch fog. Every time you think you're making progress, or maybe you see a flash of the old Jack, boom. It's gone." She shook her head and unconsciously reached for another cookie. Taking a bite, she sighed a little and continued. "If our mom was still alive, she'd have pushed past whatever boundaries he's got set up inside him. She wouldn't have accepted anything less."

Rita heard the wistful tone and responded. "She was tough?"

"When it came to her family? Oh, yeah." Cass grinned. "No one could stand in her way. But she's been gone five years and it's like the rest of us can't figure out how to reach Jack." She crumbled the rest of the cookie in her fingers. "That's why we're so glad he's got you. And the baby."

Oh, that guilt was really starting to get heavy, Rita thought. What would Cass and the rest of their family think of Rita when this three-month marriage ended? Would they blame her for walking out on Jack, never knowing the real reason behind it?

"The worst part for me is I hate seeing my dad look so…helpless over this," Cass said. "He tries to talk to Jack but just can't and he's scared. Heck, we all are."

So was Rita. In the time since Jack had walked back into her life, she'd seen him withdraw not only from her but from the family who clearly loved him. Their marriage hadn't helped. If anything, he was working even harder at avoiding her.

"I don't like feeling helpless," Cass muttered. "I'm not good at it."

Rita smiled. Here, she really could bond with Cass. "Neither am I."

"Good." Cass gave her a conspiratorial smile. "I'm glad to hear it. That means you'll push him as maybe the rest of us can't."

But no pressure, Rita thought.

Six

Rita had a sister of her own and two older brothers, so she knew what it was to worry about a sibling. To want to help and not be allowed to. She could understand what Cass was feeling; Rita just didn't know if she was going to be able to do what the Buchanan family hoped she could. Bring Jack back to them.

"I don't know if Jack told you, but I'm a doctor."

She came up out of her thoughts with a jerk. "He did mention that. Family practice, right?"

"Right. Well, speaking as a doctor, not a sister," Cass said, "I can tell you that Jack's being affected by PTSD, which you've probably already guessed."

Rita nodded.

"There are so many different levels of this syndrome," Cass said with a sigh. "I've done a lot of reading and studying on it since Jack got home. And I know that the men and women affected by it are all different, so what they go through is different, as well. Naturally, treating it is a bitch. No one can find a standard type of treatment because each case is so wildly dissimilar."

Rita had come to that conclusion on her own. And it made perfect sense, really. Obviously, something horrible had happened to Jack on his last tour. When he left her six months ago, it was with a promise of a future that had been unsaid, but felt by both of them. And he'd come home for good just two months later, a completely changed man.

"I actually don't like the PTSD label—the word *disorder* bothers me. *Post-traumatic stress* I can get behind. But *disorder*? No." Cass shook her head firmly and scowled at what was left of her cookie. "That makes these men and women seem…sick, somehow. When what they are is *hurt*." She glanced up at Rita and winced. "Sorry. I didn't even realize I was climbing onto my soapbox."

Rita studied her for a minute or two. Not only was she a doctor, but she was the very concerned sister of a man suffering silently. "No apology necessary. I agree with you."

"Good. Thanks." Cass ate what was left of the cookie. "I knew at the wedding that I'd like you. And if you can help Jack through this, I'll love you forever."

Rita's heart opened up for the other woman. If one of her own brothers was in pain, she would do anything in her power, ask anyone she could think of, to get him the help he needed. Knowing that the Buchanans, in spite of all their money and power and influence, were as close as her own family made her feel more on solid ground. She could understand the driving need to save family and she liked Cass more for what she'd just confessed. "I'm going to try."

Cass smiled. "That's all we can do."

Rita walked to the wall ovens, opened the doors, then slid the bread trays inside, closed the doors and set the timers. As she wiped down the gray-streaked white marble counter, she asked, "Would you like a cup of coffee?"

"I'd *love* one," Cass said. "If you'll join me."

"No coffee for me yet," she said sadly, giving her baby bump a gentle rub. "But I'll have some herbal tea and cookies."

"That works." Cass grinned a little. "You know, if you haven't already lined up a pediatrician, I'd love to be your baby doctor."

Since she really hadn't chosen a doctor yet, this was a gift. "Who could be better than my baby's aunt?"

With Cass's beaming smile lighting her way, Rita walked to the front of the shop for the tea and coffee. Whatever else had happened today, she hoped she'd made a friend.

"Your wife is here," Linda announced over the intercom the very next afternoon.

"What?" Jack looked up from the file he was going over. "Rita?"

"Do you have another wife I don't know about yet?" Rita asked, sailing into the office with a wide smile on her face. "Thanks, Linda," she threw over her shoulder as Jack's assistant grinned, backed out of the office and shut the door.

Rita wore jeans, a white dress shirt and a black sweater over it that matched the black boots on her feet.

Her brown curly hair was loose and tumbling around her face. Her brown eyes were shining and that smile pulled him in even as he fought against the draw.

"What're you doing here?" he asked as she walked through a slant of sunlight pouring through the windows to approach his desk.

"Such a warm welcome. Thanks. I'm glad to see you, too."

He frowned at the jab and her grin widened in response.

"I brought lunch," she said simply and held up the dark green cloth bag he hadn't even noticed until that moment.

Just when he thought he'd figured out how to survive this marriage, she threw a wrench into the whole thing.

Every morning, he drove her to the bakery because damned if she was going to be driving herself through the darkness. Once she was safely inside, he drove back to the office and caught up on the dreaded paperwork that seemed to be what most of his days were made of. At the end of the day, he most often tried to just grab something for dinner and then disappear into his office or his bedroom. Jack knew the only way he was going to make it through the next three months was to keep as much distance between him and Rita as possible.

Damned hard though when she fought him at every turn. She insisted on breakfast at four in the morning. When he could, he avoided having dinner with her and simply escaped into his room or his office and stayed there until she was in bed.

He was living like a fugitive in his own damn apartment. And now, she'd hunted him down at work.

"Nice idea, but—"

"I called Linda to check," Rita said, interrupting him neatly as she began to empty that bag onto a table set between two overstuffed leather chairs. "She assured me your next appointment wasn't for two hours, so we have plenty of time for lunch."

He bit back a curse. What good would it do at this point? Sometimes, he reminded himself, surrender was your only option. "What've you got?" he asked.

She flipped her hair back, turned her head to smile at him. "I went to your favorite Chinese place. I've got beef and broccoli, chicken chow mein and shrimp fried rice."

As she opened cartons to spoon the food onto two plates she pulled from her bag, Jack took a breath and drew in the delicious scents. Well, hell, he had to eat sometime, right?

He pushed up from the desk and walked across the room, took one of the chairs and accepted the plate Rita handed him. She grinned at him and his insides rolled over. The woman had power over him, for sure. He was achy and needy most of the time now and he had her to thank for it. Her image was always in his mind. The hunger for her never eased. And having her in his house and still untouchable was harder than he even imagined it would be.

Jack was starting to think she was deliberately trying to seduce him just by acting as though nothing was going on between them. And damned if it wasn't working.

"Think you're pretty clever, don't you?"

"Absolutely," she agreed, and sat down in the chair opposite him. She dug into the bag again, and came up with two bottles of water, two sets of chopsticks and a stack of napkins.

"So," she said, "how're things in the megabusiness world?"

The food looked delicious and smelled amazing. He took a bite, savored it, then said, "Buying, selling. How's the bakery?"

She shrugged. "Measuring, mixing, baking."

Her eyes were shining, her smile was hypnotic and she smelled even better than the food. Jack was on dangerous ground already. Having her invade the office he thought of as his own personal cave wasn't helping anything. Now he'd be seeing her here, even when she wasn't. There had to be boundaries. For everyone's sake.

"Why're you really here?" he asked. "Isn't the bakery busy enough for you?"

"Oh, it really is. But Casey's a great manager." She took a sip of water. "As you said yourself, I'm the boss, I can take a break when I want to."

Tough having your own words thrown back at you and used against you.

"I can't," he said, but he kept eating the chow mein. It really was good. "Look, I appreciate this, but it's not something that should become a habit."

"Really?" She tipped her head to one side. "Why not?"

"Because we both have work," he said and knew it sounded lame. But off the cuff it was the best he had.

"Uh-huh." Thoughtfully, she took another bite of her broccoli, then asked, "Sure it's not because you're trying to avoid being around me?"

"If that were true," he countered, "why would I have married you?"

"Such a good question." She took another bite. "Have an answer?"

This was not going well. He was losing a battle he hadn't even been aware he'd entered. "You know why we got married."

"The baby."

"Exactly. This wasn't about us having lunch or dinner together," he pointed out, but hadn't stopped eating yet. "This isn't about cozy nights at home, Rita, and you know it. It's an arrangement with an expiration date."

"Hmm. And, it wasn't about you driving me to work every morning either and yet…" She shrugged again, a small smile tugging at the corner of her mouth.

Well, he'd stepped right into that one.

"That's different," he argued. "You used to live above the bakery now you have to drive to work—"

"Six miles," she threw in.

"This isn't about the distance, it's about safety." He took a drink of water. "I'm not letting you drive through the city alone in the middle of the night when it's just as easy for me to drive you."

"So you're worried about my safety. That doesn't sound disinterested to me," she mused, taking another bite.

"Being concerned doesn't mean worried." Though he was. Hell, the thought of her driving alone through the city in the middle of the night gave him chills. What if she got a flat tire? Or the car just died? Or something happened with the baby?

She took another bite and watched him as she chewed and swallowed. Sunlight filtered through the windows and made her dark hair shine with golden highlights. Just watching her chew had his body going on red alert. It was that mouth, he told himself. That full, generous, completely kissable mouth that was doing him in.

"You work so hard to pretend that you're oblivious to me and your family, but it's not working."

His frown deepened and rather than argue, he took another bite of his lunch.

"Look it up in a dictionary, Jack. *Concerned* means *worried*. And that's exactly what you are. Worried, I mean. Oh, don't say anything," she said, waving her chopsticks when he started to deny it, "I know it bothers you to be worried, so that's almost the same as not being, unless you think about it carefully and then it's exactly the same thing and you don't want to recognize that, do you?"

Jack stared at her. "What?"

Shaking her head she took a sip of water, "Nothing, never mind. Doesn't matter right now. I didn't get the chance to tell you, but your sister came to the bakery to see me yesterday."

His head snapped up. Suddenly, her conversation was taking several different paths at once and none of them were making sense. "Cass?"

"You have two sisters as well as two wives?" she asked, teasing.

"Funny." That smile was really hard to resist and he was pretty sure she knew it since she kept flashing it at him.

"A little, maybe." She shrugged again. "Anyway, Cass wanted to talk about you, big surprise."

Well, there went the appetite. He set his plate aside, reached for his water and took a long drink. "That's what this visit is about then," he said. "What Cass had to say."

"Nope." She shook her head, sending those brown curls into a wild dance that made him want to spear his fingers through them. "I was coming to surprise you anyway. This just gives us more to talk about."

"No, thanks." He took another drink, half wishing it was a beer. "I'm not interested in conversations and besides, I have to get back to work."

"No you don't," she said, setting her plate aside, too. "You're just trying to get rid of me again."

"Again?"

She sighed. "Jack, you avoid me every chance you get. The penthouse is big, but not so big that we shouldn't run into each other more often. But you see to it that we don't." She ran one hand lovingly over her baby bump, but her gaze never left his. "Even when I trap you into breakfast in the morning, you just bolt it down and dodge every attempt at conversation."

"Four thirty in the morning, not the best time for chats."

"What's your excuse then for dinner?" Still shaking her head, she said, "Usually, you grab an apple or something and disappear into your office. Or if you do sit down with me, we don't talk. Heck, you hardly look at me directly."

It was too damn hard to look at her. To want her so badly it was a constant, driving ache inside. He was paying, daily. His atonement continued and he could only hope that he survived it somehow.

"Rita…"

"Your family's worried about you."

He scraped both hands across his face, then stood up, unable to sit still any longer. "You don't have to tell me about my own family."

"Are you sure?" She stood up, too, and faced him, toe-to-toe. A part of him admired that spine of hers.

He'd liked it right off, from the moment they met and she hadn't been afraid. But right now, he wished she was more cautious, less ready for a confrontation.

"They want to help you and they don't know how," she said. "*I* don't know how."

"I didn't ask for help," he reminded her tautly. "I can deal with things my own way."

"Not so far," she countered and folded her arms across her middle.

His eyes narrowed on her. "You don't know anything about it."

"Then *tell* me," she challenged, moving closer, tipping her head back to meet his eyes. "And if not me, Jack, tell *someone*."

"Therapy?" He laughed, shook his head and shoved one hand through his hair. "Yeah, not needing a couch, or some stranger poking around in my head. No, thanks."

"Tough marine doesn't need anyone, is that it?"

He glanced at her, read frustration clearly in her eyes but there was nothing he could do about it. "Close enough."

"Well, you're wrong, Jack," she said and this time when she moved closer, she laid one hand on his chest, right over his heart. Silently, he wondered if she felt the staccato beat beneath her palm. If she had the slightest clue what she did to him.

"Even marines are human, Jack. Even marines can't fix everything solo." She stared up into his eyes and he was unable to look away. "People need each other. That's why we *have* families, Jack. Because we're stronger together. Because we can count on each other when things get hard."

He ground his teeth together and fought for patience. He knew she meant well. Hell, he knew they *all* meant well. But they couldn't help unless he talked and he wasn't going to talk about it. About any of it.

Through gritted teeth, he said softly, "I'm fine, Rita."

"Yeah, I can see that," she said. "That's why you don't have to set an alarm to get up at four a.m., because you can't sleep but you're fine."

He jerked his head back to give her a glare. "How the hell do you know I can't sleep?"

"I can hear you, moving around the apartment, going out onto the terrace…"

Apparently, he wasn't as stealthy as he liked to think. And he had to ask himself, if he'd known she was awake, too, would he have gone to her? Tried to lose himself and the dreams that dogged him in the warmth of her embrace? Would he have given in to the insistent urge to take her, to find the heat and the welcome he'd once found in her arms? He didn't know the answer and that worried him.

"Sorry," he said tightly, rubbing the back of his neck. "I'll be quieter."

"Oh, Jack, that's not what I meant at all," she said and rested her hand on his forearm. "I'm right here. Let me in. Am I so scary you can't talk to me?"

For the first time ever, he was tempted to do just that. To just start talking and in the talking, maybe the images in his head would start to fade. Looking down into those compelling eyes of hers, he could feel himself weakening, in spite of the promise he'd made to himself. That he would never talk about the past, because doing that kept it alive. Kept it vivid. But hadn't it stayed alive despite his silence?

"I'm not going to do that." He shook his head and gave a halfhearted laugh. "Besides, one thing you're not, Rita, is scary."

"I can be, when pushed. Just ask my brothers."

Gaze still locked with hers, he lifted one hand, smoothed her hair back and briefly let himself enjoy the silky feel of it against his skin. Her emotions crowded those whiskey-brown eyes of hers and her teeth tugged at her bottom lip. God, she was beautiful. He wished...

"Let it be, Rita," he said quietly. "Just let it be."

"You know I can't."

She stared up at him and he fisted his hands at his sides to keep from grabbing her, burying his face in the curve of her neck and drawing her scent deep inside him. She made him feel too much and he couldn't allow that. He was done with caring. Done with letting others care about him. It was the safest way.

Finally, she lifted both hands and cupped his face in her palms. Heat from her body poured into his and still couldn't thaw the knot of ice he carried deep inside. "Rita, just leave my secrets in the past. Where they belong."

Looking deeply into his eyes, Rita shook her head. "They're not staying in the past, Jack. They're right here, surrounding you, cutting you off from me. From everyone. So no, I won't let it be. Not a chance."

Rita couldn't sleep. Maybe it was the confrontation/lunch with Jack two days before. Maybe it was the baby, who had decided to start training as a gymnast while still in the womb. And maybe it was just the whirring sounds of her own thoughts spinning frantically in her mind. Whatever it was, though, pulled her from bed and sent her pacing the penthouse.

It was beautiful, she had to admit, though it was a little impersonal for her. Beige walls, gleaming wood floors and comfortable, if boring, furniture. There were generic paintings on the walls and in the penthouse kitchen, the appliances were top-of-the-line, but the dishware was buy-a-box-of-plates-style.

Nothing in the place spoke of Jack. It was as if some decorator had come in, put in inoffensive furniture and left it at that, expecting whoever lived there to eventually make it their own. But apparently Jack had no interest in putting his own stamp on the place. Here, like everywhere else in his life, he was simply an observer. As if he were a placeholder for the real person who hadn't arrived yet.

Rita curled up on the forest green couch, pulled a throw pillow onto her lap and wrapped her arms around it.

For two days, she'd been determined to make Jack interact with her. She refused to let him lock himself away in his office once he returned to the penthouse. She made dinner and forced him to talk to her over a meal. She told him all about what was happening at the bakery and peppered him with questions about his work.

She didn't understand half of what he was talking about—with cargo containers and shipping schedules, but at least he was talking. She asked questions about his family and listened when he told her stories from his childhood, the fishing trips, the cabin they used to have in Big Bear.

And though she was managing to keep him engaged, it was a lot of work. The man spoke grudgingly and she had to practically drag information from him. But it was better than letting him brood alone. Still, her heart hurt because she wasn't getting to him. She wasn't any closer now to finding the real Jack than she had been when she married him.

Moonlight pearled the darkness. If she'd had company, it might have been romantic. As it was, though, she felt sad and tired and frustrated all at once.

"If he doesn't care, why is he working so hard to shut me out?" she asked the empty room and her voice sounded overly loud in the quiet. Hugging the pillow a little tighter to her middle, she told herself that if he didn't care about her or their baby, he wouldn't have so much trouble being around her.

"And if that doesn't sound backward I don't know what does." But it made an odd kind of sense, too. He was throwing himself on a proverbial sword by avoiding her. Making sacrifices she didn't want for a reason he wouldn't share.

So how was she supposed to fight it?

The week she'd spent with him now seemed like a dream. Even that last morning in her hotel room had taken on the soft edges of a fantasy rather than the warm, loving reality she remembered.

"I should go," Jack said, bending his head to take her mouth in a kiss that was filled with a hunger that never seemed to ebb.

"Not yet." Rita cupped his cheek in her palm and looked into those amazing blue eyes, trying to etch everything she read there into her memory. "Stay. Just for a while."

He smiled and threaded his fingers through her hair. Rita closed her eyes briefly to completely savor the sen-

sation of his hands on her. She'd never known a week to fly by so quickly. She'd thought only to take a week at the beach. A little vacation to clear her head after the Christmas holiday rush at the bakery back home.

But she'd found so much more than she'd ever expected. A man who made her laugh, made her sigh and made her body sing in a way she'd never known before. They'd spent every waking moment together in the last few days and even asleep, they were locked together as if somehow afraid of being separated.

And now, they would be.

Her heart was breaking at goodbye. But her flight home was that night and Jack would be leaving himself first thing in the morning. Their time was up. But what did that mean for the future?

"My enlistment's nearly up," he was saying and she told herself to concentrate on the low rumble of his voice. "This time, I'm not going to re-up. I'm getting out."

She ran her hand over his chest, loving the feel of those sharply defined muscles beneath soft, golden-brown skin. "What's that mean for us?"

He slid one hand up the length of her body to cup her breast, his thumb and forefinger tugging on her hardened nipple. Electricity zipped through her entire body and set up a humming expectation at the very core of her. One touch from this man and she was a puddle of goo at his feet.

"It means I can come up to Utah as soon as I get home."

"Good," she said on a sigh. "That's very good."

"And we'll pick this up," he said, "right where we left off."

"Even better," she said and got a smile from him. "Please be careful, Jack."

She could have bitten her own tongue off. She'd promised herself she wouldn't cry. Wouldn't worry him. Wouldn't put her own worries onto his shoulders.

"I will be," he promised. "Always am. But this time, I've got even more reason for making it home in one piece."

He was smiling as he said it, but fear nearly choked her. Rita reached up, wrapped her arms around his neck and held on, as if somehow if she held him tightly enough, she could keep him safe. Keep him from going. From leaving her. Tears stung the backs of her eyes, but she blinked like a crazy person, to keep them at bay.

She didn't want to let him see her cry.

"Hey," he soothed, rubbing his hand up and down her arm for comfort. "I'll be okay. I swear it."

She nodded into his chest, but kept her face buried against him so he wouldn't read her fear on her face.

"Rita," he said, and gently moved her head back so he could look down into her eyes. "I swear to you. I'll be back. And I'll come to you."

"You'd better," she quipped, trying to take the pain out of goodbye. "I have two older brothers who will beat you up if I ask them to."

"Well, now I'm scared." He grinned, kissed her again, running his tongue over her lips until she parted them, sighing at the invasion of her mouth. When he had her completely stirred up, he pulled back again. "I never thought to find someone like you, Rita. Trust me when I say I don't want to lose you."

"I'm glad. I don't want to lose you, either, Jack."

"You won't."

Late-afternoon sunlight spilled into the room and bathed the two of them in a golden haze. A soft, cool breeze ruffled the curtains hanging at the partially opened window.

Letting his gaze sweep up and down her body, he finally met her eyes again and whispered, "You are the best thing that's ever happened to me, Rita. Never forget that."

Oh, God. That sounded too final and she couldn't accept that. He had to come home. To her. So she smiled and fought for courage.

"Don't you forget it, either," she said.

"Not a chance."

He kissed her again and she knew it was goodbye. He had to leave. See his family before shipping out in the morning. And she had a flight to Utah to catch.

When he slid off the bed and grabbed his jeans, she sat up, dragging the coverlet up to cover her breasts. Pushing her hair back out of her eyes, she watched him dress and her mouth went dry.

"You'll write to me," she said, not a question.

"I will." He patted the pocket of his shirt. "I've got your address and you'll have mine as soon as you get a letter from me. I'd give it to you now, but I can't be sure it won't change. Hell, I'm not even sure my email address will be the same."

"Doesn't matter." She shook her head, went up on her knees and reached for him. He held her close and she locked her arms around his waist, resting her head on his chest. She heard the steady beat of his heart and prayed it would remain safe and steady until she was with him again. "Just write to me, Jack. And let me know you're safe."

He tipped her chin up with the tips of his fingers. "And when I'm coming home."

"That, too." He kissed her again, looked long and deep into her eyes, then turned for the door. At the threshold, he paused, turned back and sighed. "You take my breath away."

She covered her mouth with one hand and knew she would soon lose the battle with her tears. "Be safe, Jack. And come home to me."

He gave her a sharp nod, then turned and left, the door closing quietly behind him. Alone, Rita walked to the window, the coverlet a toga of sorts, around her naked body. She pulled the edges of the curtains back, looked down into the parking lot and saw him, taking long, sure strides toward his black Jeep.

As if he could sense her watching him, he turned, looked up at her and simply held her gaze for several long seconds. Then he got in the car and drove away.

But he never wrote. He never came to her. If she hadn't moved to Long Beach to feel closer to a memory, she might never have known he was even alive. Was that Fate blessing them? Or cursing them?

"Down! Get down!"

Startled at the muffled shout, Rita jumped to her feet and whipped her head around to stare at the darkened hall leading to Jack's bedroom. Starting down the hall, the wood floor was cold against her bare feet. With every step she took, his voice came louder, more desperate.

She ran, following his shouts, his pain.

Her heart.

Seven

Jack shouted himself awake, jolted upright in bed and struggled to breathe. The dream—*nightmare*—still held him in a tightfisted grip and he had to force himself to look around the moonlit room to orient himself. He was home, yet his heart still raced and his mouth and throat were dry. A black duvet pooled in his lap, his bare chest was covered in sweat and his gaze was wild. He scrubbed one hand across his face, rubbing his eyes as if he could wipe away the fear raised by the images still stamped in his mind.

"Jack? Jack, are you okay?" Rita hurried into the room.

"I'm fine," he muttered thickly, jumping out of bed. *Perfect. Just perfect.* He'd woken her up and now she'd stare at him with either pity or fear and he didn't think he could take either.

He wore loosely tied cotton pants that dipped low on his hips and he was grateful he'd decided not to sleep naked since she'd moved in. Damn it. Jack needed a little time to get a grip. To shove those memories back into the dark corner of his mind where they were usually locked away. He needed to be clearheaded when he talked to Rita. Jack just didn't see that happening anytime soon.

He pushed one hand through his hair and looked at her as if she were a mirage. Jack had pulled himself out of a hot, dusty dream where the sound of explosions and gunfire still echoed in the stillness around him. Seeing her here, in the dark moon-washed confines of his bedroom, a world away from the scene that still haunted him, was almost too much to compute. "Sorry I woke you. Just…go back to sleep."

He turned his back on her, hoping to hell she'd leave, and walked out onto the terrace, welcoming the brisk slap of wind. Sea spray scented the air that he dragged into his lungs, to replace the dry dustiness that felt as though it was coating him in more than memories.

"Jack?"

Damn.

She'd followed him onto the terrace and the touch of her hand against his bare back had him flinching. Every nerve in his body was firing, on alert.

"What is it?" She stood right behind him, her voice soft, low, soothing. "*Talk* to me."

He whipped his head around to glare at her. "I don't want to talk. That should be clear. Just leave me alone, Rita. You don't want to be with me right now."

"Yeah," she insisted and didn't look the least bit cowed. "I do. Or I wouldn't be here."

Gritting his teeth, Jack ground out tightly, "I'm on the ragged edge here, Rita. I need some space."

"No, you don't."

He choked out a harsh laugh. "Is that right? And you're an expert on me, is that it?"

"Enough to know that you've had enough space," she countered, stepping in closer. "Too much, maybe. Everyone backs off when you tell them to, but I won't. I'm here, Jack, and I'm not going anywhere. You can't use a nasty tone and a miserable attitude to shake me off. *Talk* to me."

His skin was buzzing, his mind racing and his heartbeat was still at a fast gallop. Jack had come out of that damn dream ready to fight, but there was no enemy to face. He needed to move. To fight. To do *something*, to expel the ghosts gathered around him, shrieking for his attention.

"Damn it, Jack," Rita said, tugging at his forearm until he turned to face her again. Her whiskey eyes were hot, burning with passion and fury and he wasn't sure which had top billing.

"I'm not deaf or blind," she said. "I heard you shouting. I stepped into your room in time to see you bolt up in bed as if the hounds of hell were after you."

She'd hit that one on the head. Scraping one hand over his face, he muttered, "They were."

"Then tell me." She held on to him, the heat of her touch sliding into his arm, moving through his bloodstream. "Let me in, damn it. What does it cost you to open the door just a crack?"

He speared her with a hard look. There was no pity, no fear in her eyes. Only concern and curiosity and maybe that was worse in some ways.

"You think it's *me* I'm worried about?" He grabbed her shoulders, giving her a little shake for emphasis. "It's *you* I'm thinking about here. I'm trying to save you, don't you get it?"

"Save me? From what?"

"God, you won't let this go," he muttered thickly.

"Not a chance."

He stared into her eyes. "Fine. I'm trying to save you from me. Okay? I don't even trust myself around you right now."

"That's ridiculous."

There was a response he hadn't expected.

"You're not trying to injure me in some way, Jack," she pointed out, her voice a little louder, her eyes a little more fiery. "You've done your best to simply avoid me at all costs."

"There's a reason—"

"Did I ask you to save me?" she interrupted, breaking free of his grip. The cold ocean air lifted her hair into a cloud of dark curls around her head and with the flash in her eyes, she looked like a pagan goddess. Even the nightgown she wore that was hot-pink with the image of a cupcake on it and the words *SWEET THING* scrawled across the top couldn't diminish her. No, not a goddess, he corrected. Instead, she looked like a short, Italian Valkyrie. She was furious and her eyes were shot with sparks.

She poked her index finger into the center of his chest. "I'm a big girl. I save myself when I need it. I don't need a knight in shining armor, Jack." She shoved her hair out of her eyes impatiently. "What I need is for my *husband* to tell me what's tearing at him."

"You would have made a great warrior, Rita," he said

softly, gaze raking her up and down, from her bare toes with their purple-polished nails up to the eyes that were so incensed he was surprised she wasn't actually shooting flames from them. "You are a Fury, aren't you? Not afraid of anything."

"Not afraid of *you*, anyway," she said, whipping her head back to shake her hair free of her eyes.

How the hell was a man supposed to win an argument with a woman like this? How was he supposed to ignore her, ignore what she made him feel?

"Maybe you should be," he said, pulling her in close with one quick move. "And if I were a better man, I'd tell you to leave. Now. But I'm not—so if you want to run, now's your chance."

She reached up, cupped his face in her palms and demanded, "Does it look like I'm going anywhere?"

"No. Thank God." He bent his head, and took her mouth in a kiss that was filled with the hunger and desperation he'd felt since she reentered his life.

With the dregs of the nightmare still clinging to him, Jack held her tighter, his hands running up and down her back and down to her bottom. He pulled her against his rock-hard body and she wriggled closer in appreciation. Expectation. His blood ran hot and fast, his heartbeat raced and his mind was fogged by the want choking him. *Need* was alive and shouting inside him.

The cold ocean wind wrapped itself around them, but he didn't feel it. Nothing could vanquish the internal heat. One hand cupped the back of her head and held her still so he could completely claim her mouth. His tongue tangled with hers and her eager response fed the flames licking at his soul.

There was no time for romance, seduction. He needed to be with her. In her. Over her. Tearing his mouth from hers, he looked down into her now-glassy eyes and fought to breathe.

"What're you doing?" she managed to ask breathlessly. "Why are you stopping?"

"Not stopping. Changing location." He bent down, scooped her up and carried her back through the French doors and into his bedroom. Moonlight followed them, the wind rushed in behind them and none of that mattered. He laid her down on the mattress and, in one deft move, stripped her nightgown off, leaving her naked—just as he wanted her. She scooted back farther on the mattress and reached for him. Jack didn't keep her waiting. He yanked off the sleep pants he was wearing and joined her on the bed an instant later. His hands moved over her, exploring every curve. Every line.

He remembered this so well. Had tormented himself over the last few months, by recalling the feel of her skin, the lush fullness of her breasts and the taut, dark nipples that he loved to suckle.

And now, because of the baby, she was so much more than she had been. She was ripe, delectable and more alluring than ever. Even as he thought it, though, both of her hands went to the mound of her belly as if to hide it from him. He drew her hands away and said, "Don't. You're beautiful."

She laughed. "I'm huge."

He shook his head. "No. Curvy. Delicious. Amazing."

She sighed a little. "Wow. When you try, you really know the right things to say."

He grinned, bent his head and indulged himself in

what he'd wanted to do for weeks now. He took one nipple into his mouth and savored the taste of her. Her scent invaded him, the soft sighs and moans sliding from her throat enflamed him. He ran his tongue and teeth across the tip of her nipple and then suckled, drawing her very essence into himself.

She planted her feet on the mattress and lifted her hips. "Touch me, Jack. Touch me."

He did. Sweeping one hand down the length of her body, he cupped her center and used his thumb to brush across her most sensitive spot. She jerked beneath him and he smiled against her breast, relishing her reaction. He suckled harder, and then lifted his head to switch to her other breast and she went crazy in his arms. As if the need that had been building between them for weeks had finally reached a breaking point for both of them, she rocked her hips into his hand.

He pushed two fingers into her heat and groaned himself at the slick, tight feel of her. It had been too long. His body was ready to explode and so was hers. He couldn't wait another minute to be inside her, to feel her body surrounding his.

Lifting his head, he looked down at her then kissed her briefly. "At least we don't need a condom now."

"Points for us," she said, swallowing hard, breath coming in short, hard gasps. "Damn it, Jack, don't drag this out. I need you inside me."

"Just what I need, too," he said, and shifted position to kneel between her thighs. He spread her legs wide and looked down at her. She was wanton, wild and everything he'd ever wanted in a woman. And for this one moment at least, she was his again—as she was always meant to be.

His mind whispered that this was temporary. That this marriage wasn't real and he was nobody's idea of husband material anyway. But he shut that nagging voice down and surrendered to the mating call trumpeting through his body.

He ran his hands over her hot, slick center, watching her twist and writhe in her own desperate need.

Her response pushed his own desires beyond what he could bear. Body throbbing, heart galloping, he leaned over her and pushed himself inside her. That first, glorious slide filled him with the kind of ease he hadn't known in months. This was what had been missing in his life. This sense of rightness that claimed him when their bodies were joined.

She hooked her legs at his hips and pulled him in tighter, deeper. Tipping her head back into the mattress, she bit her lip and moved with him. Their bodies meshed, linked in the most intimate way possible, he felt the pounding of her heart. Saw the flash in her eyes, heard her gasping breaths and experienced her body quaking, quivering as he pushed her higher, faster than they'd ever gone before.

Her nails scored his back as he rocked in and out of her body, setting a rhythm she raced to meet. "Jack! Jack!"

"Come on, Rita," He urged, barely able to frame the words as his breath sawed in and out of his lungs. "Go over. Go over so I can follow."

She clung to him and shouted his name when the first tremors took her. He felt her body tighten around his in spasms of delight and when she'd reached her peak, Jack let go and found the peace that had been denied him for months.

* * *

Rita took some deep breaths and tried to ease the frantic beat of her heart at the same time. It had been six long months since he'd touched her like that. Time in which she'd almost convinced herself that her memory was making what they shared much better than it actually had been. Well, she told herself, *that* theory was just shot out of the sky.

Her whole body was so alight with sensation she thought she should glow in the dark. And even while she tried to regain control, she was thinking about doing it all again. She turned her head to look at Jack, lying beside her. One arm flung across his eyes, his chest heaved with every breath and she smiled, knowing that he was just as shaken as she. Had she finally broken through the wall he'd built around himself? Was her Jack finally back?

"You owe me twenty bucks," he said softly.

She blinked at him, then laughed. "Seriously? You want a *tip*?"

He lowered his arm and turned his gaze on her. "Nope. A bet we made. Not only did you marry me when you said you wouldn't, you just—"

She held up one hand. "I know what I just—" then she slapped both hands to her hips as if checking for a wallet "—I don't seem to have any pockets at the moment so I'll have to owe you."

One corner of his mouth quirked. "I suppose I can live with that."

Rolling to one side, he propped himself up on one elbow and looked down at her. "Rita—"

She stopped him by laying her fingers on his mouth. Disappointment welled in her chest. Looking into his eyes, she could see that her Jack was still buried behind a shutter of ice. Maybe there were a few cracks in that cold stillness, but it was a seductive stranger staring at her through Jack's eyes. Her heart hurt for it, but she wouldn't give up. Now more than ever, it was important to find a way to completely reach him.

"Don't you dare apologize for this," she said firmly. "*Or* tell me that it'll never happen again—"

He tried to speak, but she hurried on. "We both wanted this, Jack. And I want it again right now."

"Want isn't the point," he ground out as he laid one arm across her middle.

"Then what is?" She reached up and smoothed his hair back from his forehead, just because she wanted her fingers in that thick, wavy mass. Rita needed to touch him, to ground herself and hopefully *him*. To remind them both that the threads binding them were still there. They hadn't been broken, only strained. She had to believe they could strengthen them again.

"Talk to me," she said, locking her gaze on his so that he could see how much she wanted this. That when he told his story, whatever it was, he would still be safe with her. "Tell me what you were dreaming. Why were you shouting? What made you grab hold of me and hang on like I was a lifeboat in a tsunami?"

He scowled, but she was so used to that expression now, it didn't even affect her. "I don't want to talk about it."

"Just dream about it then?" she countered, refusing to give up on him. *Them.* "Don't you see that if you do tell me, maybe it will make the dreams fade?"

"Nothing can."

Then the baby kicked and his features went blank

with surprise. He glanced down to where his arm rested across her belly and then he sucked in a gulp of air when the baby kicked again, as if reminding its parents that they weren't alone. His astonished gaze snapped to hers. "That was—"

"A good kick," she finished for him. She knew what he was feeling, because she'd felt exactly the same the first time the baby'd moved. It was magic, she knew. Staggering. That tiny life making itself known. Taking his hand, she held it tightly to the mound of their child.

On cue, another kick came and Jack's eyes went wide even as an unexpected grin lit his face. "Strong baby."

That wide smile of his tugged at her heart. "Like its father."

Just like that, his smile faded into memory. Pulling away from her grasp, he asked, "What is it? The baby, I mean. Do you know?"

If he hadn't pulled away from her, Rita would have thought that she was making more progress with him. He hadn't once asked about the baby before, so normally, she would have celebrated internally that he was feeling...linked. But the look in his eyes was cool, not warm, and so she had to admit that nothing had changed.

"No," she said sadly, sorry that he was withdrawing again. "I didn't want to know ahead of time. I wanted to be surprised. There aren't many real surprises left in the world."

"*You* always surprised me," he said. "Still do." Just for a second, she saw another crack in the wall around him. Then it was gone and as if to prove it to her, he turned and pushed off the bed.

He walked naked to the open French doors and out

onto the terrace. On the twenty-fifth floor, facing the ocean, there was no one to see them. No nosy neighbors.

He stood there in the cold wind, his hair lifted off his neck and Rita wanted to touch it, feel it against her skin again. Broad shoulders, narrow hips and long, muscular legs made her mouth water, but while her blood burned, her mind mourned because he was trying to pull away from her. Again.

But Rita wasn't going to let him. Not this time. Scrambling off the bed, she went to him and pulled at his upper arm until he turned to face her. "I'm not going to quit trying to reach you, Jack."

He shook his head. "Did you ever think that maybe there's nothing to reach?"

"No." She shook her head, too, just as fiercely determined to find him as he was to hide. "There's *you*, Jack. And I'm not going to stop pestering, pushing you. I'm not going to stop asking you what happened, so you might as well give in now and tell me."

"Damn, you've got a hard head," he murmured, with the faintest of smiles.

"That's been said before." She looked at him ruefully. "By *you*, mostly. Jack, tell me. Tell me what's haunting you."

He grimaced. "*Haunting* is the right word for it."

"Talk."

A harsh laugh that held no humor scraped his throat and his gaze swung past her to lock on the dark, roiling ocean. But he looked more as though he was focusing on something only he could see. His ghosts. His past. And finally, Rita thought, he was going to bring her into the shadows with him. Maybe then, she'd be able to hold his hand and lead him back into the light.

"You want to know?" He blew out a breath. "Fine. Here it is. Two days after I left you, I was back with my unit." He glanced at her briefly before turning his gaze to the sea. "I was actually writing you a letter when my squad was sent out to do some recon on a nearby village."

Her heartbeat stuttered a little, knowing that he had been keeping his promise to write and a little fearful of what had kept him from completing that letter. Rita watched him, judging every tiny twist of his features, trying to guess at the turnings of his mind, at the nearness of his ghosts. Her gaze on his profile, she held her breath and waited.

His voice sounded far away as if he wasn't really there with her at all, but instead, he was caught in his memories. He was somehow more a part of his past than he was a part of his life, here. She had to know why.

"We were told there was sniper activity so we were careful. Well, thought we were." He shook his head, gritted his teeth and forced the words out. "I'm not going into details here, Rita. You don't need to know them anyway. Short version. One of my guys was shot. We took cover, a couple of men breaking right while my best friend and I went left, dragging the wounded man with us."

"Jack..." She put one hand on his forearm.

"There was an IED on the left."

Tears drenched her eyes. She didn't know what was coming next, but her heart ached just looking at his stony profile, the hard set of his jaw, his narrowed gaze.

"The wounded man was killed. My friend Kevin got hit hard. His legs." He blew out a breath then dragged in another gulp of the cold, sea air. Shaking his head, he swallowed hard and continued, "Somehow, we got the sniper and then I could work on Kevin's wounds. I got tourniquets on him but he fought me." He paused, to steady himself, to distance himself from the pain? She couldn't know. But he kept talking, so she stayed quiet.

"Kevin didn't want to live without his legs—kept cursing at me to leave him be. I wouldn't listen. Couldn't let him die."

"Of course not." God, to have such scenes and more in your head. To see them in your sleep. His sister, Cass, was right. These guys weren't sick. They were hurt. Right down to their souls. Rita wrapped her arms around him and held on whether he was aware of her or not.

"We called for medics and evac. One guy dead, two wounded and Kevin, half-conscious and still cursing me for saving him." Jack scrubbed one hand across his mouth as if he could somehow wipe away the taste of his own words. Then he finally shifted his gaze to hers and when she looked into his eyes, Rita felt the sympathy he'd already said he didn't want.

"I couldn't write to you after that," he said. "Couldn't even think about you. I talked to my friend's widow after they notified her and left her broken to pieces. She loved Mike so much that losing him shattered her completely. Then I went to see my best friend, Kevin, before they flew him out for surgery and he wouldn't even talk to me.

"Hell, he wouldn't *look* at me. All those curses he'd brought down on my head for saving him were still running through my head and probably his. It was like I was dead to him."

"You never talked to him again?"

"No." Jack took a breath and blew it out again. "He contacted me a couple of months ago, but I didn't get back to him."

"Why not?"

"What's the point, Rita?" He shoved both hands through his hair. "You think I want to stand there, look at him in a chair and have him ream me all over again? No, thanks."

She felt for him. He'd saved his friend, done his best for him and the man had fought him every step of the way. No wonder he was tortured by nightmares and didn't want to talk about what he remembered. But things might have changed for his friend by now. Maybe he wanted to make amends with Jack and by not allowing it, Jack kept the pain close and fresh.

"You don't know what he wanted," she told him. "Maybe he wanted to say thank you."

"I don't need to be thanked, either," he snapped. "I did what I had to do. That's it."

The emptiness in Jack's eyes was so profound, Rita didn't know how he could still be standing. He had to be the strongest man she'd ever known. And the most alone. Even with a family who loved him, a wife and a child on the way, he was so terribly alone.

Voice brisk, letting her know this little truth-telling session was now at an end, he said, "Anyway. After all that, I had nothing left for you, Rita." Shaking his head, he said softly, "Still don't. I'm not the guy you knew. Hell, I don't even recognize that man anymore."

"Well, I do," she said, going up on her toes to kiss him. "I know him. I still see him when I look into your eyes. And I know you're punishing yourself for something that wasn't your fault."

"My squad. My calls."

"And you think I have a hard head."

He glanced at her, surprise flickering in his eyes.

"Jack, you were ordered to check out that village. You all took cover. What happened, just…happened. You're not in charge of who lives and dies. Jack, you did the best you could."

"Wasn't good enough," he insisted.

"It was, because it was all you *could* do." Now that she knew, she could almost understand him cutting himself off from her, from his family, from everything that was important to him.

He'd seen too much loss. And he didn't want to risk more of it. So by shutting down his heart, he thought he was protecting himself. Instead, he'd welcomed a different kind of pain. Rita laid her head on his chest and listened to the wild thumping of his heart. He stiffened against her and for a second, she thought he was going to shove her aside, but instead, he grabbed her tight, pulled her closer. Buried his face in the curve of her neck.

"Damn it, Rita," he murmured, "you should have left it alone."

"I can't do that, Jack. I can't leave *you* alone." She wondered if he heard the love in her voice. If he understood how much she was feeling for him or that it was so much bigger than what she'd felt for him when they first met.

She held him, rubbing her hands up and down his back, wishing she could reach past the shadows inside him, wishing she could convince him that he wasn't at fault. But all she could do was *show* him. What she felt. What she saw when she looked at him.

Drawing his head up, she kissed him, pouring everything she had into the kiss and was rewarded when he groaned and took everything she offered. Her head was spinning when he fast-walked her back to the bed, when he stretched her out and claimed her in every way possible.

Rita's mind blanked out and her body took over. Sensation flooded her. Tingles of awareness swarmed through her and curls of delicious tension settled in the pit of her stomach and spread like a wildfire. His hands, his mouth, moved over her, driving her wild, until the flames he lit enveloped them both.

She touched and stroked and kissed, wanting him to experience everything she was. Wanting him to know that he wasn't alone. That she was here. With him. Wanted him to *feel* the love she couldn't bring herself to say yet.

Oh, yes, she still loved him. Yes, she still wanted the happily-ever-after with him. But she knew instinctively that he wouldn't want to hear that now. So she kept it tucked inside and told herself that they were a matched set. Each of them locking away a piece of themselves they wanted no one else to see.

Then he entered her, and all thought fled. She focused only on what he was doing to her, making her feel. His body moved within hers and the incredible friction left her breathless and she didn't care. Breathing was overrated. She didn't need air when she had Jack.

He took her higher than she'd gone before, pushing her to reach for the completion she knew was waiting. Rita kept her gaze locked on his. She couldn't have looked away if it had meant her life. Those ice-blue eyes warmed and steamed and glowed with passion. Watching him and her own reflection in his eyes, she shattered, her body simply splintering into jagged pieces of pleasure that had her screaming his name and clutching his shoulders. And only a moment later, he surrendered to her, emptying himself into her and she held him while he fell.

Eight

"**D**on't start thinking anything's changed," Jack warned her the next morning.

Rita bit her lip and hid a smile. She had been expecting this. She'd known that after what they'd shared the night before Jack would try to pull back again. Pretend that last night hadn't happened. And she'd come up with a way to combat it. She wasn't going to argue. She was simply going to ignore *his* arguments.

Rita had had a long night to think about this. Naturally there hadn't been any snuggling or cuddling after their amazing bout of lovemaking—and that's what it had been whether he admitted it or not. It wasn't just sex. It was making love. And though Rita had spent the rest of the night alone in the guest room, she'd been more hopeful than she had been in six months.

He might not realize it yet, but there was a chink in

the wall he was hiding behind. For one brief moment, he'd let his guard down. Let her in. Sure, he'd slammed it shut again quickly, but now that she'd made it through once, she was determined to do it again. Alone in the silence of her own room, Rita had vowed to smash those walls around Jack until nothing was left but the two of them standing in the rubble.

"Okay," she said brightly. "Got it. Nothing's changed. This ship is just gorgeous."

"What?"

She looked at him, pleased to see the confusion on his features. If she kept him off balance, it would be harder for him to plant his feet behind that damn wall.

"I said this ship is gorgeous." Rita did a fast circle on the main deck of *The Sea Queen*, taking in the gleaming wood floors, the shining windows and the sweep of sea stretching out behind it. "I've never been on a cruise ship before. For some reason I didn't realize just how *big* they are."

"Yeah," he said irritably, "it's great."

"Thanks for inviting me along to see the ship."

"I didn't invite you. *You* invited you."

"True," she said with a shrug, "but you didn't fight me on it. That was practically gracious. Congrats."

He frowned again and Rita had to fight to hide the smile tugging at her mouth. "So, do you really have to meet with the captain?"

Still frowning, he glanced around, then up at the bridge. "Just to say hello, let him know I'm doing a walk-through."

"Do you want me with you or can I wander?"

"Come with me, then wander," he said, heading toward the wide open doors that led to the main lobby and reception area.

Rita was grinning as she followed him inside, then she stopped dead, her mouth dropped open and she did a slow turn to take it all in.

The Sea Queen was palatial. A tiled floor was inlaid with a depiction of what looked like a Middle Ages golden crown. There was a staircase that was so wide she suspected trucks could pass through side by side. Copper railings lined the second and third stories that looked down onto the lobby and deep scarlet rugs climbed the stairs. The ceiling was draped with pendant lights in shades of copper and brass and the walls boasted murals of what, again, looked like the Middle Ages. There was a theme here that went toward ancient royalty, with a hint of magic.

"At night, the pendant lights glow, and starlight flickers against the black ceiling."

"Wow." She didn't even look at him. "I seriously love this. It's very…magical. I half expect to see wizards and witches walk through the doors."

"Good," he said, shoving both hands into the pockets of his black jeans. "That's what we were going for. The club rooms and bars are all done with the same kind of decor. A little mystical. A lot upscale."

Now she did look at him in time to see a flash of pride cross his face. "It's really spectacular," she said.

Nodding, he said, "Let's find the captain, then I'll show you a few of the staterooms."

She took his hand and counted it a victory when he didn't shake her off, instead holding on to her fingers as if she were a lifeline.

On the bridge, Rita was stunned. It was a huge room,

with windows giving the crew an incredibly wide view of the sea. There were enough computers to make it look like a spaceship rather than a cruise ship.

Captain McManus, a tall, gray-haired man with sharp brown eyes and an easy smile, welcomed them both then took Jack to one side to go over a few things. Rita didn't mind. It gave her a chance to look around and appreciate the nearly bird's-eye view of the ocean and the Long Beach harbor.

There were two tall command chairs that reminded her of something off the Starship *Enterprise*'s bridge and counters filled with screens, blinking lights and men and women busily going over everything. She could only imagine how busy they were when they were actually at sea.

And what would that be like, she wondered. Being on this luxurious ship, sailing off to other countries, meeting new people. She looked up at Jack. "You've been on a lot of cruises, haven't you?"

"A few," he said, looking out over the water. "When we were kids, my folks liked to pile us all on one of the ships for a couple of weeks." His features softened at the good memory. "Mom used to say it was the only way she could get all of us to stay in the same place for any length of time."

"That must have been fun," she said, a little wistfully. "I've never been on one myself. Just a little too spooky, I guess. All of that water—"

He shook his head and said, "Doesn't seem that way, though. Once you're on board, it's like you're on your own private island."

"Well," she said, glancing around, "this ship is big enough that maybe even I wouldn't be nervous."

"I can't imagine you scared of anything," Jack said.

She looked up into his eyes. If he only knew that the one thing that scared her was losing him again. She'd mourned him once and now she had him back. Rita was determined that she wouldn't let him go this time.

"You ready to see other parts of the ship?"

She half turned to look up at Jack. "Sure. I'd love to. But first let me say, the bridge is amazing. And a little disappointing, too," she added.

"Really?" The captain laughed and asked, "Why?"

"Well, it sounds silly, but I sort of expected to see a wheel up here."

Jack smiled and the captain let out a laugh that had several of his officers turning to stare at him in surprise.

"No," Captain McManus said finally. "Everything's done by computer now. Not as romantic but much more efficient."

"I suppose," she said, then held out one hand to the man. "Thank you for letting me look around."

"For the boss's wife?" He shook her hand and winked. "Anytime at all."

"Thanks, Captain," Jack said. "We'll let you get back to it."

"Excellent. We'll be ready to sail on time, Mr. Buchanan."

"Good to know."

When they left, Rita took Jack's hand again and walked beside him on the catwalk surrounding the bridge. The sea air flew fast and furious this high up and gave her a chill that was dispelled by Jack's big hand holding hers.

"We'll take the elevator down and I'll show you the

theatres, the pools and a few of the club and casino lounges."

"Okay." She whipped her hair back to look up at him. "So, you're glad you invited me along?"

His lips twitched. "I didn't invite you."

"You wish you had."

"Maybe." He glanced at her, gave her hand a squeeze, then steered her into an elevator.

There were mirrors on every surface and Rita couldn't help but look at him. The man was so gorgeous, she could have stared at him for hours. His features were strong and sharp and had been honed down over the last several months, giving him the look of a saint with a wicked side.

He met her gaze in the mirror and just for a second, the power of his stare was enough to punch her heart into a frantic beat.

"You okay?"

"Fine," she said, though she really wasn't. How could she be, when she was in love with a man who didn't want to be loved?

The elevator stopped with a ding and he announced, "First stop, Deck Three."

Just like the rest of the ship, it was elegant and luxurious, from the brass sconces on the walls to the dark ruby carpet on the floor. Then her gaze focused on the solid white surface stretching out in front of them. "There's an ice-skating rink?"

He laughed. "We've got everything."

Her imagination completed the picture, with families moving across the ice, laughing, making memories. She could almost hear them echoing in the now-empty space.

"Oh, I miss skating," she said, and rubbed one hand over her belly. "But my center of gravity's a little whacked right now, so…"

"Yeah, well, you can always skate when you're back in Utah after the baby's born."

It was a slap. A reminder. *Don't get comfortable*, he was saying. *I won't let you in. I won't let you stay. I won't let myself care.*

Rita almost swayed with the emotional impact, but she locked her knees because she couldn't let him see what he could so easily do to her. She wanted to argue with him, tell him she loved him and she wasn't going anywhere. But Rita remembered that she'd made the decision to simply not engage when he pulled back. When he tried to shut her out. So she smiled instead, though that small curve of her mouth cost her more than he would ever know.

"Yes. There's plenty of time for skating after the baby." She looked around. "Where's the theatre? What movie's playing?"

"Not a movie theatre," he said, frowning at her, as if waiting for her real reaction to what he'd said. "It's for live shows. The movies are up on Deck Eight, along with a spa and a casino and stuff for the kids and—" He broke off. "Hell, who can remember it all?"

"So, show me." She started walking in the direction he'd pointed. He was still holding her hand though and tugged her to a stop.

"Rita, last night, what I told you—"

"It's okay, Jack. Whatever you tell me is safe with me," she assured him.

"It's not that. It's…" He paused, took a breath and then released it again. "I want you to know that I made a vow to myself. You keep telling me how I'm keeping my family—and you—at a distance. You're right. But it's with a purpose. I swore I would never put anyone in the position of mourning me—and now I've got you. And the baby. And if I let my family get close again, let *you* get close, then I risk causing pain. I won't do it."

She didn't even know what to say to that.

"Rita—" His eyes were shadowed. "Bottom line, I don't want to hurt you."

Foolish man. Couldn't he see that's exactly what he was doing? Did he really believe that causing pain *now* was better than later? His family was already in pain because they couldn't reach him. And she knew just how they felt. But Rita knew he wouldn't want to hear that.

"Good." She nodded sharply. "I don't want to hurt you, either."

"Great. But my point is…"

"Oh, don't worry so much, Jack." She looked at him and the sunlight filtering through all the windows threw golden light across his face. "I get it. Nothing's changed. You're still locking yourself away from the world to save the rest of us."

He didn't want to hurt her, but he didn't want to love her, either. She had to force a smile again and he would never know how much it cost her.

He frowned. "That's—"

Rita kept her voice light, as she added, "Not important right now. I said I don't want to hurt you, but I might if you don't show me where the closest bathroom is. Honestly, this baby must be camped out on my bladder."

"Oh. Right." With the subject neatly changed, he

led her down one side of the ship and waited as she went inside.

Rita hadn't really needed the bathroom, for a change. What she'd needed was a minute or two to herself. To think. To search her heart and find the strength to keep pretending that he couldn't rip a chunk out of her soul with a word.

She gripped the edge of the black marble countertop and stared into the mirror at her own reflection. Her eyes had so many things to say and she didn't want to hear any of them. Maybe she was being foolish for loving a man who so clearly wasn't interested in making the same kind of commitment.

But how could she simply stop?

Besides, the very fact that he was trying to warn her off, save her from him, told her that he *did* care. More than he wanted to.

"And, it's not like you get a *choice* about who you love," she told her reflection. And scowled a little when her mirror image mocked her. "Fine," she admitted, "even if I *had* a choice, I'd still choose him."

Did that make her a martyr? An idiot? "Neither," she decided, staring into her own eyes. "It makes me Rita Marchetti Buchanan. I love him. It's as simple as that, really."

Nodding to herself, she shook her hair back, gave her baby belly a consoling rub, then lifted her chin and went back to face her husband with a smile.

The next few days weren't easy. Jack had expected Rita to be a little more…depressed, he guessed, about the fact that he'd brushed off their night of sex as changing nothing.

Of course, it *had*, he just couldn't admit that. Not to himself and certainly not to her. But the truth was, now that he'd been with her again, that was all he could think about.

Apparently, though, Rita was having a much easier time of it. She'd moved on as if she'd felt nothing and that he knew was a damn lie. He'd watched her, heard her, *felt* her response to their lovemaking. But she'd set it all aside and rather than being relieved, Jack was just a little ticked off. What the hell?

She wasn't talking about it and he'd fully expected her to go all female on him. Women always wanted to *talk*. To *share*. The fact that Rita wasn't bugged him. He couldn't put his finger on what was happening and that bothered him, too. Jack felt off balance somehow and he wasn't sure when that had happened.

His new reality was simply marching on as if nothing had changed at all. Every morning, since he refused to have her drive across town all by herself at four thirty in the morning, he was up and taking her to the bakery. Where she made him coffee and fresh pastries and they had breakfast together while she talked nonstop, telling him stories about her family, talking about her plans for the bakery, refusing to accept his silence.

She pushed him for his opinion and when she didn't agree with him, she goaded him into an argument. Hell, he hadn't talked this much in the four months since he'd been home.

Every night, she was right there, whether she was cooking in the penthouse kitchen or they were ordering takeout. Rita made him a part of it. She poked and prodded at him until she got him to talk about his work, about their tour of *The Sea Queen*, readying to set sail. She poked her nose into his relationship with his brother, sister and father. Nothing was sacred, Jack told himself. The woman was making herself such a presence in his life, he couldn't ignore her in spite of how hard he tried.

And every night, when she was in the guest room and he was alone in his huge, empty bed, he really tried. But her face was uppermost in his mind all the damn time. He closed his eyes to sleep and she was there. The pillow she'd used still carried her scent.

How the hell was a man supposed to do the right thing when everything in him was demanding he do the *wrong* thing?

"Hey, Jack?"

He closed his eyes and sighed a little. Even shutting himself up in his home office the minute he got home didn't work. Rita would not be stopped. "What is it?"

"Someone's here to see you."

What was she up to now? he wondered. Had she brought his whole family over? Hers? Were they all going to sit in a circle and hold hands? Frowning, he pushed up from the desk, crossed the room and stalked out into the living room, half-ready for battle.

Rita was sitting on the couch, smiling at the man opposite her. Jack stopped dead when he spotted the man's wheelchair. *Kevin.* Had to be. His chest felt tight as if something was squeezing his lungs like a lemon trying for as much juice as possible. His gaze snapped to Rita. Had she done this? No. Of course not. He hadn't even told her Kevin's last name. There was no way she could have found him and arranged to get him to the penthouse.

So what the hell was going on?

"There he is!" Rita shot him a wide, bright smile of welcome. "Jack, look who's here."

The guy in the chair turned to face him and suddenly, time did a weird shift and it was nearly five months ago. The sun felt hot, oppressive. Screams tore at the air and Kevin's curses were loud and inventive as Jack worked to stop the bleeding. He felt again the raw desperation and the sense of helplessness as he shouted for a medic.

He was standing in the penthouse and yet he had one foot firmly planted in the past and no idea how to escape it.

"Dude," Kevin said on a laugh. "You look like you just saw a ghost."

In a way, he had, Jack told himself and shook his head, trying to clear the images rising up in his mind. For just a second, he'd seen Kevin as he'd been before that last mission. Tall, strong, laughing. Now reality was back and he didn't know what to say. "Surprised to see you is all."

"Yeah. It's been a while." Kevin rested his forearms on the arms of his chair and folded his hands together. His blond hair was just a little longer than it had been in the corps and his blue eyes were sharp, shrewd and locked on Jack. He'd lost some weight, but the real difference was the pinned-up legs of the slacks he wore.

Kevin Davis had lost both legs on that mission, in spite of the medics delivering fast, heroic care. And Jack hadn't talked to him since the morning he'd been evacced to a hospital ship. Even then, it had been less of a conversation and more of Kevin damning Jack to hell for saving him. Not something he liked to think about.

"You gonna say hello anytime soon?" Kevin asked with a tilted grin.

"Yeah. Sure." Jack crossed the room, held out one hand and looked down at his friend. "Good to see you, Kev."

After shaking hands, Jack sat on the couch beside Rita and asked, "So what brings you here?"

"Cut right to the chase, no bull," Kevin said, smiling even wider. "Haven't changed much, Sarge."

For a second, Jack felt a twinge. He'd been in the military for so long that becoming a civilian again had been a stretch. Now he wasn't sure where the hell he belonged. Then he felt Rita's hand sneak into his and though he told himself not to accept the comfort she was offering, his fingers linked through hers and locked them together.

Guilt pinged around the center of his chest like a Ping-Pong ball on steroids. Here he sat. Beautiful, pregnant wife. Elegant penthouse. Successful business. His life hadn't been shattered. He'd simply stepped back into it and though it hadn't been an easy adjustment, it had been nothing compared to what Kevin had no doubt gone through. Jack's tours of duty hadn't cost him what they had Kevin. And he couldn't make himself be okay with that.

His back teeth ground together and he fought against the rising tide of regret within. This was why he hadn't answered Kevin's email. Hell, why he hadn't even opened it. His memories were thick and rich enough that he didn't need a reminder—being with Kevin in person—to make them even more so. And hell, what could he say to the man? Kevin had lost his legs. Jack had come home whole, if changed. How was that fair?

How could he look into the man's eyes, knowing that it was he who had been leading that squad? It was Jack's decisions that had eventually brought about what had happened to Kevin. If they'd zigged instead of zagged, what might have changed? A man could drive himself crazy with thoughts like that.

How could Kevin not still blame him?

Jack had spent months trying to get past the memories of that one fateful day and hadn't been able to do it. How much more difficult was it for Kevin to try to move past it when every day he was faced with a physical reminder of his own limitations?

"Jack," Kevin said quietly, as if he knew exactly what his friend was thinking, feeling, *remembering*. "You don't have to do this. Don't have to feel bad for me. I'm fine. Really."

Now, looking into his old friend's eyes, Jack couldn't find any blame there, any anger. And that alone surprised him enough that he couldn't get his head straight.

Jack felt Rita give his hand a squeeze and he appreciated it. "I can see that. I'm glad for it."

"Now all you have to do is accept it." His friend nodded, kept his eyes fixed on Jack's. "Took me a long time, I admit it. For weeks after it happened, I'd wake up and try to swing my legs out of bed." A rueful smile curved his mouth. "Could have sworn I felt them there."

"Kevin—"

"I didn't come here to make things harder for you, Jack."

"Why are you here, then?" He managed to get the question out even though he was worried about the answer.

"To see you, you damn fool," Kevin said, leaning back in his chair, shaking his head. "You never answered the email I sent you two months ago. Hell, you never even opened it."

"Yeah." Jack nodded. "Sorry about that. I just—"

"I get it," Kevin said. "You still should have read it, though. Would have saved me a drive up from San Diego."

Jack smiled at that. He and Kevin had formed a friendship at first because they were both from Southern California. Just a couple hours away from each other by freeway, so they'd had a lot of the same experiences. They'd formed a tighter bond, of course, as all military in combat did, but it had begun on the California connection.

"So," Kevin was saying, waving one hand at the chair and his missing legs, "a lot of things have changed. Obviously."

Jack watched his friend, looking for some sign of anger or bitterness or blame and couldn't find any. Instead, he looked…comfortable in his skin. In that chair.

"But, hey," Kevin added, smiling at Rita. "Looks like you've had some pretty big changes, too. You're married now, having a baby."

Jack glanced at Rita, and when she smiled at him, he felt that tug of guilt again. Kevin couldn't know that this was a temporary arrangement. And there was no way Jack would let him know. He forced himself to look back to Kevin. "I'm glad you're okay."

"I'm better than okay." Kevin shook his head and gave Jack a wry smile. "If you'd bothered to open the damn email I sent you like two months ago, you would have known that."

Jack ran his free hand across his jaw. "I know. I'm

sorry. I should have. I just didn't want to go over what happened again."

"Hey," Kevin said softly, "neither do I. Look, Jack, last time I saw you, things were a little...*tense*."

Jack laughed shortly and held on a little more tightly to Rita's hand. "You could say that."

"Why don't I go make some coffee?" Rita looked at both men. "I'll give you guys some time to talk."

"Not necessary," Kevin told her. "I can't stay long, anyway, so don't go to any trouble for me."

"Stay, Rita," Jack said, looking into her eyes. He wanted her there. It surprised him to acknowledge just how much he wanted her beside him. Seeing Kevin again, watching him maneuver that wheelchair, tore at Jack and damned if he didn't want the connection to Rita to help him get through it.

When the hell had *that* happened? When had he started counting on her?

"If you're worried I'm here to cuss you out again for saving my butt, don't be." Kevin moved the chair in closer and linked his gaze to Jack's. "I remember it all, you know?"

"Yeah. I know." So did he. Every damn night, he remembered it. He always would.

Kevin smiled, nodded. "'Course you do. Hard to forget something like that—you doing your best to save me while I'm telling you to shoot me."

"Kevin—"

"Nah, man," he said, holding up one hand to keep Jack quiet. "I'm not here to go over it all again." He grinned. "Once was enough, trust me. I just wanted to say *thank you*."

"What?" Confused now, Jack just stared at him.

"Well, that surprised you," Kevin said wryly. "Yeah. Thank you. Thanks for saving me even when I was too stupid to want to be saved." He blew out a breath, dragged his fingers through his hair. "I swear, being furious at you got me through those first few days."

Jack nodded, took a breath and held it.

"But one day I realized that I like breathing," Kevin said. "So I started being less mad at you."

"Glad to hear it."

Kevin shrugged. "I'm not saying it was easy, getting used to being shorter—"

Rita smiled and he winked at her.

"But I did. And I'm here to tell you, alive is better than dead." Kevin held his hand out to Jack. "So thanks, man. Thanks for—hell. For everything."

Jack took his hand and felt one or two of those straws of guilt fall from his shoulders. He still had plenty left of course, but there was a sigh of relief to know that at least some of the burden had been eased. And Kevin *did* look good. Yeah, he was in a chair, but he looked strong and well and, damn it, *happy*. Jack had worried about his friend, thought that maybe he'd never really find any kind of contentment again.

"You're really okay."

"I'm *better* than okay, dude." Kevin slapped Jack's shoulder. "Again, man. Read your emails."

Rita squeezed Jack's hand again and in spite of the easing of the tension within, he held on to her tightly. "So why don't you just tell me what's in the email?"

"Turns out you're not the only one settling down. I'm getting married, can you believe it?" Kevin laughed, shook his head and said, "Lisa's a nurse. Hell, she was *my* nurse at Walter Reed. I showed up there all full of

myself and complaining and she just would not listen."
Still smiling, he continued, "The woman refused to let
me bitch. She ignored my crappy moods and pushed
me to come back to life when I really didn't want to."

Well, hell. Jack felt Rita's hand in his and told himself that he and Kevin had a lot more in common than
he would have guessed. Wasn't that just what Rita had
been doing to *him* for the last few weeks? Prodding,
pushing, refusing to give up and go away.

"Anyway, Lisa's a California girl—her folks live in
Oceanside—weird, huh? Go halfway around the world
to meet a girl who lived about twenty minutes from
me?" Kevin laughed a little. "So I got along so well,
they transferred me to a hospital out here and Lisa made
the move, too. We're getting married at my folks' place."

"Congratulations," Rita said, giving Jack a nudge.

"Right, yeah. I'm happy for you, man."

"Hey, there's more. We're having a baby, too."

Surprised again, Jack blurted, "Really?"

"Hey, man," Kevin said, grinning, "I didn't lose any
of the important bits over there in that hellhole."

Rita laughed and Jack just shook his head. "Damn,
Kev. You really haven't changed much, have you?"

"Older, wiser, shorter," Kevin said, then his smile
slowly faded away. "Look, I had to make this drive to
see you in person because my wedding is this weekend."

"So soon?"

Kevin's eyebrows lifted. "When I emailed you, I
gave you two months' warning."

"Right." Jack nodded. "My fault."

"Absolutely true," Kevin agreed easily. "But the point
is, I drove my ass all the way up here to ask you to be
my best man."

"Your—" Okay, Jack didn't know how many more surprises he could take. He never would have expected the man he'd believed hated his guts to ask him to stand up for him.

"Best man. Yeah. Because that's what you are." His features sober, serious, Kevin said, "We were buds before. Been through a lot of crap together. But what you did for me, Jack, I can never repay."

A twist of pain wrung at his heart. "You don't have to."

"Yeah, I know that. Doesn't stop the need." Kevin glanced at Rita. "Your man was always a stand-up. He kept me alive in a place that tried its best to kill me."

Rita reached out instinctively and took his hand with her free hand, somehow linking the two men even more completely than they already were. Kevin released her hand, and reached into the pocket of his black leather jacket. He drew out a cream-colored envelope that he handed to Rita.

"I'm giving this to you for two reasons," he said. "One, you're way better looking than Jack."

"You're a very astute man," Rita said, grinning. Beside her, Jack only sighed.

"And two, more important, you'll make sure he gets to the wedding. Right?" He looked at her meaningfully for a long moment.

Then Rita leaned forward, kissed Kevin's cheek and said, "You bet I will." She glanced back at Jack as if for confirmation. "We'll be there. Won't we?"

"Yeah." He looked from Rita to Kevin and back again. "We'll be there, Kev."

"Good." He clapped his hands together then scrubbed his palms. "Then my work here is done and my lovely

bride-to-be is going to be picking me up outside in—"
He checked his watch. "Ten minutes. We're going for
dinner, then taking the long drive home."

"Do you really have to go so soon?" Rita asked,
standing up as Kevin wheeled back and turned. "Why
don't both of you come up and have dinner with us?"

"No, but thanks." Kevin looked knowingly at Jack. "I
think we're both going to need a little time to get used
to the new us, right, Jack?"

It would take time and it was good to know that
Kevin not only understood but felt the same. Too many
emotions were churning inside him. Waves were rocking his insides like a storm at sea and he had a lot of
thinking to do. "Yeah. A little time would be a good
thing."

Kevin nodded solemnly, but his gaze locked with
Jack's. "We'll get there. But we'll see you Saturday?"

Just as somber, Jack promised, "I swear. We'll be
there."

Nine

Once Kevin was gone, Jack gave in to the tension screaming inside him. Stalking across the room, he made for the terrace, pushing open the French doors and stepping into the icy blast of wind that rushed at him. He turned his face into that wind and wished to hell it could blow all of his churning thoughts right out of his head.

"Jack?"

Teeth gritted, he kept his gaze on the expanse of the ocean streaked with the brilliant colors of sunset rather than turn to face the woman who'd become too important to him. Until Kevin had come by tonight, Jack hadn't realized just how much he'd come to depend on Rita's presence in his life. He was already in too deep, he knew that because of just how much he'd needed her by his side when Kevin was in the house. Needed her to anchor him.

And that bothered Jack plenty.

"Are you okay?" Her voice was soft, husky, filled with concern that scraped at him. He didn't want her worried about him, caring about him, God help him, *loving* him.

He'd once vowed that he would never put anyone in the position of having to mourn him. And the more she cared, the more pain she risked. How was he supposed to stand by and let her get deeper into feelings that would only carry the promise of future pain?

Damn it, this marriage was supposed to be temporary. Supposed to be emotion-free. A bargain. Yet somehow, in spite of his best efforts it had turned into more. The question now was, what was he prepared to do about it?

"Jack?" she asked again. "Are you okay?"

"Fine." He bit the word off, hoping she'd take the damn hint for once and leave him alone. Give him enough space to get himself together again. To find the center that had slipped out of his grasp the minute he saw Kevin in that chair.

"You don't sound fine," she said and came up beside him. She shivered in the cold wind and rubbed her hands up and down her arms for warmth. She was only wearing white capris and a short-sleeved pink T-shirt. Her bare feet had to be freezing on the concrete floor. But she wasn't leaving. He knew her well enough now to expect that.

When he didn't speak, she tried another tack. "Kevin seems nice."

Nice. Yeah, he was. He was also smart. Funny. And in a damn chair for the rest of his life. Jack closed his eyes briefly. "You don't have to do this."

"What am I doing?"

"Helping." He glanced at her. "I don't need your help. And I don't need to be soothed."

"That's what you think?" she asked, leaning against the railing to look up at him. "Everybody needs help sometimes, Jack. You're not a superhero."

Silently, he laughed at the idea. He was as far from a superhero as anyone could get.

"Didn't say I was and if I want help," he added, shooting her a dark look that should have sent her skittering for cover, "I'll ask for it."

Naturally, he told himself, Rita paid no attention to his warning look. Instead, she laughed and the raw, sexy sound awakened every cell in his body.

"Sure, you'll ask for help. Jack," she said with a smile. "You wouldn't ask for water if you were on fire."

The fact that she was right only irritated him further. How much more was he expected to take tonight? Facing down a friend whose life was forever changed wasn't enough? God, he needed time alone. He needed to *think*.

"You're staring out at that ocean like you expect to find answers there."

"I don't need answers, either," he ground out. "I just need some space. Time. Some damn solitude. God, I can't even remember what it's like to be completely alone anymore."

That insult sailed right over her head. She just didn't listen to what she didn't want to hear. In a way, he admired that about her. Even when it worked against him.

"If you think you can insult me into walking away, you're wrong."

Exasperated, he blew out a breath. "Then what will it take?"

"There's nothing you can do that will make me leave you alone right now," Rita said. "You've had enough solitude, Jack. Maybe too much."

"Fine. You won't leave, I will." He turned, but stopped when she laid one hand on his arm.

"I've got some of those answers you don't need." She paused and he knew she was waiting for him to look at her. Finally, he did.

"What are you talking about now?"

Shrugging, she said, "You said you didn't need answers, but you do. And here's one for you. You've been torturing yourself for months over Kevin, Jack. But there was no need. You saw him. He's happy."

He scraped one hand across his face. "He's in a chair."

"That's not your fault."

"Yeah, well, saying it doesn't make that true." He shifted his gaze back out to the water and watched that darkening surface churn with the wind. Looking out at the sky and sea was so much easier than looking into whiskey-colored eyes that saw too much. "You weren't there. I was."

"So was Kevin," she pointed out, refusing to let it go. "And he doesn't blame you."

"He should." His gaze narrowed on that wide, roiling water and he felt it replicated in his own soul. "Damn it, if I had made a different call, it wouldn't have happened."

"My God, you're stubborn," she said, sliding over to stand between him and the railing, so that he was forced to look at her. "Yes, you were in charge and you made the decisions, but making different ones might not have kept everyone safe. Maybe a different call would have killed Kevin. Or you. Or someone else. There's just no way to know and no point in continuing to drag yourself over the coals like this."

He shook his head. He couldn't speak. What was there to say, anyway? She couldn't get it and he didn't blame her. No one who wasn't there could ever understand what it was to hold men's lives in your hands. One wrong call and people died. Or lost their legs.

"Are you really so determined to carry the weight of the world?"

She made it sound as though he were being self-indulgent. Nothing could have been further from the truth. He had a right to feel like a damn bastard for what had happened to Kevin. To the new guy in their squad, DeSantos, who had *died* in that skirmish. Was he supposed to just close it off, pretend it hadn't happened? He couldn't do that. "Leave it alone, Rita."

"He thanked you for saving him, Jack."

"I was there," he pointed out, barely sparing her a glance. She didn't get it. Didn't know what it had been like to see his best friend lying wounded in front of him and not being able to do a damn thing about it. Didn't understand the guilt of coming home with both arms, both legs. Didn't know what it was to keep all of that locked inside you until you felt like you were going to explode.

This was why he'd never talked to his family. He couldn't share with them what they couldn't understand. Oh, they would try, but their pity for him would get tangled up in the facts and they'd only end up *more* worried about him than they already were.

She laid both hands on his chest and the heat of her slid inside him like a welcome balm, easing the harsh waves of regret and anger and frustration still roiling within. As much as he loved her touch, he almost resented it because it was temporary. She wouldn't be here for much longer and when she was gone it would be so much harder to be without her.

"Jack. If Kevin can move on, why can't you?"

He dropped his gaze to hers. Those whiskey eyes stared up at him with so many emotions rushing through them he couldn't begin to name them all. And it was probably better if he didn't try.

"Because," he said slowly, "if I move on, it's forgetting. And if I let myself forget, then I've learned nothing."

She tipped her head to one side and all those amazing dark brown curls fell off her shoulder to be lifted in the ever-present wind. "That makes zero sense, Jack."

One corner of his mouth lifted. Of course it didn't make sense to her. How could she untangle his emotions when they were so jumbled together even *he* didn't understand half of them. But right now, that didn't matter. She was there, pressed up against him, her curvy body radiating heat, the mound of their child between them and Jack let himself simply *feel*. If things were different, if he were different... But wishing wouldn't make it so.

She wrapped her arms around his middle and laid her head on his chest. Her scent enveloped him completely and he felt as if he were bathing in some soft, golden light. The tension she eased and soothed wasn't gone, just buried. It was all still inside him, twisting, writhing. But that didn't mean he had to find answers tonight.

He took a breath, drew her scent deep and let it ease every jagged corner of his soul. Closing his eyes, he held her close and told himself that just for tonight, he would take the comfort she offered.

And be grateful.

A couple of days later, they were in a backyard with a wildly spectacular garden bursting with blooms in every color imaginable. A rare June day of sunshine washed out of a clear blue sky and shone down like a blessing on the small group of people gathered.

The wedding was beautiful. Small, as Rita and Jack's had been, but instead of the beach, they were in a lush backyard with a small group of guests. There were tables, chairs and a wooden dance floor constructed just for the occasion. Music streamed from a stereo, an eclectic mix of classic rock, old standards and even a waltz or two just for tradition's sake.

Seated at a table in the shade, Rita looked at her husband, sitting beside her. Jack wore a perfectly tailored black suit with a white shirt and a dark blue tie. His black hair was a little long, his blue eyes a little too sharp, his jaw a little too tense. But he was there for Kevin, as promised.

Rita smoothed the skirt of her bright yellow dress across her thighs, and swung the loose fall of her hair back behind her shoulders. Reaching across their table, she took Jack's hand in hers.

"Look at them," she said, smiling. "They're so happy."

She watched Kevin, with Lisa in his lap, wheel around the dance floor. The newlyweds were laughing, kissing and completely caught up in each other. Maybe it was the pregnancy hormones, but Rita's eyes blurred with tears as she watched the two people so obviously in love.

"Yeah, they do look happy," Jack said and deliberately slid his hand out from under hers. He picked up his bottle of beer and took a long swig.

"But you don't." Sitting beside him, surrounded by strangers in a flower-filled garden, Rita felt a now-familiar darkness creeping closer.

There didn't seem to be anything she could do to lift the cloud that had settled on him since seeing Kevin again a few days ago. He wasn't angry or even unkind. He was…civil. He treated her as he would a stranger, with a cool politeness that chipped away at her heart and soul.

When they were first married, Jack had kept a distance between them, but Rita had still sensed that he cared for her. That there was something inside him fighting to get out. Now, it was as if he'd suddenly built the wall around his heart thicker and higher, defying her to break through. God knew she'd spent the last couple of days trying to do just that. But it was as if he was on another planet—one she couldn't reach.

He slanted her a long, thoughtful look. The dappled shade from the trees threw a pattern of dark and light across his face. His features, though, were carefully blank, as if he was determined to give her no clue at all as to what he was thinking, feeling.

"No," he said finally, "I'm not happy."

God, she got an actual chill from the ice in his voice. But she had to keep trying to get to him, to touch his heart, to make him see that he wasn't alone if he didn't want to be. "Jack, what is it? What's happening?"

"This isn't the place to talk about it," he said and

lifted his beer for another drink. His gaze shifted from her to Kevin and Lisa. His features were tighter, the glint in his eyes harder and Rita was more confused than ever.

She turned her head to watch the newlyweds, too, but what she saw made her smile. Made her heart lift. Kevin, in his chair, Lisa on his lap, looking down into his eyes with an expression of pure joy on her face. The two of them might have been alone in the world as the music played and a handful of dancers moved around them.

Why couldn't Jack see the happiness all around him and let himself revel in it? Why was he more determined than ever to wallow in misery? For the first time since finding him again, Rita was worried.

As it turned out, she had a right to be.

A few hours later, they were back in the penthouse. It had been a long, silent ride, with tension building between them until Rita had felt it alive and bristling in the car. Jack had given away nothing. She still had no idea what was bothering him but she was through guessing. Rita had waited as long as she could. There was no point in worrying over something when you could face it head-on and tackle it to the ground.

Dropping her taupe clutch bag onto the nearest chair, she stared at Jack's back and demanded, "Are you going to tell me what's bugging you?"

He was standing in the center of the living room, suit jacket tossed to the couch, hands stuffed into his slacks pockets. When he turned to look at her, Rita's heart actually dropped. If a man's face could be a sheet of ice, then that's what she was looking at.

His clear blue eyes glittered like shards of that ice as they locked on her. "What's bugging me? It's this." He pulled his hands free, lifted both arms as if to encompass the two of them and the apartment. "It's over, Rita. This marriage sham? It's done. Time for you to go."

All of the air in her lungs left her in a rush and seconds later Rita was light-headed. It felt as if the floor had opened up beneath her feet and simply swallowed her. Shock was too small a word for what she was feeling. Hurt was right up there, too, but temper was coming in a close third and quickly rising to the top. Forcing herself to breathe, she stared at him as she would have a stranger. "Just like that?"

"Just like that," he said and headed for the bar in the far corner of the room. Bending down, he opened the mini fridge and grabbed a bottle of beer. After opening it, he took a long drink and avoided looking at her.

Yep, temper was bubbling to the surface and Rita gave it free rein. Her family could have told Jack that when Rita was truly angry, it was best to run, but that was all right, she told herself. He'd find that out for himself.

"That's just not going to fly with me, Jack."

One of his eyebrows lifted in mild surprise. She could do better.

"You don't get to stand there so cool and dismissive and say 'time for you to go, Rita,' and expect me to start packing," she said, riding a cresting wave of what felt like pure fury. "You don't tell me to go and then not even bother to look at me."

He slid his gaze to hers and it was almost worse, she thought, seeing the blank emptiness in his eyes. Pain grabbed at her, but she shook it off.

"What the hell happened?" she demanded. "You've been different ever since Kevin came here. And today—" she broke off, shook her head and said, "the wedding was beautiful, but you couldn't see it. Kevin and Lisa were practically glowing and you sat there like a black hole, sucking in every bit of joy around you without it once affecting you. Where's this all coming from?"

"From Kevin," he snapped, then took a breath to visibly calm himself. When he had, he continued. "From the wedding and Kevin and Lisa and the damn hearts and flowers practically floating over their heads."

She just blinked at him. This was making no sense at all. "That's a bad thing? How does your friend's happiness equate to you being miserable?"

"I'm not miserable. I'm realistic."

"It's realistic to hate the fact that people are happy? To send me away so there's no chance of *you* being happy?"

"That's right."

God, it was like talking to a wall. Only she'd probably have gotten more out of a wall. He was bulletproof. Her words bounced off him and never left a dent.

"You don't want to be happy, is that it?" God, she was getting colder.

"You're damn right," he said, setting the beer down in a deliberately calm manner. Coming out from behind the bar, he walked toward her and stopped with a good three feet of empty space between them. "I told you going in that this was temporary, just until the baby was born."

She put both hands on her belly. "News flash. Still about two months to go."

He didn't even look at the baby. Hell, he barely looked at *her*. "Yeah, but we don't have to be living together to be married, do we?" he asked.

"Wow." She took a step toward him and he took one back. One short, sharp laugh shot from her throat. "Was I getting too close, Jack? Were you starting to care? Are you making me leave because you don't want me to go?"

"Think you've got me all figured out, do you?"

"Oh, yeah," she said, nodding. "It wasn't that hard. Answer me this. Do I scare you, Jack?"

He gritted his teeth, huffed out a breath and said flatly, "You terrify me."

Small comfort, she thought, but didn't speak again as he continued.

"I didn't sign up for this. Didn't *want* this," he muttered darkly, pushing one hand through his hair impatiently. "You're getting too close, Rita. I can see it. You're starting to believe this is all *real* and it's not. It can't be. I won't let it be."

She'd never been dismissed so completely, so casually and it hurt so much she wanted to keen, but damned if she'd let him see that. Her heart ached for them both. She'd gotten to him, reached him and because she had, he was cutting her out of his life with a single, cold stroke.

"*You* won't let it be real?" she asked. "You're the only one with a vote here?"

"That's right." His eyes were cold, empty and that one fact tore at her so deeply, Rita could hardly breathe.

"Why?" She stared at him, completely confused and hurt and even her temper was easing off to be replaced by an ache that settled around her heart and throbbed with every beat. "You at least owe me an explanation, Jack. How did Kevin showing up here and his happiness today make you so determined to throw your own chance at it away? *Our* chance."

"You want an explanation, fine. Sure, Kevin and Lisa are happy today," Jack ground out. "But what about tomorrow? What about when pain comes rolling down the track and hits them both?"

Flabbergasted, Rita stared at him. "*What?* Being happy isn't worth it because one day you might not be? What kind of logic is that?"

He shook his head grimly. "Perfect, that's what kind. I saw it happen. Too many damn times. You love someone—or worse yet, let someone love you—and things go wrong, lives are shattered. I heard a guy's widow sobbing. I watched parents grieving." He wasn't cool and detached now. His voice was hot, words tumbling over each other. "I saw the strongest men I've ever known break under the agony of loss. Why the hell would anyone risk that? No, Rita. There's no way I'm setting either one of us up for that."

Her own breath came short and fast, because she knew he believed what he was saying. None of it made sense but that didn't keep him from having faith in every word. "So screw ever smiling or being joyful because of what *might* happen."

He didn't even flinch.

"It will happen," he insisted. "You think anybody gets through life unscathed? They don't. The best you can do is protect yourself from misery."

"By *being* miserable?" she demanded.

"Think what you like." Shaking his head, he ignored that and said, "I'm not letting you get any deeper into this marriage, Rita." His voice was tight, hard. "You're getting too damn close, pulling me along with you, and I can't go any further. I won't let myself start coming back to life only to risk more grief. Trust me, it's not worth it. I *know*."

God, he'd already cut her off. He'd made that call a couple of days ago when Kevin visited and since then it had been solidifying in his mind until now; it was a done deal. Without talking to her about any of it, he'd made the decision to end what was between them.

"You're wrong," she whispered, and to her fury, felt tears fill her eyes. She *hated* that. Rita always ended up crying when she was at her angriest. Too much emotion had to eventually spill from her eyes and the tears were lowering. Viciously, she swiped at her eyes. "You're so wrong it's sad, Jack. Caring about people? That's worth *everything*."

"Don't cry." He scrubbed one hand across the back of his neck. "Just don't. It'll rip at me because I…*care* about you."

"You don't just care, Jack," she told him flatly. "You love me."

His gaze snapped to hers. "See? That's another reason you have to leave."

"What?"

"Love's coming, and I know that, too. So I need you gone before I love you."

Rita laughed shortly then actually reached up and tugged at her hair in frustration. This had to be the weirdest and most heartbreaking conversation she'd ever had. "Right. Don't want to take a chance on actually *loving* someone."

"I'm doing what I have to do."

"No, you're not, Jack," she said, lifting her chin and meeting that cold stare with all the heat she could muster. "You're doing what's easiest."

"You think this is *easy*?" he demanded.

"I think it's unnecessary," she snapped. "But no worries. I'm leaving. I'll be out of here tonight." Damned if she'd stay with a man who was so determined not to love her. To cut himself off from any feeling at all.

"You don't have to go tonight," he said. "Tomorrow's soon enough."

Her gaze locked on his. "No, it's really not."

A couple of hours later, Jack was alone in the apartment.

As good as her word, Rita was gone so fast, she'd been nothing but a blur. She hadn't said another word to him, but her silence came across loud and clear. He hadn't wanted to hurt her and someday soon, Rita would realize that he'd done all of this to protect her. He didn't want her hurt. Mourning him as he'd seen others mourn the fallen.

She'd cried.

He slapped one hand to the center of his chest in a futile attempt to ease the ache centered there. Jack had never seen Rita cry before. Not even the day he'd left her in that hotel to go back to his tour of duty. She'd sent him off with a smile that had no doubt cost her. But today, she'd cried.

If he could have changed it, he would have. But this was the only way and Jack knew it. He stepped out onto the terrace and let that cold wind slap at him. He finally had what he'd wanted—*craved*—most. Solitude. There was no one here talking to him, trying to make him laugh, drawing him back into a world he'd deliberately turned his back on.

"This is for the best. For both of us. Hell," he added, thinking of the baby, "for all three of us."

Didn't feel like it at the moment, but he was sure it would. One day. Rita would see it, too. Eventually.

"Damn it," he said when the doorbell rang. He thought about not answering it, but even as he considered it, the damn thing rang again.

"Rita probably forgot something," he told himself as he headed back inside. He took a peek through the judas hole and sighed heavily. So much for solitude.

Reluctantly, he opened the door and said, "Hi, Cass."

"Don't you 'hi' me," his sister said as she pushed past him into the apartment. She threw her purse onto the couch, then turned around, hands at her hips and glared at him. "What the hell is wrong with you?"

Calmly, Jack closed the door and faced his sister. She was practically vibrating with anger. Her eyes, so much like his own, were flashing dangerously and her features were set like stone in an expression of indignation. "What're you talking about?"

"Rita called me from the airport."

That threw him. "The *airport*?"

"Yeah, she found a flight to Utah and she went back to see her family."

Okay, he'd wanted her to leave the apartment—not the state. He wasn't sure how he felt about her being so far away. Was she planning on staying there? Giving up her bakery? Her friends?

"Are you out of your mind for real?" she asked.

"This is none of your business, Cass."

"Since we're family, it *is* my business," she countered grimly. "Rita asked me to come and check on you," Cass added, not bothering to hide the disgust in her tone. "She was worried about *you*."

"Which is just one of the reasons I asked her to go," Jack said calmly. "I don't want her worrying about me."

She jerked her head back and gave him a look of pure astonishment. "Y'know," she said, "that's what people on Earth do. We worry for the people we care about."

"I don't *want* her to care about me, that's the whole point."

"Right." Cass nodded sharply, paced a little frantically for a few minutes, then came to a stop and glared at him again. "And it's all about what you want, isn't it, Jack?"

"I didn't say that."

"Oh, please," his sister countered, waving one hand at him in dismissal. "You've been saying it in every way but words for *months*."

"I'm not doing this with you, Cass," he said. "Not going to talk about it."

"Good. Because I don't care what you have to say. Not anymore. All you have to do is listen." She came closer and he saw sparks dazzling her eyes. "I've tried to be patient with you. I'm a doctor, Jack. I know what's going on with you."

"I don't need a damn doctor and if I did," he told her hotly, "I wouldn't go to my little sister."

Damned if he needed *everyone* telling him what he should do and when he should do it. And he *really* didn't want his younger sister standing there like the voice of God telling him to shape up.

"Yes, you've made that abundantly clear and I've really tried to keep quiet, give you room to deal."

"There's nothing going on with me."

"You denying PTSD doesn't make it go away. My God, you're practically a textbook case." She walked to the couch, dropped onto it, then just as quickly jumped to her feet again, apparently unable to sit still. "I told Sam and Dad they had to give you time. Let you get used to being back in the world. That you'd come around eventually."

"I'm fine," he insisted but saw that his sister wasn't buying it.

"Sure you are." She snorted. "You notice Sam doesn't come up from San Diego much anymore? Or have you paid any attention to the fact that Dad almost never comes into the office these days even though he used to love it?"

He thought about that for a minute or two. She had a point though he'd never really considered it before. His brother, Sam, was a busy guy. And his father had recently taken up golf, so why would he be coming around an office he'd retired from. "Yeah, but—"

"Sam got tired of you shooting him down every time he tried to spend time with you."

"I didn't—"

"Yeah, you did. You've shot me down often enough for me to know that and I can tell you it's no fun having a proverbial door slammed in your face every time you try to talk to someone." She took a long breath. "Damn it, Jack, we're your *family* and we deserve better."

"I just needed—"

But she kept talking. "Dad gets his heart broken just a little more whenever he's with you and can't reach you, so he stays away."

Guilt dropped onto his shoulders, but he was so used

to the burden he hardly noticed. Remembering the last time he'd seen his father, Jack could admit to the sorrow he'd seen in the older man's eyes. And still... "He doesn't—"

"Not finished," she snapped. "Honestly, Jack, you make me so furious. Do you know how many men and women come home from dangerous duties and have *no one* to talk to? To count on? Do you know how lucky you are to have people who love you? Who are willing to put up with your bullshit?"

"I—"

"Does it look like I'm done?" She inhaled sharply, blew the air out in a huff and stared up at him. "You're my brother and I love you. You're Rita's husband and *she* loves you."

There was that pang around his heart again. He rubbed the spot idly, almost unconsciously. She loved him. He'd been pretty sure she did, but *knowing* it was something else again. He swallowed hard against that pounding ache in his heart and told himself that even if she did love him, he'd done the right thing.

"You don't get it, Cass." He sighed. "I don't want to be loved. Whoever loves me is just setting themselves up for a letdown later. Why do that to anybody?"

"Well, good God," Cass said, clearly stunned. "It's worse than I thought. It's not just your memories haunting you that's kept you tucked away up here in your fortress of solitude. It's something else. You're an idiot." Shaking her head, she said, "I'm so glad Mom can't see you like this, although she'd probably have kicked you into shape by now. You don't want to be loved? You don't want to feel anything for anyone? Too damn bad. Boo the hell hoo."

"What?" A choked off, surprised laugh shot from his throat. It seemed he was destined to have the women in his life constantly surprising him.

"You have a chance at something amazing, Jack, and you're letting it get away. You told the woman who loves you, the mother of your *child*," she added with emphasis, "to leave because you're scared to be hurt again. To know pain again."

"Careful, Cass," he said, voice soft. Even for his sister, he was only willing to put up with so much. He was doing the hard thing here. Why could no one see it, appreciate what it cost him?

"No, I'm done being careful. I should never have given you time to adjust, Jack," she said sadly. "That was my mistake. I should have done just what Rita did, grab hold and drag you, kicking and screaming back into life."

"It wouldn't have worked."

"We'll never know, will we?" she asked. Still shaking her head, she walked over, picked up her purse and slung it over her shoulder. "Look around Jack," she said. "You got what you wanted. You're alone. I hope you enjoy it. Because if you keep acting like a jackass— this is all you'll ever have."

He watched her go and the slam of the door behind her echoed in the stillness.

Ten

The Marchetti bakery on historic 25th Street in Ogden was in an antique brick building with sloping wood floors that creaked musically with every step. On one side of the shop was a handmade-chocolate shop and on the other, an artisan boutique that sold local artists' work.

The bakery drew customers from all over northern Utah, so they were constantly busy, which meant the entire family—except for the younger kids—were there when Rita arrived. Her mom and sister were in the kitchen while her father and brothers ran the front of the shop and handled any deliveries. This didn't change, she thought with a smile as she glanced around at the shining display cases and the customers wandering, looking, sitting at tables and sipping lattes.

Just walking into the bakery soothed the ball of

ice in the pit of her stomach. It had been the longest hour-and-a-half flight of her life to make it here from Long Beach. She hadn't told the family she was coming; there hadn't been time. She'd simply packed her things, told Casey to close up the bakery for a few days and then raced to the airport. All Rita had been able to think of was getting here, where she knew her heart was safe.

The long drive from the Salt Lake City airport had given her more time to think and she still had no answers. Hadn't she done everything she could to reach Jack? Hadn't she given him every reason to come out of the darkness? To live again?

Tears were close so she blinked furiously to keep them at bay and smiled at a woman she knew who was busily wiping chocolate off her child's mouth. Here was safety. Love. Understanding.

The joy on her father's face when he spotted her was like pouring oil on the churning waters inside her. Rita's brothers, Anthony and Marco, called out to her as she threaded her way through the crowd toward the kitchen to find her mom. Of course she had to stop along the way to say hello to people she knew and try to make small talk, while inside she was screaming.

Behind the counter, Rita was hugged hard by her dad, then passed from brother to brother before they released her.

"This is a nice surprise," her father said, then took a closer look at her face and frowned. "It *is* nice, isn't it?"

Nick Marchetti was in his sixties, with graying black hair, sharp brown eyes and a belly that was a little fuller than it used to be. Both of his sons were several inches taller than him, but it didn't matter because

Nick was, just as he always had been, a force to be reckoned with.

"It's good to see you, Daddy," Rita whispered, relaxing into his familiar hug.

He kissed her cheek and said, "Go on now, go sit down and talk to your mother. She'll be happy you're here."

"Okay." Rita nodded, slipped through the swinging door and never saw the worried frowns on the faces of the men in her family.

Stepping into the kitchen with the familiar scents and the heat from the ovens was like walking into the comfort of her childhood. Growing up, she and her siblings had spent most of their free time working in the bakery, so the memories were thick and reassuring.

Rita had gone home to Ogden hoping for a little peace and quiet and maybe some understanding. A half hour later, she told herself she'd clearly come to the wrong place for that.

"I can't believe you left," her mother said hotly. Teresa Marchetti had short black hair, carefully touched up to hide the gray every five weeks. She was a tiny woman but ruled her family like a four-star general.

Rita took a sip of the herbal tea she wasn't interested in. "Jack didn't want me there. He told me to leave."

"And so you do it?" Teresa shook her head and scowled. "I don't remember you being so obedient as a child."

Rita stiffened at the accusation. "I wasn't being obedient." God, that made her sound like some subservient fifties' housewife asking her husband for an allowance.

"Yet here you are." Her mother huffed a little, muttered something Rita didn't quite catch, then slid two trays of bread loaves into the oven. Turning back around, she reached for a bottle of water and took a drink.

It was hot in the kitchen with four ovens going constantly. Rita's father and brothers had deliberately stayed out front, leaving her mother and sister to do the heavy emotional lifting.

Gina looked up from the counter where she was rolling out cookie dough. "So Jack says go and you say okeydoke? What the hell is that, Rita?"

"Language," their mother said automatically, then added, "your sister has a point. Do you love this man?"

"Of course she does it's all over her face," Gina said before Rita could open her mouth.

"Thanks, I can talk for myself," Rita said.

"Just not to Jack, is that it?" Gina rolled her eyes as fiercely as she rolled the dough.

"I did talk to Jack." Rita broke a cookie in half and popped it into her mouth. She should have known that no one in her family would pat her on the head and simply accept what she said. They all had opinions and loved nothing better than sharing them. "I talked till my throat was dry. He doesn't listen to what he doesn't want to hear."

"Hmm," Teresa mused with a snort of amusement. "Sounds like someone else I know."

Fine, she was stubborn. Rita knew that. But this wasn't about *her*, was it?

"Mom, how could I stay if he didn't want me?"

"Oh, for God's sake," Gina blurted. "He does want you. You told us already he admitted that."

"Yes, but he doesn't *want* to want me."

"That's female logic," Anthony said when he hustled in to restock a tray of cannoli.

"Jack's the one who said it," Rita pointed out, finishing off the rest of her cookie.

Anthony countered, "He only said it because that's how men think women think."

"What?" Gina asked, clearly as confused as Rita. "That must be more male logic because it makes *no* sense."

"It does to men," Anthony argued before picking up the tray to head out front.

Rita propped her elbows on the counter and propped her head in her hands. A circus, she thought. It was a circus at Marchetti's.

"Go on, back to work," Teresa ordered, waving at her son to hurry him along. When it was just the three women in the kitchen again, Teresa sat down on a stool opposite Rita. "Don't think about what he said or what he did or even what your family thinks about all of this. There's just one thing to consider, Rita." She paused, shot her other daughter a don't-open-your-mouth look and asked Rita, "Do you love him?"

"Of course I love him, Mom. That's not the point."

"It's the only point," her mother said.

Gina kept quiet for as long as she could, then blurted out, "For God's sake, Rita, *all* men are impossible to deal with—"

"We can hear you!" their father shouted from the front.

Rita chuckled and shook her head. The heck with peace and quiet. *This* is just what she had needed.

"Am I wrong?" Gina shouted to her father. Then turning back to her mother and sister, she demanded, "See? Brothers, fathers, husbands, sons, they're all crazy. But giving up is never the answer, Rita. You have to dig in and fight back. Never give an inch."

"Your sister's right." Teresa nodded.

"It's a miracle!" Gina looked up at the ceiling to Heaven beyond and got a dark look from Teresa for her trouble.

Then, ignoring one daughter, Teresa reached out and took both of Rita's hands in hers. "I'm ashamed that you didn't fight for what you want, for what you need. Rita, we didn't raise you to walk away."

Her heart gave a sharp tug at the realization that that's exactly what she had done. In her own hurt and grief, she'd tucked tail and run away. But how could she not have?

"So I'm supposed to stay with a man who doesn't want me there?"

Gina opened her mouth and shut it again when her mother held up one hand.

"He does want you there. He told you so," Teresa said. "He wants you to leave before he loves you? What kind of statement is that? He already loves you and it scares him."

Rita laughed shortly and shook her head, denying the possibility. "Nothing scares Jack."

Although, the minute those words left her mouth she remembered Jack saying "You terrify me." Maybe her mother was on to something.

"Oh, honey," her mother said, "nothing scares a man more than *love* when it finally shows up." She gave Rita's hands a pat, then picked up a cookie and took a bite. "It's especially difficult for a strong man, because being out of control is a hard thing to accept."

"Jimmy wasn't scared," Gina muttered.

"Sure he was," her mother said on a laugh. "You just didn't give him time to think about it."

Shrugging, Gina admitted with a grin, "Okay, fair point."

"And your brothers?" Teresa laughed. "They were terrified."

"We can *still* hear you," Marco yelled.

Ignoring her son, Teresa looked at Rita. "Even your dad fought tooth and nail to keep from loving me."

"As if I stood a chance at that," Nick called out.

"Why do we have a door," Teresa wondered, "when everyone hears everything anyway?" Shaking her head again, she continued, "What I'm saying is, everything worth having, is worth fighting for."

Rita just didn't know. She'd left the penthouse in a rush, hurt beyond belief, angry beyond anything she'd ever experienced before. Heart aching, she'd had only one thought. Come home. To the family that was always there for her.

"So what're you going to do?" Gina spread a cinnamon-and-sugar mixture on the rectangle of dough then carefully rolled it up for slicing and baking. "You going to stay here? Or go back and reclaim your life?"

Well, that was the question, wasn't it? Being here with her family, she was starting to think and as she did, she was embarrassed to admit that running away from her problems, from the man she loved, just didn't feel right. She'd pulled back from him and hid away—the very thing she'd accused Jack of doing.

"Why should I leave?" she murmured, hardly realizing she was speaking aloud.

"Exactly," Gina agreed, slicing cookies and laying them on sheets to bake.

"I have a business there. And a home—okay, not the penthouse, but I was happy there and I can be again."

Rita ate another cookie while her brain raced and the pain in her heart began to ease.

"Sure you can," her mother said.

"Jack doesn't make decisions for me."

"'Course not," Gina agreed.

"He doesn't get to tell me when to go. When to stay. Sit. Heel."

"That's my girl," Teresa cheered.

"Why should I make this easy on Jack?" Rita demanded of no one in particular.

"You never made it easy on any of us," Marco quipped when he brought an empty tray into the kitchen.

"Oh, please," Gina sneered. "And you were the angel child? Do you remember shaving my Barbie dolls bald?"

"A fond memory," Marco assured her, dodging when she took a swing at him.

"I'm going back," Rita announced. "And I'm going to look Jack in the eye and tell him that he can't dictate my life."

"I feel like I should have pom-poms," Gina murmured.

"He's not chasing me away," Rita proclaimed, scooting off the stool to stand on her own two feet. "I'm going back. I'm going to tell him he's in love with me and when he's done being scared of it, he can come and find me. I'm building a life there and I'm not giving it up."

"Good for you." Her father came into the kitchen and gave her a quick hug before grabbing another cookie. "But you can stay for a couple of days, right? Have a nice visit before you go back?"

"I sure can, Daddy," she said and leaned in to the most wonderful man she'd ever known. "Let Jack miss me. It'll be good for him."

"You women are devious, wonderful creatures," her father said.

"And don't you forget it," his wife warned.

Solitude was overrated.

Three days of it and Jack felt like he was suffocating. Quiet. Too much damn quiet. He kept seeing Rita's ghost in the penthouse. He heard her laugh. He caught her scent in the guest room she'd used and ached for her in a way he wouldn't have thought possible.

It was worse somehow, knowing that she was in Utah. Jack hadn't really believed Cass when she told him that Rita had left the damn state. So he'd driven to Seal Beach, walked past the bakery and got a chill when he saw the closed sign on the door.

He'd driven her off and she'd actually left. He should be happy. Instead, he felt…hollowed out. Like a shell of the man he used to be. At that thought, he imagined what Rita would say to it and he could almost hear her. *Whose fault is that, Jack? Who keeps running away from life?*

Shaking his head free of irritating thoughts and reminders of all he'd lost, Jack turned his attention back to the stack of papers waiting for his signature. He'd been spending more time than usual in the office because it beat the hell out of being alone in the penthouse with too many memories.

"I'll get over it. Hell," he murmured, scrawling his name along the bottom of a contract, *"she'll* get over it."

"Mr. Buchanan?" Linda stood just inside the open door to his office.

"What is it?"

"Marketing reports *The Sea Queen* is now sold-out."

"Good. Great." The cruise liner would be a huge success, one more feather in the Buchanan family cap and Jack couldn't have cared less. "Is there anything else?"

"Just one thing." Linda stepped back, a smirk on her face and Rita sailed past her into the room.

The door closed behind her, but Jack hardly noticed. All he could see was her. That amazing hair of hers was a tumble of dark curls. Her eyes were sizzling. She wore black slacks, a lime-green shirt that clung to the mound of her belly and a white linen jacket over the shirt. Black sandals were on her feet and her toenails were a bright purple.

He'd never seen anything more gorgeous in his life.

Standing up behind his desk, he curbed the urge to go to her and grab hold of her. He'd done the right thing and he wasn't going to backtrack now. "Rita. I thought you were in Utah."

She tipped her head to one side and gave him a cool glare. "Hoping I'd stay so far away you'd never have to think about me again?"

"No." There was nothing on this earth that could keep him from thinking about her. "I just—"

"I didn't come to chat, Jack," she said, cutting him off as she dug into the oversize black tote slung over her shoulder. She pulled out a large manila envelope and handed it to him.

"What's this?"

"It's an ultrasound picture of your daughter."

His eyes widened, his jaw dropped and his fingers tightened on the envelope. "I thought you didn't want to know what the baby is."

"Turns out," she said, "surprises aren't as much fun as I used to think they were."

Okay, he knew that was a dig for the way he'd ended things between them. And fine, she was due a fair share of hits. He could take it. Then what she'd said suddenly hit him.

"A daughter?"

"Yes," she said, and clutched her fingers around the handle of her bag. "It's a girl. And I wanted you to know."

"Thanks for that…"

"I didn't do it to be nice, Jack," she said, interrupting him. "I came here to tell you that I'm not running away. I'm not *you*. I don't hide."

"I'm not hiding."

"Call it whatever you want to," she said, voice tight. "It amounts to the same thing."

Sunlight spilled into the office through the wide windows, lying in long, golden rectangles across the floor. Rita stood in one of those slices of light and it was as if she were glowing from the inside. Even the ends of her hair shone, and the sunlight was reflected in her whiskey eyes, making them look as if they were on fire.

"You're upset, I know," he started.

"Damn right I'm upset, Jack." She stopped, took a long breath and steadied herself. "But I didn't come here to get into another futile argument, either."

Still holding the envelope he wanted very badly to open, he asked, "Why are you here, then?"

"To tell you that I'm staying. Our daughter will be raised by *me*, in the apartment over the bakery. I'll tell her all about you, but you're not going to be a part of our lives, Jack."

"You can't keep her from me."

"Watch me," Rita countered. "You don't want *her*

or me. You just want to do what you think is the 'right' thing. Well, I don't care about that. My daughter's going to grow up loved. Happy. And if her father isn't willing to give up his self-pity party long enough to be grateful to be alive, then he just won't be a part of our lives."

"Self-pity?" He repeated the words because they'd slapped him hard enough to make an impact. Was that who he was? Who he'd become? Was she right? "That's what you think?"

"Jack," she sighed out his name. "If you ever manage to work your way out of that cocoon you've wrapped yourself in long enough to realize you love me, let me know. Until then? Goodbye, Jack."

He looked up as Rita turned around, stormed across the room and out the door, slamming it behind her.

Jack fell asleep that night, still holding the ultrasound picture he couldn't get out of his head. A daughter. A little girl. Torn between desire and caution, he wasn't sure which move to make. And then the dream came.

It was hot. So hot every breath seared his lungs. He squinted into the too-bright sunlight and signaled to his men for quiet as they approached the village.

Shots were fired. Explosions rocked all around them, making his ears ring. Someone screamed and another shot fired and Jack was down. Pain burst in a hot ball in the center of his chest. Air caught in his lungs, refusing to move in or out. Jack stared up at a brassy sky, the sun beating down mercilessly and he knew he was dying.

But this wasn't how it happened. The dream was wrong.

Then Kevin was there, leaning over him. Jack looked up at his friend. "I'm hit. I'm hit bad."

"Yeah, dude. It doesn't look good."

"But this is wrong. You were wounded, not me." Jack breathed past the pain, felt it sliding through his body. *"Help me, Kev. Do something. I did it for you."*

"Yeah, you did." Kevin grinned and was suddenly in a wheelchair. *"And I appreciate it. Wish I could help you now, bro. But it's all on you."*

None of this made sense. Jack looked around. The sand. The sun. The men. Everything was the way it always was in his dream. Well, except for Kevin, grinning like a moron at him from a chair.

"What's so funny? Do something, damn it!"

"Nothing I can do, dude," Kevin assured him. *"It's a heart shot. You're done for. There's no hope."*

Panic roared through him followed by fury. Damned if he'd end like this. *"What the hell kind of help is that? Call a medic. Slap a bandage on my chest."*

"Hearts can't be healed with a damn bandage, man. You're way past that."

Fear and fury were a tangled knot inside him. *"Then what do I do?"*

"You already know that, Jack," Kevin said. *"You're not shot, man. Your heart's broken and the only way to fix it is to find Rita and make this right. It's as good as over for you."*

Reaching down, he held out one hand and waited for Jack to take it. Then Kevin pulled him to his feet and slapped Jack on the back. *"The only way out is Rita."*

"Rita." Jack looked down at his chest. He wasn't bleeding. He was healthy enough. He was just...lost. Lifting his head, he glanced around. The dream had changed. The desert was gone.

He was on the beach, the roar of the sea pounding in his brain. And there was Rita, standing at the shoreline as she had been on the first night he'd seen her. And just like that, Jack knew Kevin was right. He felt as if his heart had been ripped out of his chest. It was over for him.

It had been over from the first moment he'd seen her.

Just the memory of her was strong enough to tear down the dream that had been haunting him for months. Rita had drawn him out, with the help of an old friend.

But when he turned to thank Kevin, the man was gone. Looking back down the beach, he saw Rita, holding a baby girl with dark brown curls and bright eyes. He started toward them just as Rita smiled. Then slowly, she and the baby faded until they finally disappeared completely. When he stood alone on the darkened beach, pain hit him like a fist.

Fix this, *he told himself,* or lose everything.

Jack woke with a start and sat straight up in bed. His mind racing, heart pounding, he realized so many truths at once, he was breathless. Maybe it made sense that the lesson he needed to learn had come from Kevin. He'd think about that later. Right now, he knew what he had to do, so he lunged for his cell phone on the bedside table. He punched in a familiar number and waited interminably as it rang on the other end.

"Dad? Yeah, it's me, Jack." He walked out onto the terrace, into the teeth of the wind and had never felt warmer in his life.

"Jack? Are you all right?" his father asked. "What time is it?"

He winced and glanced at the clock. Two o'clock. He rubbed his eyes and laughed shortly. Taking a deep breath, Jack realized that for the first time in months, he didn't have a cold stone in his belly. In fact, he felt pretty good.

"Weirdly enough," he said, "I think I am all right. Or I will be. I'm sorry it's so late, but look. I need you to do something for me."

Eleven

"So have you thought of a name for her yet?"

Rita looked at her bakery manager and shook her head. "No, but I have plenty of time."

"Yeah, you do. But just remember, Casey's a great name for a girl."

Laughing, Rita slid the tray of cookies into the oven. It was good to be home. She'd needed that visit to her family, but being here was what felt right. Back in her apartment over the bakery, doing familiar work with people she loved, it was all good.

Sure, she missed Jack desperately, and there was an ache around her heart that she was really afraid would be permanent. But she would learn to live with it. Learn to live without him, because she had to.

"Thanks, Casey, I'll keep that in mind."

When her phone rang, Rita answered, still laughing. "Hello?"

"Rita, this is Thomas."

Jack's father? For a second a thread of fear wound through her. Was Jack okay? Had something happened? Would she always be wondering about him? The answer was of course, yes.

Sighing, she said, "Hi, Thomas, everything all right?"

"Oh, yes, yes. Everything is great, really. I was just wondering, though, if you might do an old man a favor."

Setting the timer on the oven, Rita wandered to the refrigerator and pulled out a bottle of water. She uncapped it, took a long drink and said, "Of course. What can I do?"

She heard the smile in his voice when he said, "I hoped you could come down to *The Sea Queen* to see me."

"You're on the ship?"

"Yes," he said. "I'm taking the first cruise. Thought I'd get a little golf in on the islands. But there's something I'd like to give you before I go."

Rita did some fast thinking. She really liked Jack's father and just because the man's son was behaving like a loon didn't mean she couldn't be close to his family. Thomas was, after all, her daughter's grandfather. And Jack's sister was going to be the baby's doctor. Family mattered, whether Jack could see that or not. "Of course I can. What time do you want me there?"

"Wonderful," he said, pleasure ringing in his voice. "As for what time, the sooner the better."

Now she was curious. Jack hadn't said anything to her about his dad going on the first cruise. But then, she told herself, maybe he didn't know. What could Thomas possibly have to give her that was important enough for her to go scurrying down to the harbor just before the ship sailed? "Okay, I'll just arrange for my manager to take over and I'll come right down."

"Thank you, Rita. I'll leave word at the dock and they'll bring you to my suite."

"Okay, then," she said, still baffled, "I'll see you soon."

She hung up and just stared at the phone for a second or two. Rita had no idea what was going on, but the sooner she got to the harbor, the quicker she'd find out.

Half an hour later, she was boarding the ship and being met by a young man in a navy shirt and sharply creased white slacks. *The Sea Queen* was stitched onto the breast pocket of his shirt and just below, he wore a name tag that read "Darren."

"Mrs. Buchanan?" he asked and when she nodded, he said, "If you'll come with me, Mr. Buchanan is waiting in the owner's suite."

The crowds were frantic. People rushing around, having their pictures taken, waving to people on the dock. Children ran past her, their laughter hanging in their wake. The scent of the sea flavored the air and Rita lifted her face into the wind briefly before boarding an elevator with Darren.

"Everyone seems really excited," she said.

"They are," Darren assured her. "It's a great ship and it's always fun to go out on the first cruise."

Probably would be, she thought and told herself that one day she'd have to try it. Right now, sitting on an island beach with nothing to do sounded pretty good.

She had no idea what deck they were on when the

elevator stopped and they stepped off into a luxurious hallway. But it was quiet with none of the eager abandon down on the main decks. Darren led her to a door at the end of the hall, then opened it for her.

"Mr. Buchanan said you should just go on inside, ma'am," he said, then strode quickly away, back to the elevator.

Rita walked into the massive suite, closed the door behind her and for a second, all she could do was stare with her mouth open. It was more than elegant. It was opulent.

Midnight blue carpeting was so plush her feet sank into it. There was a huge living area, with a flat-screen TV, an electric fireplace and several couches and chairs all done in cream-colored fabric. There was a bar, and out on the private balcony, she could see a table and chairs as well as lounges.

She'd love to get a look at the rest of the suite before she left, but for right now… "Thomas?"

Someone stepped into the room from the terrace, but it wasn't Thomas. Even before he spoke, she knew it was Jack because her blood started bubbling and her heart leaped into a gallop.

"Thanks for coming, Rita," Jack said.

She backed up. Cowardly, yes; she'd be embarrassed later. "What're you doing here? Where's your father?"

"That's the thing. He's not here. I asked him to call you for me, since I figured you wouldn't speak to me anyway."

"You were right about that," she snapped and turned for the door. She had to get out of there. Off the ship, back to the bakery.

But Jack was too fast and his legs were much longer

than hers. He beat her to the door and stood with his back against it, blocking her way.

"Move, Jack."

"Not yet."

"You really don't want to push me right now," she warned, though she didn't know what she could do to move him if he didn't want to be moved. Gina would kick him, but Rita just wasn't the kicking kind. Too bad.

"Just hear me out. Then if you want to leave, I won't stop you."

"Why should I?"

One corner of his mouth quirked up and her heart thudded painfully in her chest. "Because you're curious. Admit it."

She hated that he was right. Hated that he could make her body burn with a half smile and hated that just standing this close to him made her want to lean in and take a bite of his lower lip. "Fine. Talk."

He shook his head. "Not here. Come in. Sit down."

When he took her arm, she pulled free of his grasp. She didn't trust herself to stay mad if he was touching her and she really wanted to stay mad. She'd earned it, hadn't she?

"No," she said. "I'm not sitting down. I'm not staying. Just say whatever it is you want said and get it over with." She felt a little wobbly. Too many emotions churning inside at the same time. Didn't he know how hard this was for her? Didn't he care at all? Shaking her hair back, she said, "Unless you've brought me here to declare undying love, then just let me go, okay?"

"That's why you're here," he said softly.

"What?" She couldn't have heard him right, Rita told

herself. Jack wouldn't have said that unless he had another agenda. "What're you saying, Jack?"

"I love you."

She swayed in place and he instinctively reached out
one hand to steady her. Tears blurring her vision, Rita
slapped at his hand. "No, you don't. You're just telling
me what you think I want to hear."

Irritation bloomed on his face. "I should have known
you wouldn't react the way I expected you to. You've
always surprised me, so why should now be any different?"

"What are you talking about?"

"I'm trying to tell you that I was wrong. That I love
you. That I want you—but if you're not going to believe
me why bother?"

"I didn't say I didn't believe you—" She broke off,
stared up into his eyes and saw, along with sparks of
exasperation, the love she'd always hoped to see. "You
love me?"

"Now will you sit down?" he asked.

"I think I have to," she said. She was shaking all over
and her heart was pounding so quickly it sounded like
a frantic drumbeat in her ears.

Once she was perched on the couch, Jack started
pacing. He glanced at her and said, "You were right."

"Always a good start," she said. "Right about what?"

"Pretty much everything." He paced away from her,
then whirled around and came back. "I was hiding. Not
just from pain, but from life. I didn't really see that despite how many of you kept trying to tell me. I guess it's
not easy for a man to admit he's been a damn coward."

"I didn't say you were a coward."

"No," he agreed, "that's one thing you didn't say.

But it's true anyway. Hell, Rita, seeing Kevin again, it shook me. Then the wedding, him and Lisa, you and me… It was like an overload or something. My brain just exploded."

"So you told me to leave."

"It seemed like the right thing to do at the time—"

She started to speak but he cut her off for a change.

"—but it wasn't. Damn it Rita, I've *missed* you. Your voice, your scent, the taste of you. Hell, I miss that loud laugh of yours so much I keep thinking I hear it echo around me."

"Loud?" she repeated.

He grinned. "Loud. And sexy as hell."

Rita took a breath and held it, really hoping this was going to keep going the way she wanted it to.

"That day in the desert almost finished me and did a hell of a lot more to Kevin." Jack stopped pacing, stared into her eyes and said, "But he got past it. Moved the hell on, found a life, while I was still stuck in the past, trying to rewrite history."

"Oh, Jack." She was glad to hear that he had done some thinking, but she hated hearing him put himself down like this, too. It was, she thought, the way of family. *I can call my sister names but if you do it, we go to war.* Well, that's how she felt here, too.

"Just let me get all of this out, okay?" He pushed one hand through his hair. "I've been doing a lot of thinking the last few days and last night, it all sort of came together."

"How?" She needed to know. Needed to believe that this was all real and that somehow he wouldn't go back down that dark road he'd been so determined to stay on.

"The dream came again."

And she hadn't been there to help him through it. Pain for what he'd been through chimed inside her as she pushed off the couch to go to him. "Jack…"

"No," he said, smiling. "It wasn't the same at all this time. In lots of ways. And it doesn't matter right now. All that *does* matter is that I finally figured something out."

She looked up into his eyes and for the first time, noticed that he seemed different somehow. There weren't as many shadows in his eyes. He looked…lighter. As if at least a part of the burden he carried with him had slipped off. And that gave her hope.

"What, Jack? What did you figure out?"

"That I was an idiot. Telling you to go when I should have been begging you to stay." His gaze moved over her face like a touch. "Hell, Rita, I should have been thanking the Fates for bringing you back to me and instead, all I could think about was if I loved you and lost you it would kill me."

Tears blurred her vision but she blinked them back. She didn't want to miss a moment of this. "So," she said wryly, "to keep from losing me, you lost me."

"Yeah." He sighed. "Like I said. Idiot."

"Agreed."

He laughed shortly. "Well, thanks."

"Hey, who knows you better than me?" She asked and reached up to smooth his hair back from his forehead.

"Nobody," he said, voice hardly more than a whisper. He laid both hands on her shoulders and stared directly into her eyes when he said, "Forgive me, Rita.

I was too messed up to see what I had. What I lost. I told you once that you had to leave before I loved you."

"Yeah," she said, the memory of that pain filling her. "I remember."

"That was a lie, too." He rested his forehead against hers. "I loved you the minute I saw you on that beach. When you smiled at me, my heart dropped at your feet. I didn't want to acknowledge it and that's the idiot part." He slid his hands up to cup her face and wiped away a single tear with his thumb. "But my heart is yours, Rita. Always has been. I love you."

She sucked in a gulp of air and held it. "Say it again."

He grinned. "I love you. More than I ever thought possible to love anyone."

"Jack..."

He frowned a little. "Is that an irritated sigh, or a dreamy one?"

Rita smiled up at him. "Dreamy. With just a little bit of irritation tacked on to the end for what you put us all through."

"That's fair," he said, nodding. "Rita, I want to stay married to you. I want to raise our daughter and however many more kids we have together. I love you. Always will. I'm sorry I hurt you. Sorry I hurt my family. My friends."

She reached up to cover his hands with hers. "I love you, Jack."

"Thank God." He sighed in relief. "You'll never be sorry, Rita. I swear it."

"I never was sorry, you dummy," she said and went up on her toes to kiss him.

Jack took her mouth like a drowning man taking his first clear breath. She leaned in to him, wrapped her arms around his neck and held on as he picked her up and swung her in a circle, their mouths still fused together.

Finally though, breathless, he broke off and grinned down at her. "I love you."

"Keep saying it," Rita told him. "I want to hear it. A lot. In fact, I'm going to send Kevin and Lisa a thank-you card for inviting us to their wedding."

"Oh!" Jack let her go long enough to walk to a table, pick something up and come back to her. "Hey, that reminds me. I brought this along for you to see. Kevin sent me an email this morning. I learned my lesson there, too, and opened it right away. Then I printed it."

Rita's eyes blurred again as she looked down at the picture of Kevin and Lisa, standing side by side. The picture was captioned "Got my new legs. I'm an inch taller than I used to be. Thanks again, Jack. For everything. Give us a call sometime."

She looked up at Jack. "That's so great."

"Yeah, it is." He took the picture, tossed it to the table again, then held her hands in his. "And one of these days, I'll thank him for waking me the hell up in time to save the only thing that matters to me." He cupped her cheek with one hand. "You, Rita. I love you."

"I love you back," she said and felt her world completely right itself and steady out. He'd been worth the fight. Worth the pain. Worth everything to get to where they were now.

Bending down, he kissed her baby belly and then stood up to face her. "You know I told you I've been doing a lot of thinking the last couple of days and I wanted to ask you something. How do you feel about naming our daughter Carla? After my mom."

Rita's heart melted. It was perfect. It was all so perfect. She stepped into his embrace. "I think I love it. You're back, Jack. Really back, aren't you?"

"Yeah." He gave her a smile. "I'm finally home. *You're* my home, Rita. I know that now." His arms closed around her and she felt the steady thump of his heart beneath her ear. She had Jack. She had her daughter. She had everything.

The ship's horn sounded and Rita jumped. "Hey, we've got to get off the ship before it sails."

He only tightened his hold on her and laughed. "No, we're not getting off."

Confused, she stared up at him. "What do you mean?"

"Just in case you didn't kill me," Jack said, grinning, "I arranged for Gina to come to town to run the bakery for two weeks. My dad's coming out of retirement to run the company and you and I are sailing to St. Thomas."

"You can't be serious," she whispered, a little panicked, a little excited.

"Absolutely serious."

"But, I don't have any clothes…"

"We'll buy whatever we need." Then he kissed her and admitted, "But I'll say I'm going to want you naked most of the time."

Oh, boy. A tingle of anticipation set up shop low down inside her. But could she really just leave? On the spur of the moment?

"But—" Was this happening? When she woke up that morning, she'd been alone and afraid she would stay that way. Now, she had Jack, a dream vacation and the life she'd always wanted being handed to her. How could she keep up?

"Oh," he said, that tempting smile curving his mouth again, "Gina said to tell you she had lots of ideas on how to 'fix' your bakery."

Rita's eyes narrowed on him. "Oh, you're going to pay for that," she promised.

"Can't wait," Jack said and bent to kiss her again. "You brought me back to the world, Rita. Let me show you some of it."

And just like that, it was all right. She'd go with him anywhere.

"Show me, Jack. Show me everything." Love shone so brightly all around them it was blinding, and Rita would never stop thanking whatever Fates had brought them back together.

"Come with me," he said and dropped one arm around her shoulders, pulling her in close to his side as he led her out to the balcony. And there they stood, wrapped in each other's arms, looking ahead as they sailed into the future. Together.

* * * * *

MILLS & BOON®

Desire™

PASSIONATE AND DRAMATIC LOVE STORIES

A sneak peek at next month's titles...

In stores from 13th July 2017:

- **The CEO's Nanny Affair** – Joss Wood
  and **Little Secrets: Claiming His Pregnant Bride**
  – Sarah M. Anderson

- **Tempted by the Wrong Twin** – Rachel Bailey
  and **The Texan's Baby Proposal** – Sara Orwig

- **From Temptation to Twins** – Barbara Dunlop
  and **The Tycoon's Fiancée Deal** – Katherine Garbera

Just can't wait?
Buy our books online before they hit the shops!
www.millsandboon.co.uk

Also available as eBooks.

Join Britain's BIGGEST Romance Book Club

50% OFF your first parcel

- **EXCLUSIVE** offers every month
- **FREE** delivery direct to your door
- **NEVER MISS** a title
- **EARN** Bonus Book points

Call Customer Services
0844 844 1358*

or visit
millsandboon.co.uk/subscription

* This call will cost you 7 pence per minute plus your phone company's price per minute access charge.

BKCB3

MILLS & BOON®

Why shop at millsandboon.co.uk?

Each year, thousands of romance readers
find their perfect read at millsandboon.co.uk.
That's because we're passionate about
bringing you the very best romantic fiction.
Here are some of the advantages of
shopping at www.millsandboon.co.uk:

* **Get new books first**—you'll be able to buy
  your favourite books one month before they
  hit the shops

* **Get exclusive discounts**—you'll also be
  able to buy our specially created monthly
  collections, with up to 50% off the RRP

* **Find your favourite authors**—latest news,
  interviews and new releases for all your
  favourite authors and series on our website,
  plus ideas for what to try next

* **Join in**—once you've bought your favourite
  books, don't forget to register with us to rate,
  review and join in the discussions

Visit **www.millsandboon.co.uk**
for all this and more today!